HERALD OF THE WITCH'S MARK

ROWAN BLOOD VOLUME THREE

KELLEN GRAVES

For Mo,
for whom I would
learn to bend light.

CONTENTS

Author's Note

This novel is Fantasy-Romance for a New Adult audience, and contains tropes commonly found in that genre. Such tropes include but are not limited to:

- themes of anxiety, depression, PTSD
- Descriptions of PTSD flashbacks
- themes of gaslighting and manipulation
- crude language
- themes of fantasy-based bigotry
- descriptions of blood, gore, and death
- descriptions of animal death and mutilation
- Descriptions of excessive drinking/drunkenness
- Explicit scenes of consensual sex
- Descriptions of (fantasy-based) terrorism at crowded/public events

Pronounciation Guide (Fictional & Inspired)

Ailir (fictional) *EYE-LEER*

Asche (fictional) *ASH*

Beantighe (irish-gaelic) *BAN-TEE*

Cylvan (fictional) *SIL-VAN*

Eias (fictional) *EYE-USS*

Fiachra (irish-gaelic) *FEER-KRA*

Gaeilge (irish-gaelic) *GWEL-GAH*

Geis (irish-gaelic) *GESH*

Kyteler (irish-gaelic) *KITE-LER*

Shamhradháin (irish-gaelic) *SHAM-RA-DIEN*

Sídhe (irish-gaelic) *SHEE*

Sionnach (irish-gaelic) *SHUN-NAH*

Tuatha dé Danann (irish-gaelic) *TOO-HA DE DAN-AN*

Title Reference (Fictional)

HE/SHE/THEY

Lord/Lady/Gentle

King/Queen/Danae

Prince/Princess/Daurae

MAY DAY! DELIGHTFUL DAY!
    BRIGHT COLOURS PLAY THE VALES ALONG.

NOW WAKES AT MORNING'S SLENDER RAY,
    WILD AND GAY, THE BLACKBIRD'S SONG.

NOW COMES THE BIRD OF DUSTY HUE,
    THE LOUD CUCKOO, THE SUMMER-LOVER;

BRANCHING TREES ARE THICK WITH LEAVES;
    THE BITTER, EVIL TIME IS OVER.

The High Deeds of Finn and other Bardic Romances of Ancient Ireland
    T. W. Rolleston, 1910

1

———

THE OFFERING

Saffron rubbed a hand up and down his neck. He rolled his tongue over in his mouth, blinked through the dark shadow of black chiffon draping his vision. A half-moon piece of silver flattened his tongue, connected to a chain tracing over the crown of his head. Two silver hands overlapping a dagger tightened around his throat, squeezing his voice, his breath. Slowly suffocating him.

It was only when he searched for silver cuffs restraining his wrists, fingers skimming over the finger-smooth edge of a woven yew bracelet instead, that his throat opened up again. His vision cleared. His mouth relaxed. He returned to reality, where none of those bad memories remained, despite how vividly he remembered them.

He saw the paper tickets clutched tightly in his hand, forcing himself to ease his grip before smoothing them down against his thigh. Those hands that weren't his, but moved like his would. Slightly paler, smoother, lacking the light scars he'd memorized like words on the page of a book. Even his cuticles were trimmed, nails shiny and smoothed down into blunt curves. Never knowing a day of work in their life. He still couldn't wrap his head around how the amethyst pendant dangling from his neck could extend a glamour of perfection all the way to the tips of his fingers; all the way down to such fine details.

Those fine details trembled slightly just as he did, though. There was no glamour to hide his anxiety. He told himself it was simply excited anticipation, knowing the day he'd been waiting for months to come finally embraced him—but there were layers to that anticipation. Elation and apprehension. Joy and fear. Relief and nervousness. Everything mixed into a bitter potion of nausea in his gut, where butterflies teemed and reminded him he was supposed to be excited. He was, he was. He was excited. He was so excited he might throw up if he opened his mouth too wide.

The day he'd waited months to come was also coated in coarse emery paper, and he was an iron pan layered with rust. Every time he heard the distant squeal of the steam engine, he tasted silver in his mouth, that emery paper scratched away a little more of his composure. Every time he saw the name of the train station on the paper tickets clutched tightly in his hand, his ears rang. He kept counting the pieces of paper, again and again, constantly worried he might lose one while waiting for the engine to arrive. One, two, three, four; one ticket, shiny with gold filigree, for first class boarding. Three plain-printed ones for beantighe-valet boarding. Cylvan had told him exactly what to buy at the ticket window, down to every step, but not how to pronounce that word. *'Beantighe vall-ae.'* The moment he uttered the wrong pronunciation and the worker gave him a strange look, his heart never stopped racing. As if the glamour costuming him as a high fey lord suddenly failed, and he was put on display for everyone to see.

It took him a few minutes to catch his breath afterward, finding an empty seat in the waiting area, closing his eyes and breathing in the fresh air of late-afternoon. He could still smell the Agate Wood. He wondered if the forest smelled the same in Avren. Ah—but it would be tinged with sea salt, because Avren was on the ocean. He couldn't imagine how those two scents would mix. He was excited.

Once his nerves settled enough to hold a pen steady, he scribbled confirmation to Cylvan in the crow book with its charmed black paper. Two months of shared messages textured the previous hundred pages, emitting a sound as he flipped through them, growing more nervous at the thought of running out of space before he had the chance to get a new one. Two months of messages, back and forth, words appearing simultaneously in the second book it was paired with, as they were written. Crow book, because it mimicked how messenger crows carried letters. As he wrote on the page, his finger rubbed the embossed blackbird pressed into the soft leather cover, gold foil worn away from months of doing the same every time his pen touched the page.

I bought the tickets. Train should be here soon. It's a few hours to Connacht, then two days to Avren. I don't think I can keep waiting.

Two months since they last saw one another. Since Saffron woke in the royal infirmary after the bloody night of Taran's failed engagement, that night of Ostara. Two months since Saffron had to be shuffled away in secret so no one would know the witch who attacked the prince and his fiancé-to-be was still very much alive. Alive, and under the protection of the royal Tuatha dé Danann.

More than under the protection of. Betrothed to. The Night Prince's intended harmonious partner, who would one day become a prince, too. Then, someday after that, even king. Saffron squeezed his eyes closed at the reminder. But it was too late to run into the woods and disappear, he repeated to himself. Even though the trees were right there. He could hop off the platform so easily. There wasn't even a railing that would slow him down...

Cylvan's handwriting responded below where Saffron wrote his own, almost instantly. He'd promised to be there and ready in case Saffron had last-minute questions, and even though it went well, Saffron still felt the tension in his chest lighten up at knowing his prince would have been ready if it hadn't.

GOOD. THAT WILL BE THE FIRST AND ONLY TICKET YOU EVER HAVE TO BUY YOURSELF WITH YOUR OWN HANDS, MY DEAR PRINCE.

DID THEY MAKE YOU BUY A STEERAGE TICKET FOR NIMUE? (HAHA)

IF YOU HAVE ANY CHAPLETS LEFT OVER, USE THEM ON SNACKS FROM THE CART THAT WILL COME AROUND TO YOUR COMPARTMENT.

Saffron exhaled a breath, unable to resist the chuckle that left him. He wrote back:

Is 'steerage' for water things? No. I made them wait on the benches so the ticket attendant wouldn't ask any questions.

How many cakes can I get with thirty chaplets?

I miss you. I can't wait to see you.

I HAVE THOUGHT OF NOTHING ELSE BUT YOU SINCE THE DAY WE MET. I UNDERSTAND NIAMH'S GRIEF MORE THAN EVER BEFORE WITHOUT YOU HERE.

SAFFRON SMILED. HIS ANXIETY EBBED SLIGHTLY MORE, heart spinning and fluttering and making him sigh under his breath.

Saffron would finally leave the Spring Court for Avren. For the very last time, and despite Cylvan's lovely promises, he had to resist the urge to write back "are you sure you still want me?" "Do you still like me?" "Is this alright?" "Do you have any second thoughts?" like he already had a hundred times before. Cylvan was so patient every time. He always replied with such certainty. Such grace. *'I've never been more certain of anything. There has never been anything I've ever wanted more than you. I have no doubts. You cannot escape me; if you try and run, I'll find you anywhere you go. That's my warning.'*

Words of love, words of reassurance and promise that helped keep Saffron's constant restlessness at bay. Words that comforted him as he wandered in and out of the Agate Wood every morning and evening by himself, sometimes exploring the Kyteler Ruins, sometimes doing his best to untie as many memory threads as he could from the trees surrounding them, sometimes just walking until he knew it was time to turn back. Always by himself except for the pixies and his crow book, and, occasionally, a nameless human from Hesper who'd crossed Saffron's path a few times. A fellow, silent explorer, who Saffron exchanged only a few words with over their weeks of mutual escape. Who called Saffron Morrígan; who Saffron greeted as Hesper in response. Saffron still wasn't entirely convinced they weren't another ghost haunting those ruins.

It was the countless memories, hauntings, regrets that lured him into the quiet woods every morning, then followed him back home again like long shadows every night. Habits he still couldn't shake, despite nothing of harm even nibbling at him since returning from Avren. He knew Beantighe Village was safe; he knew Cottage Wicklow was safe. He knew the people he cared about were safe; he knew the people he'd once feared were dead, or missing, or something else—but far away from him, nonetheless.

Still, he propped a chair beneath the doorknob of Fern Room every night, once everyone was accounted for and safe in their beds.

He scratched at his wrists whenever he left through the front door of Cottage Wicklow, as if a part of him still expected to be yanked back by silver cuffs.

He leapt to his feet and bowed whenever someone said his

name unexpectedly; he leapt to his feet and for the stairs whenever someone came into the house unexpectedly. That urge to race up to the attic and hide himself.

He turned and hid his face whenever a stranger came from Morrígan or Avren by request of Cylvan or Luvon or someone else; he always bowed his head and wouldn't meet their eyes, when he wasn't searching for somewhere to hide so he wouldn't have to speak to any of them at all. Baba Yaga did most of the talking for him. Like she understood. She never had to ask.

Since they finished rebuilding Cottage Dublin, they are now talking about repairs on the collapsed cottage at the top of the hill; they want us to choose a name for it. King Ailir had a shipment of new blankets and pillows sent from somewhere in the Fall Court. King Tross has sent you a handful of fabric samples and wants to know your favorites. Prince Cylvan sent you a gift of cakes and chocolates; do you want them for yourself, or to share with everyone else? Headmistress Elding wanted to speak with you about additional improvements to make around the village. I told her I would talk to you, first...

Lifting his head again, Saffron searched the waiting area, seeking his friends who waited on the other side of a gate with the rest of the beantighes and other servants. He wished they could join him on his side. He hated sitting all by himself, vulnerable, perceivable, wearing a face that was his but wasn't, with ears that were pointed despite how many times he reached up to feel for himself. Sharp only to the eye; still rounded like moons under fingers. All the while trying to remember to sit up straight, relax his furrowed brows, make his expression neutral. The natural state of a high fey lord. Catrín mag Shamhradháin's voice echoed in his head whenever he realized he slouched, scolding him just like she did in person. He could practically feel the sharp snap of a reed across his shoulders.

Letty, Nimue, and Hollow looked caught up in an intense conversation by their expressions and body language. Saffron knew what they were arguing about, and knew it didn't constitute such aggression. Saffron had planned to order meals for each of them to eat on the train, and Nimue was annoyed because her fish was only offered cooked. She'd snuck a raw fish into Letty's bag that morning, right before they left. Hollow found it on the way out of campus and did what anyone would have—he flung it into the woods, stating you can't take a raw pollan on a fucking train. Nimue shoved him off his horse and threatened to gut him in revenge. Letty cried. No one could quite decide whose fault it was for upsetting her. Clearly the debate raged on.

DID YOU HAVE A CHANCE TO BE INTRODUCED TO THE HIGH LADY SEER BEFORE YOU LEFT?

Saffron wasn't expecting the new question to appear on the crow page. His quill hovered before responding as those words made his heart thump in another wave of anxiety.

Yes

He started, before having to close his eyes and inhale through his nose. He didn't want to think about it—and maybe Cylvan realized his mistake in asking, because he immediately started writing something else, but it was too late. Saffron thought about those three oracles from Avren as they arrived early that morning, wearing navy blue veils with silver embroidery, smiling at him once Baba Yaga introduced him. Baba Yaga, who knew that Saffron's throat closed up the moment he saw them and couldn't speak even his own name.

He thought about those oracles administering weaverthistle tea to every living soul in Beantighe Village as soon as Saffron left. All of those who had ever walked side-by-side with him to and from campus through the Agate Wood; who asked him for favors from the woods; who stood next to him in the assignment office and mopped, scrubbed, cleaned every inch of Morrígan Academy while sharing in hushed conversations. His hand shook over the crow paper, unable to read whatever Cylvan had written to him. He swore there was a black veil hanging in front of his face, again. The oracle's voice whispered in the back of his mind.

We won't be pulling many threads at all, except from those who you shared a cottage with; it's quite lovely in here, by the way. I'm so glad to see repairs happened quickly after the unfortunate fire on Ostara.

We'll be using charmed weaverthistle tea to blur the memories of everyone else who didn't know you so closely. We finished up on Morrigan's campus last night, and it went as smoothly as Danu could bless it to be. I pray Ériu will ensure the same this morning. Thank you for entrusting us with this sacred duty, Lord Saffron. Remind me again who you've requested not have their memories tampered with...?

For Saffron's protection. For Cylvan's protection. To ensure no one would make any connections after he arrived in Avren to enroll at Mairwen Academy; to ensure no one caught on to his true identity and turned it into a scandal. A human beantighe wearing a high fey glamour while attending a high fey school and accepting invites to high fey galas, executable crimes in themself, who also not only tricked his way into Mairwen, but also the Night Prince's heart and bed...

Saffron closed his eyes. The sound of a wailing steam train cascaded over the trees, closer than the first time.

Hollow wouldn't be forced to forget. Neither would Letty or Nimue. Neither would Baba Yaga or even Adelard, at Saffron's request. But Fleece, Silk, Blade, the other henmothers, they might not have their entire memory of him plucked, but—he would cease to exist as anything more than a blurry memory. Like a childhood friend with a forgotten face, nothing more intrusive than that.

He tried to remember how calm that oracle woman's smile had been. He kicked himself for how, despite how reassuring and kind she was, he hadn't been able to speak to say thank you. He must have looked so ungrateful, so uncaring at what was about to happen.

It was just—

He'd already been a ghost, once. And while that time it was different, that time it was for good reason, he was no longer trapped in any house, he wasn't forced to be silent, he didn't have to pretend to have lost all his memories, he was to be a ghost in the minds of some in order to be able to make an impression on others—there was something awful about being rubbed away from the minds of everyone he'd spent the last ten years of his life alongside. They who he became a ghost for the first time, making the deal with Taran to protect them from the wolf stalking the woods. He gazed down at his forearm at the thought, and although glamoured away, he knew they were there. Those scars from the night of Ostara, when he'd cursed Taran with a true name that Saffron, himself, owned. *Icarus,* carved into his arm in an ogham stele, that healed over but never healed away.

The people he had done all of that for—would forget about him. They probably already had.

Something thick dripped from his nose, making him jump. Digging the handkerchief from his shoulder bag, he quickly smeared the blood away, shoving the thoughts back in the same motion and hoping he'd done so quickly enough to avoid a worse reaction. He sensed eyes from across the platform, offering a reassuring smile and wave to Hollow, who watched him as he wiped the blood from his nose. He was as used to it as Saffron was by then, as used to it as Letty, Nimue, Baba Yaga, Adelard all were by then—the way he would spontaneously drip blood from his nose, his mouth, sometimes even his eyes and ears if unbridled emotions struck him hard enough. If he had nightmares terrifying enough; if he pushed himself too hard for too long physically; if he sensed something shift within the veil nearby, like a sudden tear or something else.

Baba Yaga claimed it to be a known side-effect of being a valley witch, or a rowan witch without a bridge partner. It was only his body straining beneath the overwhelm of the oath he made. His rowan magic, which was more emotionally-rooted than standard arid magic, and feasted on Saffron's already overfilled and spilling emotions at any given time.

He was getting better at sensing when they started digging their claws in, at least. He was getting better at keeping his emotions tamped down. Something he'd purposefully tried to master during his two months healing in the village so that, hopefully, Cylvan would never have to witness something so pathetic.

I AM COUNTING THE MOMENTS UNTIL I GET TO SEE YOU AGAIN, PÚCA. I SWEAR YOUR LIFE WITH ME WILL BE A HAPPY AND FULFILLED ONE. YOU WILL KNOW NOTHING BUT JOY FROM THIS DAY ONWARD.

LET ME KNOW WHEN YOU ARRIVE IN CONNACHT. I DREAM OF THE MOMENT I CAN HOLD YOU AGAIN.

Someone cleared their throat from next to him, and Saffron turned quickly. He almost apologized, thinking maybe he'd accidentally taken someone's seat—but then he smiled, exclaiming Hesper's name in surprise. His ghostly companion from the woods.

"You left without saying goodbye," they said, smiling at him with curious eyes. "I like your glamour."

Saffron stiffened. He forgot about his glamour. Already, he'd forgotten he was even wearing one. His mouth dangled open in panic, petrified with the thought of what to do next, but Hesper just chuckled and shook their head.

"I won't tell anyone, Morrígan. Just wanted to give you something before you go. Are those your friends over there?"

"Huh? Oh, yeah—" but in the time it took Saffron to glance over his shoulder and back, Hesper was gone. Gone as quickly as they came, vanishing into the growing crowd. In their place on the bench, Saffron smiled at the sight of a bright red apple, then a matching red card hidden beneath it. Biting into the sweet fruit, he read the words on the card just as the train to Connacht pulled into the station, deafeningly announcing itself for all to board.

"Once silver sows their longest day,

"Iron reaps its bloody night;

"As yew trees pin our suns in sleep,

"Rowan tears the moon shall weep.

"Not once, nor twice, nor thrice—

"Six knocks aloud, they scatter like mice."

Saffron didn't move, not until Hollow meandered up and nudged him, saying it was time to go. Saffron's eyes lingered on that final line, trying to make sense of it, of why something about it rang familiar. Until, for the first time since leaving Avren, he was reminded of a memory he'd tried so hard to forget. That man who visited him in the infirmary, who knew him by name, who knew about the oath he made. Who left through a sudden tear in the veil, chased by a distinct sound only Saffron had heard. Ryder Kyteler.

Knock, knock.

2

THE GLAMOUR

Connacht's docks on the river were surprisingly bustling so late in the evening, setting sun painting the sky in shades of orange and lavender that reminded Saffron of flowers illuminated in candlelight. He focused on the sky. Just the sky. Not the people. Not the sour memories Connacht reminded him of. Not the tightening knot of thorny vines in his chest making it hard to breathe.

Had he not been joined by his friends, he might have been even more self-conscious. Had his amethyst pendant not glamoured his ears with points and the rest of his features with all the soft, pretty loveliness of a high fey, he might have been even more self-conscious. Had he not fought so hard to keep his shoulders squared and his back straight like he'd been taught, he might have even had the ability to swivel and see exactly how many people really looked. But even though he still wasn't a *perfect* high fey specimen by any means, pointed ears alone made it so people didn't stare too long. A passing appearance was all a fey pedestrian needed to ignore the group of four loitering there, one presumed fey with two beantighe-humans and one wild undine thing that perhaps drew more attention than Saffron ever would have. Maybe that was a gift in itself. Could he have Nimue follow him from class to class at Mairwen, too? The way she hissed at anyone who looked Letty's way a little too long was apparently just what a high fey needed to scurry off down the road again.

Saffron kept his eyes peeled for a specific carriage that seemed to never come, though he knew the antsiness stemmed more from being perceived after months of being a ghost in the woods. And to do so wearing a skin that wasn't his. Glamoured skin. Altered features. Antsiness and eagerness.

He wanted to be in Avren. He wanted the multi-day journey by ship to be over with so he could arrive even earlier. He wanted to see Cylvan. God, he wanted to see Cylvan again.

When Luvon's carriage finally clattered up the cobblestone street and halted in front of them, Saffron breathed a sigh of relief. It wobbled back and forth as the driver hopped from their seat, but the side door flew open on its own, accompanied by a booming voice of greeting. Luvon emerged with a massive grin and splayed arms, and only then did Saffron realize exactly how tense he'd been standing. He melted instantly, nearly bursting into happy tears and having to resist racing into his patron-father's arms like he really wanted to. His brief time being taught high fey manners in the Winter Court with Catrín a month prior had taught him that much. *Proper high fey of noble class don't erupt with emotion and cling to one another in public. Unless you're my husband, but he is a bad example.*

Saffron instead offered Luvon a polite but shallow bow while the rest of his friends—Nimue excluded, because she insisted on being rebellious—bowed from the hips. Luvon, meanwhile, wrapped Saffron in a suffocating hug and swung him back and forth with enthusiasm.

"Oh, *a leanbh,* I was so sad I couldn't be there while Catrín whipped you into shape! I kicked myself over and over again! I'm sure you look lovely! I can smell the cologne you're wearing, was it a gift? Ah, your hair is even brushed back for once, isn't it? Did your henmother give you a haircut before you came? You're quite the young lord, aren't you?" He rumpled fingers through

Saffron's hair, making Saffron groan as he'd spent so much time trying to style it. "You've always been so careful to dress as well as you can, even under your veil; I know those skills certainly apply now as well. I can tell by the outline of your aura, you must be so handsome. I'm sure you take after my distant sister—or whoever it is we decided—off in Alvénya. You know, I've been pondering the perfect backstory for all of that, filled to the brim with proper scandal and intrigue and all other sorts of court shenanigans—"

"Sir!" Saffron groaned, wriggling in Luvon's grasp until Luvon finally put him down.

"Please, I must do all I can until it's too late. To embarrass a king is to lose my tongue."

Saffron squeaked. *King.*

Another bittersweet reminder that once they boarded the ship, *Saffron dé patron dé Luvon mag Shamhradháin* no longer existed. He'd been replaced by someone called *Harmonious Crown Prince of Alfidel, Saffron dé Tuatha dé Danann*, even if no one else knew it. Oh, god—oh *god*. Despite Catrín's best efforts to desensitize him to the title during their short time together, it still clawed at him.

It was obvious by the lacquered wood and bone-white sails of their chartered ship that it wasn't anywhere near the most cost-effective option of travel, despite everyone always going on and on about the importance of not drawing too much attention to themselves. Saffron could only smile bitterly to himself, knowing Cylvan probably worried himself into a lather at the idea of his dear harmonious beantighe-prince traveling like a beantighe-peasant. One ticket on the grand vessel probably cost more than Saffron's earnings working an entire year as a servant at Morrígan. Meanwhile, Luvon, who had plenty of wealth of his own, gladly enjoyed every perk of patronizing a future king. Traveling in comfort and style on the royal family's dime did not go against anything he stood for. Nor did it go against anything Hollow, Letty, or Nimue stood for, as they vocally whooped and hollered in glee at the sight before scurrying off for the servants' ramp.

Upon finally boarding themselves, Luvon sought out the passenger liaison, searching for the special charm all attendants wore so they could be identified through opaque aura glasses like his. He moved like a beast on the hunt, using his cane to swat other guests out of his way. Saffron, meanwhile, sought a place to sit that was off to the side of all the foot traffic, pulling out his crow book to re-read Cylvan's previous messages before scribbling a new note:

Just boarded the ship in Connacht. I think I will spend the second half with my eyes closed so I do not see the ocean for the first time without you.

Cylvan responded instantly. As if still waiting.

I AM GLAD YOU MENTIONED IT BEFORE I HAD TO ASK. PLEASE RESERVE YOUR FIRST TIME FOR ME. I WILL MAKE IT WORTH YOUR WHILE.

Sighing with a smile, Saffron closed his eyes and leaned back. He gazed over his shoulder across the river, appreciating the fresh scent of the water mixed with the town one last time, wondering exactly how long it would take before it turned salty and rumbling sea waves crashed against the side of the ship, instead. He hadn't been able to see it the last time he was in Avren, having remained in the infirmary until he was well enough to barely walk, only to then be snuck straight away to the nearest train station to escape the city while rumors tore through the streets. *Taran mac Delbaith was attacked by a witch at his engagement fete.*

A human witch? Did anyone see who did it?

It was too dark. Apparently they wore a red veil.

Like a beantighe?

It couldn't have been a beantighe.

Did you ever hear of the rowan spirit haunting Morrigan

Academy? I believe it was attached to Prince Cylvan. Perhaps he summoned it to harm his betrothed.

Why would he do such a thing? Lord Taran was the best thing to happen to him. They were madly in love.

I hear Lord Taran died.

I hear he turned into a horrible beast.

Was it a curse?

I thought it had something to do with his family's opulent silver?

But could Proserpina's Silver change a person's appearance entirely? More than just a glamour? To physically change them...

Surely it had something to do with the witch.

Prince Cylvan must be heartbroken.

He killed the witch who did it, you know. He shot them right through the heart. They buried the body in a silver coffin stuffed with yew branches and dill weed.

I can't remember the last time they went to such lengths to bury a witch... why not just burn them like all the others?

Something about fear of scattering bone ashes.

Is this a sign of what's to come...?

Fondling the yew bracelet on his wrist, it was thin enough to keep his otherwise untethered magic under the surface, not enough to hurt. To keep the glowing halos of opulence from blinding him, like they once did on Ostara. Not unlike Cylvan's citrine ring that kept his Sídhe magic at bay while at Morrígan. Saffron realized he'd never asked if citrine rings were required at Mairwen, too—before remembering they'd already decided to claim he was ashen. No opulence in his blood at all, in order to explain how he couldn't compel or do anything else a high fey could. Still, the yew bracelet might stand out while otherwise glamoured and dressed in all the fancy clothes Luvon picked out for his new wardrobe.

When he wasn't fondling the woven bracelet, Saffron pinched the ring on his finger. A ring he never wore while wandering Beantighe Village or the Agate Wood, not even on a string around his neck as he was terrified of losing it. A ring he only wore to bed, appreciating it in the moonlight or candlelight while everyone else slept peacefully around him. Only when he intended on rejoining the rest of the world, glamoured and perfect, could he finally put it on for good.

It was prettier than the fern ring had been, with slender silver branches weaving around a shiny, teardrop-faceted green emerald. Cylvan had apologized for its "simplicity" while tucking it on Saffron's finger in the infirmary, only hours before Saffron was whisked away from Avren. But even a plain band of bronze would have been enough to make Saffron's heart race every time he looked at it. Cylvan said he chose emerald because of how much Saffron loved the woods; then, in a secret whisper, explained that the woven branches were inspired by rowan trees. Saffron's heart thumped every time he thought about it, simultaneously cursing Cylvan for calling it *simple* as if it wasn't something to be treasured for the rest of his life.

His courting ring—not quite an engagement ring, Cylvan constantly insisted—that would also be his new patron ring, his new anti-aging ring. Ensuring, as it gradually found rhythm with his creeping life, he would age at the same rate as Cylvan whenever he wore it. One less worry out of millions when it came to what he would face in the coming days, weeks, months, years, eternities. At least, with that ring, he could rest assured all of it would be done with Cylvan right next to him.

He just—wanted to be perfect. To be everything Cylvan would ever need, no matter how many charmed bracelets or rings or glamours he had to wear to do it. Perfect enough for Cylvan, perfect enough to be a prince, and one day a *king*. Perfect enough that, until then, he would never be mistaken as anything but a noble fey like he claimed to be. He had to live up to the expectations of the glamour he wore; he had to live up to the expectations of all the high fey around him.

I am a distant relative of Luvon mag Shambradháin. I come

from a high fey family from the Lelfe Court in Alvénya across the sea...

I am engaged to a powerful fey noble in my hometown, and therefore am not actively seeking courtship in Avren...

I am attending Mairwen Academy to expand my worldly experience...

I am a full-blooded fey of distant nobility...

I have never met Prince Cylvan before, but I think he might be the loveliest, most handsome high fey I've ever laid eyes on... someone from such humble roots as me could never win his favor... though if I did, I might even consider leaving my Alvényan fiancé to pursue his hand, instead...

Saffron sighed down at his ring, appreciating the color of the stone. He couldn't wait to be stolen away, as soon as possible.

THE VESSEL TEASED BACK AND FORTH BENEATH Saffron's feet until he had to cling to the corridor railing. Making their way down to where he and Luvon would be sleeping on the two-day long journey, the sight of the room's interior reminded Saffron how he was definitely in too far over his head. With extravagant wallpaper depicting wild fey skipping through fields of wildflowers; the gold metal accents along the walls, the wash-basin, the rim of the window; the matching gold sconces that flickered with candlelight and smelled of natural perfumes, Saffron was... wholly unprepared. But there was more. There was even more—and he was forced to reckon with every luxurious detail he'd never even thought about, before. All the while feeling so very, very out of place.

The soft sheets and pillows for him to sleep on that night; the hot meal delivered to his room once they set sail; the freedom to wander above and below decks to watch the passing landscape on the edge of the river when he felt like the churning below deck was going to make him hurl; how everyone who wasn't another passenger bowed deeply in greeting and referred to him as *my lord* or *my gentle* before asking if there was anything he needed. Every time, he resisted the urge to ask if he could be shown to the servants' quarters to see his friends. That would have been strange. They would have asked him *'why do you need your servants, my lord? Is the staff aboard not meeting your needs? Please tell me how else we can help you.'* He'd never felt so helpless while surrounded by such grandeur put on display for... people like him. For people like him, Saffron dé mag Shamhradháin de Lelfe of Alvénya, who only came into existence the moment he stepped foot on that very ship.

He gulped back an apothecary of seasickness tonics every other hour, even late into the night, clearly having cursed himself somehow. He took the never ending nausea and wavering balance and puking over the side of the ship or in the sink or in the bathtub as payment for his luxurious quarters and treatment compared to what he knew the others were experiencing. God, he just hoped they were being fed. He hoped it was warm below-deck. He hoped they wouldn't hate him too much when they finally saw each other again upon docking in Avren.

When morning of arrival finally came, Saffron thought of nothing and everything at the same time. Emerging from the haze of the dozens of tonics he choked down—on top of two nights of so little sleep—the sudden, plummeting, crushing weight of what waited for him as the ship slowed on arrival into Avren's port just made him sick all over again. For a different reason. For a million reasons.

Even with the window sealed shut and curtains drawn over it, Saffron knew when they arrived. He heard the shouts and hurrying feet on the deck overhead and in the corridor, the flap-ping of cruising sails lowered in favor of smaller ones, the addi-tional shouts and clamoring of people who weren't on the ship, but rather the dock on the other side. Crowds on the pier. Would there be a lot of people there to witness his debut? Whether they meant to or not?

He could only picture it because the day prior Cylvan had

drawn him a little map of what the bay, the port, the dock all looked like from above, explaining all the places he could stand above deck and never see the ocean if he really wanted to avoid it. Saffron had been partially joking when he first wrote it, but the nausea that nearly killed him on the actual journey made it come true either way. Cylvan would be thrilled to be Saffron's first.

He took another few minutes to stare at himself in the mirror. To fix his hair that was a little blonder, to gaze into his eyes that were hazel rather than green, to run his hands over his cheeks that were too smooth and perfect and didn't show any hint of the scars he was used to seeing. A stranger whose face moved as he did. Would Cylvan recognize him? Would Cylvan like that face? If not, could he get it changed? It had been an oracle who did it the first time, placing a charm on the amethyst in all the ways Saffron had no capacity to understand. He only felt better about being in the dark when even Cylvan admitted anything but the most basic details of glamour charms went far over his head, too.

He'd almost kneaded himself back into a state of glamoured-human-shaped calm when Luvon arrived at his door with a knock, clearly avoiding a comment on what Saffron was sure was a slurry of colors in his aura that gave away every emotion he battled. But then he noticed how Luvon hesitated before saying what he meant to—like he knew it would only make Saffron's emotions erupt into something worse:

"Have you decided on your new name, *a leanbh?*"

Cylvan had warned Saffron about that. He'd even given Saffron some ideas for what to call himself while wearing that glamour that lightened his hair and smoothed his skin and turned his green eyes hazel and pointed his ears. *Seraphine. Seraphiel. Seraph, which is a human term for 'angel'. Oh, sorry, you don't know what angels are, do you? I'll have to tell you all about them when you get here. Until then, just trust me when I say it's a good fit.*

"Oh," Saffron whispered. A question of *'do I really have to?'* lingered on his lips, unsure how to word it in a way that wouldn't get him scolded on why it was so important. He knew why, already. But he liked his real name. He liked it because Luvon chose it for him. He liked being named after a flower. He liked the way it sounded when Prince Cylvan said it.

But he knew why. And he knew exactly what Luvon's answer would be if he pushed back. *Because it's a beantighe name.*

Before he could decide how to answer, Ériu blessed him in the form of Hollow, who appeared at the door and knocked with the back of his knuckles. Saffron leapt to his feet in a mix of surprise and relief, racing to hug him and sigh his name and express how glad he was to find him still alive and not suffocating below-deck. Hollow chuckled, hugging Saffron back as Luvon quietly excused himself, but not without a gentle warning in the way of, "I'll wait for you above deck, Saffron, so don't take too long."

"Gotta help unload or whatever," Hollow said once Luvon disappeared, before digging through his back pocket. "Luvon said Letty and Nimue and I would head straight for the palace once your things are unloaded, but, uh—I thought you might want to see this."

He handed Saffron a red card. The same one Hesper had left on the bench for him at the station outside of Morrígan. Saffron took it, stomach flipping in surprise. He patted around his own new, fancy, embroidered doublet before grabbing his shoulder bag from the bed and removing his crow book. He first thought the card had fallen out from where he tucked it between the pages— only to be more surprised when he found the first card where he'd put it originally.

"Where did you...?" he asked, turning the card over and back.

"One of the other beantighes below deck gave it to me right as we docked," Hollow said, returning Saffron's gaze with matching uncertainty. A hint of apprehension. A sign that, whatever the card meant, it was more intentional than a fun little greeting to be left for people at random. Why did that make Saffron instantly restless?

"Did they say anything?" he asked.

"Just 'welcome to Avren,'" he answered in a low voice, meant only for Saffron to hear. Saffron frowned, turning the card back and forth again, hoping the one given to Hollow might have even a little bit more information. A tiny bit more context. But like the first one, there was only that poem on the front—and the same apprehensive knot in Saffron's stomach.

Hollow shuffled slightly more into the room, out of the way of passengers in the corridor who kept throwing looks to where the massive beantighe could have been mistaken for blocking his fey lord's way out. "Let's talk more later, when there aren't so many, erm... pointy-eared gossips around."

"Yeah." Saffron nodded, before tugging on Hollow's shirt. "Be careful on your way to the palace, alright? I'll come see you as soon as I can."

"No rush." Hollow smiled. "I know how nervous you are to see your prince. And how difficult the next few days are gonna be for you. Take care of yourself, first. In the meantime, I'm gonna be eating and drinking everything the royal family has to offer. All while not working a lick harder than I have to to keep my bed."

"Good," Saffron laughed, though the acknowledgement of his anxiety made him realize perhaps he wasn't hiding it as well as he thought. He might have instantly burst into nervous tears had Hollow not pinched his cheeks and pulled, spreading his mouth into a strained smile. Saffron swatted him away, offering one last hug, a promise to see him soon, and another goodbye.

Watching Hollow hurry down the corridor, stepping aside for fey passengers, bowing to any of them that met his eyes, was bitter on Saffron's tongue.

3

THE INTRODUCTION

Saffron was the last one to enter the corridor and make his way for the stairs to the upper deck, which was equally empty of other patrons. Other passengers were eager to get off the ship and back onto dry land. Saffron should have been the same, but when the moment came—his feet were made of lead. All of him was made of lead. He'd never felt so heavy and unsure of every step until that very moment, all the way until he approached and greeted Luvon above. From there they would walk to the gap in the railing and descend the ramp down to solid ground. Where everyone was waiting for them. And everything would be fine. Everything would be fine. Just fine. Perfectly fine. Nothing would go wrong. Ever. Nothing would ever go wrong. And Saffron would live a long, simple, peaceful life where nothing ever went wrong at all.

But the moment he broached the edge of the deck to make that very descent into a life of simple fineitude, Saffron stopped short, causing Luvon to bump into him from behind.

"Everything alright?" he asked, touching Saffron's shoulder before his cane tapped the heels of Saffron's fancy shoes in encouragement. But Saffron only stared across the massive crowd of people waiting alongside the edge of the dock. At the single clearing in the center of the throng, speckled with a handful of bodies. A handful of bodies and a royal carriage, glimmering in the overhead sun. He knew that carriage—he'd once seen it through the windows of Danann House the night Prince Cylvan first arrived on Imbolc. He didn't have to see the faces of those who dotted the clearing to know exactly who they were, either—and he knew the most important one by their obsidian horns in the sun and all-black attire. Saffron would know that silhouette in an instant, even if only with his hands searching in pitch darkness.

Panic devoured him, reducing his nerves to dust. Cylvan. For the first time in months—Cylvan. For the first time not wild-eyed and mad on veil magic, or drunk on pain tonics and blood loss in the royal infirmary. Finally, as a person who could take his hand and meet his eyes, who could smile and speak. No longer a ghost choked by silver hands and trapped by silver cuffs.

Saffron would finally be reunited with his prince, his raven—in front of all those people.

"I—" he choked. "I thought—you said we were meeting them at the palace?"

Luvon chuckled like Saffron was only being shy. He gently nudged Saffron forward again, and Saffron had to obey, else he look strange to the people observing from below. Oh, god—there were so many people. All looking at him, watching him. As if waiting for him, too. All of those strangers seeking him out, when he really thought his arrival in Avren could be a quiet one. Maybe he should have known better. Of course he wasn't meant for a simple life of predictability. He was marrying Cylvan dé Tuatha dé Danann, after all, who was the most dramatic creature to walk on two legs.

With his heart swelling in the back of his throat, at the very least it kept him from screaming. He took his first, then second, then third steps down the roped boarding ramp. Saffron hated how so many curious faces turned to look. How they gawked, gazing him up and down, as if searching for any place the glamour had a weakness. He had to bite back the urge to reach up and touch his ears, to subtly cover them, just in case. Was he about to approach the royal family of Alfidel with all the dressings of a fey noble, moon-round ears blatantly on display? No, no—Luvon would be able to tell. He would be able to tell something was off through his glasses, even the smallest thing. He would say something. Definitely.

The thought was a relief for only a second before Saffron nearly tripped over his feet again the moment he wondered if anyone else in that crowd also wore aura glasses. Someone who would look at him and see something strange. Notice there was an additional layer of magic coating every inch of him. Oh, god. Ériu above, watch over him—No, goddamnit, not Ériu, he was a high fey, he should have been praying to Danu—but wouldn't the goddess know? She would know he was a farce as well. She would know he was only a human wearing high fey skin. Would she curse him? Would she rebuke him? Would Ériu shield him against her sister as he prayed to the other for protection, or would she be angry and accuse him of treachery? Would they both wail on him with holy fists for trying to be something he very, very, very, very, *very* much was not?

"Oh my god." He didn't recognize his voice; he didn't know they were even his words. When had he become as shrill as a pixie? Had they managed to follow him all the way to Avren despite his best attempts to keep them out of his bags? "Oh, god, Master Luvon, who do I pray to?"

Luvon's hand found the small of his back, offering support as they walked. Somehow, they reached the base of the walkway, crossing onto the hard ground of the passenger dock where stones clacked beneath Saffron's heeled boots. They excused themselves between onlookers, many of whom, up close, had no interest in Saffron at all. But there were others who did. Some who even pushed their way to the front of the crowd to get a better view of him, which only made his nerves heighten. A few called out to ask his name, to ask where he'd come from, what his business was in Avren—but Luvon kept nudging Saffron along. He'd already warned about those people, saying Saffron would be able to recognize writers for gossip columns by the intrusiveness of their questions. Would they have tried so hard to accost him if the royal carriage hadn't been there to welcome them? Didn't anyone think of that? Why didn't anyone consider how Saffron had never been under so much scrutiny all at once, after years of spending every day hidden beneath a veil, a ghost, something meant to be neither seen nor heard...?

Something thick and warm raced up the back of his throat, and a thin ribbon of blood dripped from his nose. He scrambled for his handkerchief, quickly wiping it away as a few people gasped quietly before scribbling on palm-sized bundles of parchment. As if it was the most interesting thing to happen all morning in a city as big and grand as Avren. His face went red, burning and boiling internally until surely no more overwhelmed, magical blood would be able to drip out. He'd cooked all of it from the inside out.

His mind raced endlessly, mercilessly, until the world tipped, nearly toppling beneath him. He felt only the digging gaze of every curious onlooker on every side, searching him up and down, whether to understand him or to find something wrong. Something else to scribble on their little notepads. There was already so much wrong with him, he knew, even with the glamour doing its best to make him pretty. He knew he didn't walk with the perfect elegance of a fey lord. His hair never stayed perfectly in place, no matter how much he tried to comb and coif it. He didn't look straight ahead and hold himself upright with squared shoulders like he should have, unbothered by the crowd because he was used to getting looks back home. He was meant to be a noble fey lord, one accustomed to all the excitement and cacophony of court games, even those in Alvénya which were, according to Catrín, less grandiose but even stricter than in Alfidel. But he wasn't. He didn't. He was never meant to be anywhere in proximity of nobility unless it was washing their sheets or scrubbing their floors or polishing their shoes. How could they have ever believed he could do anything to pass as one of them?

He should have turned around. There was still time. The ship was still docked. He could get back on it. Demand to be taken home. He could shove his way through the crowd and disappear into the city. He could steal a horse and ride back to Morrígan. He could flee into the woods never to be seen again at all, to become one with the wild fey, it would be so easy, it would be so much easier than—

The crowd parted, and Saffron's eyes found the shadowy leanan sídhe waiting on the other side. Prince Cylvan, whose stiff tunic was perfectly smooth and upright at the collar. Whose silver belt cinched him at the waist, whose legs held him straight and upright with squared shoulders and all the perfect regality of a member of the royal family. He wore his hair loose, adorned with braids and beads at the crown and cascading in waves over his shoulders and down his back in the way Saffron liked. He wore a silver rapier on his hip, one hand resting on it. His makeup was shimmery and light, making the color of his eyes vivid and impossible to ignore. His horns were shiny, polished and newly carved with what could be ocean waves or swirls of wind. Slates wiped clean of their previous vines and leaves, like symbols of a new, fresh start.

Saffron's eyes landed on the absolute perfection of Prince Cylvan, and the noise of the crowd fell away.

Suddenly there was only the clattering of bone-white sails and creaking ships. There was only the lapping of water against the dock and wooden planks. There were birds singing in the trees and the trickling of a fountain. A breeze through long grass and the smell of fresh morning air right after rain. The sensation of flying and falling, heart racing as strong arms held him with surety. The soft laughter of water nymphs splashing in a crisp mountain lake at the base of the grassy hill, decorated with aromatic fields of lavender plants.

And then Cylvan smiled at him—the tiniest little twitch of his perfect mouth. So small no one else would notice. But Saffron did. He'd memorized every inch of Cylvan's face, he'd never forgotten even the tiniest details of it, even in their time apart. He wouldn't have had such vivid dreams, otherwise. He wouldn't have been able to draw him from memory onto the pages of his sketchbook with such accuracy, otherwise.

Saffron offered a tiny smile back, overcome with the unbearable urge to race forward and throw his arms out; to embrace his Night Prince and taste his mouth again for the first time in too long. It was only Luvon—Luvon, who could read Saffron's mind and sense his every want—who stopped him with the gentlest touch of a hand on his shoulder. A reminder to *wait, compose yourself.* Just a moment longer.

Reaching the edge of the crowd, the edge of the little clearing around the royal family, Saffron knew it was rude to never offer a glance to King Tross or Daurae Asche who also stood there, even as he followed Luvon's lead and gave a bow in greeting. But Saffron couldn't pull his eyes from Cylvan and Cylvan, alone. Cylvan, who bowed in return, though not as deep. Who moved with grace Saffron had never seen before, grace he himself could never fathom owning for himself. The grace of a prince on display. One who'd learned from the day he was born how to be perfect in every movement and word. It left Saffron breathless.

"Welcome to Avren!" King Tross exclaimed, putting out his hands and approaching Luvon to pull him into a hug. "It's been too long since you came to see me, friend. I see your relative has made it safely across the sea as well."

The king turned to Saffron, smiling in a way that was both familiar in its friendliness, while also perfectly formed to regard Saffron as a stranger. Perfectly practiced, another pinching reminder that Saffron was in over his head. All he could think to do was offer another bow as Luvon answered in his stead. His voice was calm enough to be casual, while simultaneously declaring it to everyone who listened. Perfect. Practiced.

"Indeed he has, all the way from Alvénya. His dear mother asked me to see him to Mairwen, so scared of her poor son traveling to such a grand city on his own. It was my honor to accompany him here. And what an honor for him to meet you right away, your majesty. Go on, child, introduce yourself properly to the King of Alfidel."

Saffron stiffened. He smiled awkwardly at Luvon, then cast a brief glance to Cylvan, who wore the same kind of smile King Tross did. He broke into a cold sweat.

"Y-your majesty," he stammered, bowing for a third time, as deep as a beantighe would go. He hadn't decided about his name, yet. He hadn't given enough thought to it. He thought he would have more time. And—he still didn't want to change it at all, from the first moment it was suggested. He liked his name. He didn't want to give up his name. He swallowed the nervous lump in his throat. He would have to decide—immediately.

"My name is... my name is Saffron, your majesty," he finally said, voice shaking. "Saffron of Lelfe, of Alvénya."

By some grace of the goddess, whichever one decided to bless him, the sky did not fall down. The earth did not rent open beneath his feet. Cylvan did not throw his head back and groan in exasperation, Luvon did not put his face in his hand in disappointment. King Tross didn't even flinch. In fact, he grinned ever brighter, revealing a golden ring pierced through the skin over the front of his teeth, a matching gem in his tongue.

"A lovely name! I imagine you'll be coined the *Flower of Alvénya* in all the gossip columns by morning."

A hundred whispers cascaded out around them like a stone thrown into a pond, and Saffron understood why Luvon always praised Tross as a master of publicity. He couldn't help but smile in return, overcome with relief.

"Shall we head back to the palace?" Tross went on, glancing over his shoulder to Cylvan and Asche, who both nodded. Asche looked ready to tear out of their skin in excitement, biting back a huge grin of their own as they hadn't quite developed the practiced expression of their brother and father. "I would be honored if you would join us for dinner, Master Luvon. Lord Saffron. I'm having the finest Alvish cuisine prepared to celebrate your arrival. I think you will be impressed with our breads especially, Lord Saffron. They pair beautifully with Alvényan cheeses."

"Of course, your majesty," Luvon nodded. Saffron mimicked the motion, then offered another slight bow as Tross clapped his hands and turned back to the carriage.

"Father, there's no rush," Cylvan interrupted, putting up a hand and flashing the handsomest smile Saffron had ever seen. His knees almost buckled. "Why don't you and Master Luvon appreciate the market for the rest of the afternoon? The other guests won't be arriving until this evening, anyway. Saoirse and I can escort Lord Saffron back to the palace for now"—Saffron glanced at the massive armored fey woman standing behind Cylvan, vaguely recognizing her as his personal guard from the last time he was in Avren—"...and ensure his things are delivered to Master Luvon's townhouse in the meantime. Take the daurae with you as well, I know they are on the hunt for more embroidery beads—"

"I'm ready to go home as well!" Asche interrupted, practically shoving Cylvan out of the way to grin at Saffron properly. "I'm Daurae Asche. It's a pleasure to meet you. I love your outfit, do you mind if I look at it a little closer?"

Saffron smiled in uncertainty, but nodded, offering one of his arms so Asche could run their fingers over the ornate beading on the pointed cuff. They mumbled something to themself, then pulled a notebook from a pocket, before being swiftly bumped out of the way again as Cylvan returned with a few black hairs out of place.

"Asche, stay with father—"

"You can't make me."

"Asche—I swear to Lugh himself, *on grounds of being your*

crown prince"—his voice lowered to a threatening hiss—*"stay with father or I will snap those horns clean off your head for a third time, you little brat."*

Saffron burst out laughing without meaning to, throwing a hand over his mouth in embarrassment. Asche swiped for Saffron's opposite hand the moment they had the chance, tugging him toward the carriage. Saffron barely had a chance to offer a goodbye to the king and Luvon, then threw an apologetic smile to the simmering Night Prince as they passed him on the way. He didn't know what the formality was for that sort of situation. He thought the gossip pamphlets might write that he and the daurae got along right away, at least, which couldn't hurt first impressions.

He climbed into the carriage exactly how Catrín had taught him, ensuring he led with his right foot on the metal step, then his left into the carriage itself, based on some old fey legend about how leading with the right meant a safe journey. Behind him, Cylvan hissed something that sounded a lot like *'those horns are mine'* as Asche scrambled in on Saffron's heels, claiming the seat alongside him. Cylvan perched on the edge of the cushion across from them as the carriage door clicked shut, bumping his knees with Saffron's and slumping back in the seat with crossed arms to pout. Saffron kept smiling at him, even as Asche grabbed at his amethyst pendant to look it over, before squeezing Saffron's cheeks and ears and complimenting how flawless his glamour charm had been made. Saffron bit back giggles the entire time; it was all so very much exactly what he could have expected. What a relief. Like he hadn't been away at all.

"This is my first time in Avren, your highness," he said as the carriage driver climbed into the seat at the front with Saoirse. Saffron maintained the polite, humble, innocent lilt of someone surrounded by strangers, someone in unfamiliar territory facing down a dangerous Night Prince who was not to be disrespected. He bumped his knee against Cylvan's again as Cylvan glared daggers at his younger sibling. "I appreciate your warm welcome.

You're as handsome as they say, you know—Ah, but perhaps that's a little too forward of me so soon."

Cylvan's crystalline eyes flickered back to him, and he smirked. Saffron's dark prince finally sat up, smiling wickedly like Saffron had whispered something naughty in his ear.

"You've heard of my beauty even in Alvénya?" he asked, voice low and cool. Sharp nails reached out to touch Saffron's knee, before drawing a line up the center of his thigh and making Saffron bite his lip. "What else do they say of me there?"

"They say you have beautiful eyes of amethyst and hair of raven silk," Saffron teased, embarrassed at how breathless he was the moment Cylvan offered even the slightest touch. "And you control storms at your fingertips. Is that true?"

Asche scoffed, but Cylvan ignored them. He lifted the hand that wasn't tracing up and down Saffron's leg, twirling his fingers and summoning a tiny thundercloud from nothing. Saffron's excitement was genuine, sitting forward and grinning in appreciation.

When he finally met Cylvan's eyes again, they watched each other for a moment—before bursting out laughing. Then the raven prince swept forward, wrapping Saffron tightly in his arms and taking his face to kiss him. It drew all the breath from Saffron's chest, and he claimed Cylvan's face in his hands in return, gasping against his demanding mouth and kissing him back with two months' worth of anticipation. Fingers tangled in his hair, sliding back on the cushions until Cylvan was on top of him. The taste of Cylvan's mouth wiped every thought from Saffron's mind, past, present, and future; he'd never known anything except the taste of him, the softness and warmth of his lips, how it felt for the tip of a familiar tongue to trace Saffron's bottom lip and tease him. He'd never known anything else, and he never wanted to.

Asche complained and attempted to kick Cylvan away, crushed by one of their brother's legs as Cylvan held Saffron pinned against the cushion. Saffron pulled from Cylvan's mouth only because otherwise he would choke on his growing laughter, all while Asche gave up and moved to the empty seat on the other side of the carriage. They grumbled under their breath and brushed the wrinkles from their tunic, while Saffron returned to where he belonged. Hands on Cylvan's face. Holding him. Kissing him. Exactly where he was always meant to be.

4

———

THE REUNION

Saffron held Cylvan's hand the whole time they traveled through the city. He saw none of it on the other side of the window, except when Cylvan would point something out to him specifically. All the bakeries Avren was best known for, trinket shops, Cylvan's favorite places to get coffee and books. But even in those moments, Saffron barely took his eyes from Cylvan's face longer than an instant. Cylvan, too, never glanced away longer than a handful of seconds. Sometimes they would meet each other's eyes and gaze into them in silence, smiling like idiots, until a bump in the carriage or a long, exasperated sigh from Asche broke them free of one another again. It was hard not to constantly slip into that silent, still moment with Cylvan right on the other side of him. Finally. Finally, again, Cylvan was right there. Saffron had to keep squeezing his hand, reaching out to touch his face, kissing him to make sure it was real and not only a dream. He'd had those dreams so many times, only to wake up in Cottage Wicklow staring at the ceiling overhead. He wasn't sure he could do it again. He wanted that time to finally be real.

"You're real," he whispered more than once under his breath. Every time, Cylvan would smile, pressing Saffron's hand against his cheek before kissing the center of his palm to prove it.

They talked about Cylvan's classes, as well as how the beginning of the semester was going for him. He was sure to brag about already being top of the class again, as well as re-joining the hurling team as one of three star players. He pressed Saffron's hand to his chest to prove it, and Saffron made a noise of *oh-so-impressed* when he felt how much firmer the prince's muscles had grown during their time apart. He couldn't help but trail both of his hands over Cylvan's shoulders, down his arms, his stomach, his thighs, all the while complimenting every dip and curve of the body underneath. Cylvan's ears flushed pink even while he kept the cocky composure on his face. Saffron then stretched out his leg to brag about how he'd actually gotten stronger since they last saw one another, too, on account of spending nearly every day of their two months apart hiking in the woods or doing manual labor around Beantighe Village. That made Cylvan narrow his eyes, asking if Saffron was still climbing tall trees with no one there to keep an eye on him—and Saffron lied straight away. *Of course not. I promised you a long time ago, no ladders and no tall trees.* But then Cylvan's amused smile faded slightly, eyes lingering on the center of Saffron's chest. That place where, compelled by Taran, he'd shot a metal bolt on Ostara. Saffron took Cylvan's hand, pressing it to the puckered scar tissue beneath his tunic.

"Barely hurts anymore," he reassured. "I promise."

Cylvan didn't look convinced. Saffron talked about himself a little bit more, trying to change the subject. Trying to summon that sparkle back into the prince's eyes. He told Cylvan about his work cleaning up the threads around the Kyteler Ruins and how Baba Yaga promised she would continue the job whenever she had a chance while he was away. He talked about the improvements to Beantighe Village under Headmistress Elding, and Cylvan nodded the whole time like he was taking mental notes.

As the buildings on the street slowly dwindled into well-groomed trees in a line along both sides of the road, Saffron's attention was finally claimed from Cylvan for longer than those briefest moments. At the top of the hill, the briny smell of the sea filled the carriage through the open windows, mixing with fresh mountain air and the distant sound of gusting wind. They passed through the first gate into the palace, where someone was in the process of fighting against a nail embedded deep in the wood. Saffron watched in curiosity, only for Cylvan to take his hand and pull his attention away from it. Wanting him to see what was on the other side.

Leaning out the window, Saffron held his breath at the landscape that swelled open in front of him. Mountains encircled the white stone palace in a lush green embrace on three sides, the fourth plummeting to a deep valley that opened up to a view of the sea. Beneath the long bridge they crossed, a river ribboned between the heights to empty into the waves below, and Saffron wondered how wide the water actually was with the height at which he saw it. The bridge was hardly more than a ribbon itself crossing the great expanse to the palace on the other side, and Saffron couldn't help but worry the strong winds summoned by the ravine would pick up the carriage like a kite and whisk it away. At least they had an air nymph who could float them right back again if needed.

Within the embrace of the valley walls, the white capitol palace of Avren stood like perpetual snowcaps amidst the warm summer air. Built from marble and gold spires that clawed at the sky like gilded fingers, windows speckled every part of the exterior that didn't jut out with sprawling rooms and towers, enclosed staircases, and arcading walkways, draped in vines and other wild greenery borrowed from the surrounding hillsides. Perhaps the only thing bigger than the palace, itself, was the courtyard that encircled it, partially groomed for parties, partially left wild for privacy on the terraces and walkways.

He'd witnessed the exterior of the palace twice before. The first was the night of Ostara; the second was at midnight while fleeing Avren only a few nights later. Holding Cylvan's hand as he was carried on a cot toward a side-exit where Luvon's carriage waited for him. He mostly recalled smiling at Cylvan, floating in an ocean of numbing tonics to keep the pain of the wound in his chest at bay enough to be moved. How Cylvan looked so concerned, yet tried so hard to smile through it whenever he glanced down at Saffron grinning drunkenly up at him. Promising they wouldn't be apart for long. Saffron was going to be safe. Cylvan was going to make sure he was taken care of. They would be together again in Avren, soon.

His final memories of the palace were nothing more than blurry pigments like paints on paper soaked with too much water. Cylvan kissing him goodbye, holding his hand through the window of Luvon's carriage until he absolutely had to let go. King Tross and King Ailir offering blessings of safe travel. Asche quickly stuffing a hand-beaded unicorn talisman through the window at the last second, which Saffron later used as a book-mark. Luvon held his hand as they left, then all the way to the Avren train station. Transported in secret. In silence. And for Saffron, nearly entirely fast asleep.

But that morning, he was wide awake. He was holding Cylvan's hand, headed toward the palace on the mountain rather than away from it.

He glanced at Cylvan one more time, nerves easing right back down again the moment he reminded himself—Cylvan was right there. He would be there for as long as Saffron needed him.

"You're real," he whispered, squeezing Cylvan's hand to prove it. Cylvan smiled at him, handsome and perfect and exactly how Saffron remembered it.

"I'm real."

As they reached the secondary gate at the end of the bridge and passed through the first stretch of expansive court-yard, Asche reclaimed Saffron's attention to point out every type of flower, shrub, and tree growing there, detailing which ones they'd personally used in creating charms, as well as which others had special properties. They held Saffron's hand the entire time to ensure Cylvan couldn't reclaim it again, all the way until they reached the main gate. Cylvan sighed and groaned and mumbled curses under his breath whenever Asche continued speaking, and even more each time Saffron showed genuine curiosity in what they were saying—all culminating the moment they arrived past the third gatehouse onto the cobblestone drive of the inner palace wall. Cylvan scooped Saffron into his arms the instant the carriage door opened, leaping into the sky and soaring high overhead with only a gasp and a shriek of surprised laughter from Saffron.

"I've had enough of sharing you!" Cylvan announced over the wind, grinning when Saffron threw arms around his neck to hold on tight. "Keep your eyes closed or else you'll see the ocean before I can make sure it's perfect, púca!"

Saffron laughed again, obeying the command and nestling his face into the crook of Cylvan's neck. His heart refused to keep in his chest, lifting into his throat and fluttering with every rise and fall of their dance in the sky.

"Are you going to drop me in?" he called out. Cylvan's arms pulled him closer.

"I'm going to introduce you to someone very important."

"What!" Saffron's eyes snapped open, before laughing again when Cylvan's hand flew to cover them.

"You're just going to have to trust me. You have nothing to worry about."

"Oh, god, that only makes me worry more."

"Apart for only two months and you already lack faith in me?" Cylvan pouted. Saffron took his face, squeezing his cheeks until his lips puckered.

"You know we have been apart nearly as long as we knew each other at Morrígan? Do I really have reason to trust you?"

"You trust me enough to be carried through the sky in my arms." Cylvan smirked. "I think you trust me more than you tease. Besides... plenty of high fey get engaged within a week of courting one another. I actually went easy on you."

"A week!" Saffron gasped, kicking his legs. "It should be the other way around, since fey live for so damn long! You should be courting one another for years, not weeks."

"Big talk for someone engaged after only two months."

Saffron pouted, but grabbed Cylvan's face to squeeze it again.

"Only because you're so handsome." He mumbled. "If you were any uglier, I would have said no. I wouldn't have put up with you and your personality for so long."

"I could say the same for you."

"Hey!" Saffron punched him in the chest, laughing when Cylvan pretended to nearly drop them. Below, a blanket of trees spread far to the horizon as Cylvan held Saffron specifically so the sea was at his back. Saffron wrapped his arms back around Cylvan and pulled himself close, pressing a kiss to the side of his neck.

"I missed you so much," he sighed. "I don't care that we haven't known each other long, either—no fated lovers I've ever read about in myths knew one another for long before falling in love."

"I am worried which fated lovers you mean. Most of them end in tragedy."

"Not us," Saffron said, though he knew how dangerous those words were. All things considered. But then pressing the curve of his nose into Cylvan's skin, breathing him in, sensing his pulse, Saffron couldn't help but think maybe it could be true. *Not us. Not us.* "I know I'll only ever be happy with you."

"I'll do everything I can to ensure that." Cylvan smiled. "And this is how I'll start."

Cylvan prompted Saffron to close his eyes again. Saffron did, clinging to Cylvan's hand even as they descended lightly and his feet returned to solid ground. Cylvan then coaxed him forward, up a slight incline, where he could smell the thick trees and fresh air, hear the birds and breeze, and in the distance, what he knew to be crashing waves. He couldn't stop smiling. Cylvan even noticed and teased him, pinching his cheek and asking what could possibly have him looking like that when there was nothing to see yet, but Saffron squeezed Cylvan's hand and bounced on his toes.

He was just—happy. He was just so happy to know that time, when he opened his eyes, Cylvan would still be there. It wouldn't be his imagination.

When Cylvan finally settled to a stop, he stepped behind Saffron, running fingers up through the back of his hair.

"Alright."

Saffron had to blink against the bright sunlight—but once his vision cleared, he gasped, taking a step forward in awe.

He knew the ocean was endless. He'd seen paintings of it, read descriptions of it in books; he'd been told about it by Luvon and Adelard and even Letty whose patron family regularly visited their private island. He wasn't so foolish to think he would see something unexpected—but finally witnessing it firsthand still took his breath away. An infinite landscape of water, like navy-blue grassy fields tousled by the wind, blown into jagged caps like a thick quilt speckled with green and white embroidery beads. Standing on the cliff overlooking it, he gaped first at the endless sight straight ahead, breathing in the smell of heavy rain threatened by storm clouds on the horizon, before appreciating how waves crescendoed endlessly against the snakelike cliff sides stretching long in either direction. Forming the shape of the eastern edge of all of Alfidel, one Cylvan had once drawn for him in their crow book. One he'd seen so many times on the giant map in Adelard's office, never once believing he might get to see it for himself one day.

"Oh..." was all he could say. There weren't words big enough to describe it, to do something so large and alive and humbling the justice it deserved. Cylvan wrapped his arms around Saffron from behind, pulling him close.

"This will be your view every day here, if you wish," he whispered. Goosebumps kissed Saffron's arms. "For as long as you're here with me, you'll get to see the ocean whenever you like."

There was only one thing that could compel Saffron's eyes away from such an astounding sight—and he turned to kiss it. He took Cylvan's face, holding it, kissing him until he had to stop breathing just to be close enough to satisfy him. There was the slightest tinge of sea salt on his lips from the spray. The wind tangled his hair around them. And Saffron wanted to have all of it, to keep in his hands and take for himself.

"It's going to have competition for my attention every day," he whispered. Cylvan grinned like that was the most satisfying thing he'd ever heard. Like a part of him had been jealous.

"Careful. We wouldn't want you upsetting the gods of the sea."

"Let them hear it. I'm sure they already know they don't hold a candle."

"My prince is willing to start a war with the sea over my beauty," Cylvan smirked, tucking a piece of windswept hair from Saffron's eyes. "Perhaps we are fated to be as lovers in myth, after all..."

He trailed off, eyes skimming up the length of Saffron's body, lingering on the skin beneath his ear. Saffron's cheeks were already flushed before Cylvan ever reached out to flatten his hand against the back of Saffron's neck, squeezing slightly.

"This is going to be a problem," he mumbled. "Most high fey have long hair, or wear high collars... there's something sensual about the back of the neck. Something dominating about being able to see it. Since only short-haired, bowing beantighes usually show it off."

Saffron flushed hotter, averting his eyes before swatting at Cylvan to let him go. Cylvan chuckled, taking Saffron's hand in his own again, then turning him back toward the trees.

"I said I was going to introduce you to someone. Come on, then."

He nodded over his shoulder, pulling Saffron from the edge of the cliff. Saffron searched the greenery as they walked, about to ask how far it was from where they landed, when something appeared through the foliage and piqued his curiosity.

The structure came into view around a bend in the trees, and Saffron's mouth dropped open slightly in surprise. It nearly scared the shit out of him at first, staring up at a man carved into the trunk of a living tree at the center of the altar, branches sprawling tall and out of the circular roof overhead. An older fey man with a long beard, he reverently held a spear between two hands. A hound at his feet gazed out across the sea. On his hip, a harp dangled alongside a sheathed sword, every minuscule detail carved into the still-living wood with precision. He almost asked how the figure kept such a detailed shape in a trunk still thriving, before realizing the offerings on the stone altar at the man's feet were fresh. Garlands of pine and silver bells, flowers, bowls of fruit and fresh water, amphoras of sweet-smelling wine, and an array of burning candles poured with pine needles and flower petals in the wax—but then Saffron stumbled backward with a sharp gasp, pressing a hand to his mouth to swallow back his alarm.

In one of the offering bowls, drenching the fruit in crimson, a mutilated barn owl curled with wings outstretched, feathers wet with blood, beak and talons chipped with signs of fighting. Tucked into the soiled breast feathers—a red card donning the same words as the one left for him at the train station.

5

THE SEA

Cylvan didn't let Saffron stare for long. He swept Saffron into his arms and leapt over the edge of the cliff without warning, making Saffron yelp and scramble for something to hold onto. He squeezed his eyes closed and held his breath until they returned to the earth, wet sand shifting beneath Cylvan's boots and ocean spray piercing through Saffron's tunic to kiss his skin. Even once they landed, though, Cylvan still didn't put Saffron down, instead taking long, graceful leaps on the lift of his wind to skate toward a nearby inlet in the cliffside, dampening the chill of the crashing sea and the sound that came with it.

"What was that?" Saffron finally asked as Cylvan let him down, boots scraping against the stone ground dusted with sand from the beach. Wind tousled his hair, smelling of salt and incoming rain, hardly giving them another few moments before drops speckled the ground.

"Not what I meant to show you," Cylvan sighed, raking fingers back through his hair before leaning out from the inlet to gaze up at the edge of the cliff overhead. Saffron followed suit, as if expecting there to be a face peeking down to search for them.

Cylvan's eyes lingered long enough for Saffron to grow suspicious, grabbing his tunic and jostling him to break him out of it.

"What's going on?" he asked. "C'mon."

"This really is not the way I wanted to spend my first hours alone with you," Cylvan said, growing more and more annoyed as it sank in. Saffron could practically see the images of him tearing a stranger apart behind his eyes, like the fantasy would soothe his nerves for the time being. He ran fingers back through his hair again, before pressing Saffron into the uneven stone to shield him from the growing rain. "It's... it's nothing. Nothing for you to worry about—"

"Oh, don't you dare even try."

Cylvan scowled. He ruffled Saffron's hair in frustration. "Can't you be cute and innocent and meek for me, just for a little bit? Let me sweep you away from a gory sight, then reward me for being so chivalrous."

"I'll reward you all you like. But you have to tell me if something is going on, first."

"Gods above," Cylvan grumbled. "Like I said, it's nothing. There have always been dissenters in Avren, it only caught me off guard."

Saffron narrowed his eyes. Cylvan narrowed his back, and they played a silent game of intimidation until Cylvan finally threw his head back in a defeated groan.

"Some dissenting groups have been particularly loud and troublesome, lately. That's not the first barn owl that's been killed in the name of sending a message. Three others have been nailed to the front gates of the palace in the last few weeks." His voice lowered. "Which was... part of the reason I chose to leave you at Morrígan for one more month. But the royal guard still haven't found who's behind it, and I'm a selfish creature, so I didn't want to wait any longer... I knew you might see something eventually, but—damnit, I didn't expect it to be right away. Within a hour of your arrival."

Saffron sighed, closing his eyes and pressing a hand to Cylvan's chest. He took a few purposeful breaths, before shaking his head. He almost said what he was thinking—but decided he would much rather give Cylvan his wish. Someone cute, innocent, meek. Someone who would not question if Cylvan knew anything else about who was mutilating birds and organizing the passing out of red cards with strange poems; or if there was any chance it involved one specific man Saffron met in the palace infirmary months prior. In fact, Saffron was more than happy to keep Ryder Kyteler's name as far from his mind as possible. He would gladly pretend he'd barely seen anything at all. Just for a little bit longer.

"Thank you for sweeping me away to safety so quickly, your highness," he said, running his hands up the back of Cylvan's neck, into his hair. "It was very chivalrous of you. Will you tell me what you were trying to show me?"

"What, you didn't recognize him?" Cylvan smiled smugly. "I thought you'd be the one telling *me* everything I needed to know the second you laid eyes on the old king."

Saffron pursed his lips, but scoured his memory at the challenge. Someone he should have recognized. Someone Cylvan assumed he would know plenty about. He thought about the harp on the carving's belt, the sword, the spear...

"Would you like a hint?"

"No. Is it Oisín? After accidentally touching mortal earth."

"No."

Saffron frowned. "Then... King Lir?"

"His children would have been carved around him if that were the case, don't you think? Come on, there's something you're missing. Why would the royal family have a private altar to an wrinkled fey grandfather, unless...?"

Saffron jumped, stumbling over his words before finally declaring: "King Lugh! That was King Lugh!"

Cylvan grinned, grabbing Saffron's face and smooshing their noses together, before kissing him again and again on the cheeks.

"Ohh, beantighe, you're so good, so smart, the smartest little beantighe ever, I'm so proud."

Saffron attempted to shove him away, squealing with laughter when Cylvan pressed him harder against the stone and groped him all over, planting more kisses against his face, then down his neck.

"Yes, I was hoping to introduce you to old King Lugh Lamhfada, who is the patron deity of the Tuatha dé Danann," Cylvan went on, still teasing and tickling him, before taking Saffron's face under the chin and smiling at him. "I wished to show you to him, to see if you pleased him enough to bless our marriage."

Saffron gulped. "O-oh... and? How would you know whether or not he did?"

"They say if anyone unfriendly to the Tuatha dé Danann enters his presence, the spear in his hand lights into flames and burns down his ancient tree," he said, before shaking his head. "Obviously, considering what actually waited for us there, it's just a myth, but... I was fully prepared to let you believe it. I wanted to hear what you might say to someone who would know if you were lying."

"Say about what?" Saffron smiled nervously. Cylvan's eyes were deep and rich in the overcast light, strands of dark hair beginning to cling to his skin as rain saturated him from above.

"About your intentions with me."

Saffron's breath caught, searching Cylvan's face for a silent moment. His lips parted, speckled with drops of rain as he gazed up at the perfect fey lord hanging over him.

"I would have told him everything," Saffron whispered. Cylvan's sly smile softened. "I would have told him that... while I'm not much... I'm only starting school for the first time in a few days, I've been a beantighe my whole life, I don't know anything about how to be a high fey... I care about Prince Cylvan with my whole heart. My whole being. And..."

His hands found Cylvan's chest, pressing flat against it,

absorbing his warmth. Feeling how his heart beat beneath Saffron's touch.

"And how I think I can help him be a good king one day. Even if everyone thinks he's going to bring a Night Court. Even if he actually does. I don't care about any of that; it doesn't scare me. I would tell him about how much I missed you while I was away, and how excited I am to be here. And how grateful I am for the chance you're giving me. And how I've thought about you every single day and night since we last saw one another, to the point of obsession. I thought of nothing else at all. And now that we're finally together again—I'm afraid you might still be the only thing I ever think about, until the day I die."

Cylvan's expression gentled further, smiling in the softest way Saffron could never have imagined possible. The prince lifted a hand to cup under Saffron's jaw, gliding a thumb over his cheek where his most prominent scar was hidden beneath the glamour. At the thought, Cylvan's hand slid down to hook a nail beneath the chain of the amethyst pendant, pulling it away and revealing Saffron's real face underneath.

"Beautiful," he whispered, touching Saffron's cheek again, tucking wet hair behind his ear. "I missed your face so much. I dreamed of it every night. Just like this."

Saffron smiled weakly. He put his hand into the crook of Cylvan's arm, standing on his toes to kiss him gently. Cylvan's mouth tasted of rain and ocean salt, like the woods and everything else Saffron needed to feel satisfied again. Filling the gap in his heart, the last little bit that never healed over even when the rest of him did. That place where Cylvan belonged, where he fit so perfectly.

As their lips glided effortlessly against one another, as Cylvan's breaths grew heavier, sharper, a hand returned to the back of Saffron's neck. Squeezing it again, cupping the back of his head, before nails slid up through his hair.

"Cylvan," Saffron breathed between their mouths, feeling

how Cylvan's touch intensified as he did. "Touch me. Please. Don't make me wait anymore. I don't want to have to wait..."

He found the line of buttons down the front of Cylvan's tunic, slippery in the rain, fingers growing clumsy as Cylvan's hand slid down the front of Saffron's waistband to tease him. The prince's knee nestled between Saffron's legs, opening them, pressing him back against the wet stone and making his breath catch as a warm palm found and stroked him.

"I thought we might do this in my bedroom," Cylvan whispered into Saffron's ear, smiling to himself when Saffron's hands halted on the buttons of his tunic in growing overwhelm. "I was going to feed you cakes and sweets, wine, undress you slowly, worship every inch of you. Properly refamiliarize myself with every part I've missed most. Until you were clutching my bedsheets, begging..."

"Fuck," Saffron gasped with a crack in his voice. Cylvan noticed exactly how sensitive he was to simply being touched, smiling mischievously and pushing Saffron's tunic open to kiss his chest, rolling a hot tongue over one of his nipples while his opposite hand pushed his pants down a little more, revealing the bare skin of his legs to the chilly air.

"I don't think I've ever met a beantighe who whimpers so easily under my hand."

"G-god," Saffron wanted to curse him, but Cylvan was right. While he'd touched and pleasured himself plenty during the previous two months, it simply wasn't the same. Saffron thought about Cylvan the entire time, every time; he could count the number of times he'd been able to be intimate with Cylvan on one hand—and it made the anticipation of every new opportunity sweeter than the last. Saffron wanted to feel it again. He wanted to have it again. He'd been withheld from for too long. He was going to tear apart in hunger. He wanted to writhe and beg and whimper beneath Prince Cylvan's hands and mouth and weight on top of him.

"Did you wait for me? Even though I said you didn't have

to…" Cylvan asked breathily, hand sliding further between Saffron's legs, teasing entry as Saffron shivered at the sensation of sharp nails. "No matter how many parties I went to, suddenly there was not a single courtier I had any care to spend the night with… not after learning how soft… and warm… and needy human beantighes can be."

"I… thought of you," Saffron panted, tensing when Cylvan's wet fingers gently pushed inside, careful not to scrape with their sharp ends. "Every time I—touched myself, when I was alone."

"What did you think of?" Cylvan lifted one of Saffron's legs, and Saffron instinctively curled it around Cylvan's waist. Cracking open his eyes, his cheeks were hot against the chill of the air. Cylvan slid another finger inside, invited deeper with Saffron's leg lifted out of the way—and Saffron could only cling to the front of his tunic in tighter hands.

"Y-your fingers." Saffron said pathetically as Cylvan purred against the side of his neck, thrusting such things deeper into him, in and out and making Saffron's toes curl. "And your—m-mouth!"

He clung to Cylvan as the fingers opening him up stroked faster, nearly making his leg buckle, gasping and clenching as rising pleasure coiled in his stomach. As fingers grazed the tender place inside of him, deep enough that only someone else's fingers could reach. Cylvan's fingers were gentle but demanding, careful with their sharp tips to not hurt him—though the gentle trailing of their points along his insides summoned a pitiful, bubbling whimper from his lips. Teasing him, tickling him, making every inch twist and itch with desperation for relief.

Cylvan pressed a hand to the small of Saffron's back, curving his spine, tilting his hips and allowing his fingers to stroke deeper. "You're so tight… it must have been agony, waiting for me to touch you again."

"I—" But Saffron couldn't summon the words. He didn't know the words. He wasn't sure they even existed. "Oh, Cylvan—please…"

Cylvan chuckled again. He pulled his fingers out, slow enough to drive Saffron to near insanity, before kissing him again while working down the front of Saffron's tunic.

"I'm going to take my time with you," he whispered. "I'm going to refamiliarize myself with every inch of you—so your skin won't forget how it feels beneath my touch, alone. Until you're begging for me."

"F-fuck," Saffron groaned. "Th-they warned me... you were a Night Prince. I never thought... it would be like this."

Cylvan smiled darkly like that was his favorite thing to hear. He pushed Saffron's tunic off over his shoulders, baring his skin to the biting wind and sea spray. Saffron shivered as he was exposed, then again as Cylvan's mouth returned to his nipples, firm and sensitive from the cold and the anticipation of what would come. In the center of his chest, the scar from Ostara was warped and ugly, and Saffron attempted to say something—but Cylvan kissed it, instead. He kissed it, trailing the tip of his nose over the edge as if offering reverence to something so horrible. Saffron felt the same emanating off of him, hating how he knew Cylvan still blamed himself for it. Even though he shouldn't. He shouldn't, he shouldn't—Saffron never did. Cylvan hadn't had any choice.

He trailed fingers back through Cylvan's hair, drawing him from the quiet distraction.

"Please touch me more, Cylvan," he whispered, and Cylvan obeyed. The prince's mouth explored Saffron's skin like he promised, trailing his lips, his tongue, his hands over Saffron's ribs with all the care of appraising a priceless treasure; his fingers puckered the skin over Saffron's waist, cupping and squeezing the round of his ass and sighing into Saffron's mouth as he did. They trailed down the tops of Saffron's thighs, before creeping upward again, always barely skimming past his needy erection with an impish smile.

Saffron felt like he was going to tear out of his skin. He channeled the waves of frustration into his own hands, pulling a little too greedily at Cylvan's own tunic, accidentally popping some of the buttons off and sending them to the sand. He hardly noticed, hardly pulled his mouth from Cylvan's that tasted exactly like he remembered, that moved against his like it was made for him. His forbidden fruit; his pomegranate full of ambrosial seeds that he would devour without care for the consequences. His dark prince, his lord of the underworld, his king of the forest, his raven—

"I missed you so much," he whimpered. He shoved Cylvan's tunic away, pressing hands to his chest, tracing them down his stomach, pausing only when he realized how much that body had really changed in their time apart. He pulled from their mouths, breathless and flushed as he fully appreciated Cylvan's physique. They'd teased about it in the carriage—but Cylvan hadn't been exaggerating. He'd always had cuts and dips between the muscles of his chest, his stomach, his shoulders—but since they last saw one another, he'd broadened out. He was firmer beneath Saffron's hands, stronger, slightly more refined. Saffron couldn't help but trace fingers over every line between Cylvan's muscles, down the center of his chest, his arms, before weaving their fingers together. He pulled Cylvan back to his mouth, kissing him for a long time.

"I missed you," he repeated softly. "I missed you, I missed you..."

"We never have to be apart again," Cylvan whispered. His hands grasped Saffron's hips again, and Saffron's own found the front of Cylvan's pants, undoing the laces and pushing them away from his hips. The prince strained beneath the fabric, and Saffron took his cock in his hand, watching how Cylvan's expression twisted in pleasure as he stroked and rubbed the end, the length. How he bit his lip, inhaled sharply, furrowed his brows, clenched his teeth—before heavy eyes lifted to gaze at Saffron through dark lashes, wanton and pleading.

"I've waited long enough," Saffron said, kissing Cylvan again before pulling away. He turned, placing his hands on the face of the stone cliff, gazing at Cylvan over his shoulder and curving his back. "Haven't I? Cylvan..."

Cylvan's hands hooked beneath Saffron's hips, pressing into the backs of his thighs and stroking his length against his tailbone. Saffron bit his lip, a silent sigh escaping as Cylvan's tip kissed between his legs—then pressed slowly inside. It spread Saffron open, making his legs tremble and his breath stutter. He turned his head, catching Cylvan's lips over his shoulder and drinking him in as the shocking pleasure of penetration consumed him. Made it hard to hold himself upright, to think straight. Rendered drunk without a sip of whiskey or a taste of fairy fruits—Cylvan was enough. Cylvan was all Saffron needed.

Cylvan's thighs met the backs of Saffron's, leaning into him until Saffron was pressed flush against the stone. Pinned there as Cylvan complimented him, hands encompassing his narrowed waist and teeth biting Saffron's ear. The prince moved carefully at first without oil to wet Saffron's insides, knowing his own pleasure would spill inside and ease the effort soon enough. Saffron felt as every thrust came smoother, slipping in and out of him without drawing such a sharp line from the base of his tailbone, until Cylvan's restraint thinned and his movements grew more demanding.

Harder and harder, thrusting into Saffron with months of pent-up frustration, kissing and biting at the curve of Saffron's neck as his hand gripped his hips harder. Saffron tried to bite back his moans and whimpers, curling his fingers against the stone, breath hitching with every churn inside of him. He pressed a hand to the base of his stomach, sure Cylvan was going to pierce straight through him. Filling him to the brim, again and again, pinned by his arms into submission.

When Saffron's knees buckled from the overwhelm, Cylvan caught him, pulling him into his chest. Saffron laid his head back over Cylvan's shoulder, bending an arm behind his head as his legs were pulled open again. He gasped and moaned into the side of Cylvan's neck, pressing his face beneath the prince's ear as sweat beaded on his forehead and his eyes watered. His opposite hand stroked between his legs, begging to be fucked harder as warmth tightened in his stomach. He bit back more fervored cries of pleasure, before breaking with a gasp, arching his back and clenching over every inch as the ecstasy between his hips swelled and spilled out of him.

He slumped back into Cylvan's arms, breathing heavily—but Cylvan grunted, pulling him closer and planting a hand over his mouth as he slammed harder, deeper, faster, making Saffron claw at the silencing hand as he almost screamed in overstimulation. He moaned and begged in the form of whimpers, though even he didn't know if they were pleas for mercy or *more more, more, more—!*

Cylvan came inside of him with a moan and squeezing arms —then gave Saffron no chance to catch his breath, pulling away only enough to sink to his knees on the beach. Cylvan clawed at his tunic balled up on the sand, sloppily spreading it out before grabbing Saffron with one arm under his back and dragging him onto the soft fabric. Saffron barely threw his arms out to claim Cylvan back again, kissing him roughly between battles to catch their breaths—all while Cylvan pushed his legs open once more, thrusting inside with an eagerness that jolted the rest of Saffron's body upward. He whimpered into Cylvan's mouth, still holding his face, rolling his hips against the hardness entangled within him. Cylvan fucked him like a wild fey in heat, until Saffron dripped onto the tunic under his back, until he couldn't feel his legs, until he couldn't remember his name or the name of the demanding weight on top of him. It whittled him down to a weeping, drooling, begging mess, just kissing him, groping at him, wrapping his legs around Cylvan's waist to keep him inside, to beg him to keep going when words failed him.

Cylvan fucked him until there was nothing left—and then did it again. And again, then again, until Saffron collapsed over the prince's shoulder while riding him chest-to-chest. Exhausted. Wholly devoured but spilling over. Cylvan cooed at him, cupping the back of his neck in one hand, petting the back of his hair, gently easing in and out a few more times before planting a row of kisses up the side of Saffron's neck in what felt like praise. *You did so well. You've done so well.*

Saffron smiled to himself, drunk and empty, aching and flushed, throbbing and overflowing and littered with love bites, teeth marks, bruises where Cylvan gripped him too tightly for leverage. He shivered as sweat mixed with humid sea spray on his skin, finally closing his eyes and releasing a long, weary breath. Cylvan pulled out slowly, carefully, before sinking with him onto the dirtied tunic beneath them. He pulled Saffron close, and Saffron only had the strength to offer one more kiss to his sweat-sheened chest, before sinking into the velvet darkness of pure bliss.

6

THE MORNING

A feast at the palace may have been lovely, but Saffron wouldn't know. Afternoon tea might have been nice. Dinner may have been an entire spectacle. Saffron wouldn't know. Saffron was too busy gazing at the great expanse of the sea from the beach where Cylvan made a meal of him for hours. Where they rested still naked, Saffron wrapped in Cylvan's tunic as the rain picked up, spilling against the stone over their little inlet that only offered the slightest protection. With his head on Cylvan's chest, listening to his heart, Saffron extended a hand outward to cup at the falling water, sipping it from his palm. He told Cylvan it tasted like the rain in the Agate Wood, which was a reassurance. Cylvan gazed down at him like he was the most interesting thing in the world.

They hid on the edge of the ocean until time lost all meaning, lost in conversation after getting lost in one another's mouths and hands. When they weren't chatting, they sat in comfortable silence as waves crashed a hundred feet against the beach ahead of them. Until the sun went down and even midnight came and went. Until the sea spray and sweat clinging to Saffron's skin left him shivering, though he tried to hide it. Until Cylvan finally uttered the words Saffron was afraid to hear, but knew were inevitable: *I suppose we should go back.*

Carried in Cylvan's arms, Saffron clung to him as they lifted into the rainy sky over the city, only a few hours shy of sunrise. Below them, Avren might as well have been a sun on its own merit with the brightness of its lights, street lanterns and warm interiors glowing to show them the way. A part of him wished Cylvan would change his mind, to turn and soar off in the opposite direction, back toward the sea—but he kept reminding himself, it wasn't the last time they would see each other. Never again.

Rather than taking Saffron back to the palace, perhaps because he secretly dreaded Asche monopolizing him all over again, Cylvan carried him to Luvon's townhouse in the city. He didn't bother with the front door, instead lighting down on the railing of the third-floor balcony, landing on the ball of one foot with all the weight of a feather. He let Saffron down first, then landed both feet on the balcony, only for Saffron to wrap him up in another kiss.

"Will you stay a little longer?" He asked. Cylvan smirked, tucking a finger under Saffron's chin.

"I will do anything you ask," he breathed. "... Starting tomorrow. Luvon's waiting for you on the other side of the door, there. I can see him in the shadows."

Saffron glanced nervously over his shoulder. Sure enough, his patron father sat in an armchair on the other side of the balcony doors. He didn't look their way, but Saffron knew he knew they were there. He offered Cylvan a heartbroken smile, tugging on the front of his tunic one more time. Then grimacing at how wrinkled it was, covered in sand and other things, a few buttons torn away near the collar.

"There actually is something I wanted to ask... since the next time we see each other, it'll be at Mairwen," he said, avoiding Cylvan's eyes because it was embarrassing. It took Saffron a few moments to finally speak it out loud. "When we finally see each other on campus, will you... tell me I look handsome in my uniform? Even just in passing. Like a stranger might..."

The sincerity of his request appeared to catch Cylvan off guard, and he tilted his head.

"I don't have to see it to already know—"

"I mean it," Saffron interrupted, before shaking his head, still too timid to meet Cylvan's eyes. Perfect, handsome, flawless Cylvan. "Even with the glamour, I'm worried I'll look out of place. Like it'll be obvious I don't belong there, like I have no idea what I'm doing—and the last thing I want is to look foolish, and make you look foolish, so that everyone wonders why in the world someone like you would ever want to court someone like—"

Cylvan kissed him, silencing the words. His fingers on Saffron's cheek were so gentle.

"I am eager to fall in love with you at first sight," Cylvan whispered. "All over again."

"Don't lie," Saffron mumbled in embarrassment. "You definitely did not."

"How would you know?" Cylvan countered with a coy smile. Saffron shook his head, recalling how he'd looked in the mirror right before leaving Cottage Wicklow the morning before they boarded the ship to Avren. Something about that human face gazing back at him, hair a mess, eyes puffy from restless sleep the night before—it only emphasized how little he believed someone like Cylvan could fall in love at first sight with someone like him. But, perhaps once glamoured, wearing his tailored uniform, existing in the same world as Cylvan dé Tuatha dé Danann—it might actually be believable.

"I love you," Cylvan went on. "I'll see you soon, púca. I'll make sure you fall madly in love with me all over again, too."

Saffron laughed. He kissed Cylvan one more time, before finally having to let him go. He stood on the balcony and watched until his raven vanished entirely into the early morning sky.

. . .

"GOOD MORNING, LUVON," SAFFRON GREETED UPON finally entering the room, habitually running fingers back through his hair as if Luvon would be able to see it. Wanting to look nice even if it didn't matter. "I'm—I'm sorry for missing dinner with the kings..." or was it lunch? "Prince Cylvan and I just... lost track of time..."

"Ah, yes, I'm sure you did, a leanbh," Luvon sighed, getting to his feet and brushing himself off. "I figured you would be easily distracted by your prince. King Tross and I gossiped about it all night. You know Prince Cylvan is only third in his class? And third best on the hurling team. He didn't even apply to be a prefect for his dormitory."

Saffron rolled his eyes, though couldn't resist smiling a little bit.

"If he was too perfect he wouldn't be real, I think. Everyone needs flaws."

"Not my future son-in-law," Luvon said threateningly. As if Cylvan merely being the Crown Prince of Alfidel wasn't enough. "We'll talk about it more, later. For now, wash up, then..." he pointed his cane toward the bathroom door, where a buttoned garment bag hung from a hook. "... try those on and come downstairs."

"Oh, alright," Saffron said in surprise, glancing at the bag before back to Luvon. He'd really been hoping to spend his last day before starting classes in bed, maybe reading, or drawing, or exploring Avren—but perhaps that was naïve of him. Of course Luvon would be dolling him up for something or other every chance he got.

Once Luvon left, Saffron approached the mystery bag hanging from the door, unbuttoning the line down the front. What waited for him inside made his heart skip.

He was so used to Morrígan's dark maroon blazer and slacks, the off-white high-collar cravats and neck scarves, the dark brown shoes. Mairwen's design followed a similar silhouette, but Saffron was charmed in an instant by a rich forest green jacket, matching slacks and waistcoat, an off-white button down shirt with sharp, high-collared lapels, and shiny black derby shoes that reminded him of those he wore as a beantighe. Above all else, though, he was captivated by the lapels of the jacket.

Blue, shaped like elongated butterfly wings that wrapped around the back of the collar. Embroidered along the veins, they shimmered slightly with a sheer layer of fabric that allowed light to shine through, just slightly, like the sun catching a thick pane of colored glass. On the breast pocket was the school crest, a matching blue butterfly overlaying a tree of swirling branches and roots that circled around the edges. Touching the embroidered patch, all he could think was—weren't butterflies... delicate? They were nothing like the raven of Morrígan, or the barn owl of the royal family, or the unicorn of Danann House, or the stag of the mag Shamhradháins...

With nervous hands, Saffron fully removed the articles of clothing from the bag. He pulled each one out carefully, finding them to be perfectly tailored to his measurements, though it didn't help the overwhelming sensation that he wasn't suited to wear them. They weren't meant for him. Whoever tailored them probably had no idea a human beantighe-turned-witch-turned-royalty-in-a-fey-glamour would be sliding his scarred legs, arms, body into the well-crafted fabric. He squeezed the amethyst pendant for strength, then tucked it down into the shirt before he could completely give in to the feeling of drowning.

AFTER A WASH TO REMOVE SAND, SWEAT, AND OTHER unmentionables from his skin, Saffron dressed in the clothes that were perfectly tailored for him. As to be expected. He perceived nothing of the room around him, or the room where Luvon had been waiting for him, or hardly anything else at all—he only saw how the uniform had looked in his hands. How it felt to touch. His eyes would constantly flicker to where it hung on the door. Again and again and again, until he finally pulled them on carefully, as if delicate. As if made of paper, afraid of tearing them. And even though they fit perfectly, he was too self-conscious to look in the mirror again.

He found Luvon in the dining room eating breakfast, and Saffron offered the same three-knocks on the entryway door he always did while at home at the Winter Court, not wishing to startle his patron father.

There was something surreal about being in such a strange place, that, in many ways, was familiar by the choice of interior design. Luvon always leaned toward warm, earthy colors, like natural wood and furs and woven knits. His townhouse there in the Mid Court was no different, except for the lighter weight of fabrics, less need for thick floor rugs, sheer curtains to allow sunlight in instead of fighting to keep warmth in the rooms where it belonged.

While Saffron wished he could find comfort in such small, familiar details in such an unfamiliar place, one thing blanketed it with cold self-consciousness—and that was the presence of beantighes puttering around the house in every direction, even in and out of the dining room as Saffron stepped in. Saffron wished Luvon would have warned him first, but—beantighes were a normal, everyday occurrence in Luvon's life. Like any other high fey who could afford to employ and patronize them, they were hardly more than decor on the wallpaper, or little breaths of wind that fluffed pillows and steamed linens. He probably hadn't had a second thought about them at all.

There weren't any familiar faces from his Winter Court estate, at least, Saffron noticed right away. He almost asked if they were new, if they were all patronized by someone else in the city, or if Luvon had registered ownership of a handful more to watch over the house while Saffron was in Avren attending school—but didn't know how, especially as they kept sweeping in and out. Paying him no mind. A normal high fey wouldn't have any reason to ask anything like that, anyway.

On the table, crystal glasses stood perfectly polished alongside plates already laid with food, and the smell made Saffron's stomach growl in hunger he didn't realize he had. Perhaps it made sense, considering all the ways he'd been eaten alive for the entire night before. He flushed at the thought, hurrying inside. Just wanting to confirm to Luvon the uniform fit, so that he might—carefully—strip it all off again and spend the rest of the day preparing himself for the giant thing about to happen. To remind himself why he should be more excited. Not so nervous. Ah—damnit.

"Good morning," he finally greeted as Luvon bit into a piece of toast softened by a layer of butter and jam. "I'm... I'm wearing my uniform, Luvon. It fits perfectly."

"I knew it would," Luvon smiled, wiping his hands off on a napkin and rising to his feet to seek out where Saffron stood. Dark brown hands brushed over the stiff shoulders of Saffron's blazer, then down the soft lapels as Luvon memorized every detail. "It has blue lapels, doesn't it?"

"Yes."

"Good." Luvon nodded. "I had to remind the school tailor a number of times, since they kept thinking you were a prep-school student. Those uniforms have monarch-colored lapels. You may see the daurae wearing one."

"I'll go change then join you for breakfast," Saffron went on, the anxiety making his skin itch. "I'm sorry for taking so long—"

"No need," Luvon interrupted, patting Saffron's shoulders again before motioning for him to take a seat at the table. "I'm actually taking you to campus this morning. I figured you would want some extra time to get used to everything before your first class tomorrow."

"O-oh!" Saffron squeaked, digging his heels into the wood as Luvon shepherded him to the table. "Th-that's—! Oh, that's not —necessary—!"

But his patron father won out, and Saffron took his seat, staring down at the plate of food waiting for him.

Oh, god, what was he going to do? No—no, he was thinking

about breakfast. He was going to think very, very hard about breakfast, and not about the world-turning thing Luvon had just finished telling him.

He thought he was ready. He wanted to be excited, but—the moment it was placed in front of him, Saffron felt more like a mouse petrified by the eyes of a snake.

But then the amethyst down his shirt warmed, and Saffron's racing, panicked thoughts slowed to a trickle. He closed his eyes, breathing in deeply, wishing he could clutch the pendant in return. To send Cylvan a thousand little pulses to ease his blood-melting panic. But he couldn't—and that forced him to accept his fate. It forced him to breathe. Forced him to eat, and to sit with the discomfort.

He wasn't ready—but he might never be.

But—that was also the one thing he'd always wanted. It would have been the *only* thing he'd ever wanted, had he never met Cylvan dé Tuatha dé Danann. And no matter how much it scared him, Saffron knew, it would all be fine knowing Cylvan would be there. He would be there—and they would never have to part again. From that point onward. Saffron would get to have the two things he'd always wanted most in his life—to attend school, and to have a love like those in myths.

Saffron took a deep breath. He lifted his fork to eat. He sat up straight, used a napkin after every bite, and spoke in a polite tone and volume while he and Luvon shared casual conversation over the meal. Just like Catrín had taught him. Just like he'd been preparing for.

All Saffron could do was his best.

7
____

THE ACADEMY

They'd long since left the outskirts of the city, crossing a swath of countryside before the rolling hills gave way to trees as thick as the Agate Wood, when Saffron yanked the carriage window down to breathe it in. Allowing the fresh air mixed with nearby sea-salt to cleanse him from the inside out. It helped, at first. But the tightness returned the moment they approached the gates.

Cast in gold, words embellished a metal banner over the gates:

MAIRWEN ACADEMY OF OPULENT ARTS;
AVREN, MID COURT.

"You should have an entry token on your pocket chain," Luvon said, tapping the foot of his cane against the carriage floor. "It should be attached to the buttons of your waistcoat."

Saffron undid his jacket, searching for what he knew Luvon was referring to. A thin, silver chain wrapped around one of his waistcoat buttons, a matching silver pendant donning Mairwen's crest dangling off the end.

"I have it," Saffron said, patting around his waistcoat.

"Very good. Why don't you go let us in?"

Saffron hesitated, before climbing out of the carriage. He held the chain in one hand, staring at the locked gates for a long time, wondering exactly what he was supposed to do—but then he spotted a small mark on a silver plate where the two gates latched. Touching the pendant to the metal, he grinned when it hummed, then clanged, swinging open wide enough for the carriage to pass through.

"It works like Morrígan's rings!" Saffron exclaimed as he clambered back inside, and Luvon patted him on the back with a smile.

They continued another hundred yards before the trees thinned again, then finally gave way to an expansive clearing boasting more buildings than Morrígan twice over. Grander, brighter buildings, though built with similar stone, metal, and glass styles as those Saffron spent so many years cleaning.

There was more color in the trees, the bushes; the landscape nearly obscured each building from one another, providing a sense of coziness connected by cobbled pathways and students whose green blazers and slacks blended into the surrounding foliage. To their left, the trees gave way to plummeting cliffs over the ocean, the land sweeping downward until it leveled out with the shoreline, and Saffron breathed in a lungful of that salty air he was quickly coming to love. Unlike Morrígan, whose campus repelled the trees, Mairwen appeared to have built itself amongst them, only chopping down the ancient trunks where necessary. And of those stone buildings, the similarities with Morrígan stopped at the silhouettes. Windows glistened with colored inlays. Ornate glass paneling replaced rooftops and clerestories in the larger structures. Some were built entirely in shiny glass crystal, reminding Saffron of the greenhouse alongside Lake Elatha. His breath caught each time he spotted something else more stunning than the last, heart full as he couldn't keep the smile off his face.

Amongst all of it, students milled to and fro, perhaps heading to early morning classes, making their way to the dining hall for breakfast, Saffron wasn't sure, but it reminded him so much of Morrígan. That time, though, in an exciting way. In a way that made his heart swell and spin as he reminded himself with every glance down at the green cuff of his sleeve—he was one of them. He would walk with them on the paths, an equal. He would know what students normally did between classes, where they relaxed, where they studied, what they talked about. No longer forced to witness such stunning architecture beneath a white veil, knowing it only in its smallest details and by the way it dirtied and had to be cleaned.

"Why don't you tell me what you see?" Luvon asked. "You've gone silent. Are we in the wrong place?"

"No! Not at all," Saffron said excitedly. "Ah—I think this must be the main campus."

He dug around in his new, stiff leather shoulder bag, finding the parchment map illustrating each building and different paths to get to them.

"That way to the south are some of the dormitories, on a lake called Lake Morain," he described as they passed by. "I think there are other dorms on the other side of campus, and then more back behind those trees, then some that overlook the ocean. I wonder which one I'll be in...?"

The campus gardens; the grand theater; various lecture halls; the dining hall; the grand library; the stables; paths to the wild meadows; other paths to the sports fields; a road down to the docks and tide pools; a dirt road to the nearest town, a tiny outskirt of Avren called Fullam, labeled as a place to buy school supplies, treats, or find somewhere to drink as alcohol was banned on campus except during certain events. One specific location caught his attention above all the others, which was the cluster of small buildings labeled *Beantighe Dormitories*. Saffron almost asked if Luvon knew anything about them, wondering if they were anything like Beantighe Village—then wondering if they, too, were renovated student dorms from a nearby, burned out human school. He smiled bitterly to himself, though his eyes skimmed around the rest of the map in search of anything that might pass as *'human school remains we don't talk about.'* He suddenly wondered if those were simply the Finnian Ruins Sunbeam and Asche used to talk about so much. The ruins Ryder Kyteler invited him to visit, before disappearing into the floor of the infirmary...

The carriage came to a sudden halt, nearly knocking Luvon from his seat had Saffron not thrown his hands out to catch him. Cursing under his breath, the fey lord threw the carriage door open, clearly not opposed to causing a scene in the middle of a bustling morning campus, even as Saffron begged him to get back inside before anyone saw—but then Luvon's tone changed in an instant, and Saffron's curiosity flickered.

"Oh, dear! Is that Gentle mac Carce? Sionnach!"

Luvon hurried from the carriage door, nearly walking straight into a group of Mairwen students passing by. Saffron groaned internally, hurrying to follow, clambering out onto the cobble-stone path and searching for his patron master. He found him at the head of the carriage with the driver, kneeling over someone who was in the process of being helped back to their feet. Clearly nearly trampled on such a crowded pathway.

But while Saffron's first curiosity was how Luvon knew the person at all, it was quickly swallowed whole when Saffron got an eyeful of every part of them. They wore a green Mairwen uniform like everyone else, down to the blazer and the morpho-blue butterfly lapels—but instead of slacks, they wore green bloomers that ended mid-thigh. Their thighs—that were covered in fur. That extended into legs like those of a fawn, capped with shiny dark brown hooves. Their hair was wavy and wild, shorter on top with longer pieces hanging over their shoulders, and like natural, warm-cream linen in color; they had tan skin, wide honey-brown eyes, freckles, and—horns that curled around short, deer-like ears that twitched with every sound. As they returned to their feet, a tail swayed behind them, the same color as their brown fur with a tuft of creamy-white hair at the end. Oh, god—were they a satyr? A real satyr—attending Mairwen Academy?

Saffron couldn't hear what they and Luvon talked about—his ears were ringing, completely distracted first by the tail, then by the person's ears that were so, *so* very pinchable, having to resist lifting his hand to squeeze them and see if they were as soft and velvety as they looked. He only snapped out of it when both of them suddenly turned to look at him, making him jump and utter an inelegant *"huh?"*

"I was telling Gentle Sionnach that Catrín might have told them about my relative coming from Alvénya," Luvon said, putting out a hand to search for Saffron's shoulder. Saffron took it, placing it where he intended. Luvon smiled at Sionnach the whole time. "Would you be willing to extend some friendship to him?"

"Oh—" Sionnach's smile sank in an instant, before perking right back up again. They glanced at Saffron briefly, though Saffron could see the immediate apprehension in their eyes. "Of course, I'd be happy to show them around."

"Your name is Sionnach?" Saffron asked, putting on his polite beantighe voice in an attempt to cut through the waxing tension. "I'm Saffron."

"What title do you prefer?" Sionnach asked with the same polite smile that made him wonder if they had ever been a beantighe before, too. Or perhaps they had their own reasons for putting on a polite mask when clearly uncomfortable.

"Oh, um—Lord is fine. It doesn't really matter to me."

"Do you have your dorm assignment and class schedule already, Lord Saffron?"

Saffron nodded, digging through his increasingly-disorganized bag to pull it all out. He dropped a few sheets in the process, quickly kneeling to grab them—surprised when Sionnach kneeled down to get them, too. Even more surprising was how Sionnach looked like they weren't expecting Saffron to reach for them, either. They quickly stood back up again, and Saffron followed, attempting to put everything back into a holdable stack.

"My—my dorm is Muirín Dorm. Um, Noon-North, whatever that means."

"Oh," Sionnach's delicate smile twitched. "I'm also in Muirín Dorm. That's convenient. But—did you say Noon-North?"

"Yes."

"Oh... gods help you," they whispered, before turning back to Luvon and assuring him they would help Saffron find where he needed to go. As they did, their tail continued sweeping back and forth, and Saffron suddenly understood what made cats chase the ends of string. Luvon nodded in appreciation, inviting them to come visit Amber Valley again soon, before glancing back to Saffron. He asked Sionnach for a moment alone, and Sionnach nodded, stepping off the side of the path as Luvon turned to pull Saffron into a long, firm embrace.

"Luvon?" Saffron questioned softly, embarrassed by how quickly the emotions overtook him, then how people turned to look as they passed by.

"I won't be far, a leanbh," Luvon said gently. "A certain friend of mine has already had a horse delivered to campus for you, so use it whenever you want to stay at the townhouse. It'll always be there should you ever need a safe place to rest from it all. Gods know attending a high fey academy isn't easy—even for the most prepared of us."

Saffron pulled away with cheeks already tear-streaked despite his efforts to keep the emotion at bay. Of course Luvon could sense it, or perhaps he just knew Saffron too well, because he immediately wiped Saffron's face before ruffling his hair affectionately.

"Today marks the beginning of every great thing you're destined to do," he whispered. "If there's anyone who can temper a Night Court, child... it's someone from humble beginnings. Don't forget that."

Saffron sniffed, holding Luvon's hand against his cheek before leaning in to hug him one more time.

"Thank you, father," he whispered. Luvon's arms around him tightened, and Saffron felt his body shudder with an exhale. A hand brushed comfortingly up and down his back, before they finally parted again. Luvon gave him a kiss on the forehead, then nodded over his shoulder to Sionnach, who silently nodded back.

"Go on, then. I'll see you in a few days for your first gala. Until then, don't fall in love with anyone who doesn't deserve you. Top of the class at minimum—" he paused, glancing back Sionnach's way. "Is that still you?"

Sionnach cleared their throat. "Yes, actually..."

"Who is second?"

"Lady Maeve dé Bhaldraithe."

"... Nevermind, then. Perhaps third is acceptable in this case only."

"I think you're referring to someone in particular when you say that," Saffron blubbered while attempting to wipe his face on his sleeves.

"You're welcome to assume."

Laughing under his breath, Saffron wiped his eyes for good, and made his final goodbyes. He watched Luvon go, feeling like he used to when in the carriage leaving Luvon's estate at the end of a holiday, headed back to Morrígan by himself. He remained where he stood a few moments longer, even after Luvon was out of sight, patting his cheeks and taking in as many deep breaths as he needed to recompose himself. He didn't know how much of his puffy face would be visible through the glamour, but he didn't want to risk the embarrassment when it wasn't even technically his first day. Finally, he turned to Sionnach with an awkward smile.

"Sorry," he said, before internally kicking himself for it. High fey never apologized for shit. He knew that much. Sionnach shook their head, but Saffron still added: "I promise I'm not such a crybaby all the time."

"I always cry at the beginning of a new semester, too," Sionnach said like they meant it to be reassuring, but it told Saffron more than perhaps they meant to reveal. He scoured his mind for something else, anything else he could say to change the subject. But with so little to go off, he scraped at slim offerings.

"Um, your name, 'Sionnach,'—is it Alvish? It's really pretty," He said, recognizing it as the same pronounciation as a Gaeilge word.

Sionnach cracked an uncertain smile.

"Um, no—it has Old Alvish spelling but it's actually not an Alvish name."

"It's Gaeilge, right?" Saffron couldn't resist. "An old human language... Erm—not that I know anything about that, or anything. I mean, obviously I know a little bit, but not, like—a lot. It's something that interests me but I know better than to talk about it too much—erm..."

"Oh... yeah..." Sionnach smiled awkwardly again—and Saffron realized what was so strange about it. Every time, it was full of apprehension, like they weren't used to it. Smiling at people. "My father named me. Lots of satyr languages use Gaeilge words. Though technically Gaeilge is close to Old Alvish, too, so —don't worry about trying to justify anything to me."

Saffron smiled a little too uncomfortably. "Well, my name is neither Gaeilge or Old Alvish, which I guess is good because I don't think I'd ever remember how to spell it otherwise. I mean— it's spelled like the normal spice. Or the flower, I guess. Did you know saffron is also a flower? I didn't, until a few months ago..."

"Where do you think the spice comes from?"

Saffron gaped at them, only clamping his mouth back shut when it made Sionnach laugh. A genuine laugh, even lifting their hand over their mouth in an attempt to hide it. It had the same veneer of uncertainty as their cautious way of smiling.

Leading him toward their shared dorm building, Sionnach asked what classes Saffron was taking, and Saffron dug through his bag for the hundredth time to find the parchment that listed them. He eventually found where it had mashed into the corner of his worn sketchbook, whining and cursing himself for being so careless.

"Do you draw?" Sionnach asked as Saffron pinched at the pages to try and smooth the wrinkles out. He struggled to answer, not wanting to imply he was any good at it, but he didn't want to say no, either. He mostly didn't want to have to admit he was self-taught from wild fey in the woods on pages stolen out of student books. All while he internally panicked in search of a reply, Sionnach was polite as ever, smiling with sincerity that grew a little more every time.

"You're not taking any art classes, though?" they went on as Saffron handed over his schedule for them to see. "Why not?"

"Art classes?" he asked, instantly disappointed. "I—Well, Luvon actually put together my schedule for me, and I don't think he really knows about my drawings..."

"It's probably too late to change now, but you can always audit classes if you like. They won't count toward credits until you enroll properly, but if you have time in your schedule, you can sit in on the instruction and get all the same lessons." Their mouth remained parted like there was one more thing to add, before closing it with a polite smile. Deciding against it. Saffron tried to keep the mood light, hoping they might eventually say whatever was on their mind anyway.

"Well—maybe I'll do that, then. Um, do I need to bring supplies? I only have my sketchbook—ah, I should actually probably get a new one... and I've only ever drawn with charcoal before, but I could probably get some more as soon as... well... I could probably get some, soon, I just have to ask Cyl—erm, Luvon for some money."

Sionnach chuckled again, like Saffron kept surprising them.

"You can just come and join. They have all the supplies you'll need, so don't worry about bringing any of your own unless you want to."

"Alright!" Saffron exclaimed, hurrying to keep up with Sionnach's pace. "Speaking of Luvon—you know each other? How?"

Around the corner of the Administration Building, they took a right, heading south. Buildings continued on either side of them up ahead, but Saffron could still smell the ocean nearby. He could hear the crashing waves, practically feel the sprinkle of saltwater on his skin. He wondered where Cylvan was on campus, then what he was doing, if he was in class or maybe on break, or maybe visiting that nearby town Fullam for breakfast. He adjusted his jacket and smoothed down the front at the thought, hoping it still looked alright. That, if they did happen to unexpectedly cross paths, Cylvan really would think he was handsome and fall in love at first sight. Just like they'd joked that morning.

"You probably already know Master Luvon's wife, Mistress Catrín, is an adjunct professor at Ambegun in the Winter Court. She gave me permission to study in their archives during the end-of-semester break."

"Oh! That's really interesting." Saffron hurried to keep up again. "What were you studying? Can you tell me? Ah—I know the archives are usually for restricted information, like the stuff they don't want everyone to know, right?"

Saffron's rush of curiosity caught Sionnach off guard, looking surprised as if Saffron spoke nonsense while waving a burning torch in reach of a grain silo. Like they still couldn't decide if he was being serious or trying to make fun of them. Saffron was definitely being very serious.

"You must have stayed with them in the Winter Court then, right?" he tried to ease their worry. "Luvon's estate is so beautiful, don't you think? Did you visit Lake Corsecca at all?"

"Um..." Sionnach trailed off, eyes locking on a group of students on the path ahead of them. They approached on the backs of horses, wearing what Saffron could only guess were sport uniforms. He swore something close to *oh no* escaped Sionnach's mouth, before they suddenly grabbed Saffron's arm and turned him to face one of the bulletin boards they passed.

"Why don't you look and see if there are any clubs you want to join?" they asked, motioning to the flyers of parchment on the board. Saffron frowned, about to ask what had gotten into them, but stopped once he felt how Sionnach's hand on his elbow trembled.

"Is everything alright?" he asked quietly, instead.

"Oh, it's just..." Sionnach began to answer, glancing over their shoulder again toward the approaching group.

Deciding he didn't want to push Sionnach's clear discomfort, Saffron pretended to do what he was told, gazing over the flyers dancing in the morning breeze. Something about the approaching students made Sionnach nervous—was it the horses? Was it the people on the backs of them? Saffron wouldn't blame them if that was the case—though he wondered again if Sionnach had been a beantighe once in their life in order to have that instinct. Or maybe something else? Some other kind of servant, before finding grace in the eyes of some powerful fey lord who offered them a chance at attending school, too? Saffron smirked. How ironic, he thought, letting the scenario play out in his head as the group on horseback passed behind them.

"The field was positively horrendous this morning... ah, perfect. A place to wipe my shoes."

Sionnach suddenly slammed into Saffron's back, sending them both toppling into the mud. Sionnach scrambled backward to ask if Saffron was alright, but Saffron's head spun and his crushed chest ached too miserably to answer right away. Only when he could slowly push himself up did he see the sorry state of his uniform. His new uniform. Wet and caked in mud.

Behind them, laughter intermingled with horse hooves clopping against the walkway. Saffron turned over his shoulder to memorize the face of whoever had kicked them and ruined his clothes, swearing vengeance—only to meet eyes with a pair of equally surprised amethysts.

Prince Cylvan went completely pale, staring at Saffron with his mouth hanging open. He wore a sport uniform matching the others behind him, and Saffron realized they must be on their way back from hurling practice. Cylvan's foot, still somewhat extended, divulged the proof of smeared mud on the sole.

Saffron glared at him in a wave of fiery bloodlust. Instantly, he'd never seen Cylvan look so fucking terrified, paling further and gulping back a lump in his throat that Saffron wished would choke him. The prince never broke eye contact while wordlessly lifting his leg over the saddle, planting his feet to the earth. He stared at Saffron a moment longer, mouth hanging open like he really thought he was about to beg for his life.

Instead, he reached stiffly into a pocket on the inside of his sport tunic. He pulled out a handkerchief, whiter than a ghost when he realized nothing so small would ever make a difference on the mess he'd made. All over Saffron's brand new uniform. He stared at the handkerchief in his hand for a long time, desperately trying to fathom a single thing he could say or do for Saffron to spare his life. Saffron saw the words clicking by behind Cylvan's eyes. *I fucked up.*

"I'm sure this fey lord just didn't see you, Gentle Sionnach. It must have been an accident." Saffron offered Cylvan a single lifeline. He would get one chance. Sionnach, meanwhile, stammered while insisting there was nothing to worry about, how of course it was only an accident, but Cylvan jolted back to life like a doll struck with sudden consciousness from the finger of Danu.

"Yes," he said stiffly. "Yes. It was my mistake. Are you alright?"

Sionnach stared at Cylvan in a way that told Saffron it was the first time they'd ever heard anything like that from such a pretty, royal mouth. But Saffron wasn't going to give Cylvan any more time to figure out what to say or do to make it better—he just approached, plucked the handkerchief from the prince's white-knuckled grasp, and turned to wipe mud from Sionnach's face.

"You were going to show me to my dorm?" he invited, as if nothing had happened at all. "There's probably a bath in my room too, huh? I love hot baths. You'll have to show me somewhere I can buy some nice-smelling oils to put in it, that's always my favorite part. My fiancé in Alvénya would always draw me such luxurious baths, it makes me miss him so much. Perhaps I'll write him tonight and tell him all about how there isn't a single fine fey lord in all of Alfidel."

Cylvan might as well have turned to stone, watching as Saffron hooked an arm through Sionnach's and walked away from him. Saffron hoped his heart stopped.

8

———

THE ROOMMATE

Approaching the far end of campus, Sionnach's voice was far away, but Saffron's feet still moved without the rest of his mind following. He thought only of Cylvan's face, how if Saffron hadn't been there to put the fear of Ériu in him, he would have kept laughing and trotted on with the rest of the hurling team members with him. He regarded Sionnach's endlessly nervous, uncertain smile, stomach turning when he realized, perhaps there really was a pattern.

He followed close behind his newest friend, feeling a sense of protectiveness, like he might lash out at anyone or anything that so much as gave them a weird look. Sionnach noticed, and kept quickening their pace like they weren't sure who Saffron's ire was directed toward. That only made Saffron more annoyed.

They eventually came to a halt in front of a black wrought-steel gate, enclosing a wide courtyard on the other side. Saffron stepped in close, squinting to perceive the light-colored stone chateau in the center of the wide lawn, butting right up against the cliff's edge overlooking the ocean below. Shaped like the letter U, repeating windows claimed the facade of the whole building, three stories high with an additional row of dormer windows lining the light gray, sloping roof. Some windows were pushed open, curtains sweeping outward in the wind, while others were shut and closed off. Around the side of the building, Saffron thought he could see bodies moving around in a back garden, their voices carrying somewhat over the sound of crashing waves. Around the wide perimeter, a stone wall kept the open courtyard protected, a gravel driveway circling a patch of grass and hedges in the middle.

Sionnach prompted Saffron to use one of his new access tokens to open the front gates, giving him a few moments to try and find it himself before offering a polite suggestion. Saffron thanked them under his breath, scrambling to press the silver icon to the magic plate and compelling the ancient bars to creak open and let them through.

Inside they stepped into a grand common area bustling with students coming and going from late-morning classes, eating decadent plates of breakfast foods from the house kitchens, yawning and drinking strong coffee with a scent that permeated the air. At the back of the common area, a few high fey entered through a rear door wearing the same sports uniforms as those who had harassed Sionnach by the bulletin board, and Saffron scowled at them. Cylvan was not among them, at least.

The Muirín dormitory was set up like Pallas, Erce, and Nemain dorms at Morrígan, less like Danann House which had been more of an estate house than a place for a number of separate flats. Sionnach showed him the sitting area, smoking area, open restrooms, dining hall for house events, and the kitchens, where Saffron lingered. At least a dozen beantighes washed dishes and scrubbed the counters between prepping plates of food. Sionnach explained that each dormitory had its own kitchen for meals, though they were hardly more than snacks and appetizers compared to what was served in the main dining hall. Saffron wondered if that was what Danann House once looked like, too —staffed by so many people who slept in the cramped attic rooms when they weren't scrubbing or cleaning. Carving protective arid marks into the floors and wall beams.

Mairwen beantighe uniform tops were the same shade of stark white as those at Morrígan, though with a little less ruffling, as well as black slacks instead of gray. It was all similar enough that Saffron's mouth went dry. At least they didn't appear to have to wear veils, too. At least there was no chiffon pulled out of the way of their faces, except it seemed on those who wanted it. A choice they were allowed to make for themselves, rather than a mandatory one.

It was the same in the house laundry. It was the same in the back gardens, where humans scurried between bushes, walkways, a white gazebo in the back corner, primping and preening the plants so they would be perfect. Always, always perfect. Saffron returned to Danann House's attic, gazing out the window as white-veiled ghosts cleaned up the back gardens, never knowing he watched them at all. Was that how the fey always felt? But their secret witness was rooted in power—while Saffron had only ever known how to be hidden.

"All Mairwen dorms have three living floors, labeled according to times of day. Ground floor is Dawn, first floor in Morning, and top floor is Noon," Sionnach went on as they climbed the stairs. "So your room in Noon North Corner isn't too hard to find once you have that in mind. Come on, just up this way... gods, I hope Copper hasn't trashed the place..."

Sionnach knew they spoke too soon as Saffron used a third access token to open the door, the smell of rotting meat hitting them like a wall. Saffron's eyes watered, throwing up his arm to cover his nose as Sionnach audibly gagged, reaching for the knob and yanking the door back closed again.

"I knew it!" someone shouted from the opposite end of the hallway, both of them turning to watch as a fey lady shoved something into the hands of another fey she was talking to, before stalking in Saffron and Sionnach's direction. Sionnach stiffened, pulling on Saffron's arm to reel him out of the way before he was flattened. "I knew that smell was coming from him—dé Bricriu, open this fucking door! You there—you have an access token? Give it to me."

"Wh—" Saffron jumped like any other confused beantighe caught off guard. The intensity of the lady was enough to suck all the air out of the corridor, a cloud of bitter ice encircling her, long white-blonde hair braided down her spine nearly as long as Cylvan's. Her eyes were equally icy blue, cutting into Saffron like carving knives and whittling him into something useful. Something she could shove into the ancient keyhole that would allow her into the room that smelled like a morgue.

"Is he dead?" Sionnach squeaked, by then cowering behind Saffron rather than defending him.

"I doubt it. He's impossible to kill. Like a fucking curse," the lady replied, snatching the access token from Saffron as he cautiously offered it.

"Who is she?" Saffron asked as the lady turned and slammed the token against the plate on the door, kicking it open without flinching against the wave of stink on the other side. Sionnach answered with a hand over their mouth.

"Lady Maeve. She's the Muirín Dorm prefect."

"Oh... second in class rank..." Saffron recalled that name. "What's a prefect?"

A sudden crash from inside the room made Saffron jump, hurrying inside as he pictured a wild animal loose in the room that was meant to be where he slept.

But instead of a wild animal—the room on the other side was suspiciously pristine. No, not suspiciously—beantighe-clean, clearly scrubbed and organized by knowing hands in all the ways Saffron immediately recognized. The perfect position of every pillow on the couches; the perfect stack of unused wood logs in the fireplace; the pristine wiping of the windows both inside and out. Still, despite the clear layers of scrubbing, the stink lingered. Like something existed in the ceiling. The walls. The floor. Saffron's nightmare incarnate, the beantighe in him crawling beneath his skin with the itch to tear the room apart in search of the source.

By Lady Maeve's own behavior, it was clearly a recurring issue, and the crashing sound Saffron heard had been one of the bedroom doors slamming shut as the perpetrator fled the fey lady storming into the room. Still, despite the near-feral levels of fury in Maeve's voice, the way she held herself physically was as pristine as the rest of the room. Even while pounding a fist on the door, her hair never slipped out of place, her uniform never wrinkled, the collars of her shirt never creased. Saffron could only fantasize about ever reaching the level of perfection she carried herself with —not to even mention the stunning beauty of her face, with angular features, upturned eyes, dark eyebrows, pale skin, and those sharp blue eyes that reminded him of the thickest slabs of ice on the surface of Lake Corsecca in the Winter Court's true season. Even clenched in a bloodthirsty rage that reminded him a little too much of Cylvan.

She grabbed the knob of the bedroom door, and Saffron saw exactly why a cloud of chilly air followed her around—ice emerged from her touch, kissing the metal with frost until it grew brittle, allowing her to snap it off and shove the door open. On the other side, the person attempting to hide shrieked, before being dragged out by the hair. Shirtless, enormous, wet and muddy, Saffron recognized the pants he wore as the same ones Cylvan did in his hurling uniform. Saffron's eyes narrowed, all sympathy he might have felt leading up to that moment snuffing in an instant. He even hoped Lady Maeve might freeze the man alive and break him apart like glass like she did the doorknob.

"Show me what you've done," Maeve hissed, yanking Copper dé Bricriu into the middle of the common room and throwing her hand out in invitation. "Where's that horrible smell coming from, fox!?"

"Oh, hey!" Copper ignored her, honey-gold eyes going bright and sparkling when he spotted Saffron lingering near the entry-way. "Hey, I know you! You were knocked over by the goat earlier

—oh, the goat's right there. You're actually not welcome h—*urk*—"

Maeve took him in a headlock, which may have been humorous if Saffron wasn't so immediately terrified of her. Maeve, who was only a few inches taller than Saffron, both of them easily a foot smaller than the ginger giant she handled like a house cat.

"Prince Cylvan actually knocked me over," Saffron corrected, anyway. "By kicking Sionnach in the back."

"Oh, right—" Copper wheezed as Maeve continued dragging him around the room in search of the smell. "He was really torn up about that. It was hilarious. You really showed him what."

Saffron furrowed his brows. He didn't know how to reply to that, deciding to keep quiet until Maeve got what she wanted. He didn't really want to sleep in a room that smelled like pure ass, either.

But no matter how Maeve pressed him, choked him, tossed him around, Copper laughed the whole time, declaring she would never find it, it was none of her business, he would clean it up himself. He would take care of it himself if she'd just *get out.* Something about that pushed her over the edge, finally releasing him, telling him she would be back with someone from administration to expel his ass. Copper rubbed the back of his sore neck with a cocky little smile, wishing her luck. She whipped him in the face with her braid as she turned and finally stomped out. Before she slammed the door behind her, she planted a heavy hand on Saffron's shoulder, meeting his eyes with all the intensity of a high fey seeking vengeance.

"I'll pray for you," she said with total sincerity, before snapping at Sionnach to join her. It sent chills down Saffron's spine, making him stiffen before turning slowly back to Copper who watched Maeve's every movement. Only when she finally left did he loosen his shoulders, letting out a howl of relief before stretching his arms.

"Damn, close one. What exactly can I help you with? Can't

imagine you were the one to tattle on me to the ice queen. Right?" He spoke as he crossed the common room to a corner nook furnished with a small table, icebox, basket of fresh fruits, a cabinet for bread and crackers. Saffron didn't answer at first, watching as the man climbed on the table and yanked a metal grate from the opening of an air vent, reaching inside and pulling out a sloppy handful of rotting meat. Saffron might have puked, had the urge not been instantly overwhelmed by what came out with it—a small flurry of rainbow pixies, biting at Copper's hand and squeaking at him in annoyance.

"Why..." he started. Copper glanced at him before going to the nearest window and tossing the meat right out. Saffron heard it splat to the ground three floors down. "Why are you putting raw meat in the vent?"

"Because otherwise they try to pluck out my eyes while I sleep," Copper answered, papping one of the grappling pixies in question, leaving a puff of glitter residue on his fingers. "Can't seem to figure out what they like, though. The ones I grew up with in the Autumn Court loved chewing on fresh blood. Dunno why these ones have to be so damn picky."

"They're rainbow pixies. They like sweet things," Saffron corrected before realizing he'd said anything. Copper gazed at him with continued curiosity, before eyeing the colorful winged insects in question.

"That true?" he asked the buzzing cloud. They squeaked angrily at him in reply. "Why didn't you little shits tell me?"

"How long have you been trying to feed them raw meat?" Saffron went on, unable to resist smiling and putting his finger out as a few of the pixies bumbled over to him in curiosity. He'd been careful not to bring any of his own Spring Court rainbow friends with him, which broke his heart, so there was something wistful about how those ones instantly crawled around in his hair and chewed on his ears. Copper was equally intrigued at how Saffron never flinched, unfazed by their tiny hands and the way they crawled under his blazer, up his sleeves, into his shoulder bag.

"Since they moved in about a month ago. There was a windstorm that knocked some trees over in the woods nearby, I think their hollow might've been destroyed."

"Ooooh," Saffron cooed, rubbing the tiny face of the yellow one sitting on his finger and kicking its legs back and forth. "Poor things."

"I've been letting them stay while they recover and find each other again. I was gonna take them out to find a new tree eventually, but obviously I'm not providing the right kind of food to keep them satisfied. People are starting to notice."

"The smell?"

"And signs of them being around. Folks are talking about a pixie infestation, which is the worst thing that could happen."

Saffron frowned, but realized that was why Copper refused to reveal anything to Maeve. He wondered if the high fey of Mairwen would treat pixies the same way as the ones at Morrígan. Like insects to be squashed under shoes and between hands.

"Well..." he mumbled. "In my experience, rainbow pixies really like raw honeycomb. It lasts them a while, too. Puts them into sugar-sleep."

"Sugar-sleep? Is that the scientific term?" Copper teased, making Saffron's cheeks go red in embarrassment.

"No... I don't know... it's just what I always called it..."

Copper regarded him for a long time, long enough for Saffron to shift uncomfortably between his feet, before finally perking up again. Something about it reminded Saffron of a fox perking up at the sound of a rabbit in the grass—but perhaps only because of Maeve calling him such a thing earlier.

"You my new roommate?"

"Huh? Oh—yeah. Sorry, I guess I could have..." Damnit. Damnit—*stop apologizing!* He clamped his mouth shut, kicking himself internally. But Copper didn't mention it, he just smiled unevenly.

"Hey, alright. You said something earlier about the goat

showing you to your dorm, but I never imagined it'd be this one. Oh, let me double check there isn't anyone already in there."

"What?" Saffron asked in surprise, following him to the opposite side of the room. "There's—there's already someone here? But my paperwork said this was mine...?"

"Oh, it is, but there are these cats... oh, you'll see. Hold on. This is your room," he said despite it all, grabbing the handle of the second room and pushing the door open, only to curse when there were, in fact, two people fully comfortable on the bed inside. "Fucking cats—Neva, Aven, come on! This room's taken again. You gotta go. Go on, scram."

Saffron peeked around Copper's broad middle, watching the two elegant things in his new bed stir from all the noise, tangled up in one another, stretching and yawning and—waving their tails. Flicking their ears. Like cats, their eyes were hardly more than slits on yellow irises, black ears and tails matching their short black hair. Two of them, identical, flicked open their eyes and gazed at Copper, then Saffron.

"Who is that pretty one?" one of them asked with a coy smile, putting out a hand. Saffron didn't know why, but he reached back in response. They grinned, gently coaxing him forward until his knees bumped against the side of the bed and they could touch him all over. Like two leanan sídhe, they gently brushed fingers over his dirty uniform, through his hair, smiling and cooing compliments about how handsome and pretty he was, how good he smelled, how they'd never seen anyone like him before.

"You... you have ears," Saffron whispered in captivated delight, reaching up to touch, but his hand wafted straight through them.

"They're just glamours," Copper said, suddenly grabbing Saffron and pulling him back, breaking the twins' spell in an instant. Saffron blinked a few times, snapping out of the hypnosis with a jolt and a nervous, embarrassed laugh. "Dunno why someone would... Dressing up like animals... what the fuck."

"They're cute," Saffron said anyway as Neva, or maybe Aven,

reached out for him a second time, but Copper snapped at them to cut it out. They giggled and slithered away, but still didn't leave like Copper demanded. Instead, they piled on top of one another again, eyeing them both with swishing tails in curiosity.

"Copper, why are you covered in mud?" one of them asked. Saffron turned to look for the first time, remembering his new roommate was shirtless—but also still wearing his hurling pants. He hadn't looked close enough the first time, but sure enough, there was drying mud on Copper's face, his arms, in his hair.

"Oh—Prince Cylvan was being a real ass this morning, so I bodied him into a big puddle in the middle of campus. Normally he squeals the whole time, but this time was so melodramatic and didn't fight back at all... so I was able to really bury him... he looked like a real lake monster by the end of it. Hilarious. What an asshole. Hate that guy."

He nudged Saffron as he spoke, as if implying he'd done it all in Saffron's favor, to make up for what Cylvan had done to him and Sionnach. Saffron might have thanked him, though a part of him was positive Copper really just liked any reason to 'body the prince into a big mud puddle.'

"Are you also in this room?" Saffron turned back to the twins.

"Sometimes," they answered with mischievous smiles that matched their ears and tail. "Is that alright with you? You look like someone who would be heavenly to cuddle up with at night."

Saffron blushed, opening his mouth to politely refuse, but Copper threw his hands up and swatted the twins off the bed and out of the room before he could. Saffron secretly thanked him, watching as they were herded back to the door. Sionnach was unexpectedly on the other side, holding a few pieces of clean clothes for Saffron to wear until his actual luggage was delivered. Saffron scampered over to them before Copper could give them any trouble, taking their hand and pulling them in.

· · ·

SIONNACH HAD THEIR OWN CLASSES TO ATTEND, BUT Saffron thanked them endlessly for the borrowed clothes in the meantime. Something to wear while his uniform was sent to the house laundry, where Sionnach promised they could get any stain out of anything. Saffron knew that. Saffron knew that, but he didn't want to think too much about why. He couldn't handle that tiny, silly detail, of how he knew exactly the lengths which beantighes went to to scrub mud and blood and everything else from uniforms. He wondered if Muirín dorm beantighes had their knuckles switched if they didn't get their clothes spotless, too, just like at Morrígan.

Once all the excitement finally died down, once Saffron was allowed a single moment alone in his new dorm room, he pressed his face into his pillow until it nearly suffocated him, allowing the pressure to build in his chest until his old wound ached. Teasing the edges of the hole in his heart where that metal bolt had burrowed and he'd been forced to recover on his own merit and whatever little tricks Baba Yaga could stir up from herbs and her dilapidated grimoire. She still wasn't allowed to perform arid magic in Beantighe Village, even though it might have healed Saffron faster. Not unlike when they tried to save Berry. It would have been the same sort of spells to ease the pain, even if something about his rowan magic got in the way of being healed entirely—but even though she offered, Saffron only ever shook his head and refused. No matter how badly it hurt or however many times the stitches in his skin strained and popped open. He wouldn't put her in harm's way. Not again. Not when they didn't know if it would work on someone whose magic was so empowered like his. Not when he wasn't sure how much pull Cylvan could have if the aged henmother was caught doing taboo magic.

Once the exhaustion had gone, he was finally able to sit up and breathe. He was finally able to gaze around his new room—*his dorm room!*—and memorize every part he hadn't seen in all the excitement.

That space was for him alone; Copper had his own room on

the other side of the common area, on the other side of the door. In comparison, Saffron was used to having anywhere from three to six other people crowding a cramped little room all at once at any given time. Being alone made him restless in all the worst ways, and he truly realized how bad it was as, even in that brief amount of time in the dorm by himself, he constantly checked the doors to his bedroom and the main room to make sure they weren't locked behind his back. He habitually scratched at his wrists to reassure himself there weren't any silver cuffs to trap him. He kept tucking a chair under his bedroom latch whenever he had to turn his back for something.

He meticulously observed every inch of that dormitory to try and ease his nerves. The common area had a grand fireplace with a decorated mantle, overseeing an ornate rug on the floor, dark-wood coffee table, sitting couches, and a few other pieces of furniture closer toward the main door. There was a connected washroom with a full tub and overhead shower, though it wasn't anything like the one in Luvon's townhouse by size and luxury. Copper's room was the blatant opposite of the pristine condition of the rest of the space, cluttered with dirty clothes and uniforms, books and parchment stacked in haphazard piles by the windows, bed undone, smelling of too much cologne and sweat. Saffron only had the strength to peek his head inside, before slowly backing out again.

Saffron's bedroom boasted a wide, comfortable bed with sage-green blankets and embroidered pillowcases; at the foot of it, an empty cushioned chest meant for linens, or maybe finer clothes that should be particularly folded; an empty dresser; an empty standing wardrobe; a fireplace of his own, though not nearly as large or decorated as the one in the main room; sconces that lined the walls, as well as a single overhead dangling light that wasn't quite a chandelier, but not quite a plain fixture. The lights were all electric, and took a few crackling seconds to turn on after the switch by the door was flipped; when they burned, the light was dim and orange and buzzed incessantly. Saffron decided early on he wouldn't use them unless he absolutely had to. It wasn't like there was a dearth of candles and oil lamps throughout the dorm to use, instead. Electric light was so... dead. Lifeless. And *loud*.

Once his nerves were satisfied enough, he found the strength to dig the crow book from his shoulder bag, completely unsurprised to find multiple messages waiting for him. Only growing more frantic as they went on.

Saffron, I want to apologize for my behavior this morning. Please let me know if you are free this afternoon, we can meet somewhere private.

Saffron, my love, please let me know if you are alright. I am worried sick after seeing how hard you fell.

Púca, my lunch hour is at one P.M. Please let me know if you can meet me somewhere in private so I can make sure you're well. Did you find your new dormitory? I am eager to know where they assigned you.

Saffron, my prince of the sun, I know I have done something wrong. Please answer me just so that I know you're alright. I will go mad with worry, otherwise.

SAFFRON FINALLY TOOK HIS PEN AND SPECIAL INK TO the page, pressing the nib a little too hard into the paper and tearing a line into it with the first stroke. He wondered if that detail passed through the pages for Cylvan to see, as well.

I'm sorry, your highness, I think you must be mistaken. I don't recall crossing paths with you this morning. I only crossed paths with a royal cock who was the ugliest fey lord with the frizziest hair I've ever seen.

A response came almost immediately, but Saffron snapped the book shut and shoved it under his pillow. Only then did he notice the poem card from the train station had fluttered out from between the pages to the floor, making him bend over to quickly scoop it back up and return it to the pages again.

The front door in the common room opened and slammed shut. Saffron clutched the card in his hand with a sudden new urge to find something to keep himself busy so no ravens he was angry with would fly in through his window and bother him. He pushed himself to his feet and followed the sound of his roommate rummaging around on the other side.

"Did you have a nice—oh!"

Copper shouted and whirled at the sound of Saffron's voice, clutching his chest as he slammed back into the wall in fright. Saffron stared at him, before covering his mouth, but he couldn't hold back the sudden rush of laughter bubbling up the back of his throat.

"I'm sorry! I didn't mean to surprise you."

"Gods above and below my feet, I thought you were a ghost," Copper croaked, catching his breath before shrugging away from the wall to gather the things he spilled in his surprise. "Lord god, I thought you'd come to take my soul from me. Forgot already that I had a new roommate. What was your name again?"

"It's Saffron."

"Two beantighes in Noon-north. Love it." Copper smirked.

Saffron's awkward smile hovered on his face, and Copper stared right back at him like he was waiting for a reaction.

"Um... beantighes?" Saffron questioned. He hoped Copper couldn't hear how his heart pounded nervously in his voice. Copper smiled awkwardly, realizing his joke hadn't landed.

"Erm, it's just 'cause... I'm always getting teased because I have a beantighe name... um, Copper, you know... and, well, no offense, but Saffron's sorta a beantighe name, too."

"O-oh!" Saffron choked, before forcing a laugh. "Oh, haha, that's... that's funny." He really had to change the subject before the relief in his voice could be considered suspicious. "Hey, um, I have a list of things I need to get before my first class tomorrow, and I was wondering... the person who was originally going to help me is really getting on my nerves, so I was wondering—"

"Who, Sionnach?"

"What?" Saffron frowned. "No, not Sionnach. Do you think you can help me or not?"

"Oh, you bet. I gotta go talk to a guy in Fullam about a barrel of whiskey, anyway. And some honeycomb, I guess. Different reasons. Let me change really quick and we can go. Gotta hurry before it gets too late."

Copper raced into his bedroom, slamming the door behind him. Saffron bit his lip, unable to resist a breathy laugh and a smile at the absolute unpredictability of the man he was meant to live with for the next—who knew how long. Normal fey students attended school for, what, a few decades by human standards? He didn't know if the feeling in his stomach was pure giddiness or apprehension at the thought. At least, for however long he would study amongst them in secret, Saffron could rest assured his roommate was nothing more than a more excitable Hollow. Something about that—was so comforting.

9

———

THE SHRINE

Fullam was carved from the same slab as Avren, smelling of fresh bread and ancient trees and ocean water, salt-water canals snaking between the roads and buildings, feeding the myriad of sculpted fountains spotting the town corners. It only lacked the towering cathedrals of stone and glass, buildings instead reminding Saffron of Connacht. Made of wood and ceramic tiles, with warm cobblestone walkways that clattered with wheeled carts and hooves. Some walkways off the main streets were even unpaved, flattened into hardened dirt paths that hardly felt any different beneath Saffron's shoes.

He and Copper made their way first to the market so Copper could find someone selling fresh honeycomb for the pixies in the vents, while Saffron scoured every little shop and stall located within the massive, rectangular, open-air block. More than once he swore he spotted a dark, horned shadow trailing him, but every time he looked, there was nothing except a suspicious little breath of air. Every time. Saffron made sure to pretend like he didn't notice, pretended like he was having the time of his life without anyone there to bother him at all. Just in case.

Trinkets and snacks, shoe repair, makeup and perfumes, hair-cuts, crafting materials, Saffron couldn't help wandering from where Copper bartered with a vendor in order to explore further into the town, knowing it wasn't big enough to lose his way even as a first-time visitor.

Most shops seemed to exist for the sole purpose of fulfilling the needs of Mairwen students, evident by constant displays of bags, embroidered patches, stationery, branded clothing. There were even entire stores dedicated to Mairwen-approved uniform goods that could be worn and used in class, including quill boxes and inkwells, tunics, doublets, sweaters, even hair clips and thick pads of parchment.

In the first bookstore he crossed, when he spotted a leather-bound sketchbook embossed with the school's crest, he almost screamed, grappling for it like it would vanish if he didn't move fast enough. From there, he couldn't resist anything else that caught his eye, grabbing books on figure drawing, calligraphy, even Alvényan romantic myths which he was sure he could justify to Cylvan as a requirement. He also found a handful of those he'd once picked out in the bookstore in Connacht before being introduced to Pimbry Scott. He stared at the cover of one in his hand as those memories came rushing back, before closing his eyes and shaking his head, tucking it away again. He wasn't ready for any of the books that reminded him of that terrible day.

He could have spent the rest of the evening in that shop alone, picking everything he wanted and buying out their entire stock, until he realized he didn't have any money. He wasn't sure where to get money. Cylvan and Luvon both said Saffron would want for nothing while attending school, he simply had to ask—but should he have asked for money to carry around in case he crossed into a bookstore? One of the members of staff noticed his internal turmoil, offering to hold on to the books for him if he needed more time, and Saffron timidly agreed. If anything, the next time he saw his raven, he would push him into the mud and steal all the money he had on his person. As payback. To get even. And so he could come back and get those books he wanted so badly.

Outside the shop, he searched up and down the street for

Copper, wondering if he'd already gone back to Mairwen after losing track of Saffron for so long; then he wondered what the odds were that Cylvan, as petty as he was, hadn't actually followed them into Fullam and wasn't quietly stalking Saffron from behind at every turn. He whipped around at the thought, thinking he might spot a shadowy raven peeking out from behind the corner of a building, but Cylvan must have been better at blending in than Saffron thought. He knew for a fact the prince would not have let Saffron wander off—perhaps out of a sense of protective duty, but mostly out of jealousy that someone else would be allowed to join Saffron on his first trek into the nearby town. He couldn't help but smirk at the thought, digging into his bag for the crow book and flipping through the pages.

"As yew trees pin our suns in sleep... we're meeting at the old shrine of Ériu at the top of the mountain at sunset."

Saffron's head snapped up. Heart pounding, he recognized those words from somewhere, needing only another moment before remembering. He flipped through the pages of his crow book in search, finding the red card from the train station. Hollow had been handed one as they arrived in Avren, too. Saffron was sure it was also the same card tucked into the feathers of that dead owl at Lugh's altar—which meant, if Saffron heard someone quoting it, it meant they were probably the same one handing the cards out. The same ones killing owls and nailing them to the gates of the palace. Humans, human dissenters.

Searching the street, it wasn't hard to spot those in question when he knew what to look for. A group of people huddled together beneath a tree across the street. One of them handed another a red card, before hurrying away again. Their ears were covered by a hooded cloak, but Saffron knew without having to see. Saffron didn't have to witness rounded ears to know, it was humans passing them out, and with intention. The one Hesper gave him at the train station. The one given to Hollow. The one in the owl's feathers. And Saffron just watched it happen.

Perhaps Hollow hadn't had a chance to ask what the card

meant, but Saffron wasn't going to let his own sudden opportunity pass.

He glanced up the length of the street once more; that time, Copper being nowhere to be found was a relief. Saffron hurried around the side of the bookshop, down a narrow alleyway, quickening his pace as one of the people handing out the cards passed by at the opposite end. When he reached the neighboring street, he peeked his head out, first, watching the stranger hurry away. Toward the edge of town, where a path opened up into the trees. *We're meeting at the old shrine of Ériu at the top of the mountain at sunset.*

Knowing there wasn't a single person in that town who would know him by his real face, Saffron took a deep breath, reaching down inside his shirt to pull out the amethyst pendant glamouring him. Tugging it off over his head, he nearly tucked it into a pocket before a hand suddenly grabbed his wrist, twisting it backward.

"I don't recommend that," Cylvan mumbled in his ear. Saffron instantly lurched away with a yelp of surprise, putting his hands up in defense. Cylvan watched him with a pinched expression, clutching the pendant that'd come off in his hand. He'd been tailing Saffron, after all. Saffron should have known.

"It's not what you think!" he exclaimed, before panicking and grabbing his irritated prince by the front of the tunic, tucking him back into the alleyway before anyone could see.

"You have exactly three seconds to tell me what it is, then," Cylvan growled, keeping the pendant out of Saffron's reach as he attempted to snatch it back. "Before I throw you over my shoulder and fly you straight back to campus!"

"There's something strange going on with the humans here!" Saffron hissed, standing tip-toe and crushing Cylvan against the wall as he stretched for the pendant held high over his head. "I only—meant to go see for myself!"

"Already betraying me so early?" Cylvan asked. His tone was only partially playful. Saffron's heels hit the ground, and he grabbed Cylvan by the front of the tunic to yank him in close. Even Cylvan looked surprised.

"Don't you dare even joke about that," Saffron told him. Cylvan's frown remained, but his tense brows softened slightly. Despite his clear unhappiness, he conceded enough to offer the pendant back. Saffron snatched it, tucking the necklace securely in his pocket. He almost turned on heel and left Cylvan right there, but then closed his eyes and sighed. Against his better judgment, he pulled the red card from his back pocket.

"We promised not to keep secrets from one another ever again," he said. Cylvan's eyes narrowed, but he nodded, straightening up slightly. Saffron flicked the card nervously between his fingers. "I was given this randomly by someone I met in the Agate Wood before coming here. Then Hollow was given one like it on the ship as we docked. And I don't know if you saw it, but there was another one in the feathers of that owl on Lugh's altar. You said there are humans causing trouble in Avren lately, and I think these things are all related. I just watched some humans across the street who were discreetly handing them out. They said there is a gathering happening tonight at Ériu's old shrine at the top of the mountain—and I'm going to see if it's something I should be worried about."

"Oh, are you?" Cylvan muttered.

"Yes. I am," Saffron countered, pushing him.

"Then I'll go with you."

"Wh—what!" Saffron punched Cylvan in the chest on reflex, apologizing sharply as the prince grunted. "No! No—you know what? If you want to do me a favor, you know—or, you know, pay me back for kicking me in the mud earlier—I put a bunch of books on hold at the shop right next to here. Why don't you go buy me those things instead? Hm? That would be so nice of you—"

But Cylvan ignored him, reaching down to smooth his tunic, his sleeves, before glamouring himself suddenly as a human. It happened so fast, Saffron had to blink a few times to make sure he wasn't imagining it. Wavy brown hair, brown eyes, pale skin, objectively plain features, despite still being so ethereally beautiful as ever—Saffron thought he might be the only person in the world who would be able to recognize Cylvan's smallest attributes within the disguise. It was purposefully simple, he thought, to avoid drawing attention.

"I'll send a bird to buy your books when we get back to campus tonight," Cylvan added as simply as ever.

"You have to be kidding me," Saffron breathed in frustration, but curiosity prickled over it. He couldn't resist cupping either side of Cylvan's face, turning him this way and that, then sweeping a hand over the crown of his head. It bonked against his invisible horns, making Cylvan grumble and swat Saffron away.

"It's only a visual glamour, I don't have the energy for a physical one," he said, hands moving through what Saffron could imagine was his long hair, braiding it over one shoulder without anything to see. It was absolutely surreal, and he couldn't help but reach out and try to touch him through the disguise, again.

"Amazing," he whispered. "But—you can't really expect anyone to believe you're a human, looking like this."

"Like what?" Cylvan asked, sounding insulted. "Am I not just a boring human man?"

Saffron would have laughed if he didn't think Cylvan was being serious. Cylvan, who, even glamoured, was the most unnaturally beautiful creature on two feet. Saffron pinched the bridge of his nose, weighing his options—but knowing it didn't matter. Cylvan was going to do whatever he wanted, no matter what Saffron said. It was one of the biggest things they had in common, after all. Finally, he sighed in defeat.

"You've never glamoured yourself like this in front of me before, you know," he said, before frowning again. "Oh—saying that out loud, I'm actually shocked."

"Shocked? What for?" Cylvan countered. Saffron shrugged, knowing Cylvan already knew exactly what he meant. Cylvan scoffed and flipped his invisible braid over his shoulder. "Glamouring to play tricks is below me. I much prefer people to know exactly who is bullying them."

"Don't say that after what you did this morning."

"Ah, right, about that." Cylvan's eyes suddenly softened, practically fluttering his eyelashes and reaching for Saffron's hand.

Saffron snatched it away. Cylvan more aggressively tried to take it back, demanding Saffron hear his apology, he'd spent all day thinking of the perfect way to say it, but Saffron played keep-away before racing out into the street. Cylvan chased after him, screeching to stop being so immature, to listen to him, he was about to offer a rarely-given apology with his own mouth—but Saffron just kept running, until he couldn't keep the laughter at bay.

THEY RAN UP THE MOUNTAIN PATH UNTIL SAFFRON HAD to bend over his knees and catch his breath, pressing a hand to his chest as his wounded heart throbbed and complained. Thankfully, despite being on the hurling team again, Cylvan's own endurance was challenged by the heeled boots he wore, buckling at the knees when he finally caught up and held up a hand for Saffron to wait. Saffron thought the prince might puke from the effort, patting him on the back and whispering reassurances, before taking his hand. Cylvan squeezed it until Saffron squealed, attempting to yank it away again, laughing as Cylvan clawed into it and hissed threats of reclaiming ownership.

It was strange to hold Cylvan's hand so freely, even as people passed by them, walked ahead of them, trailed along behind. As the mountain path slowly populated with more and more humans following the same invitation that drew Saffron to go see what it was all about. Many of them even smiled and said hello. Saffron said hello back every time, perhaps out of surprise, perhaps out of habit. It reminded him of Beantighe Village—and those feelings warped into something he couldn't describe every time he recognized the uniform of a Mairwen beantighe, or a palace beantighe, or some other establishment he didn't yet know. But he knew the ruffled shirts, the different styles of veil pinned out of their faces or to the veil-buttons on their shoulders and sleeves. All the while, Cylvan remained silent. He only squeezed Saffron's hand every now and again between interactions, as if it was the only way he could keep his obvious thoughts to himself.

"I didn't realize there were any shrines to Ériu in Avren," Saffron whispered as a gap in the passing foot-traffic allowed. If anything, to distract Cylvan from his clearly-growing uncertainty. "But there are a lot of other shrines to fey gods, aren't there? Like the one to Lugh on the mountain behind the palace."

Cylvan feigned shock. "You know of the family shrine to Lugh, beantighe? How? You must be highly favored by someone very powerful."

Saffron pretended to swoon, collapsing into Cylvan with a hand over his forehead. "Oh, I cannot speak of it—but yes, I am being courted by a member of the royal family. The most hand-some of them all, as a matter of fact. And the most frightening and powerful, of course—oh, but he is such a treasure in bed."

"I hear that Night Prince is well-endowed and has a favor for humans. Apparently he enjoys how soft and warm and vocal they are."

"I think you're right—but that also makes him easily manipu-lated, you know. I get on my knees for him and he offers to make me his king."

"I would call him a fool, except I think I would offer you the same if I had it. In an instant."

"That is very kind of you—but there is only one person whose kingdom I would take, and it belongs to a seelie prince."

Cylvan's hand lifted Saffron's, pinching the emerald ring set in the silver rowan branches. "Not your fiancé from Alvénya, then?"

"Not if a prince offers me his world while fucking me silly."

Cylvan finally laughed, tugging Saffron closer and nearly kissing him in a rush of amusement. He barely pulled away before the urge won out, but Saffron tucked a hand around Cylvan's jaw and pulled him down to peck his cheek.

"Will you take me to see all of the other shrines in Avren?" he asked. "So I can give them all a proper greeting. A better one than King Lugh got, at least."

"I'm sure the other gods are all envious of the greeting we gave the sea." Cylvan smiled wickedly. "Perhaps we should offer the same to every other temple in Alfidel, all hundreds of them."

Saffron smirked in agreement. Even behind his human glamour, Cylvan was so handsome—but perhaps only because Saffron knew who really hid beneath the mask. Saffron couldn't help but smile back at him, losing himself in those eyes that were different, but exactly how they should have been. He would lose himself in any way Cylvan changed his face, he would sink into his raven's eyes with ease no matter what color gazed back at him.

"I will gladly travel all over Alfidel to pay respects to your gods, if you promise to apologize to my friend for what you did this morning."

"Oh, you're already calling the goat *'friend'*, are you…?"

Saffron elbowed Cylvan in the ribs. "I mean it. Otherwise I will only feel worse for wishing I could forgive you so badly. Do you want to make me feel terrible?"

"That's the last thing I want. I'll bow on my knees for Gentle Sionnach's forgiveness."

"Hm," Saffron sniffed. "You have to do it in front of me, then. So I know you aren't lying to me."

"I would never lie to you."

At the top of the mountain path, Saffron was surprised at exactly how many other humans gathered to hear what those at the head of the throng had to say. At the crown of the incline stood a cracked marble statue depicting a woman in robes, holding a lamb in her arms, long grass and broken fern leaves carved from the same stone rising from her feet. Behind and on each side, withered white columns stood in varying states of decay, and Saffron wondered if the goddess had once had a whole temple with a roof to shield her from the rain, too.

While it was not a reassuring sight to find her in such disrepair, especially after the care he saw put toward Lugh's shrine—when there wasn't a butchered owl on the altar—Saffron could find at least one ounce of relief in the way there were no signs of fire damage around her or on her columns; she hadn't been destroyed purposefully, like so many other things that once belonged to humans. She'd simply gone abandoned, forgotten by those who were tasked to watch over her. Slumbering rather than ruined.

Keeping near the back of the crowd, Saffron and Cylvan found a place to huddle between two trees where no one could hover at their backs. In case of need for a quick escape, which both of them seemed to understand and seek without having to say so out loud.

Someone approached the crowd from the stone platform beneath the goddess, putting up their hands. Illuminated by bowls of fire on each side of the statue, something about it was simple, humble, unintimidating—but at the same time, unsettling. Saffron held his breath to better listen.

"Welcome, friends," she called out over the throng. "You've heard our call, and came to listen. I know it is not safe for any of you to be here with us tonight, but I promise I will not take too much of your time. Simply put... your high fey gentles, lords, ladies, and masters have been withholding something awe-inspiring from all of you, for the sake of protecting their own luxurious ways of life. With the intent of keeping you in the dark and docile, to perform as beantighes and obedient possessions for every day you live. But—we are here to shine light upon those fey-spoken lies."

Saffron squeezed Cylvan's hand again, but couldn't look away. The woman at the front turned to the person next to her, offering them a nod. They nodded back, before crouching and, as perhaps only Saffron in that moment understood, taking a piece of chalk to the stone ground to draw a circle. They added feda markings around the rim. Saffron's heart pounded until it hurt.

Bracing for something to erupt from the arid circle, perhaps a bang or a flare of light, something intense and exciting—instead, there was only a sudden rush of wildflower growth that spilled from the center, like a meadow tearing through the old stone and reclaiming what it once had. Around them, gasps rang out in alarm, pushing one another for a chance to get a better look. It was painfully bittersweet for Saffron to witness so many humans' first time realizing it wasn't only the fey who were capable of magic—all while he held the hand of the fey prince right next to him.

"Humans are capable of magic, and always have been," the woman continued. "Each in our own ways, rooted in ancient rituals, in individual family lines, in our respective cultures. While we of Finnian can only teach you the ways of Arid-Ogham magic of the Celts, if you wish to later learn the ways of your own historical rites, stay here with us. You deserve to know where you came from, whether born here in Alfidel, found here, or brought here as an innocent changeling baby. We will house you, feed you, protect you, as you abandon the life of a beantighe forced on you by the high fey in this city, and in this world.

"Even if you do not wish to pursue magic with us, know this —we will not leave you behind. We intend to liberate more than only those who learn with us, and far more than only those who can safely join us. These high fey have oppressed us and our rightful ancestry for centuries, now, all while stealing us as babies. To work us to the bone, and bury us in their mounds. But that is not the world Verity and Virtue Holt wished for us; this is not the world they fought so hard to give us. They may have freed us from the reaping of the Night Queen, but they were not able to show us the sun. We know where to find it."

She put out another hand. From behind the statue, a third person approached carrying a shrieking animal. Golden wings thrashed and flapped as the barn owl fought wildly against the bindings around its ankles. It clawed at the man's gripping hand, tearing at him with its beak, but stood no chance against the leather gauntlet he wore.

The bird was tied to the stone carving of a fern at Ériu's feet, and the woman put her hands up, drawing the audience's attention back to her.

"This, the creature that represents the royal family, and therefore all of Alfidel and her luxuries we ourselves have never known... Let me show you exactly how we may tear them from the sky. To pin them beneath rowan, as their yew has pinned our suns in sleep."

Saffron's heart skipped.

As yew trees pin our suns in sleep,
Rowan tears the moon shall weep.

The bird shrieked again, flapping its wings and attempting to tear away from the stone perch. Saffron watched in horror as, from another ogham-circle drawn around the base of the fern carving, vines of rowan leaves, thin branches, bright red berries emerged and crawled like snakes up the stone. Creeping closer and closer, until finally kissing its thrashing talons. Wrapping around and knotting against the bird until it was pinned. Disappearing into the thick, pillowy feathers of its stomach, then curling and looping as the bird could only screech and snap its beak in an attempt to tear them away.

"Why bother with an innocent creature?" Someone ahead of where Saffron and Cylvan stood whispered to the person next to them. "Tie Prince Cylvan to a perch and strangle him, instead. Save us before he kills all of us."

The other person chuckled. "Feed him fairy apples first, get him drunk and gasping..."

A line of crimson dripped from Saffron's nose. He stared at them, at every other human who faced away from him and watched the demonstration of human magic at the feet of the goddess Ériu, deity of earth and abundance and peace. Strangling that innocent animal for the sake of making a statement, to prove themselves and their cause.

The arid marks forming Taran's true name on Saffron's forearm itched. Cylvan whispered something, but Saffron didn't hear it. He flexed his hand, skin growing tight like it was about to split apart. On the verge of tearing open, to spill his wild rowan blood across the ground, to release something thrashing in his bones.

When Saffron could no longer stand to watch, as the rowan branches reached the owl's throat and encircled it—Cylvan said his name just as he lunged into the crowd.

Shoving past the bodies in his way, bystanders gasped and yelped, growling at him and attempting to grab and yank him back. But Saffron shoved past each of them, tasting blood in his mouth as even more dripped from his nose, soaking the front of his shirt.

All the way to the front of the crowd, where he met the head woman's eyes as she took an uncertain step backward. Unsure what to expect of him, perhaps sensing the wild rage like a tempest burning in his blood. His blood of iron and rowan, barely contained from tearing free and drowning each and every one of them.

He felt the heartbeat of the summoned rowan branches. Felt their life, despite being inanimate. Given intention by the arid magic written on the ground, given life and animation and reason for being. But Saffron could see, could feel that magic as strongly as he once did after exhuming himself from the earth at the edge of the palace on Ostara. After making his oath with the veil. He saw the glowing red aridity encircling the base of the stone perch, along the branches moving like venomous snakes made of iron.

Blood spilled from his nose, filled the inside of his mouth— and the yew bracelet around his wrist erupted in a flash of light, smoldering in an instant. Extending his hands, he could feel them, the branches. He felt his fingers curl beneath them, despite never stepping closer. Holding the air, but tousling their fibers. Their magic. He burrowed his touch through them—before tearing them away without ever physically grasping them in his hands. Shredding their magic apart until the glow flickered out, until even the magic circle from where they grew disconnected, a crack forming in the stone where it was drawn. He shredded the branches where they strangled the owl on the perch. Until they were nothing but remnants of leaves and bark scattered across the ground.

The crowd behind him surged, screams ringing out as they thought he was a high fey using opulence to interfere. He didn't care, he just lunged forward, that time tearing at the broken remnants of rowan with his hands. He ripped the owl free, throwing it into the sky where it tumbled for a moment, before snapping open its wings. With a shriek into the night sky, it disappeared like a streak of moonlight. Saffron watched it go, before snapping around to those responsible. Blood gushed from his nose, his mouth, as he cursed at them:

"You will not use rowan to perform such cruel acts ever again —especially not at the feet of Ériu, herself. Else you'll have to deal with me."

Hands grabbed him from behind. They wrenched him backward, off the stone platform, and into the woods.

10

———

THE MANIFESTATION

Dragged into the trees, not knowing in which direction or how far they went, Saffron kicked and thrashed, world spinning as a hand smacked him and demanded silence. Pinned face down in the grass and dirt, another hand found his hair, yanking his head upward.

"Is he some high fey or something?" one of them grunted, and Saffron strained his eyes to look.

The one pinning him with a knee to the back cursed as Saffron nearly managed to tear away. Saffron's eyes watered as the hard ground burrowed into the scarred-over wound in his chest, crying out through his teeth as his weak ribs creaked beneath the weight. It halted his offense just for a moment, hands planted on the earth as he desperately tried to relieve the pressure of the man kneeling on top of him. The pain, the adrenaline, coursed through his body in an attempt to fill his muscles with enough strength to shove them off—but it was no use. He didn't have enough in him to physically overpower anyone, especially not while so much pain radiated from the center of his body.

"Get me those berries!" Another shouted.

"*Silence,*" Saffron mocked with compelling intention, grinning with bloody teeth. A hand returned to his hair, pulling back roughly. Someone knelt in front of him, grabbing his face and turning him this way and that.

Grabbed by the shoulders of his tunic next, the fabric tore as he was turned roughly onto his back. Throwing out his hands, Saffron smashed a fist into the nose of whoever was on top of him, then spit a mouthful of blood into their eyes, only for the others to grab his wrists and ankles and flatten him before he could break anything else within reach. One of them shoved something into his mouth—and Saffron choked on a laugh when he recognized the taste of rowan berries. They really thought he was a high fey—they thought rowan berries would poison him. By then, they tasted sweeter than candy.

Spitting them back into the face closest to him, Saffron's thoughts scrambled for what he could possibly do to defend himself, to free himself—but he'd spent all his time only practicing the basics of arid magic. Iron magic, the kind that required rowan berries, ironick blood, ogham circles and lines. He'd never had a chance to learn anything of rowan magic; he didn't know how to control it, how to use it—or even how it was meant to be used. He didn't even know why the surge happened to free that owl—but not again right then when he needed it.

"Why didn't it work! Damnit!" One of the humans snarled, slamming the heel of their boot against Saffron's stomach. Saffron grunted, curling up on instinct, searching his mind for anything, anything, anything he could draw in the dirt to help him—but the moment he extended his hand, another foot came down, crushing it. Crushing his forearm with the jagged scar of Taran mac Delbaith's name, making him cry out and claw at the boot as electric pain rocketed up his arm to his shoulder, making his teeth crack together. But the toe of the shoe ground into him, scraping the soft skin away, bending the bone beneath its weight.

"Was that other person with you hiding pointed ears, too?" The person pinning his arm glanced to somewhere Saffron couldn't see. "Hey, Sav, go see if you can find them!"

A bolt of terrified heat like lightning erupted from Saffron's aching chest, spreading into every limb at the thought of Cylvan being dragged into the woods alongside him, identity revealed, put in danger by Saffron's own hubris. The adrenaline spiked his nerves, and he felt everything at once. The warm, early-summer air; the grit of dirt between his teeth; the pressure on his back; the pain of his chest; the blood pooling under the skin in his arm pinned beneath him, the jagged scar of Taran's name throbbing with his pounding heart, even as he managed to finally jerk free from the foot that crushed it. Saffron buried his fingers into the soil, before thinking of nothing else except how the scars burned like white hot metal. Pleading for relief, straining his opposite hand to claw at them, as if to release whatever venomous thing coiled behind it—

Something crunched in the bushes behind them. The agony in Saffron's arm didn't lift—but it eased slightly. Every human around him paused, every mouth going silent, down to the breath. Saffron took his chance by whatever distracted them, pulling his arm into his chest and scrambling away, kicking himself as far as he could up to the bushes. Staring at the other three humans standing there in the darkness, breathing heavily. Standing there, silent, motionless, and—staring, directly over Saffron's head.

Saffron heard it, too. *Crunch.*

The sound of spindly leaves raking through thick fur.

The smell of wet rot.

He petrified in an instant. His lungs turned to stone, refusing him breath, refusing him any more chance to inhale that stench. He swore he felt the weight of silver on his wrists, around his throat. He swore he smelled a distant bonfire, swore he felt that tingling, irresistible affliction of moonhunting enchantment in the back of his throat.

He glanced slowly over his shoulder—and witnessed the profile of a giant wolf blacker than the night sky, eyes glowing a low crimson. It was so close, hanging over his shoulder, close enough that he would have pressed his cheek into the animal's snout with a mere tilt of his head.

The only thing that kept him from screaming—was the way the beast moved, as if it weighed nothing at all. How its shoulders rose and fell with breath—but there was no heat emerging from its mouth, despite foaming and dripping with delirious, blood-thirsty spit.

"What—the hell is that thing?" One of the humans choked out. The wolf's ears twitched—and then it lunged. Without a sound. Without a gust of wind. Without hardly a shift in the leaves at all.

Paws the size of saucers slammed the first human to the ground, claws tearing them open at the chest. They shrieked, but were cut off when a mouth lined with teeth crunched down on their collarbone. Around them, the others screamed, scattering, abandoning their friend who was pinned, then thrashed back and forth like a cotton doll in the beast's mouth.

"Stop!" Saffron cried—and the instant the word left his mouth, the beast halted its assault. It didn't release its jaw, it didn't step off the body it crushed beneath its massive weight, but it stopped. Its nose wrinkled, lip curling back as if furious to be commanded. Saffron didn't know what else to say, what else to do —only that he knew that beast. He knew that monster. At least— he knew the origin of the form it took for itself.

Rising slowly to his feet, holding his aching chest, nose and mouth and ears dripping with warm blood, crimson splattered down the front of Sionnach's borrowed tunic as he forced himself to speak. That name that haunted him. Like poison on his tongue, making his throat tighten as if clutched between two silver hands.

"I-Icarus," he said, voice cracking in restrained terror. *"Stop. Leave them."*

A thousand dormant fears flooded, plaguing him, carried back to the bonfire on Ostara with such vividness he nearly forgot where he was. Witnessing the halos of opulence behind every fey courtier's head. Their true names that glowed crimson on their chests. Remembering the searing pain of giving that name to Taran's bones, the old wolf king's opulent bones, to trap him in a beastly form just like that one. But there was no glow of magic around that animal in front of him, like Taran once had—the one Saffron summoned from the shadows was sewn from nothing but pure darkness and the pain under his skin.

The beast reacted to the sound of Saffron's voice saying that name that tasted like blood and bonfire smoke and wild fairy fruits. More bloody bile rose up the back of Saffron's throat as it turned to perceive him, eyes bright red and glowing like rubies in firelight. Lifting its head, it dragged the lifeless body of its victim for a moment longer, before finally letting go. Allowing the human to thump back to the earth. The world spun as the beast then turned fully to Saffron, summoning every terrible, agonizing memory to surge back into all the places he'd been so careful to find and tuck away. His breaths came weakly, heart pounding in his ears. Smelling its rotten fur, tasting ash on the air, iron over his tongue as the blood from his nose and the back of his throat collided like opposing tides in a river.

"Icarus," he croaked. *"G-go. Be gone."*

He expected the animal to turn and leap back into the trees, to race off and disappear like Taran had on Ostara—but it melted into thin air. Vanishing like black smoke without a sound, just as it had first come. Saffron whimpered, still clutching his chest and searching in every direction, blinking through the darkness, desperate to find where it had gone—but there was nothing. It had simply vanished.

Sinking to his knees, he shuddered with a certainty that his heart had split apart. He had to grope at his chest in search of a metal bolt. Fighting to keep himself in reality, he turned his focus to the injured human a few yards away. He forced himself onto his knees through the pain, dragging himself toward the motionless body. Bleeding from their chest and throat, clothing torn open over their wounds, stained and wet. Saffron had seen that before.

Saffron had witnessed that same horrible, awful sight before. He'd heard that gurgling of trying to breathe through blood-drowned lungs. And like the first time—Saffron knew it was all his fault.

He placed his hands on the human's chest, sinking his palms into the wounds. They groaned miserably beneath his touch.

Saffron closed his eyes. Baba's words echoing in his mind felt ancient, like spoken by something a thousand years old. Not only a few months prior.

Recalling when he'd once tried to save Berry, that time too disoriented to draw an ogham circle around them, Saffron begged his magic to be merciful. He placed his hands on the human's slippery skin, careful not to dig his fingers into the wounds. He summoned the agony into his own body like Baba had once taught him—hunching forward and shuddering as the pain manifesting in his already-sore chest erupted like stone tearing through ice. Beneath his hands, muscle and skin stitched itself back together, painfully slow, but clean. He fought to keep his hands where they were for as long as he could, to deliver his spell with everything he had left in him, to give that person their best chance at surviving—but soon he couldn't blink away the exhausted darkness rimming his eyes, the pops of color, the turn of the earth beneath him, and Saffron had no choice but to pull back.

He slumped before knowing for sure whether or not he'd saved them. Closing his eyes and sinking, expecting to feel grass and dirt beneath his cheek—he instead fell into a pair of arms. They pushed hair from his sweaty forehead. Then lifted him off the ground entirely.

He couldn't see where they carried him—only that the trees changed. Their shadows shifted, sometimes creeping by, sometimes stretching out their limbs like they wished to claw at him. Had he not been so exhausted, he might have put out his hands to fight back. He barely had the strength to lift his eyes to seek out the face of whoever carried him, knowing beneath the blanket of dulled senses that it couldn't be his prince. No—that person smelled of leather and tobacco. Their hair was lighter. Even their breath was wrong. Saffron would know Cylvan even by his breath.

He didn't know exactly how long they walked—it could have been moments, it could have been days—but the stranger eventually stopped, kneeling to carefully tuck Saffron against one of the trees that reached for him. Saffron groaned as he returned to the earth, forcing himself to lift his head again.

"Who are you?" he asked weakly. God, he just wanted to close his eyes and drift away.

"Ah, you wound me. Don't you remember?" The stranger answered, and Saffron could hear the smirk in their voice. That voice that strummed along strings of familiarity, though Saffron didn't quite know the instrument. He attempted to squint through the darkness, but his vision was too blurry. "My name is Ryder Kyteler, your highness. We've met before."

Saffron's eyes bulged open. He nearly lunged, eliciting a laugh from the man who put his hands out to grab and right Saffron against the tree, again.

"Easy, I'm not going to hurt you. Just wanted to get you away from there. Wouldn't want your prince seeing the bloodbath you caused, right?"

"Wh...at?" Saffron croaked. His thoughts swirled like muddy creek water. He pressed a hand to his forehead, but it only throbbed more painfully.

"Don't worry about it for now—we'll have a chance to speak again soon. Ideally when you're feeling a little more like yourself." Ryder Kyteler tucked a finger under Saffron's chin, nudging it upward. "Until then, try to avoid hurting anyone else, alright?"

"I didn't..." Saffron said on instinct, before clamping his mouth shut. Blurry memories told him otherwise. The crimson stains on his hands, his shirt, his pants told him otherwise. He released a frightened, trembling breath, then lifted his eyes again to ask if the man really was Ryder Kyteler, who once visited him in the royal infirmary—but when he did, there was no one. Only the foreboding trees leaning over where he sat, hungry and wishing to claw at him. And then—the sound of wind, tearing through the branches in descent.

"Saffron!" Cylvan cried, feet slamming to the earth, followed by his knees. He pulled Saffron close, pushing hair from his eyes and touching his face. Saffron struggled to find the means to react, but forced himself to part his lips, to whisper Cylvan's name as if it would be a comfort. Cylvan said nothing, just searched Saffron all over, only exhaling again when he was sure none of the blood soaking into his clothes belonged to him.

Lifting Saffron from the earth, Cylvan turned, rushing deeper into the woods, away from anyone who might see—away from Ryder Kyteler. Away from the other humans at Ériu's shrine. Saffron grabbed at his tunic, before turning and spitting blood to the ground. He forced his eyes open, focusing on the passing trees as Cylvan pushed through their wall of fingers and suffocating darkness. That time, they leered away, as if frightened by the Night Prince who owned the wind.

"I'm sorry," Saffron croaked—not knowing to whom or exactly what for. For all of it. For the grave sin he'd just committed. *Until then, try to avoid hurting anyone else, alright?* "I'm sorry... I'm so sorry..."

Cylvan pulled Saffron closer. Only when he was sure they were far enough from the shrine, did he finally shirk his glamour and take off into the sky. Only then could Saffron close his eyes, knowing the wolf's gnashing teeth wouldn't bite anywhere near his prince so long as they remained above the trees. Cylvan wouldn't see what Saffron had done so long as they remained above the trees.

11

THE MESSENGER

"Wake up, my love."

Whatever deity beckoned to Saffron so warmly also pressed a kiss to his forehead. It brought back a blur of memories—returning to Mairwen in the dark. Muirín Dorm. Cylvan locking the bathroom door and silently washing the blood from an equally silent, petrified Saffron's face, neck, chest in the warm water of the bath. Carrying him to his room. For his first night's sleep in that bed. Clean. Exhausted. Protected.

"Please don't go." The words bubbled from Saffron's mouth before he realized he was coming-to. Barely broaching the surface of the thick pond he slept beneath, feet tangled in unseen vines and a lilypad forest to keep him under just a little longer.

"I have no choice," Cylvan answered. "Your roommate will wake up soon for hurling practice, and it would be quite the scandal to already be in your bed, púca. But I will see you tomorrow night at your first gala. I'm sure you will be stunning."

Another kiss, that time to brush Saffron's lips. Saffron sensed how Cylvan held something back, like there was so much more he wanted to say, but wouldn't. He resisted. As if worried speaking something out loud would make it real. His following reassurance told Saffron as much:

"You're safe. Enjoy your first day of classes. Forget about what happened last night."

Forget about what happened last night. Saffron liked that idea. Still—the words summoned another unwelcome glaze of memories to drape behind Saffron's eyes, making his breath catch as he was forced to remember. The gathering at Ériu's shrine. The barn owl. The wolf that manifested from Saffron's arm. Ryder Kyteler, who was supposed to stay gone until summer was over. Had he not been so tightly knotted in underwater roots, Saffron might have torn out of the water in a rush of panic. Another still submerged, heavy part of him wondered if Cylvan had slipped something into the hot tea he helped Saffron drink after bathing the night before. Perhaps to help him sleep. If that was the case, Saffron wouldn't blame him. He would thank him, later, perhaps on his knees.

"I love you," he mumbled through the water, not wanting Cylvan to leave without hearing it. "Don't forget... you promised... Sionnach..."

"I haven't forgotten," Cylvan chuckled. He placed one last kiss to Saffron's forehead. Saffron wished his head wasn't so heavy, wished he could sit up and kiss him back properly. "A part of me hoped you might, but I haven't forgotten. I'll be sure to make amends with your newest friend."

"Thank you." Saffron managed an exhausted smile. "You're a good king."

Cylvan's ghostly laughter was the last thing he heard before drifting off again, back beneath the water where nothing had happened the night before at all.

SAFFRON EVENTUALLY EMERGED BACK INTO THE AIR, lying on his back in that bed that embraced him for the first time the night before. A familiar, unfamiliar place. That dorm room in the Muirín Building. Noon-north. The one he'd hardly seen the inside of at all.

Remaining on his side facing the window, he pressed a hand to his head as it throbbed. Banging against the inside of his skull like how Baba used to bang on the bottom of the attic trap door when all her chicks were smoking weed in the attic without her.

The light through the window was still muted so early in the morning, and perhaps for the better, for the sake of his throbbing head. He trailed his hands over the soft white blankets draped over him, clean of even the slightest hint of any of the blood he'd left the woods covered in. Ah—no, that hadn't really happened. Just like Cylvan said. He wanted to believe that, even while simultaneously knowing it was foolish to do so. Perhaps even selfish.

He thought instead of how it felt for Cylvan to hold him all night long, never once removing both hands from Saffron's back, his waist, his shoulders, his face, for longer than a moment, and never both at once. Never once asking what happened, what he'd done. Not even scolding him. Just wiping him clean, holding him, giving him something thick and floaty to drink, then burying him within the blankets and pillows of the bed and sliding in right next to him.

What he'd done. What he'd done. What had Saffron done?

"Nothing," he whispered to himself, squeezing his eyes closed. "I did nothing. Nothing happened. Nothing for me to worry about." Nothing he had the capacity to worry about. High fey Saffron of Alvénya knew nothing of arid magic at all. And that was who woke in Saffron's Noon-north bed.

Still, he stared down at the glamoured scars on his forearm. Those feda letters spelling out the true name he'd given Taran mac Delbaith—given to his opulent bones.

Icarus.

No, not him. It wasn't him, not really—that wolf had appeared out of thin air. He'd disappeared into the same. There was no way it was actually Taran. Surely, if it had been, he would have done more to Saffron than turn and vanish. Maybe a manifestation of his own magic? A glamoured beast summoned by his panic, his fear, taking the form of something that'd once terrified him so much, in an attempt to defend against those attacking him? After what he did to save that owl from the choking rowan branches, renting them free without ever touching them, witnessing the halo of red glowing within them like on Ostara—was it so hard to believe? His magic was wild. It was uncontrolled, out of hand, a mystery. A mystery no one had yet been able to help him solve.

A mystery—and a danger. Saffron was... dangerous, wasn't he? He pressed his hand into his wrist, covering the scars. Wrapping his fingers around where the yew bracelet had once been. In all the time he'd worn it since waking in the royal infirmary, he hadn't witnessed even a flicker of glowing opulence or aridity anywhere. He hadn't felt any sensation in the scars on his arm, except the dull ache of them as they healed. But whatever he'd done the night before, before ever summoning that beast at all—it had been powerful enough to eviscerate the circlet in an instant.

He pressed his face into a pillow, breathing in deep as it still smelled of Cylvan's hair and skin. Waiting for his racing heart to slow, he wished he could open his eyes to find Cylvan still lying next to him. If not that, then to find himself somewhere safe. Comfortable. Familiar. He wished his dorm room was already all of those things, trying to imagine all the little details he'd found while exploring the day before. Wondering if it would reassure him it was a place he knew all the secrets of. There was nothing unexpected waiting for him.

Sage-green floral wallpaper. Light-colored herringbone parquet floors. Plaster motifs along the crown molding. Windows that rattled slightly on worn-out hinges against the early-morning sea-breeze on the other side, clouds thick and overcast and turning the view of the shoreline gray and soft. Exhaling through his nose, he pulled the pillow away, gazing toward the window to witness exactly that. Breathing in the smell of the sea, silently appreciating how easily he really could see it through the window. He wondered if Luvon got him that room on purpose. He wondered if his patron father knew him enough to consider how much it would calm him to see it, smell it, hear the sound of the crashing waves from where he woke every morning.

Finally, he sat up. Rubbing his hands into his eyes again, he kicked his legs over the edge of the bed, wishing to shove the window open even wider and drench the room in the salty morning air—only to ram his toe into something hard, cursing and yanking his feet back up again.

In the dull blue light, he regarded the room in breathless surprise, finally seeing everything he hadn't imagined with his face buried into the pillow. Cluttered wall-to-wall with more than furniture from the day before—it was suddenly piled to the brim with boxy shadows.

Saffron grabbed and lit the oil lamp from the nightstand, mouth dangling open in surprise at the swathe of new belongings in front of him, more than just the luggage he'd expected. Probably delivered while he was in Fullam the night before. Unfamiliar boxes and bags cluttered around the foot of the bed, the nightstand, the dresser, the floor. Saffron couldn't fathom why, or from whom, or for what reason there would be so much—but then he recalled how many gifts had been sent to Cylvan at Morrígan when he first arrived, too. From anyone and everyone who ever wanted to be known by the prince. Saffron couldn't believe he himself would ever be *someone by whom people wanted to be known* —but perhaps Luvon was. King Tross, who Luvon was close friends with, definitely was. It eased his apprehension enough to slip silently from the bed, crouching to his knees to pull open the first gift within reach.

Lots of stationery, stacks of expensive parchment, a pocket watch, fancy clothes for fetes, shoes, makeup, hair pins; perfumes, flowers, cloaks and articles of clothing, new boots, a swath of paints and other art supplies, leather bags, and books—so, so many books that Saffron could barely keep track of, gifted from names he knew and names he didn't, and including the ones he'd asked Cylvan to buy for him in Fullam the night before. Lots of handwritten notes wishing him well in Alfidel and at Mairwen. *Lots* of Alfidel-specific trinkets and charms meant to give luck and abundance in school and his travelings around the country, probably to impress the alleged Alvényan part of him. Despite knowing each and every one of the trinkets wasn't anything special, it almost brought him to tears to be given them at all. He never thought, as a beantighe, he would ever be given anything like that.

The first gift to leave Saffron actually, physically stunned, mouth hanging open like a fish in shock, was a gorgeously crafted, white, thick-furred cloak, lined and hooded with shiny crimson silk, which he immediately swept onto his shoulders and pulled over his head. Embroidered with bright, colorful threads down the edges, he found openings in the front panels for his arms to slide through without having to let any warmth out. It even had *pockets*, both inside and out. In one of them, Saffron discovered a card addressed to him—and he almost screamed at the reveal of who sent it. The Danae of Alvénya.

King Ailir insists on being coy with the details, but I love the thought of him (and you) owing me a favor. Almost as much as I love keeping a secret. I have been assured you are someone exceptionally kind and ambitious, and I am pleased to have you represent Alvénya at Mairwen Academy, at least in the interim. I look forward to meeting you at your future coronation, or sooner if you wish to see me first. I can always make room at my table for the future Harmonious King of Alfidel. Your Primary is not invited until he returns the books he stole from my archive the last time he was here, however. Let him know.

Best wishes to you and your endeavors. Cheers to the earliest start of your reign being one draped in secrets.

— Danae Ruvslana av Nadia Emilia.

P.S. If you decide Prince Cylvan is not your type, I have

twelve sons you may consider, instead. Gods bless and godspeed.

Saffron buried his face into the fur cloak in embarrassment.

Rifling through the rest of his gifts, he gushed over the thick paper and art supplies, wrote a thank you note to Cylvan for the books, then sprayed way too much perfume while pulling on his newly-washed uniform and setting Sionnach's borrowed clothing —that had to be washed of blood before being returned—to the side.

A sudden screech made him nearly tear out of his skin in surprise, whirling around and searching the mountain of gifts for something he might have missed—before finally finding the source perched on the edge of the window, left open a crack as Cylvan left early that morning.

A barn owl. With wings the color of dark honey, face white and round like the moon, eyes dark and as deep as polished obsidian. Saffron didn't know what else to do but stare, wondering if there was some sort of mistake, or maybe it was a hallucination— but then he saw the injuries wringing the bird's ankles, angry and red and swollen.

"It—it's you!" he exclaimed. The bird screeched and flapped in warning when he stepped forward, compelling him to jerk backward again and throw his hands up in apology. "Sorry, I'm sorry. I'm—I'm glad you're alright, though. I don't know how you found me, but... but I'm glad you're alright. Um, do you want something to eat? Hold on, maybe I can..."

He scrounged around in the delivered gifts at first, before deciding it probably wasn't ideal to feed the bird chocolates and candy. He recalled Copper's misguided stash of raw meat for the pixies in the vent, hurriedly checking his appearance in the mirror before cracking the door and peeking into the front room to search for his roommate. When it appeared to be empty, he slipped out, moving straight for the ice box in the corner nook near the front door. He hoped Copper hadn't thrown any of the remaining morsels away, especially since Maeve threatened to string him up by the toes over it, relieved when he cracked open the box and uncovered a few bacon strips hidden at the back. Saffron claimed a handful like a thief in the night.

"Hey! What happened last night?"

Saffron banged his head against the pantry shelf, groaning and rubbing it while glancing over his shoulder. Copper smiled at him in uncertainty, dressed in his hurling uniform that was still muddy from the day before. Saffron scowled, fighting the beantighe-born instinct to demand he strip down so Saffron could scrub it clean, as no proper fey lord should be seen looking like such a mess—but he bit it all back.

"Last night?" he asked, getting back to his feet. The moment he realized what Copper meant, the blood drained from his face and he grappled for the fey lord's sleeves. "Oh—oh my god, Copper! I left you in Fullam! I'm so sor—erm, I wasn't planning on that, I promise! Something came up and I had to come back to Mairwen unexpectedly... I probably could have sent you a bird, I just didn't think of it. It was so rude of me."

"Whoa, hey, relax," Copper laughed, putting one of his hands up. "I'm just glad you're alright. Kinda worried you got wrapped up in some weird tourist shit or something. People are always handing out weird pamphlets and stuff in Fullam, trying to recruit new students who don't know any better into all sorts of cults and all that... but it looks like you made it back unscathed. That's good."

"Um... yeah..." Saffron trailed off. Thank god he was still capable of lying. "You heading to practice?"

"Was gonna grab breakfast, first. Erm, that all you're gonna eat? On your first day?"

"Oh!" Saffron accidentally squished the cold bacon in his hand. "No! I mean—yes, but—oh, I don't know how to explain. Do you know anything about owls?"

"Owls? Not really, we were more of an eagle-messenger family.

But I guess it's all sort of the same thing. Feathers are feathers no matter the weather, or whatever. What's the matter?"

Copper followed Saffron back to his room, where Saffron peeked inside. His stomach sank when the owl was no longer perched on his windowsill, only to sigh in relief upon spotting her pecking at something shiny on one of his trunks, instead. Copper peered in behind him, making a small noise of surprise.

"You got a new messenger bird?" he asked.

"It's a wild bird, I think," Saffron corrected. "It just, um, randomly appeared at my window after I woke up. It's hurt though, so I want to see if I can help it."

"I don't think that's a wild bird," Copper said with consideration. "Looks more like someone's lost messenger. S'way too pretty to be a wild thing, you know? Like it looks a little too pampered."

"You think so?" Saffron finally stepped inside, pausing only a moment longer when the bird's white head swiveled around to look him and Copper up and down with dark eyes. "Is there another way we could tell?"

Copper claimed one of the bacon strips from Saffron's hand, flapping it around between his fingers. "Yeah. How it reacts to food will be an easy way to tell. Come on then, birdy, c'mere."

The owl tilted her head, adjusted her feet on the edge of the trunk, then opened her wings to lift off—but instead of landing on Copper's extended arm, she *fwumped* clumsily on Saffron's shoulder, smacking him in the face with a wing and nipping at the back of his collar with her beak to regain balance. Saffron didn't dare move, groaning internally as she attempted to right herself again, losing her footing and burying sharp talons into his shoulder. Once composed, she thankfully loosened her grip, before settling with all the comfort in the world. Saffron took Copper's lead and raised another piece of bacon to her in offering, barely keeping his fingers clear as she snapped out and swallowed it back whole.

"Definitely trained," Copper concluded. "At least a little bit.

There's no token around her neck, though, so maybe someone let her go or she got lost. Seems to like you enough, though."

"What do I do with her?" Saffron asked, risking a finger to scratch under her beak. When she chirped and purred in reply, he couldn't help but giggle in surprise.

"You could take her to the aviary master and let them find her a new home, or... s'pose you could take her for yourself."

Saffron offered the bird a second piece of the meat, thoughts trailing in and out as he considered it. Was something like that... alright? Was he allowed to do that? He'd never known a beantighe to have a personal messenger bird—let alone even know how to send a messenger bird in the first place—ah, but he wasn't a beantighe anymore, was he? Even Cylvan had a personal bird. His grouchy, one-eyed raven, Balor.

His eyes trailed down to the wounds on the owl's legs again, making his stomach turn in a surge of anger and protectiveness. He ran the back of his hand over her head, then allowed her to nibble on his fingers in search of more to eat. She never bit hard enough to hurt him. As if she knew who he was, even when glamoured. As if she thought she could trust him, enough to seek him out in the last place anyone would expect the rowan witch from the night before to be sleeping.

"How do I do that?" he asked. "How do I make her mine?"

"Let's go to the aviary," Copper said, glancing at the clock ticking on the fireplace mantle. "There's some time before classes start, shouldn't take long at all."

"What about practice?"

"Eh, I'm already the best player on the team. I mostly only go for the excuse to throw the prince into the ground."

"Right..." Saffron couldn't help but laugh. Apparently there was more than one reason Cylvan didn't want to be found by Copper in Saffron's bed. Copper might very well throw Cylvan over his shoulder and body him out the window without ever making any connections about them and their relationship at all.

· · ·

THE LAST PERSON SAFFRON EXPECTED TO FIND IN THE aviary was Sionnach, who looked just as surprised to see Saffron— then practically horrified when Copper walked in behind him.

"What, can't afford the tuition on your own?" Copper said in lieu of a greeting. "Gotta work a campus job? Or did you finally realize they don't accept payments in straw and leaves?"

Saffron turned and looked at him in long, drawn out silence. Copper grew visibly uncomfortable as he didn't get the reaction he was looking for.

"Erm... because... goat."

Saffron didn't even roll his eyes. He just turned back to Sionnach and smiled again. As if Copper was nothing more than a honking goose in the middle of campus. "I want to register a new messenger bird, or... or something. Er, however that works. I don't know."

"This one, I assume?" Sionnach, thankfully, was equally practiced in going right back to normal after someone said something rude about them. Saffron felt Copper deflate behind them, mumbling something before going to pull faces at some of the birds resting in their cubbies. "What a pretty girl. What's her name?"

"I want to name her Fiachra," Saffron answered, thinking about it since leaving the dorm. After the fourth child of Lir missing from the painted mural on Morrígan's Grand Library ceiling, the one only present in human versions of the myth. A secretly human name for the messenger of a secretly human high fey.

"I'll get a messenger token for you. Do you already have a letter you want to send?"

"I was going to write it here, if that's alright."

"Of course. There's paper and ink at the table, over there."

Saffron found the table Sionnach indicated, letting Fiachra down to skitter across the surface and peck at the paper he pulled and flattened to write on. He knew what he wanted to say, he knew exactly what he needed to ask, but he also knew better than to do so outright. Especially if he had no proof Fiachra would deliver the message where he wanted it to go at all; especially if he had to write it right there, out in the open. He recalled what he and Baba Yaga had once agreed on, should that ever be the case.

Grandmother,

Today is my first day of classes. I'm very excited. However, I am still feeling very ill and have not yet found anyone who can help me in Avren. Last night was particularlly bad. I will not go into detail, but it ~~frite~~ frightened me, how sick I was. Have you learned anything else since we've been apart? Any sort of advice you can give me will be a releif, even if it takes some work for me to get.

I hope you and everyone else is well. I will write you again soon.

—Your little spice.

P.S. Assuming this letter makes it to you, it means my new messenger bird is a good fit for me. Her name is Fiachra (after the child of Lir). She may be able to help your orange cat hunt some mice around the house until you are able to reply.

Folding the letter over itself, tucking it into an envelope, then rolling it into a scroll, he tied the letter off with string like Cylvan had once taught him. When Sionnach provided a messenger token and harness to wiggle over Fiachra's head, Saffron couldn't help the nervous tremble in his hands. For many reasons, only some of which were written on that piece of parchment. He couldn't keep his eyes from lingering on his glamoured forearm where Taran's name had produced something horrific the night before.

12

THE STUDENT

Double-checking his schedule for the hundredth time, Saffron thanked Copper for his help finding the building for his first class—*High Fey Theology and Opulence*—before realizing maybe he should have asked for help finding the right classroom, too. But, no, that would be strange. He should know how to find a classroom with a provided room number and everything

Well—he did. He did know how to do that. He had Morrigan Academy memorized, even still. If someone wrote him a letter asking how many coat closets were in the Nemain Dormitory, or how many staircases were in the Pallas Lecture Hall, or how many back doors there were to the Administration Building... Saffron wouldn't even flinch. He wouldn't have to think about it at all.

Saffron knew how to go to school. He knew what to expect. Ironically, out of everything else that had happened since just arriving in Avren a few days earlier, attending class might have been the thing he knew how to do best. He'd watched academia from afar for his entire life. The only difference that time was he would be sitting in one of the seats instead of mopping the hallway on the other side of the door.

Still, despite all the self-reassurance, Saffron practically screamed with joy when he stepped into the lecture hall and, very first thing, spotted cornsilk-blonde hair braided over one shoulder, black horns curling from the crown of their head. Hurrying to reach the empty seat alongside the daurae, Saffron had to stop and think, first, about whether or not it was a good idea to be spotted next to one of the royal family when that wasn't part of the plan yet. But they'd already been seen introducing themselves to one another at the docks, so perhaps it wouldn't be so unusual? Or would people think it was strange for them to already be so friendly? Thoughts and worries hounded him, but then Asche turned, their own pale expression brightening as they practically leapt to their feet and motioned for Saffron to join them. Oh, god, Saffron couldn't resist. Still, he put on an act, just in case anyone was watching.

"Is this seat available?" he asked in his most demure transfer-student voice. Asche nodded, patting the table.

"You're welcome to sit here," they said with equally perfect acting. "I am surprised you have the courage, everyone else in this room seems afraid of me."

"I can't imagine why." Saffron hurried maybe a little too quickly.

They sat at the far back of the lecture hall, a dozen other rows of long tables descending down the terraced platforms to the podium at the base. Setting his books on the table and sliding out the chair, he settled into it with a pleased exhale. Thankfully, no one gave him more than a second look, though their eyes did flicker to Asche and linger. He assumed it was because they were the daurae, but then noticed the lapels on Asche's uniform jacket. They resembled the orange wings of a monarch butterfly, rather than the blue of a morpho. He vaguely recalled something Luvon said about the difference, but still thought it would be a natural conversation starter to ask again. Anything to get the required back-and-forth theatrics out of the way so he could relax with a familiar face.

"Why are your collars different?"

Asche pinched the lapel, before averting their eyes like it was something embarrassing.

"I'm actually enrolled in Mairwen's Prep School on the other side of the trees... I'm an advanced student, so I get to take some upper classes here at the Academy, too."

"Oh!" Saffron raised his eyebrows. "Why doesn't that surprise me? You're one of the smartest people I know. Erm—that I know *so far,* of course, your highness." He laughed under his breath. Asche blushed slightly at the compliment.

The professor who joined the lecture was a tall, curvy fey lady with red hair styled upright like a beehive, wearing a long skirt that trailed behind her with every step along the base of the hall. As the class began, an image was projected behind her from what Asche explained to be a piece of charmed glass over an open book that could be moved and changed as the professor spoke. It reminded Saffron of the brief glances he would sometimes get into Adelard's lectures, how there used to always be strange things projected on those walls, too. Schematics of bones, brains, bodies, colorful watercolors depicting auras or different forms of opulence surrounding the drawings in all the ways that mattered to students of high fey anthropology. Adelard had referred to his tools as "lenses" or "opaque projectors," but never explained much more than that. As Saffron had come to expect.

"Let's review what we discussed last time," the professor announced, turning the page beneath the projector light and replacing the charmed glass. Saffron's heart fluttered at the next image to appear ahead of him. Swirling lines interlacing through one another, like woven ribbon, like the trail of a drunken sprite circling a flower field in search of sweet pollen. Saffron had seen something similar before. Similar, but different, and just enough to make his insides tangle like it was full of sprites, too.

"Now—have any of you ever had a conversation with your family oracles outside of asking whether your courtship will be successful or not?" she asked, and the room chuckled slightly. "Can you tell me what this represents?"

There was no reaction from the class at first, until a few people slowly raised their hands—but Saffron was more surprised at how quickly Asche scribbled down their answer on the parchment in front of them, rather than offering the answer, themself. *'Celtic knots.'*

"They're Celtic knots, professor," the chosen student announced matter-of-factly. "They have to do with the veil. Our family oracle placed a similar one made from stone in our garden to keep tears from forming."

"That's right," the professor nodded, adjusting the presentation glass again. Saffron scribbled the student's statement word-for-word on his parchment, instantly enchanted at the thought. "Also called knotted stones, this form of ancient epithet is older than any high fey records, older than even the oldest of written language we still use today. The only way we know they were once used in regard to the veil comes in findings of veil fingerprints left behind after a tear is closed. Fingerprints such as charred stone beneath layers of newly deposited minerals, signs of phantom-formed foliage, and, occasionally, similar shapes included in some of our oldest oracle texts."

Epithets. Oracles. The veil. Goosebumps flushed Saffron's arms. He squeezed his hands together under the desk, noticing Asche's stiffness as well. As if they recalled the same memories Saffron did, performing those spells in the Kyteler Ruins outside of Morrígan. Using Taran's knotted memory threads that resembled what was on the wall ahead of them.

Saffron's instincts told him to look away, as if it was some sort of trap, as if just looking at those markings would unravel his own memories.

"Now—celtic knots are a well-documented cultural staple on the human side of the veil, as well, though it's unclear if they fully understand the connection to the veil as we do or if they are simply used as religious tokens. 'Celtic' is actually a human word. Who knows if their own uses of such knots were ever as advanced as our own—such as placing knotted stones in gardens to keep veil tears at bay." She nodded at the student in question. A few more people chuckled.

Saffron frowned, only then realizing there was an insult somewhere in that statement. He raised his hand in what he knew to be a misguided attempt to defend himself and other humans like him, ignoring the voice in the back of his head already begging him to just let it go.

The professor nodded at him, and he stood up, for some reason. Perhaps because he wasn't sure what else to do. Perhaps because he wanted to make sure she heard him the first time, as he didn't want to have to repeat himself.

"Aren't knots like these also used in preserving memory threads?" he asked. The room dipped into silence, followed by whispers and what he swore were tiny bouts of laughter. The professor smiled awkwardly, then shook her head.

"You are Lord mag Shamhradháin, right? I haven't had the chance to welcome you to Mairwen, yet. That said, I don't know what they were teaching you in Alvényan schools, my lord, but I have never heard such a claim."

Saffron frowned, surprised at how curt her response was. A part of him sensed an insult buried within that statement, too. He didn't mean for there to be a sliver of beantighe-politeness in his response, only realizing it as the words escaped his mouth in a continued attempt to validate himself.

"I only ask because I've seen memory knots that looked like—"

"Common memory thread manipulation has been taboo in this country since Evening King Elanyl came into power," the professor interrupted, and Saffron felt his first twang of embarrassment. "Only the highest oracles weave memories here in Alfidel, and any discussion otherwise is a quick way of getting yourself in trouble with the high guard. If someone claimed to be showing you knotted memory threads, I'm afraid it was likely a tourist trick. I do hope you didn't pay that street-swindler too much money to take one home."

More giggles filled the room. Saffron almost insisted further, but the nervous tug of Asche's hand on his sleeve stopped him. Glancing down at them, they stared back at him with wide, nervous eyes in the low light, shaking their head. Saffron pressed his lips together in frustration, but reclaimed his seat without another word, and the professor went on. He returned his quill to the parchment in front of him, ignoring how other students glanced over their shoulders, turned in their seats to look at him. At the new student who, to them, had said something foolish in front of everyone. He clenched the quill tighter.

"It wasn't a trick," he muttered. Wishing he could scream it.

Asche slid their parchment toward him, donning a scribbled sentence that squeezed Saffron tight with every looping letter. *I still think about them sometimes, too.*

Saffron might have turned to look at them again, had a line of overwhelmed blood not slid from his nose and dripped to the back of his hand. Hating how all the courage he'd had at the shrine the night before had disintegrated the moment he put his glamour on again that morning.

His second class of the day was an instant relief from the first, both because it was a lecture on Alvish Myths, which he had at least something of a foundation in—and also because Prince Cylvan of all people waltzed into the hall right at the start and claimed a seat at the front. Saffron quickly scrambled for his crow book, scribbling out *'you're in the Alvish Myths class with me!'*, then had to resist the giant grin that wanted to split his face the second Cylvan saw it and snapped around to look. When his eyes landed on Saffron, he cooly let them slide right off again, aloof and like any other bored prince even as he flirtily wrote back:

I KNEW DANU WOULD ANSWER MY PRAYERS WHEN I PLEADED FOR AT LEAST ONE OPPORTUNITY TO SEE YOUR FACE DURING THE WEEK. HOW ARE YOU FEELING?

I'm fine. I slept so well last night. I think I was visited by a wild fey of some sort who put a spell on me.
   Isn't this a low-level class for you?

I'M TECHNICALLY HERE TO ASSIST THE PROFESSOR. BUT I AM OPEN TO BRIBES FOR PASSING GRADES, IN CASE YOU FIND THE MATERIAL TOO DIFFICULT TO KEEP UP WITH.

What will it take to have you as a private tutor?

I'M EAGERLY LOOKING FORWARD TO WHATEVER YOU COME UP WITH, FLOWER.

DESPITE THE NATURAL RELIEF IT WAS TO HAVE CYLVAN there with him, studying myths at an academic level was nothing like what Saffron had scraped together as a beantighe hiding in the barn or the attic of Danann House. The text was too high-level even for his improved literacy, and even the terms the professor used when speaking went over Saffron's head so fast they pulled his hair in the process. What started as pure glee quickly melted into desperate note taking as he fought to keep up, struggling to write and keep pace on the page all while avoiding any risk that he might be called on to answer questions. Sometimes because whatever was being asked evaded him entirely—sometimes because, even when he thought he could give a response, his experience speaking up in the previous lecture was too raw in the back of his throat. Thankfully the professor ignored him in favor of a few others who seemed to have all the right things to say, though Saffron soon realized why that class, specifically, appeared full to the brim with students who always had something to offer. All of them wanted Cylvan's attention; all of them wanted to impress the crown prince, who was top—third—in his class. The prince who Saffron was sure everyone already knew had a penchant for myths and the study of old books and lore and language and dissecting it all as philosophically as possible. He didn't know whether he wished to shrink smaller and disappear at the thought, or try and join the flock in offering every thought that came to him in an attempt to impress the handsome Sídhe lord seated at the front of the room, too. It would only make their future courtship more believable, anyway.

Saffron spent lunch in the dining hall with Sionnach, eating a little bit of everything as his friend stuck to a plate of salad and a bowl of fruits. But Saffron had never had such unsupervised access to a student buffet, and he was going to take advantage of it until it made him sick. Chestnut and apple soup, braised veal, shepherd's pie, sugar glazed onions over roasted potatoes, rosemary and buttered thyme scones—Saffron whispered the name of each thing he'd ever prepared, himself, but never tasted before, all while piling it high on his plate. He ignored how many other people watched him in curiosity, or perhaps disgust, exchanging words under their breaths like he was something strange to witness. He didn't care. Damn—he really didn't give a shit. He was going to eat until he burst.

Anthropology of Wild, Lesser, and High Fey was assigned to meet outside the edge of campus within the treeline, where Saffron spotted Copper's red hair and hurried over to join him— but not before staring far longer than it was polite at the tall professor with round wings that shimmered like those on pixies, long ears that curled at the ends, blue-tinged skin, and pointy teeth that poked out beneath round lips every time he smiled. Despite knowing it was probably rude, Saffron couldn't resist asking Copper if he was a wild fey of some sort, only to gasp with a fluttering heart as Copper replied, "Yeah, Professor Lyna is part nymph or something."

Most of the lecture was spent crawling around in the grass, between plants and around trees, plucking bugs from bark and sprites from flowers and taking notes on everything that caught their eye. Copper admitted it was his favorite class, mostly because it was impossible to fail, though by the way he and Saffron talked to each other—and then with Professor Lyna, whose enthusiasm was contagious—it was clear the fey lord was more interested in wild things than he put on. Saffron could have guessed that much from how he talked about the pixies hiding in their dorm room, though.

Saffron sensed that class would quickly become his favorite as well, especially as Copper explained how it mainly consisted of wandering around in the woods and finding, identifying, and doing write-ups of wild fey behaviors compared to the sociological and learned behaviors of high fey in comparison—and while Saffron didn't know what *sociological and learned behaviors* meant, he was thrilled at the chance to chew on leaves and chase down pixies for a grade. He wondered if Luvon would allow him to re-take that class four times, too, like Copper said he had.

After his Anthropology class, the rest of the day was Saffron's to spend how he pleased, and he very much pleased to do so in Mairwen's Grand Library.

Copper joined him, and it was harder than he expected to pretend like walking through the doors—without requiring any fey deals or geis or stolen access rings to do so—was nothing new. Nothing special. Not, in its own way, the singular proof he needed that everything he'd been through until that point was worth it. When he actually teared up and had to clutch his chest as it squeezed, he blamed it on allergies as Copper panicked and asked what was wrong. It was only dust. It was only pollen from their last class. It definitely wasn't a huge, defining moment for Saffron and his life and everything he'd ever wanted. A welcome visitor to a school library, where he would be able to peruse all the books and read any of them that he liked. He could borrow and read them in bed in his dorm. He could study them at his own pace. And he would never have to burn a single one in fear of being caught and punished ever again.

Mairwen Academy's Library was the same as the Morrígan Grand Library, except in two ways: Mairwen's library's ceiling was made entirely of glass, allowing for sunlight—or, in the case of that day, overcast rainy light—to fall across the floor below and reduce any need for daytime lights at all. Second—there were hardly any places to hide while searching for books, with only shallow corridors of shelves, no corners to step behind while reading something questionable. Just like the Grand Library, though, rows upon rows of study tables filled the main atrium, with shelves of books lining every wall surrounding them. There were a few narrow corridors on the second floor balcony overhead, but for the most part, everything and everyone was visible to those studying on the floor below. Somehow, still, the ambient noise inside hardly grew louder than a muffled lull of whispered conversations and scooting chairs.

Despite the events of the night prior and how badly Saffron was tempted to search for answers while waiting for a reply from Baba, he also knew better than to seek out anything as blatant as *arid magic* or *arid witches* or *rowan magic* on his literal first day. He would have to be satisfied with exploring—and Ériu knew he was. To familiarize himself with the layout, the location of different sections, even thumbing through one of the register tomes and smiling to himself when he found them to be exactly the same as Morrígan's had been. He remembered how Cylvan first taught him to use them, how they stood in front of the giant book at one end of the room with Cylvan's hand on Saffron's waist to ensure he paid attention. It was embarrassing to blush so easily at the thought, pressing his hands to his cheeks and hurrying away before anyone noticed.

He was on the hunt for the *Genre Literature* section to scour their mythology offerings when he spotted a familiar face perusing an area closed off from the rest of the floor, locked behind a shiny gate that kept Saffron out of reach. Still, he approached, grabbing the bars and rattling them just in case.

"Sionnach!" He called out when it didn't work, pressing his face between the gap in the bars. Sionnach jumped at the sudden sound of their name, nearly dropping the book in their hand as they turned and searched him out. When they smiled weakly in greeting, Saffron grinned right back.

"What are those books in there?" He asked, gently rattling the bars again before sticking his arm through to point. "Can you let me in?"

"This is... the restricted section." Sionnach smiled awkwardly, lifting the book in their hands to show how the volume was attached to the shelf by a bronze chain. It reminded Saffron of those in the archive beneath the Kyteler Ruins, only making him hungrier for access. Sionnach, perhaps seeing how close Saffron was to drooling, added: "Um, you need special permission from the headmaster to get access, so I really can't let you in right now."

"You can't? Not even just this once? I promise I won't be naughty. No one will even notice."

"No, Saffron—it could get me expelled!" Sionnach squeaked, stepping a little closer like they thought it would get him to lower his voice. Not close enough for Saffron to grapple for them through the bars and hold them hostage, though. Like some sort of prey instinct. Smart satyr.

"Well then how do I get permission from the headmaster?" He conceded.

"You have to get an endorsement from the administration, first, which is only offered to top students... um, then you have to write a letter of intent and prove the work you're doing, then provide regular updates... Is there something specific you're looking for, maybe...?"

"Uh..." Saffron scrambled for anything at all. "Just... erm... G-Gaeilge. Remember how I mentioned Gaeilge when we first met?

It's sort of one of my special interests. Um—you're doing work? Is it like what you researched with Madame Catrín?" he quickly changed the subject, and Sionnach's awkward smile remained. But it was different that time, somehow, as if they genuinely weren't expecting Saffron to ask.

"Well..."

"Ah. A goat in its pen." Cylvan's voice came out of nowhere, making Saffron jump and turn. Instantly, Cylvan's mouth popped closed again, staring at Saffron with the same pure dread as when they first met eyes after he'd kicked Saffron into the mud. They stared at each other for a long time, until Sionnach's breaths came so fast they nearly hyperventilated.

"Your highness?" Saffron prompted. Cylvan cleared his throat in an instant, flipping hair over one shoulder like nothing was awry at all. But Saffron saw the stiffness in his movements.

"O-oh... I recognize you from my Alvish Mythology and Classic Literature class," Cylvan said. His voice was tight, as if trying to reason with a bear in the woods. "Is that right? What was your name again?"

Saffron narrowed his eyes. Panic flickered over Cylvan's expression.

"Are you sure it was only from class?" He asked. Cylvan flinched like he lost another year off his life.

"Ah, of course... we also met at the docks when you first arrived from Alvénya, didn't we?"

Saffron's smile tightened. Bloodthirsty. Cylvan smiled back, though simultaneously grew a little paler, perhaps finally realizing there was no salvation for his ego after all.

"I distinctly remember getting kicked into the mud by someone who resembled you yesterday morning," Saffron finally said outright.

"S-Saffron!" Sionnach wheezed.

"Now that you mention it, I do think I recall that. How unbecoming of me—the Prince of Alfidel." Cylvan tried one last time to win Saffron over with a calm voice and dazzling smile, though it dripped with undertones of *'I'm so fucking sorry. Please don't do this.'* When Saffron didn't react, the Prince of Alfidel cleared his throat. "What a shame to meet that way—especially when you do look quite fine in that uniform. I think Alvish styles suit you. I will be sure to be more careful with my feet in the future. Tell me, do you enjoy studying Alvish myths—"

"Thank you," Saffron offered shortly, though still held Cylvan's gaze. Cylvan knew Saffron had something else to say, eyes flickering so fast to Sionnach then back again, Saffron could have imagined it. Whether or not he did, he went on: "It was actually my friend Gentle Sionnach, here, who was struck by your foot, first, your highness. I merely cushioned their fall. Perhaps you'll be more careful with your feet with them in the future, as well?"

"Saffron—!" Sionnach begged, voice shrill and tight. Cylvan looked paler than ever—but to Saffron's mild surprise, the prince immediately turned to Sionnach. So fast that Sionnach jumped in surprise. Like their prey instinct kicked in again.

"Gentle Sionnach," Cylvan started, speaking with all the politeness of a prince desperate to win back the affections of his secret fiancé. "To you as well—I will be sure to be more aware of my feet in the future. It was unbecoming of me, as the... the Prince of Alfidel."

Sionnach looked like they'd been petrified by the eyes of a gorgon. Which was a shame, because it meant they never saw exactly how Cylvan looked that way, too. Saffron decided to set both of them free from such a pathetic display of common decency, sighing and touching Cylvan on the shoulder to get his attention back.

"I'm a big fan of Alvish myths, actually. I'm very much looking forward to the class we share together. Will I see you in the next one?"

"Yes!" Cylvan said with slightly too much enthusiasm, realizing and straightening up again. "Yes, I will be in the next class as well. If you ever wish to discuss the readings, please don't hesitate to ask."

Saffron nodded. Cylvan waited a moment longer, then cringed as Copper's voice suddenly rang out through the atrium, shouting for Saffron to *be careful, that's the one that kicked your ass into the mud yesterday!* Cylvan threw Copper a dirty look, then smoothed down the front of his blazer, offered Saffron a nod, and hurried from the library.

Saffron watched him go, then gave a small wave to Copper, an exasperated little *'thank you'* motion that satisfied the giant lord well enough for him to lumber off back into the shelves. He decided to give Sionnach a moment to catch their breath as well, wishing them luck in their research and finally taking his leave. He turned down the first row of shelves without anyone in it, stopping to sigh again then pinch the bridge of his nose. He didn't have to open his crow book to know it was already being flooded with Cylvan's incessant apologies.

He focused on the books. He just wanted to wander the shelves and, maybe, get a second chance to feel like any other student studying between classes. God above. God help him.

Two hours of peaceful silence passed of Saffron touching, appreciating, choosing books at random, flipping some open, actually pausing to read others. He skimmed and explored until students at the study tables slowly diminished, until the sun started to set outside the glass domed ceiling. He lost himself in the silent excuse of simply touching every book he could, and was in the middle of mumbling a page of poetry to himself when a library-beantighe meekly rolled a personal cart Saffron's way as the stack by his feet steadily grew taller. He thanked them, dumping the books in the top rack while simultaneously spotting another and reaching for it. The beantighe was kind enough to neatly organize his choices in the cart as he did.

"Do you work in here often?" he asked as the human turned to leave, startling them. They briefly met Saffron's eyes, which made Saffron unexpectedly emotional. Beantighes weren't forced to wear veils at Mairwen, he knew that already—but something about being able to meet the eyes of one was strangely bittersweet. He put on his softest, most polite smile in return, not wanting to intimidate them by accident.

The beantighe returned a practiced smile, one Saffron knew well. The rosy tint in front of his eyes broke in an instant, the moment he saw it, the moment he was on the receiving end. The beantighe just wore that empty smile, nodding once before motioning to the books to silently ask if Saffron needed anything else from them. Saffron's own smile felt awkward, so he put it away.

"Do they let you read any of the books here?"

The beantighe raised their eyebrows, before averting their gaze again and shaking their head quickly.

"Sorry—I don't mean like I want to tell on you. I was only wondering. Erm..." *Damnit.* He'd apologized again. "Where I last went to school, only elevated beantighes were allowed into the library at all, and only a few times a week to clean. I didn't mean to make you uncomfortable."

The beantighe's polite smile remained. They offered a bow.

"Why don't you say anything? It's alright," he encouraged, but they kept shaking their head and smiling. They bowed one more time, then turned to hurry away like they couldn't wait any longer. Saffron turned over every word he spoke, churning through them, trying to figure out if it was something he said to make them so uncomfortable—or if it was simply his presence, period. His addressing them at all.

It was a swift reminder—he was no longer a friendly, safe presence to be with, for the people he once worked alongside.

He couldn't stop thinking about the beantighe in the library, even after Copper showed him how to borrow all of his books and then helped him carry them back to their dorm. Cylvan complained in the crow book about how jealous he was, how he wished Saffron would stop allowing Copper to be his first-for-everything, to which Saffron coyly replied '*Not my first everything.*' Cylvan took a long time to reply after that, eventually offering a defeated *'please for the love of gods do not fall in love with the likes of Copper dé Bricriu.'*

"So do they not have libraries in Alvénya or something?" Copper asked while offering Saffron a glass of smuggled whiskey, which Saffron downed faster than he should have. He was worried Lady Maeve, the dorm prefect, would suddenly burst into the room to catch them in the act. "Since you cried the whole time you were in there."

Saffron flushed. He held out his glass to request another drink.

"Of course there are libraries," he said, but opted to be vague. He'd never actually been to Alvénya, of course, he'd only received a few surface-level culture lessons from one of Catrín's Alvényan friends during his stay in the Winter Court. He assumed they at least had libraries, though. "But the one here was just so big and pretty. I also just really like reading, I don't know..."

"Well, do me a favor and wait a few weeks before you rise in class rank, I don't think I can handle a roommate who's part of the top-three club."

"The what?"

"Top-three in the school. That's the goat, the prince, and the ice-queen. Maeve, I mean. Or is Maeve second right now? Gods know. They all flop around so much. Well—I mean, Prince Cylvan and Maeve always flop around so much. The goat is always number one."

"I think Lady Maeve is second."

"No wonder Cylvan's being such a touchy bitch lately, then," Copper chuckled. Saffron asked for another drink. He knew the real reason Cylvan was being a *touchy bitch*—that being how the new Alvényan student was constantly, publicly bullying him whenever he bullied someone else. "They're always bickering and fighting one another over maintaining it, it's annoying. Neither the prince or Maeve have ever held the number one spot for very long, though. The goat always wins out. They must absorb information by eating the books, or something. Um, you know... like a goat."

"Just now. You really didn't say Sionnach's name a single time."

"You knew who I was talking about, though."

Saffron frowned. He swirled the drink in his glass. "Is it just out of jealousy, or what?"

"What?"

"The reason you're so mean to them. Prince Cylvan is, too. Maybe my real question is why you're all so mean to *each other*, I guess." Saffron was fully aware of general high fey temperament and how much that included bullying for bullying's sake, but he never thought he'd witness them being cruel to anyone who wasn't just a beantighe.

"Oh—I mean, isn't it obvious? They're stuck up. Snobby. Not an ounce of respect for anyone else. Sorta rubs you the wrong way after a while."

"But Sionnach is high fey, aren't they? I thought all high fey stuck together." Saffron chose the easiest argument to make, knowing the rest of Copper's complaints were clearly based in some sort of deep-rooted resentment. Cylvan's treatment of Sionnach probably was, too. Like he was jealous of someone else on campus not only being smarter than him, but also having horns like he did. Except they also had a cute tail. And soft ears. And pretty legs.

"The goat is only part fey, obviously," Copper muttered into his drink. "The other part is centaur, or whatever."

"Satyr, I think."

"Same thing."

"It's not. And I know you know it's not, because earlier you were telling me all about how much time you used to spend in the woods as a kid making friends with the wild fey creatures there. You've also literally taken our anthropology class like a hundred times. I think you're just being cruel on purpose. Is it because they're smarter and cuter than all of you combined? Or because they have horns and ears and a tail and that bothers you? Since you were so put off by Aven and Neva's cat glamours, too... where are they, actually...?"

"They don't even go to this school," Copper muttered, before shaking his head. "But, alright, and so what? I don't know what's got you so protective of the goat so quickly, Saff. I'd actually tone it down if I were you, just in case someone overhears—"

"Ah, perhaps you're right," Saffron said, finishing off his drink and setting his glass on the table between them. "In that case, I'll be silent from here on out. Goodnight."

"Whoa, wait, hold on—that's not what I meant! Saff, c'mon."

"You told me to tone it down, so I will be toning it down indefinitely."

"C'mon. C'mon. That's not what I meant! Don't be so dramatic."

"I have no interest in being friends with bullies."

"What, but you're gonna attend one of the prince's galas tomorrow night? He's the biggest, stupidest bully of us all."

Saffron narrowed his eyes, hand already on the knob of his bedroom door.

"How did you know about that?"

"Letters brought by birds are left in the box outside the room. There was an invite in there for you. The prince of darkness really didn't wait even a second to try and drag you into his eternal night, did he?"

"And you call me the dramatic one?"

Copper rolled his eyes, getting to his feet to grab the small stack of letters off the side table by the door. He handed one to Saffron, before stuffing the rest into his back pocket like he only then cared to actually take them for himself. Saffron didn't hesitate, ripping open the envelope. Already knowing what it would say, but heart fluttering nonetheless. Inside was a piece of cream parchment, note written in velvety green ink. A ribbon matching the words slipped out with it.

Saffron dé mag Shamhradháin de Lelfe of Alvénya
You are cordially invited to attend the upcoming suitor's gala hosted in honor of
High Crown Prince Cylvan dé Tuatha dé Danann of Alfidel
Beginning at dusk at the Avren Capitol Palace.
Please don the included ribbon as proof of invitation.

In slightly different handwriting below the first message, Saffron read:

Master Luvon has your outfit at his townhouse. I designed it especially for you. I cannot wait to see how it looks.
-King Tross.

13

THE GALA

Classes at Mairwen repeated every other day, which meant the following morning, Saffron was forced to re-experience the bittersweet process of trying to locate all of his classes all over again, finding somewhere to sit, worrying he was in the wrong room, worrying he was forgetting something. He was already enrolling halfway through the first quarter, which only made it more difficult to jump right in to conversation or find a place to land his feet in terms of readings and homework he would have to eventually catch up on. But he wouldn't complain. He finally had what he'd always wanted, and he wasn't going to complain.

Even better—the first of his three classes scheduled that day was so serendipitously appropriate for what he was dealing with outside of campus, with the human, rowan-witch part of him beneath the glamour, that he almost rushed all the way back to Luvon's townhouse to kiss and thank him: *Ashen States and A History of the Veil.* After which would come *Introduction to Charms and Wild Magicks* then *Ancient Alvish Reading and Arithmetic.*

But the thrill didn't last once Saffron took his seat in the first lecture hall and opened the textbook—finding nothing but pages and pages of art and annotated poetry and nothing about the veil at all. Nothing about how it worked. What made it tick. He glared at the pages as the professor read aloud from the sonnets.

Tell me why my History of the Veil class is just a bunch of poetry?

Saffron scribbled into his crow book under the desk. For the first time ever, Cylvan didn't reply until his own class was over, and by then Saffron was steaming. Bursting at the seams in frustration. More and more feeling like he'd been tricked.

*I DIDN'T REALIZE YOU WERE IN PROFESSOR LONGMONT'S CLASS. I COULD HAVE WARNED YOU. YOU'RE NOT LIKELY TO GET MUCH ACTUAL, APPLICABLE INFORMATION ABOUT THE VEIL OR OTHER *TABOO TOPICS* SITTING IN A LECTURE HALL. MOSTLY JUST THE ARTS AND OTHER METAPHORICAL DISCUSSIONS. WHICH ARE IMPORTANT TOO, BY THE WAY, SO PAY ATTENTION.*

Would they be mad if I raise my hand and ask if there are any poems about humans making veil oaths to overthrow the coward Queen Proserpina?

I CAN ALREADY SEE THE AVREN GUARDS FLOODING CAMPUS IN SEARCH OF YOU. MEET ME BY LAKE MORAIN AND I'LL SNEAK YOU AWAY.

I got in trouble for asking a basic question in a class yesterday as well. She mocked me in front of everyone. She said memory knots weren't real. Maybe I should have incisted a little more.

———

WHO? I'LL HAVE HER STRIPPED OF ALL HER RESEARCH GRANTS.

———

You're only saying that because you want me to like you.

———

WHAT? OF COURSE NOT. I'M JUST YOUR MYTHS AND CLASSIC LIT STUDENT ASSISTANT. I ONLY WANT TO MAKE SURE YOU RECEIVE FAIR TREATMENT HERE AT MAIRWEN ACADEMY OF THE OPULENT ARTS.

———

Funny you should say that when

———

I APPROACHED SIONNACH AT BREAKFAST THIS MORNING AND OFFERED THEM AN INVITATION TO TONIGHT'S GALA. THEY REFUSED, BUT I DID IT. IT WAS VERY KIND OF ME. IF YOU KNEW THE DRAMA AROUND THEIR FAMILY YOU WOULD UNDERSTAND WHY.

———

What's the drama?

Maybe I'll tell you later. If you come to my party tonight. Nothing big, just a little get-together where I hope to find my future spouse. All those up until this point have been so boring, I am praying someone new comes and sweeps me off my feet.

I'm actualy already engaged to a fine fey lord back in Alvénya, I don't think I can accept this inviteation.

I will declare war on Alvénya. I'll find your fiancé and cut off all his fingers.

Why his fingers?

I know how much you like how they feel.

SHUT UP

Saffron's second lecture, *Introduction to Charms and Wild Magicks,* would eventually make a good companion to his anthropology lessons as after a few weeks of classroom instruction it would apparently transition to also wandering around in the woods searching for signs of wild magic, like discolored berries or leaves, sounds like buzzing or chimes that couldn't be explained, clusters of wild things like pixies obsessively cleaning or hovering around a specific rock. Saffron couldn't complain. He even wrote down a few things to ask the daurae when he got the chance, though could already hear Asche's voice insisting everything the professor and field textbook said was wrong, they actually knew everything that was right, they would be happy to take his hand and show him in person.

Ancient Alvish Reading and Arithmetic, while intimidating in name, turned out to be Saffron's smoothest introduction to a topic considering the level of shared traits Old Alvish had with Gaeilge. While it was harder than he expected not to raise his hand and say something that would give him away, he couldn't help but grin the entire time he worked through the reading for the day and could pronounce most of it with relative ease, even though he was still hardly the best in class. The professor still complimented his 'diction,' saying his 'articulation' was impressive for his level— and once Cylvan explained what those words meant, Saffron was over the moon with pride. He couldn't stop smiling. Cylvan used lots of exclamation points while complimenting him in the crow book as well, which only made Saffron more giddy. He giggled and sighed and grinned all the way to Luvon's townhouse later that afternoon to prepare for his first gala, perhaps subconsciously knowing the elation would soon give way back to anxiety. He would hold onto it for as long as he could in the meantime.

SAFFRON KNEW, AFTER AT LEAST THREE HOURS, HE would never get used to the feeling of being dressed and dolled up by a flurry of beantighes. He was supposed to be the one holding the fine fabrics and draping them over bodies. Not the other way around.

He was supposed to be the one watching from the back corridor as the pretty fey waited in the front room for the carriage to arrive. Not the other way around.

Surely other high fey never felt so anxious right before a big event.

"Ah, King Tross wanted me to ask if you would be part of the opening ceremony at the Midsummer Games this year. On the solstice. Seems he's interested in you shooting the opening arrow into the bonfire... Pace like that much longer, a leanbh, and you'll carve a trench in my floor," Luvon warned, realizing any other attempt at conversation was a lost cause. Around them, beantighes scurried to and from the courtyard to prepare the carriage for their journey, and Saffron couldn't find a moment of peace with how they buzzed in every direction. He couldn't stop mentally thanking or critiquing how they dressed him hours prior; he couldn't stop noticing the smallest things out of place all around Luvon's parlor room; he wanted to comment on how some of them weren't wearing house uniforms at all, perhaps because they knew Luvon couldn't technically see them. He wanted to scold them—but he bit his tongue, knowing it wouldn't be a beantighe scolding other beantighes. And he was not about to be a picky fey lord demanding perfection from tired humans.

As Luvon spoke, Saffron heard the words, but barely registered them. He agreed to whatever King Tross wanted. He kept walking, pacing back and forth, partially to try and get used to the feeling of the heeled boots beneath his feet. Definitely not adjusting how the lamp sat on the side table with the quickest flick of his wrist as he passed by. Definitely not nudging Luvon's drink to be perfectly centered on its wooden coaster. He was simply practicing moving around with the train of his blouse. Forcing himself to walk upright with his back straight. Not noticing the things only a beantighe would all around him. Just like Catrín taught him.

"Won't they be able to tell?" he finally asked, unable to take the anxiety any longer. Luvon let out a breath, getting to his feet to place hands on Saffron's shoulders and halt his incessant walking. Perhaps he did it on purpose, but Saffron found himself stuck staring at his own reflection in the tall mirror perched over the burning fireplace.

That night, there was far more to him than just the glamour that gave him the basic appearance of a high fey. Gloss in his hair made it shiny and well-behaved, earrings costumed the false points on the ends of his ears, eyeshadow made his glamoured hazel eyes appear more like his natural green ones, like fresh moss. He wore a dusty pink sheer blouse that hung off his shoulders from a deep sweetheart neckline; a separate high collar in gold draped chains down the bare skin of the plunging back and tinkled with every movement. The flowing fabric tucked into the waist of a pair of dark green trousers clinging snugly to his legs, disappearing into knee-high boots with golden heels that clacked with every step. The layered puff sleeves of the blouse came to points over his hands, his left wrist wrapped in the forest-green gala invitation ribbon, followed by the silver and emerald engagement ring on his finger said to have been given by a fey lord across the ocean. He tried not to think about how naked his wrist felt without the yew bracelet. That night, especially. Knowing the stress might eat him alive. He didn't want to think about it. He couldn't—else he might summon a reaction before ever arriving anywhere at all.

He could stay calm. He could keep calm. He would. He had to.

He focused on his appearance. His outfit that sang with grandeur, shimmering with gold embellishments in an attempt to make him look more affluent than he really was. An attempt to make him stand out, on purpose. He was supposed to have every eye on him that night, from the moment they stepped into the palace ballroom, while at the same time not being too obvious. To stand out, but just enough to be noticed. Not enough to cause a stir. Master Luvon mag Shamhradháin's distant relative visiting from Alvénya, the flower who was engaged to a far-away nobleman, but who would eventually, inevitably, be courted by the crown Prince of Alfidel, instead.

Cylvan wasn't meant to approach or flirt with him at all that night; Saffron was only meant to make an impression as a newcomer. But he still had to put on a perfect performance. To be eye-catching enough to get people's attention, but not enough to make a scene. To be remembered. Just enough to make people talk, maybe, but only positive things. To make little comments at brunch the following morning. *Did you see that relative of Master mag Shamhradháin's? The country-boy who looked so lovely in that dusty pink tunic. I heard it was designed by King Tross himself. Perhaps because the king and Luvon are such good friends...*

Intrigue purposefully designed to be irresistible. Saffron was engaged to someone else in Alvénya, how juicy it would be for the prince to break off that engagement to take the visiting stranger for himself.

Closing his eyes, Saffron let out a long exhale through his nose. He could hardly think straight. Could hardly think of anything at all, except what was expected of him. Of all the ways he couldn't make a mess. Make a mistake. All the things he'd practiced with Catrín during his two months apart from Cylvan, all the ways he'd practiced keeping his magic under control with Baba Yaga and Adelard's help, as limited as it had been.

He thought of the letter he sent with Fiachra the day before. He wondered how long it would take for Baba Yaga to receive it, if she even did. He wondered when she'd be able to reply. Until then, he would just...

He gazed down at his forearm where wicked, dangerous, wild magic was carved beneath the glamour. Wild magic that had once already laid violence upon innocent people as Saffron couldn't control it. He pressed his hand to the scars.

"Stay," he whispered under his breath, directing it to the beastly manifestation beneath his skin. "Never show yourself again. Ever. So maybe I can find happiness. So I don't embarrass

him. So I don't..." he trailed off. A lump formed in his throat, unable to speak the words out loud.

"So I don't accidentally hurt him, too."

HE THOUGHT OF IT STILL, ENDLESSLY, EVEN ONCE THEY climbed into the carriage and began the journey through Avren to the palace. He thought of it while watching the streets pass by through the window. Turning the plans and suggestions and warnings over and over relentlessly in his mind. Not wanting to mess up. Not wanting to ruin anything before it even started. Not wanting to disappoint anyone and make them regret all the help they'd already offered.

Despite knowing every step of the night and how the performance would go, Saffron was terrified. He felt nauseous, but didn't know whether it was his nerves or the swathe of enchantments all over his body. Perhaps being within the embrace of such thick opulence like ocean waves made his insides turn as his arid-tinged blood bubbled against it. He pressed his hand to his forearm again, knowing he only had to keep his emotions under control, especially without a yew bracelet to keep the urge under the surface. So long as he kept his emotions under control, so long as he never once saw the glow of magic on anyone or anything...

He would not get overwhelmed. He would not do anything to disrupt, or embarrass, or—*hurt* anyone at Cylvan's suitor gala. Not like he'd done with the humans at Ériu's shrine in the mountains.

Cylvan would even be there with him; Cylvan would be right there all night for Saffron to gaze upon and find comfort in the sight of, even at a distance. There would be no reason to get overwhelmed at all.

God—he just hoped Baba Yaga's letter would come soon, where she'd lay out all the ways she or Adelard or someone else had figured out a way to help him.

Luvon could sense the tension emanating off of him—the

people they passed in the streets could probably sense the tension emanating off of him—placing a hand on Saffron's clutching the fabric of his blouse. It helped relax him a little bit, closing his eyes and exhaling before offering Luvon an apologetic smile. Luvon spoke before Saffron could.

"Saffron," he started gently. "Everyone in Avren will fall in love with you as effortlessly as Prince Cylvan already has."

The encouraging words made tears swell in Saffron's eyes, quickly wiping them away before they blurred his makeup. He took Luvon's hand, squeezing it tight, before kissing the back of it in silent gratitude.

Arriving at the gates, Luvon slid the carriage window down for them to both extend their wrists and show the invitation ribbons. The guard bowed and wished them a pleasant night, never knowing how hard Saffron's heart pounded. Suddenly worried he'd forgotten something, or he'd already done something wrong without realizing it, worried it was all over in that moment. But the carriage continued without event. Luvon left the window down as the carriage continued through the gates, perhaps so the fresh air could cure Saffron's sudden rush of rapid breathing.

Arriving in the wide palace courtyard, stepping from the carriage with a hand over Luvon's arm, Saffron's pace stopped right outside the doors as a tight sound escaped him. His heart leapt into his throat. He tasted bile—or perhaps blood—in the back of his mouth. But Luvon didn't miss a beat. Sensing the sudden halt of Saffron's gait, his seeing stick swept around and bumped into Saffron's ankles, locating where he stood frozen and placing a hand on his back to encourage him forward again.

"The prince will not let anything go astray," he promised for what felt like the hundredth time. Saffron grew more embarrassed the more often it was implied he wasn't hiding his anxiety as well as he thought. "And if he fails you, I surely will not."

"I'm—scared," Saffron managed to whimper, but allowed himself to be shepherded into the grand entrance behind an ocean of other well-dressed fey courtiers who barely cast him a second look. While it was proof of his successful glamour, it also tilted his nerves in the opposite direction. He was supposed to turn heads. He was supposed to be eye-catching. Breathtaking. Even if that wasn't the night Cylvan was meant to notice and begin courting him—

Oh, gods—what if Saffron truly was plain, even with the glamour and the nice clothing? What if someone else caught Cylvan's eye altogether, and Saffron didn't stand a chance? Would he, alone, really, always be enough to impress the prince, who never looked anything less than immaculate even when standing naked, even when wearing a 'plain' human glamour trying to appear as boring as possible? Who was the top of his class, the smartest, most powerful, most cultured, well traveled, interesting, captivating person to ever exist?

"You have been preparing for this moment for months, a leanbh. You are no less prepared than any other high fey suitor here looking for a spouse."

"You mean—looking for *my* spouse," Saffron squeaked. "They're all here looking at *my* spouse, Luvon, how am I ever meant to outdo them!"

"I have never met someone as madly in love as Prince Cylvan," Luvon said, and Saffron knew he had to be exaggerating. "He will have eyes for no one else but you, even if he must pretend otherwise. You could arrive in beantighe rags and I would still say so confidently." He smirked. "Consider again how you first met, after all."

"...I don't look like I'm in rags, do I?" Saffron sought the obvious validation, despite catching his reflection in passing mirrors and hardly recognizing himself again. Who was the middlingly-attractive high fey on Luvon's arm? Still so plain despite the hard work of the glamour, compared to every other luxurious and stunning work of art around them? Would it even be convincing that Cylvan would choose him over anyone else? Other suitors. Also seeking a partner. Cylvan, the prince of Alfidel, attending and single. Seeking a harmonious person to one day rule beside him. With Taran mac Delbaith out of the picture, surely other families vied for that potential power. Surely they wouldn't allow someone so plain and boring as Luvon's long-distant relative nobody from Alvénya to get in the way—

"Oh, fuck," Saffron croaked. "Ohhhh fuck, shit, oh god, oh fuck—"

"Yes, good, get it all out while you can," Luvon encouraged calmly. "Fuck, fuck, shit, damnit, cock, bint. Go on."

Saffron clawed at Luvon's sleeve, hissing more curses through his teeth as he made eye-contact with the first group of strangers randomly turning to perceive the incoming crowd of guests. He expected any one of them to recognize him, somehow, from the Ostara previous when Taran mac Delbaith was ruthlessly attacked by an arid witch before going missing. What if someone had seen Cylvan dé Tuatha dé Danann declare the same arid witch his true fiancé before Danu and only a few chosen trustees, a human witch would eventually ascend to the throne over all of Alfidel? Who—

"I'm going to pass out."

"No you're not," Luvon smiled and nodded at the guards posted at either side of the entryway to the bright ballroom. He was a high fey noble, which meant his arrival was announced as they reached the doors and stood at the top of the split-wing stairs leading down to the main floor. Saffron didn't even hear it, too taken by the grandeur of the sight in front of him.

He'd never seen a room so magnificent, except perhaps the main atrium of Morrígan's Library. He knew he probably looked foolish with the way he gazed up at the impossibly high ceilings, mouth hanging open in silent awe at the painted murals filling every inch of flat space between pillars and ornate vaulting, tiny details continuing down the chains of all eight hanging chandeliers in the forms of pixies and púcas and gnomes and other small, wild things carved to look like they climbed and descended the dangling lights. Windows as tall as the ceilings claimed the majority of the outer walls, latticed with equally decorated strips of gold and shimmering in enough candlelight to make the room feel like it was the middle of the day. That was Tír na nÓg. It had to be.

Luvon whisked Saffron through the room faster than he could actually regard any of the details, taken out into the impossibly expansive gardens at the back of the palace, instead, stretching farther than Saffron could see in the darkness. Strings of candlelight wove between flowery garlands stretching over a glossy stone terrace floor, in the distance dipping into steps leading down into illuminated walkways between a maze of plants and trees and other decor. Plenty of places to hide, just in case.

None of the party turned to look when they were announced at the entrance, and once again Saffron felt nails scraping down his back in a whirlwind. They were supposed to look. He didn't want them to look. Why didn't they? He was glad they didn't. Damnit...

Scratching at the green ribbon around his wrist, he searched the crowd for anyone he might recognize. He couldn't help but feel even more self-conscious upon realizing his was one of only a handful of outfits designed specifically so the color of the ribbon didn't clash. King Tross had chosen the ensemble on purpose, just like the letter said, and Saffron silently thanked him for being so thoughtful. He would do any sort of solstice ceremony thing the king asked for in gratitude. Even if he didn't know a hot fucking thing about shooting arrows into bonfires.

Luvon, the social butterfly he was, didn't take too long before leaving Saffron to his own devices on the outside terrace, but not before reassuring him one last time that he would be fine, everything would be fine, he looked so beautiful, he had nothing to worry about, if he wished to simply stuff his face all night at the buffet table, that would be perfectly acceptable. Ah. Good. Saffron wouldn't argue.

But the longer Saffron stood at the buffet table littered with cakes, candies, fairy fruits, wine, water, juice, and everything in between, the more his nerves crawled like spiders beneath leaves. Eyes—he could definitely feel eyes. Everyone's eyes, whether they lingered or not, scaling down the low-cut back of his outfit where his glamoured skin was as smooth and flawless as the rest of him. He couldn't help but bitterly wonder why, as soon as Luvon fluttered off, leaving Saffron by himself, giving him even less reason to be noticed at all—suddenly everyone was so curious to know exactly who he was?

He was definitely going to be sick—but then someone approached him from behind, clearing their throat so that they might set a tray of finger-foods down right where Saffron stood. Saffron stepped out of the way, nodding his head slightly in apology, before kicking himself because no high fey in their right mind would be so submissive—until he realized, he knew that *beantighe*. He knew her curly blonde hair and freckles. It was all Saffron could do not to scream and embrace her.

"Well, don't you look like a little doll." Letty grinned, settling the tray before pretending to adjust all of the treats that had gone out of line. "I almost didn't recognize you, my lord."

"Letty—oh, Letty, thank god. Please know I'm spiritually hugging all the air out of you right now."

"Careful, witch. I can actually feel it."

Saffron's eyes went wide, making Letty laugh and shake her head. Her uniform that night was beautiful—a stiff dark green tunic with a high collar and fitted sleeves, delicate silver chains draping over her chest from the collarbones all the way to the bottom seam. Despite only being apart for a few days, her hair already looked healthy and shinier than ever, curls bouncing and rich with color Saffron had never seen before. Her cheeks were slightly rounder and flushed with color, proof she was finally being fed well for the first time in her life. Oh—Saffron really did want to squeeze the life out of her.

"You look beautiful," he said, unable to help it. She blushed, and then so did he. "You don't even need a glamour for it, either. Are they taking good care of you, here?"

"Oh, yes—night and day difference, really. I would be lying if I said I still didn't wish I could get dressed up and drink and dance at a fancy party like this, too, though. Serving at fetes is more enjoyable than doing chores at Morrígan at least."

Saffron grimaced. He sucked down some of the wine in his glass. "Are Hollow and Nimue here, too?"

"Nimue's in a holding cell at the moment," Letty answered so casually, Saffron almost didn't realize what she'd said. He jumped, and she bit back another chuckle. "Don't worry—she was being naughty. She knows it, too. Dumped a whole basket of King Tross' expensive fabrics in a vat of bleach water because she's sick of all the rules. It was indeed very funny—and King Tross was surprisingly patient about it all, since, well... he knows her history, and her history with the prince. You know."

Saffron barked a stiff, awkward laugh. He didn't know what else to do.

"And Hollow is... well, he's alright, I guess... I think he's serving the party tonight, too, but trying to stay out of sight. Um, he grew up as a foundling in Avren, remember? I think he's worried someone might recognize him from his... wilder days. He's already had a few run-ins with some other beantighes who recognize him, so it's been... a little touchy."

"Oh," Saffron's amusement faded instantly. He thought immediately of Ryder Kyteler and the humans at Ériu's shrine. He almost asked, but stopped himself, not sure who might overhear. Instead, all he could think to say was: "But he's here under Cylvan's patronage, so even if someone tries to cause trouble, just... just get me or Cylvan or Saoirse, alright? Tell Hollow that, too. I won't let anyone bother him."

"I will." Letty smiled, before nodding her head over her shoulder. "I should get back before people notice. You should come see us at the servants' quarters when the party starts dying down though, alright? We're having a little party of our own over there, sort of like we used to during events at Morrígan. If Hollow's there, I'm sure he'll want to see you."

"I will," Saffron promised with a nod and a tiny smile, holding it on his face to hide how his heart broke the moment his friend had to leave him again. Incredible, the way he could feel alone in such a crowded room.

14

THE SUITORS

Saffron busied himself with a glass of wine. And then another. And then a plate of plum white cake with a honey glaze, surrounded by a handful of berries he scooped onto the side with his hand, not sure how else he was supposed to get them out of the bowl. Not entirely sure they were meant to be eaten at all. Palace buffet tables were far more confusing and extravagant than anything he'd ever done at Morrígan or for visitors to Luvon's estate, and he regretted not asking Letty for guidance. He didn't know what half the things on the plates even were—and his discernment only weakened the more he drank. There was no question what would inebriate him, at least.

Watching the high fey guests, those members of court nobility, dance around one another and gossip and converse wasn't an unusual sight for him, but in more than the food and how it was served, it was all so different from the ones Saffron had the displeasure of witnessing at Morrígan. Students at Morrígan wore their nicest clothes to drink and fuck, while court nobility wore long gowns, shimmering fabrics, entire jewelry boxes worth of gems and gold. They jingled with every step. They wore their hair long and perfectly shiny, strings of gold and more glittering gems interlaced throughout the strands, crowns of matching shimmer pinned onto the back of their heads. It made him more aware than ever of his own short hair, remembering the things Cylvan said about showing off a bare nape. He couldn't help but rub it anytime he swore he felt eyes raking down his skin again.

When he wasn't seeking out something else to indulge in, Saffron tried to mimic those around him with every movement. He stood up straight, never leaning against the palace exterior or against a bannister even though his feet were beginning to hurt. He practiced eating strawberries with the tiniest goddamn forks he'd ever seen, which apparently only had the lifespan of one bite before meant to be dropped into a matching gold bowl in favor of another. He watched other fey guests use five or ten little one-bite forks or spoons at a time. He followed their lead, though admittedly felt a little silly each time, always careful to never let the bite touch his lips so it wouldn't smudge his lipstick. He tipped the edge of the wine glass into his mouth with an equally gentle touch for the same reason, though his instinct was to throw it back and glug down as much as he could at once. Especially when strangers started approaching him, trying to make conversation. Trying to ask his name, who he was there with. Saffron was so far in over his head.

But he'd promised to make a good impression. To do everything he could to blend in. Even with his full plates of indulgent food and apparently erotically-trimmed hair.

Saffron could be a high fey, he decided, growing more confident the more he ate, the more he drank, the more the minutes passed without anything terrible happening or someone seeing straight through him. Maybe it really would be so easy. It wasn't like he hadn't spent his entire life waiting on the high fey hand and foot; he knew what they liked, how they acted, how they talked, how they bitched and moaned and sucked each other off verbally and literally, at any opportunity. He'd spent most of his life observing them from a distance, serving them up close, learning everything about them that he possibly could. He only had to apply all of those things to his own mouth, his face, his movements.

When he managed to hold a conversation with one handsome fey lord for longer than two minutes, Saffron's confidence heightened. Sure, they spoke only of how warm it was in Avren, how Saffron's outfit was one of King Tross' designs, how pretty the flowers were in the decor, but perhaps that was all it took. God knew Saffron had never overheard any conversation deeper than that surface-level tripe while attending Morrígan fetes, either. Perhaps he should be more worried about dying of boredom rather than embarrassment.

When he impressed someone else enough that they asked him to dance, Saffron nervously agreed, telling them he'd never danced with anyone in Avren before. His partner found it endearing, apparently, the way Saffron tripped over his own feet and constantly babbled apologies that he then tried to play off as anything else. They said his clumsiness was cute and his laugh was musical—but Saffron wasn't trying to be charming. Saffron was just trying to be normal.

His self-awareness escalated the moment he and his dance partner passed by Prince Cylvan and his own on the dance floor—and the look on Cylvan's face was pure, white-hot striking ice, clearly wishing Saffron's partner would drop dead. It was the first time Saffron had actually crossed paths with Cylvan at all that night, having been so focused on being *aloof* and *blending in* and doing literally everything in his power not to search out the one person he wanted to see. Even in that brief moment they spun past one another, Saffron tried not to let his eyes linger too long. He saw only the pretty dark blue-green color of Cylvan's tunic, but none of the details. Why did that make him so sad? Like he'd missed out on witnessing some rare beauty in the woods.

Either way, he excused himself at the end of the dance in an effort to allow the fey lord a chance to keep his life. He might not have seen the entirety of Cylvan's reaction to the sight of him dancing with someone else—but he'd certainly felt it. He'd promised himself he wouldn't be the cause of any bloodshed that night, and keeping Cylvan tame by minding his own business was very much a part of that.

But there were others who wished for death, as Saffron suddenly couldn't find a moment's peace without fey lords and ladies and gentles and everyone else approaching to ask his name, compliment his outfit, ask how he was enjoying Avren, congratulate him on his enrollment at Mairwen. Luvon had hinted at something like that happening, something about how courtiers loved new things, new sights, new guests at their fetes, and once they spotted him, Saffron would have to simply do his best until something else inevitably came along to claim their attention in another direction. Where was his own bloody, brand new rowan witch to stumble from the trees and cause a stir, just like he'd blessed those same people on Ostara? The wicked little thought made him grin into his wine, before fluttering his eyelashes at the next nameless, forgettable fey lord who tried to flirt with him at the buffet table.

An equally wicked part of him even began to enjoy catching Cylvan's eye across the open patio—and Cylvan's gaze was always on him. Even while dancing with his own partner, socializing in the corner, tipping back a glass of champagne, he never seemed to take his attention from Saffron for long at all. Something about it was comforting, something about it was exciting, something about it was—enticing, as, especially the more Saffron drank, the more he wondered exactly how jealous he could make the prince who had everything. Everyone. Except the pretty little Alvényan visitor who he had to wait a few more weeks to show interest in.

But Saffron was quickly reminded of his natural, human place in the eyes of courtiers every time those mingling around unwittingly included him in conversation simply by standing too close. Every time, his stomach turned with annoyance, or boredom, or anger, or disdain, as every word was exactly as he'd come to learn while working as a beantighe. Flagrant gossip about other people at that same fete, whispers of untrue rumors about Cylvan himself, speaking ill of anyone the prince danced with or even briefly spoke to, rooted in jealousy or something else. People who didn't care for Cylvan as a person, but would clearly still fight for a chance to win his favor. Who just wanted to be his harmonious partner, who wanted to be part of the royal family, so that they and their own family could live in luxury for the length of Cylvan's reign. Night Court or not. So many of them, all sharing that same sentiment—*I don't even care if he's destined for a Night Court. If you're powerful enough, not even the Night can hurt you.*

Saffron managed to avoid involving himself with those conversations. He snacked more on the food, eventually agreed to dance with whoever asked again, made boring conversation with anyone who approached to speak. He rarely engaged with them first. He never engaged once all the longer the party went on. He already knew there was nothing for him to say. There was nothing they could say that would keep his attention for as long as it took to finish a sentence. It was nothing but parties, clothing, beach houses, holidays, family drama. Saffron didn't care. As midnight came and went, Saffron just wanted to go to bed.

"How long do you think a human can go without eating?"

He tried to bite back the way his attention snapped at those words, coming from a small group of fey mingling on the other side of the decorative plant he hid behind. He sipped his wine. He tried to ignore it.

"I don't know. A week? It's different for all of them. I can't tell you how many my mother has accidentally starved to death after putting them in the basement. She just forgets they're there."

They laughed. Saffron tipped back more wine. He begged it to saturate his mind a little bit faster. It kept wearing off too quickly. There wasn't enough wine in the entire palace to inebriate a chronically-exasperated beantighe like him.

"We once left two beantighes at our lake house in the Fall Court. Didn't realize until the following year when one of the dogs found their bones in the woods."

"They didn't eat your whole pantry?"

"It was empty when we left, since it was the end of the season. We still wonder whether the starvation or the cold got them first."

"I wouldn't be surprised if one ate the other to try and live. Beastly."

"We once 'accidentally' left a beantighe on my uncle's private island, too. They were asking for it, though, with all the threats of reporting my father for indecency."

"Ugh—those are the worst complaints, aren't they? As if I would put my hands on a beantighe."

"Sometimes you just need a body to take care of a passing urge."

"Which would be more harmful, the slap on the wrist or the rumors you like to fuck humans?"

"Gods above—I'll take a slap on the wrist, any day."

The glass in Saffron's hand shattered. Wine drenched the front of his blouse, but Saffron didn't react right away. He stared at the floor, fighting the crashing wave of anger swelling in his chest. His fingers twitched as a burning twinge flared in his forearm. He tried to breathe through his nose, slowly moving his hand to press into the scars.

"Are you alright?" One of the fey ladies in the group asked, leaning around the plant to look Saffron up and down. She regarded him with a level of sincerity—but Saffron knew it was only because she thought he was one of them. He was one of them, a high fey, a fey lord who might have laughed alongside them had he been invited to join the conversation. But he had nothing to say, even when the lady grabbed a replacement glass of wine from a passing beantighe and offered it to him with a smile. Meanwhile, a handful of human servants hurried over to address the mess Saffron made. On their knees, wiping wine from the floor and cleaning up broken glass with bare hands.

"You're visiting from Alvénya, right?" the lady went on, reaching out to gently take Saffron's arm and pull him closer. To invite him into the circle. She stepped on one of the beantighe's hands as she did, hardly flinching as the human hissed and pulled away quickly. Saffron's eyes lingered on them, how they only had a moment to bite back the pain of fingers crushed beneath heels before returning to the glass that pricked their skin. "We haven't been introduced yet. What do you think of Avren?"

"You just stepped on that beantighe's hand."

"Hm? Ah, that's nothing to worry about, I barely felt it," she said, extending her foot slightly to observe her shoe. "No scuffs. I would have gladly done much worse if there was. Sometimes I think they have steel wool for hands, which is why they are born to be beantighes."

Everyone around her giggled, but Saffron couldn't suppress what came over him. Like the wolf in his arm manifested through his own movements instead of tearing free with teeth and claws. He turned his fingers in her hand, clutching it, then bent the lady's fingers backward. More and more and more until she cried out in alarm and Saffron felt her fingers click beneath the pressure. She yanked herself free before Saffron could pop them out of place, swearing at him, demanding to know what his fucking problem was—

"Is everything alright?"

Prince Cylvan wore Saffron's favorite perfume; Saffron only knew once he stood close enough. Saffron, mind nothing but drunk gnashing of teeth fighting the urge to do worse, turned and stared wordlessly at him. A part of him wondered if he was only imagining it. If he'd actually heard Cylvan speak. But then their eyes met, and he saw how Cylvan resisted every urge to reach out and touch him, as if he could see exactly how close Saffron was to snapping.

"This farm boy tried to attack me!" The lady shouted, cradling her hand as if Saffron had actually shattered bone. He sneered without thinking, which only set the lady off more. Hissing at him, she took Cylvan's arm, wrapping her hands around it with a pitiful sound. "Your highness, I do not mean to cause a scene, of course, but please be careful. He attacked me out of nowhere."

"I've had a lot to drink," Saffron answered, before frowning because that wasn't exactly what he meant to say. Cylvan looked like he was about to split open from holding back a sudden rush of laughter. Saffron pointed at the beantighe at their feet, fighting to keep his thoughts in line.

"She stepped on that beantighe's hand," he said what he originally intended. The beantighe in question, who was still collecting glass on their knees, went still. They stared up at Saffron with apprehension, but Saffron only partly regretted bringing them into it. "She didn't acknowledge them. It made me angry."

The lady scoffed, throwing a look at the other high fey with her, before pretending to swoon over Cylvan once more. Before she could say anything, though, Cylvan glanced down to acknowledge the beantighe as well.

"Did Lady Callan step on your hand? Surely it was only an accident."

The beantighe, who had clearly never been spoken to directly, especially by one of the royal family, immediately bowed their head and averted their eyes. Their mouth remained tightly shut, clearly knowing better than to say anything at all. But Saffron didn't have to keep to those rules. For the first time since donning his fey glamour, he felt fully empowered to finally do some good. Even something so small.

"She did," he said. "It was unbecoming of someone from Alfidel. I know that much."

Cylvan met Saffron's eyes again. His expression was an amusing mix of hesitation and smugness, as if a war raged inside him, trying to decide whether to brush Saffron off—like a good, aloof prince who had no reason to care about the Alvényan visitor yet—or to verbally reprimand the fey lady like a bad prince who hated parties and would love to cause a scene of his own. Saffron knew which he would have preferred.

But Cylvan chose neither. He turned back to the beantighe, motioning for them to get to their feet. "Your duties are done for the night. Go to the infirmary, tell them I sent you. They should bandage you and offer something for the pain."

The beantighe stiffened. Saffron thought they might have even stopped breathing. They stared at the prince, then glanced to Saffron, then to the fey lady, then back to Cylvan, before bowing deeply and hurrying in the other direction. Saffron had to resist taking Cylvan's face and kissing him. God—why was he so turned on?

"Have you tried anything on the buffet table yet, Lord Saffron? We have some of the finest Alvish treats here. I myself am fond of the dark chocolate and raspberry truffles." Cylvan addressed Saffron again, and Saffron pressed his lips together. Cylvan definitely knew he had, in fact, tasted at least one of everything—but there was more to those words. Goosebumps flushed Saffron's arms, wondering if he was supposed to be putting on a different kind of performance. He shook his head, and Cylvan stepped out of the fey lady's reach, gently tucking a hand into the small of Saffron's back and leading him to the table of food with a light touch. Saffron's heart raced like they did something forbidden.

Regarding the dark chocolate truffles in question, Cylvan plucked one from a circling tower, taking a bite for himself before touching under Saffron's chin. Saffron reacted instinctively, opening his mouth for Cylvan to tuck the rest of the treat onto his tongue. Saffron's cheeks went hot, suddenly unable to meet Cylvan's eyes at all. His gaze had shifted from one of theatrics, to parted lips and lowered eyes of interest while he watched Saffron's lips close over the sweet bite.

"What do you think?" he asked, voice low and alluring. People were definitely staring. Oh, god, every single one of them was staring, even if they pretended not to. Saffron had to pretend like he didn't notice.

"I like the flavor of it a lot," was all Saffron could think to say. Cylvan smirked like even such a plain response was charming, and Saffron wished he could elbow him in the gut. The prince knew exactly what he was doing, like some sort of special punishment. "I'm sorry, your highness, I did not mean to draw you away from—"

"Impossible not to draw me over while you are dressed like this," Cylvan reassured, before taking a strawberry from the table and biting into it.

"Thank you, your highness. It's one of King Tross' designs."

"It flatters you," Cylvan complimented, indulging a little too seductively in the fruit. It reminded Saffron of the last time they shared strawberries like that while a crowd watched, though back then he'd been on his knees between Cylvan's legs, feeding them to the prince surrounded by a bustling fete in Danann House's front parlor. Saffron wanted to pull his hair. Perhaps Cylvan knew that, too, because he returned a dark, wicked, uneven smile, before bowing to excuse himself back to the party. He took the fuming Lady Callan's hand on the way, like he knew he had to make amends with her, too, for Saffron's sake. She smiled the whole way back to the dance floor.

Saffron watched him go. He watched all the other partygoers return to their conversations as if nothing had happened at all. Saffron could only turn his back to the rest of them, pressing his hands to his face and trying to breathe as his whole body felt hot. God, he needed a moment. He needed fresh air, even though he was already outside—he needed something even fresher. He needed a chance to recover from the memory of Cylvan's smile, his face while biting into that ripe strawberry, how his mouth stretched over the fruit. God, god, god, god, *god,* Saffron was going to kick his ass later.

But then whispers caught his ears, and the embarrassment gave way to an unsettling rush of shame.

No surprise, coming from the moonstruck prince. The beantighe lover, just like what happened in Connacht.

Saffron glanced back to where Cylvan had returned to dancing. Either he didn't hear the whispers or he ignored them—but Saffron felt like the rug had been pulled from under him. A humbling reminder that every single interaction between him and his raven could result in passed rumors, gossip, scandal.

THE MOMENT SAFFRON SPOTTED ASCHE AT THE opposite end of the crowd, he grabbed and downed another glass of wine, then made his way toward them. A perfect distraction. He was just drunk enough to pester them about a new woven yew bracelet, prepared to blame his behavior on his wild magic or the amount of wine he'd had. Anything to get people to stop looking at him. Anything to keep those fey he'd verbally accosted from cornering him in a darker part of the gardens to return the favor.

"Your highness," Saffron greeted, making Asche jump as they were clearly attempting to skirt away from the festivities. They gave Saffron a stiff, awkward smile in return.

"Lord Saffron, erm, hello. I mean—your name is Saffron, isn't it? That's what I've heard. And you're from Alvénya, aren't you? I myself have never visited, but I've heard it's lovely—"

"We have a class together, Asche," Saffron murmured. "You don't have to do this."

"Um, right, of course," Asche said, speaking very quickly, fanning themself with a stiff napkin in their hand, constantly glancing around like they were being hunted for sport. "Are you enjoying the party? I saw Cylvan talking to you. Erm, Prince Cylvan, I mean. My brother. Ah, your outfit is so lovely, it was designed by my father, wasn't it? Have you met my other siblings? They're technically only my half siblings, we don't look much alike, so it's easy to miss the relation. Here, I'll introduce you, they're over there with their mother. See? Erm, not Gentle Naoill, who is my mother. Eoine is the harmonious progenitor. She's actually King Tross' sister. Erm, King Tross didn't father my other siblings with her, of course, that would be strange, but—"

"Oh my god," Saffron muttered. "Are you going to be alright?"

Asche returned a strained smile, but clutched the front of

their tunic in agitation. "People keep asking me when I'm going to start having my own suitor galas. They keep asking me to dance. Like they already know Cylvan is out of reach for them. I've been introduced to seven suitors by their mothers already."

"Oh, god," Saffron tried not to laugh, but it was impossible not to. He practically saw the flames of anxiety charring finger-holes in the front of Asche's top where they clutched it. "Letty invited me to a beantighe party at the dorms. Why don't we crash it?"

It was like Saffron offered Asche permission to set the party and all its decor on fire. Their mood flipped in an instant, grinning and grabbing Saffron's hand, twisting their grip to dominate whatever Saffron had in mind. "Thank the gods. Thank the gods for you. You're going to make an incredible harmonious king one day. Come on, beantighe parties are way more fun anyway."

15

THE FOUNDLING

Perhaps Saffron should not have been so surprised at how well Asche bypassed guards and main palace thoroughfares on their winding journey to the beantighe dorms, impressed at their extensive knowledge of every hallway, back corridor, hidden staircase, garden path, even servants' passageways. They even showed Saffron the quickest way to sneak into Cylvan's dark bedroom through a route inside the walls, where Saffron wished he wasn't so drunk and wobbly on his feet, wishing to explore every inch of that room without Cylvan there to catch him. Asche attempted to nudge Saffron along, not wanting to have to wait, but Saffron was too captivated by that place where his prince slept, studied, lived. The collection of violins on the wall, the swords on display, the familiar clutter of clothing and empty wine bottles and jewelry scattered about. Saffron wondered if his silly, pretty bird prince had rules prohibiting beantighes from cleaning up that room, too. Just like the Aon-adharcach suite. Little did the pretty bird know there was a secret beantighe right there judging his mess and making plans to rectify it.

The windows were detailed with gothic wrought steel, rising and swirling in spiking curls at the mouth of lancet caps. The walls donned dark wallpaper with silver accents, bedsheets black as ever, bed frame built from dark wood that matched the other pieces in the room. It smelled of perfumes and incense, illuminated only by a handful of clustered candelabras around the room. Saffron could tell it hadn't been fitted with electric light, yet, and loved Cylvan even more for it. Saffron much preferred candlelight. He hoped to properly show his appreciation later once the courtiers left.

God, he wanted to sink into the prince's bed. To smell him, to roll around in the blankets where Cylvan had slept every day while they were apart—but Asche's nagging was insistent, and Saffron had to eventually turn away, again. The only consolation was knowing he would be right back there again soon enough, hopefully with Cylvan's arms wrapped around him.

Rifling through the prince's wardrobe for something less shiny and shimmery to wear to a human party, Saffron settled on the pants he was already wearing and one of Cylvan's baggy shirts, though had to cinch a belt around the middle so the wide collar didn't open and slump off his shoulders entirely.

Even in the back gardens where high fey courtiers wandered arm-in-arm with one another, Asche knew exactly where to go to slip by them unnoticed. Between trees, along the outer fence, down the bank of the creek that ran through the middle.

Out a back gate, up a set of worn steps, Saffron could already smell a warm fire and see the glow of flames illuminating the exterior of a cluster of buildings he assumed to be the beantighe dorms. It made his heart race—he hated that orange color so close to where he knew his friends slept.

But cresting the top of the knoll, there was no fiery destruction to greet them, only familiar faces—and if not faces, then rounded ears—crowding around a series of individual fires where they danced, played instruments, drank and roasted foods on sticks and racks. The sight made Saffron grin, yanking his glamouring necklace over his head, eager to be one with them for the first time in what felt like an eternity. God, he'd missed being surrounded by round ears so much even after just a few days.

Asche appeared to be a welcomed guest—or at least an unsurprising one—at the human fete, hardly a note skipping, hardly a head turning as they arrived. Asche introduced Saffron as the beantighe of a guest at Cylvan's suitor gala, and Saffron was immediately embraced and brought into the fold like a sheep who'd escaped the wolves' den. It might have just been the alcohol, but the warmth made him emotional, thanking them enthusiastically and gratefully accepting any and all food and drinks stuffed into his hands.

When he spotted one of the faces he wanted to see most, he was back to being more than a little buzzed, stumbling past one of the fires to collapse into Hollow's surprised, outstretched arms. Saffron squeezed him tight, commenting on how he'd gained weight, the palace must be treating him well—to which Hollow grabbed him by the scruff of the neck, muttering about how it'd only been a few days since they last saw one another. Saffron blinked at him, mouth hanging open, before slurring every insistence it had definitely been at least an eternity.

"Of all the places to be a slave, I suppose the royal palace isn't the worst," Hollow finally conceded with a sigh, letting Saffron go and pulling him to sit. He tucked a beer bottle into Saffron's hand.

"Of all the things I ever expected to hear from your mouth," a stranger seated opposite Hollow laughed, before throwing back whatever was in the bottle in his hand. Saffron leaned forward, vaguely recognizing their voice—but his face was a lightning strike of familiarity. Another bolt struck Saffron with tight adrenaline, squeezing his insides until he sprung back to his feet, nearly toppling into the fire had Hollow not thrown his arms out to catch him, first.

"You!" he exclaimed, wriggling in defiance as Hollow pulled him back down onto the log. "You—fucker!"

"Ironically the same way Hollow first greeted me tonight,"

Ryder Kyteler replied, smiling into the mouth of his bottle, casual as ever. Saffron sneered, finally shoving Hollow off. He pushed away the urge to run into the woods like a nervous jackrabbit, the last remaining pricks of sobriety knowing he likely wouldn't make it so far on such wobbly legs. He chose vicious stubbornness, instead.

"I suppose it makes sense that you work in the palace," Saffron said. "You're not actually the liberated king of humans at all like you claim to be, are you?"

He didn't mean to meet Ryder's eyes again, but it was almost impossible to avoid them—so he opted to stare directly into them, instead. Then tried to understand why the man smiled the way he did, before offering his own explanation.

"I don't work in the palace," he said with a dusting of arrogance. He swallowed back another mouthful of beer. "I only come to these parties to check up on the people who do."

"Ryder," Hollow growled his name like a threat. Ryder kept smiling.

"Who are you, exactly?" Saffron asked outright. "I didn't get a chance to ask last time, before you disappeared through the floor. Or the other last time when we saw each other in the woods."

"I wondered how much you remembered from our first meeting. You were, understandably, so very out of it back then. You weren't particularly *in it* last time in the woods, either. Nor right now. When will we ever be able to meet on solid ground?"

Saffron's grasp on his bottle tightened.

"You said I wouldn't have to worry about you until after the summer ended," he answered, sarcastic and annoyed and stubborn. "I'm trying very hard to keep it that way. And I would like you to try a little harder to keep that promise, too."

"Yes, I did make that promise. And I originally had no intention of bothering you until then," Ryder agreed. Something about it only annoyed Saffron further. "But then you maimed one of my people outside of Fullam. I thought maybe you were eager to chat."

"You what?" Hollow snapped, but Saffron only stared. His fingers briefly touched the scar on his arm. His heart pounded.

"But I know you didn't do it on purpose, did you, Saffron?" Ryder went on, lowering his voice and leaning in slightly. Saffron didn't move, nauseatingly captivated by how knowing the man's smile was. "It was just an accident, wasn't it?"

Saffron's mouth had gone dry. He stiffly licked his lips, then cleared his throat, before answering: "Y-yeah."

"I suppose, then, there's no better time for me to let you know... my offer still stands." Ryder's eyes never left Saffron, intense and blue like the sea. "The one I made when we first met. Do you remember?"

Of course Saffron remembered—it had plagued his nightmares during his two months in Beantighe Village. But he couldn't bring himself to say that, which, somehow worse, compelled Ryder to reiterate.

"I can help you avoid future *accidents* like the one that nearly killed an innocent human... when you finally realize these fey have no intention of helping you understand that special magic in your blood. No intention, and no knowledge of it at all. But I think you know that, don't you? That's why you were wearing that yew bracelet. Because you've decided to just try and hide it, ignore it, rather than control it, right? Because that seems easier? Safer?"

A drop of blood slithered from Saffron's nose, but he was too slow to notice. Hollow did, though, using the cuff of his sleeve to wipe it away. Saffron barely looked at him, clenching his hands into fists around the bottle on his lap.

"And what exactly do you think you know better than anyone else?" he asked. His hand cupped around his naked wrist, over the scars. His voice shook, and he hated it, but—he hated that man's arrogance more. He hated how those words made him curious. How they also filled him with guilt and shame for what he'd done outside of Ériu's shrine—and how he then tried to forget about it entirely.

But he also hated that he was promised a peaceful, romantic

summer, before anything else could possibly be stirred up. All he'd wanted was one, just *one* romantic summer, after everything he'd already been through...

"I'm not about to bare my whole chest for you." Ryder's smile remained unfazed. "I already told you, if you want to know, come visit me—"

"At the Finnian Ruins," Saffron finished, a misguided attempt to prove he wasn't foolish.

"Don't bother with him, Saff," Hollow grunted, clearly growing equally annoyed at the tense conversation happening on either side of him. "Ryder's a real coy dick."

"I've always been Hollow's favorite," Ryder grinned, nudging Hollow in the side. Saffron's attention turned to his friend, looking at him in confusion. Hollow clearly didn't want to talk about it, but perhaps could tell Saffron wasn't going to let him leave until he did. He cleared his throat.

"I was a foundling in Avren before working at Morrígan," he mumbled, despite knowing Saffron already knew that. Saffron realized maybe it implied something else—that Ryder was a foundling, too. Clearly, he still was. "Ryder and I... ran in the same circles before I got picked up and contracted to be a beantighe. That's all."

"That's all," Ryder mimicked, laughing and finishing off his drink. "Way to discount all the fun we had and all the hell we raised back then, friend."

"We're not friends."

"All the what you raised?"

"Then why did you offer me a drink as soon as you saw me here?" Ryder smiled, ignoring Saffron's interjection. "I know you missed me, big guy. And we have so, so much to catch up on. Maybe you and Saffron, both, can pay me a visit at the ruins. I'm sure you remember how to get there."

Hollow didn't say anything, just glared into the fire. Saffron didn't say anything, either—just glaring at Hollow. He didn't know why, but that revelation—made him angry. He got to his feet, about to say something about going to find Letty and sit with her, instead—

"Eventually I'm going to stop offering nicely, Saffron," Ryder commented before Saffron could begin his escape, getting to his own feet and brushing himself off. Saffron glared straight ahead, but could picture Ryder's calm, handsome smile right over his shoulder. As if he knew his words sent chills down Saffron's spine; as if he saw the moment they did, with Saffron turned away from him.

Saffron should have kept walking. He should have turned up his nose and left that man right where he stood, not even worth a roll of his eyes. But Saffron was drunk. Saffron was frustrated. Saffron had been withholding every emotion possible for days while trying to navigate every new and stressful thing in his life. Three of the most stressful days of his life—that he knew were only going to get worse in the future.

What would he do then?

Gritting his teeth, furrowing his brows, Saffron whirled on heel so fast he lost his footing, tripping into a nearby stranger who'd only just wandered up. Probably to see what all the fuss was about. Saffron held on to the man's loose shirt for balance all while snapping at Ryder with all the inebriated rage he could muster.

"Who says I need help?" he asked pointedly. *'Who says I need* your *help?'* his tone really insisted. *'Who says I didn't maim one of your people outside of Fullam entirely on purpose?'* was the ruder thing he really wished to say. Still, to his annoyance, Ryder's smile remained uninhibited.

"If you would come see me, I could show you."

"Why should I believe your stupid ruins are even as useful as you claim?" Saffron snapped. "If you really knew as much as you claimed, you would be able to show me right here. You wouldn't have to lure me into your weird dungeon."

"Yeah," the stranger behind him suddenly chirped. Saffron gave them a look of question, vision far too blurry to know if he recognized them or not. They were mostly a blur of brown hair and pale skin. Still, he turned back to Ryder with a small stomp of his foot in insistence. Ryder just kept smiling.

"Then why don't you come with me now? A handful of these palace beantighes are preparing to defect as we speak. Come with me and see the ruins for yourself. You don't even have to go inside."

"Wait," Saffron and the stranger said at the same time, before Saffron finally pulled away from them. He blurted: "You're what? Tonight?"

"Why else do you think I'm here?"

"You said you came to check on your friends, or—!"

"Exactly. Do you want to come or not? It's not far."

"How do you expect to get past the guards?" The human behind Saffron asked, voice a mix of curious and accusatory. Saffron turned to squint at them, trying for the life of him to swim through the alcohol making it hard to think straight. He definitely knew them from somewhere, but couldn't figure it out. "There's only one way in and out of the palace grounds. You can't expect to cross the valley bridge and not—"

"There are veneers all over this place," Ryder said. He smiled like he knew exactly who he spoke to, even though Saffron was still uncertain. "Would you like to see as well?"

"Yes," they answered without hesitation. It caught even Ryder off guard, before he grinned again.

"Alright. Meet me by the gnarled oak behind the north dorm. I'll go gather the rest who are so happy to leave this place."

As Ryder turned to leave, Saffron turned to the man standing behind him. The stranger cleared his throat, muttered something, then turned his face this way and that, as if he didn't want Saffron to look too closely. He might have even wandered off, had Saffron not snatched him by the arm and clung tightly. When the man refused to stay still, Saffron even reached up and grabbed his face, squeezing his cheeks until his mouth puckered while Saffron focused.

"Oh my god!" he gasped, shoving Cylvan away before yanking him back again just as roughly. It was his own prince draped in a similar human glamour as the one he'd worn to Ériu's shrine. His wobbly hands hit and whapped Cylvan all over in frustration, nearly losing his balance and toppling backward into the fire had hands not flashed out to catch him. "What the fuck do you think you're doing!"

"I should be asking you the same thing!" Cylvan hissed. Saffron pursed his lips, before grabbing one of Cylvan's invisible horns and dragging him into the shadows next to one of the dorm buildings. Cylvan complained the whole time, cursing at him, calling him a nasty little moon-ear and trying to yank himself free. But Saffron was always stronger the drunker he got. "Who exactly is that man you're so passionate with?"

"What?" Saffron scoffed, pushing Cylvan against the building. "You think that was flirting? Are you really so—oh, god, Cylvan! I've never met a prince more jealous than you. Bold to act all possessive after you twirled around with other courtiers all night long!"

"Perhaps—but I had my eyes on you the whole time."

The boiling irritation in Saffron's blood simmered, and a pathetic, drunken smile appeared on his mouth instead.

"Ah—really?"

"Yes. Of course," Cylvan mumbled, face flushing and averting his eyes as if suddenly embarrassed. "Just—tell me who that is. Before I have him arrested for treason."

Saffron blabbered something he hoped was at least somewhat comprehendible, doing his best to describe over how Ryder was the man who appeared in the infirmary and subsequently disappeared through the floor; how Saffron had briefly seen him at Ériu's shrine a few nights prior; how he kept insisting he could help Saffron reclaim his magic. Or, at least, understand it better. How, despite Saffron's stubbornness, there was a part of him that was curious. A part of him that was, maybe, just desperate enough to see what he had to offer.

"Even after what they did at the shrine?" Cylvan asked. His tone was calculating, unsure, but not argumentative. Like he only wanted to make sure Saffron had an ounce of sobriety enough to make a single clear decision. "Even though they're the people handing out the red cards, the ones causing trouble in Avren? If anyone sees you... if anyone recognizes you, Saffron, it would be the end of..."

He trailed off, pressing his lips together like he didn't want to say it. Like he didn't want to utter a single potential curse out loud, risk some higher deity hearing it and feeling curious enough to manifest such a thing. Saffron took Cylvan's hands, holding them, smiling at him as gently as his buzzing blood allowed.

"No one will recognize me," he promised. "Or you. Since you're coming with me, right? Since... we agreed to do all of this together no matter what, right?"

"Of course," Cylvan said with intensity. "Like hell I'm letting you wander off alone with someone like that man."

"Like *what?* That's the second time I've heard that word tonight."

Cylvan opened his mouth like he was going to explain, before closing it again with a tired chuckle. "I'll tell you later. When you're not so wobbly. Maybe the next gala will be a dry one for you, hm?"

"Hm," Saffron mimicked, pouting. "I don't think so. Sorry. I much prefer to be stumbling over my own ass surrounded by high fey than completely sober and subjected to their inane chatter. If I have to hear about another beach house on the Koryna Isle I'm going to jump off the nearest cliff."

"A fey lord after my own heart."

Saffron giggled. He had to resist standing on his toes to plant a kiss on Cylvan's mouth, still perfectly shaped and soft even with his glamour. He didn't know who was watching. He didn't know who could see. Instead, he squeezed his raven's hands one more time, before pulling him from the wall and asking to be taken to the gnarled oak tree Ryder mentioned.

. . .

Because he couldn't hold human-Cylvan's hand, Saffron instead held Hollow's, who gripped him like a parent grappling a toddler prone to wandering. All the while, Hollow and Cylvan bickered like parents every time Saffron stumbled over rocks or upturned roots in the dark, or tried to point something out past the light of the beantighe dorms that neither of his companions could see. Hollow scolded Cylvan for letting Saffron drink so much at his stupid party; Cylvan scolded Hollow for thinking he had any right to talk like that to a prince. Every insult thrown low under their breaths so the others wouldn't hear, every word making Saffron laugh as he cooed and asked them to please get along.

Cylvan seemed to know exactly the tree Ryder first mentioned, leading them straight to it without having to rely on any of the directions Hollow attempted to offer. That only irritated Hollow more, swiping his hand out at Cylvan's back until he finally found the prince's invisible braid and tugged on it. Cylvan spun on heel and screeched at him, only halting the assault when Saffron laughed so hard his knees buckled and he tumbled into some brambles.

At the gnarled tree in question, Saffron gazed up at the size of it in awe, cheek and palms scuffed from his fall, Cylvan's borrowed shirt a little dusty and pricked with holes where thorns had nabbed at him. Ryder clearly found it amusing, approaching him through the small group of gathered humans with a lantern in hand. He nodded at Hollow, then motioned to Saffron.

"Why don't you let me hold onto him for this next part?" He said. Before Hollow could refuse, Ryder was already dumping the lantern into his hands, forcing him to release Saffron in order to catch it. The moment Saffron was let loose, Ryder's arm found his waist, pulling him back to the head of the group. Saffron could only glance over his shoulder to offer a reassuring smile to Cylvan, who could do nothing, who prickled with instant rage at the sight of anyone touching his moon-eared prince.

"Is everyone ready?" Ryder asked the group of defecting humans, and Saffron had a moment of clarity as he gazed across them. Many wore the uniforms of servants from the same gala he'd come from; one of them he even recognized as the beantighe whose hand was crushed by Lady Callan. Saffron was glad to see it bandaged, smiling slightly at them, though they avoided his eyes. Not recognizing him. He didn't mind.

Ryder's hand never left the small of Saffron's back, even as he claimed another lantern from someone waiting behind the ancient tree. Into the dark woods they crossed, like passing through a barrier of the ether where the temperature dipped into nearly a chill, light from the lantern penetrating only a few feet ahead of them. Saffron's waning inebriation didn't pass quickly enough, forcing him to walk close to the man if he wished to remain upright and accounted for. He nearly asked how far they would have to go, recalling how Ryder insisted it wasn't far, then wanting to know how that was possible—but before any of those questions came, something appeared ahead of them. Indistinct from the rest of the woods, neither on a path nor donning any recognizable markings at first glance. A place one would have to know to find. He wondered if even Cylvan knew it was there, considering how far they'd come from the palace, from the beantighe dorms. Far enough that, when looking back, Saffron had no idea which direction he would have to go to find his way back.

The structure was an ancient hovel of some sort, a worn wooden door pressed into the face of piled stone, wood, and mud, a blanket of grass and moss covering most of its face and making it appear more like a living burial mound than a little house. Saffron instinctively kept his hands close to his chest despite the wiggly urge to reach out and comb his fingers through the coating. Ryder chuckled under his breath like he could sense Saffron's battling instincts, pulling him slightly closer as they approached the door.

Saffron's breath hitched. He might have snapped at him to *cut it out*, had something on the front of the door not snagged his attention, first.

Carved into the wood, a series of marks both strange and familiar. Circles interloping with one another, accentuated with what he instantly recognized as feda markings on an ogham circle. Two additional circlets wove into the bottom of the main epithet like coins on a keyring, and Saffron couldn't help the small sound of realization when he recognized them as celtic knots, like the ones he'd seen in class. Stepping closer, Ryder followed, holding out the lamp and saying nothing as Saffron touched the markings with curiosity. He appreciated the flawless balance of it, the perfection of every mark, how the two rings connected at the bottom actually wove into the main circle like the carver never once lifted their tool while drawing them. A single line for three interweaving rings.

"What is it?" he asked, trailing the pads of his fingers up and down one more time, before pulling away as it suddenly prickled beneath his fingers. Ryder extended his own hand instead, touching beneath the epithet with a sense of reverence.

"*Knock, knock,*" he whispered, indicating the two celtic knots. "This is a spell for passing through the veil."

16

THE KNOCKS

Saffron jolted backward. He would have crashed into the crowd of humans behind them had Ryder not kept his arm locked around his waist, pulling him close again while whispering reassurances.

"Shhhh, Saffron—it's alright. Relax. It's anchored. It's safe. It's not going to whisk you off somewhere—"

"Let go of me!" Saffron gasped, voice cracking in a rush of fear. Behind them, someone shoved through the crowd, but Saffron couldn't turn to see if it was Cylvan or Hollow before Ryder pulled him even closer, breathing directly in his ear.

"As someone who made the first veil oath in centuries, you know more than anyone, this is nothing to be afraid of."

Saffron's mouth dangled open slightly, unsure what to say to that. His heart pounded hard and fast, surely punching new cracks into his sternum where it'd once been shattered by a metal bolt. Ryder extended his hand holding the lantern again, illuminating the veil epithet, all while never allowing Saffron to pull away even an inch. Their cheeks nearly touched; Saffron felt every breath Ryder took, pulled partially against his chest.

"Knock, knock," he whispered again. "That's what those additional knots on the bottom are called. This is a two-knock epithet. It allows us to pass between two anchor points in the veil, but only on a single side. I'm not tricking you into passing over to the human side, Saffron. I promise."

Saffron's panic ebbed slightly. Just slightly. He wanted to believe that. God—he wanted to believe that. Ryder continued speaking, explaining, like casting a spell that eased the fear Saffron harbored in his body at any mention of the veil at all.

"There are seven types of veil epithets—six of them are done using knots like these in tandem with an ogham circle. They're called knocks because of the sound they make when someone delivers to activate them. This one here is as stable as they get— you can tell because there are no wild fairy fruits growing anywhere nearby. None of the veil is spilling out. There's no chance of it taking us somewhere we don't want to go. This one, specifically, will take us to a place just outside the Finnian Ruins. It was actually put here by human rebels back during the War of the Veil. During Proserpina's Night Court. That's how you know it's strong—it was put here by the same people who fought along-side Verity and Virtue Holt."

He spoke quickly, but not in a rush. With a confident rhythm, fast enough that Saffron's nerves never had a chance to spike in a lull, keeping him afloat on his own nerves until the explanation was finished. And once those final words left Ryder's mouth, once his spell was complete—Saffron's racing heart had slowed. Hardly back to normal, but enough that he could breathe normally, again. Perhaps he had the alcohol to thank for any calm flowing through his body at all.

"H—" he started, but it caught in his throat. He swallowed against the swelling at the back of his tongue. "How does it work?"

"I'll show you," Ryder said like a reassurance. "Will you hold this?"

Saffron stiffly nodded, taking the lantern from him. Ryder pushed up his sleeves, approaching the epithet on the door. He paused for a moment, bowing his head and closing his eyes, before pressing a hand flat against the wood, in the center of the main circle.

Perhaps no one else did—but Saffron sensed an instant shift around them. A buzzing energy overcame him, kissing his skin, the smell of burnt sugar and mint infiltrating his nose. Warming the air from the ground up, making the hair on the back of his neck stand up straight. It took him back to the Kyteler Ruins. The abandoned library filled to the brim with wild fairy fruits, untouched and unbothered for a century since the last time humans had formed a veil circle on the floor. The frenzied buzz of the air, the pinkish-orange veil bees, the taste and sticky-sweet smell of sugar—perhaps none of those things were from the fruits at all. Perhaps it was the reverberation of the veil, from a place where it had once thrummed with life for so long. All of those same sensations washed over Saffron as he stood there in the dark, extending the lantern for Ryder, though the energy was not nearly as powerful as he once felt when the beannighe stepped over the line of the circle in the Kyteler library, opening the door for Saffron to subsequently make his own oath.

You know more than anyone, this is nothing to be afraid of.

Saffron gulped. The lantern in his hand trembled, but he didn't move. He didn't dare even glance over his shoulder again as Ryder threw him a look, cracking a smile before taking the ancient handle of the door and pulling it open. On the other side, where there should have been the mud-and-stone interior of the structure—Saffron saw only more thick forest. In the distance, a dim glow of light barely illuminated crumbling stone towers.

Ryder put out his hand. Saffron, awestruck, took a hesitant step forward, and put his hand into the one offered to him. He allowed Ryder to pull him through it—to pass through the veil as easily as a person passed through a doorway between rooms. There wasn't even a tickle on his skin as he broached the invisible separation. There was simply—no separation at all.

The rest of the humans followed behind, equally hesitant and cautious at first, though Saffron didn't wait for all of them to pass through before curiosity got the better of him. He wandered around the little structure on the opposite side as if he still thought he'd find some sort of charm or trick to explain how it worked. To brush off Ryder's claims of veil magic as only fibs. But the fiery curiosity ignited brighter as Ryder closed the door on the heels of the last defector, performing no ritual more complex than simply letting the rusty latch click shut. As if sensing the bug-eyed shadow that was Saffron behind him, he then motioned for Saffron to feel free to poke around the door, itself. Was it that obvious on Saffron's face?

Still holding the lantern, Saffron approached the door, examining the epithet in the wood and determining it was exactly the same as the first one. He grabbed the handle and pulled it open, next, only a little bit surprised to find the veil had closed itself off on the other side, that time opening up to the inside of the structure like he expected the first time. He closed and opened the door a few times as if he could trick it into going back into effect, all while Ryder bit back a laugh next to him. Saffron ignored him. He stepped into the leaning hovel, trailed his hand over the inside of the door where there were no additional markings to be found, before scurrying out again to search for the wild fairy fruits Ryder insisted didn't exist. He was right. There was no sign of a tear in the veil there at all.

"Satisfied?" Ryder asked, finally taking the lantern back. He didn't give Saffron a chance to reply, calling out to the rest of the group to follow. He slid a hand back around Saffron's waist, pulling him along before Saffron had a chance to search for Cylvan or Hollow on their heels.

The defecting humans at their backs chattered amongst one another, partially excited, partially apprehensive, and Saffron felt the same swirling feelings in his body. Both for them, but also for himself. A mild relief that there was somewhere for beantighes to go if they no longer wished to be beantighes—but at the same time, a tousled worry that none of them knew what they were getting themselves into. A feeling that perhaps everyone was trusting the man called Ryder Kyteler a little too easily. Especially when Saffron knew as well as the rest of them the consequences of abandoning a contracted job.

He glanced up at Ryder again. He was nearly overcome with the urge to ask outright all over again: *who are you? Why are you doing this?*—but then he was reminded, he had plenty of reasons not to trust him, already. Those things he said in the infirmary, implying Saffron should consider him a threat. The things he said about Sunbeam, about Chandry. The things his people did to Fiachra at Ériu's shrine—not to mention all of the slaughtered barn owls they'd killed before then and nailed to the palace gates or left like a warm feast on Lugh's family altar.

Ryder Kyteler was not someone Saffron could trust—but that didn't mean he didn't have experience with arid magic like he kept promising. He could be a liar and mentor. There might be a way for Saffron to mistrust him, while also still learning from him. What other choice did he really have?

Right there, he decided he wouldn't step foot into the ruins. Not until Ryder was someone he could trust. He probably shouldn't have followed him through that tear in the veil so easily, either, but there was no going back on that drunken little misstep.

"The sudden silence makes me think you're deep in thought, witch," Ryder spoke, making Saffron jump. The man smiled down at him, relaxed and confident, obvious even in the low orange light of the lantern he carried. It made Saffron frown; which made Ryder smile more. "Or are you just speechless with how impressed you are with me?"

"Hardly," Saffron said, turning away again. "A veil circle doesn't impress me. I watched Sunbeam carve one for weeks, once."

"Ah, right. Her stolen circle in the Kyteler Ruins, yes, I know all about that one. It's the same one you used to make your veil oath, right? Did you notice how many knocks were on it?"

Saffron's frown deepened. He couldn't remember exactly what every mark had been—else he would have tried to recreate it already, just for a chance to speak with the veil about his magic again—but he at least knew there hadn't been any knots woven into the outer ring.

"I don't know," he scoffed. Ryder was intrigued by that, evident by the slight quirk of his eyebrow. He never looked away from Saffron once. Only when he suddenly chuckled and shook his head in disbelief did Saffron look back at him again in annoyance.

"What's so funny?"

"I just can't get over it. You, the special veil-witch; me, someone the veil has never given the time of day to, except with my circles and knocks—ask anyone who they think would know more about veil magic and who do you think they would pick?"

Saffron elbowed him in the side, making Ryder grunt and stumble. He yanked Saffron back in by the waist again. "Sorry. Can't help it. You wouldn't, either, if you were me."

"How do you know any of this?" Saffron asked, voice flat. Ryder *hmm*'d and *ahh*'d and *well...*'d for a minute, clearly only for the purpose of driving Saffron crazy, before finally flashing another handsome smile and sighing.

"I've been around. That's all I'm going to say. For now."

"Why?"

"You're not the only one trying to decide how trustworthy this dynamic is," he said bluntly. "Though, with all due respect, I believe my hesitation is a little more justified. Considering your choice of lover."

"He has nothing to do with this," Saffron said through clenched teeth, keeping his voice low.

"Doubtful. Whether you think so or not, I don't know if I can trust you not to tell him everything during your nightly pillowtalk. Which is exactly why I booted him back through the door before closing it."

Saffron's head whipped around in surprise, nearly tripping over himself as Ryder kept his hand where it was. Saffron scoured the crowd for his glamoured prince, then for Hollow, heart thudding in alarm when he realized Ryder wasn't lying about that, either. Saffron hadn't even noticed. He immediately felt terrible, knowing Cylvan was probably losing his mind on the other side of the door on the palace outskirts—if he wasn't tearing the structure apart with his bare hands in search of Saffron who'd waltzed right through without a care in the world.

"Hollow knows where we are," Ryder went on in a reassuring tone. "I'm sure your prince will come crashing down from the sky like a meteorite any second now. Which is exactly why... this is where I leave you."

His feet suddenly stopped, pulling Saffron to a halt with him. As he did, three additional lanterns appeared in the dark distance, where someone called out for the rest of the humans to continue to the road. Saffron bit his lip, watching them go, listening as their feet crunched through the thick undergrowth.

"You're just going to leave me out here?" Saffron asked—though his first instinct had been more of *'what's a meteorite?'*—sounding nervous when he meant to be accusatory. Still, he pulled away from Ryder's reach, and Ryder didn't try to pull him back. He kept his calm smile, holding the glowing lantern between them.

"Of course not. I'm going to wait with you. It's the perfect time to chat a little more, anyway. Privately."

"Go on, then," Saffron muttered after they both fell silent. "Clearly there's something you want to say."

"I know you still don't have any reason to trust me." Ryder caught Saffron off guard with the forwardness of it, no more beating around the bush. No more flirting. "And I understand why. I know you've been burned before, especially by people you thought you could trust. I don't fault you for that. I never will. Especially not you, with how much you've already been through."

Saffron wanted to ask what he meant by that, before deciding it must have just been more romantic words from the snake's mouth. He crossed his arms. He never stopped frowning.

"But ever since Sunbeam left us… we've needed someone to look to for hope. For reason to continue."

Saffron stopped frowning. Instead, his lips parted in surprise. "S-Sunbeam? What does she have to do with any of this?"

"You know as well as I do, she used to live here with the rest of us. But she left for Morrígan, for the Kyteler Ruins, to try and find a passage back to the human world. Right?"

Saffron nodded. His heart raced, like Ryder spoke something that was always meant to be kept secret. Something the man wasn't supposed to know, emphasized by how Sunbeam had always been so hesitant to share anything specific with Saffron at all. She'd always acted like someone was chasing her, right on her heels. Like she didn't think she could trust anyone, either. What did that say about Ryder?

"The first time we met, you said something about Chandry. You implied—you had her. That you were holding her against her will, or something," Saffron said.

Ryder's smile turned embarrassed, and he rubbed the back of his neck while averting his eyes.

"You're going to make me admit I was being an ass back then."

"Hm. Admit it, then."

"I was just being an ass. I haven't seen Chandry in months, obviously, since she's already in the human world. A part of me thought Sunbeam might be back at Morrígan, and you would go back and see her and tell her, and she would come rushing back to Finnian."

Saffron scowled, shaking his head. "I should just turn and walk away right now."

"You won't, though."

Saffron glared at him in defiance. Ryder's meek smile lifted at the corner.

"You need me, whether you like it or not."

"You keep saying that, yet you've said and done nothing to

prove it, except that little trick with the veil circle. Well, thank you for that information, I'll take it and go now."

"You're right. Hey, c'mon! I'm admitting it," Ryder laughed, reaching out for Saffron's arm as Saffron actually did turn to leave. "How about this—I'll give you something else. Another suggestion, an honest one, to prove I know my stuff."

"And then what?"

"Then... well, I imagine you'll take it to your nearest high fey curated library, find zero information, run into dead end after dead end, maybe get scolded by your prince for trying to research taboo magic at all, maybe garner some weird looks from a professor or two you try to confide in... only to come crawling back my way, finally, for a little more information. And I'll give it. And the cycle will continue."

"There's not a single pleasant thing about you, you know that?"

Ryder laughed a little more, running fingers back through his wavy blonde hair. "I'm aware. I don't even try to hide it anymore. I'm sure you find it at least a little bit charming, though, since I've heard the same thing about your Night Prince."

"I told you not to speak about Cylvan. This has nothing to do with—"

"Just give me until the summer solstice, yeah? That's like, what, a few months away? Just give me a few months of your free time, come visit me between your classes and your fancy parties and your drunken nights at the palace... and I promise I will teach you whatever I can. After the solstice, you can decide whether or not I'm any good for you, and I'll respect whatever you decide."

Saffron straightened up, squaring his shoulders. "So after the solstice, if I ask you to leave me alone forever, you'll actually do that?"

"Yes."

"A reminder that you already promised me my romantic summer before you'd come to ruin my life."

"Yes, and like I already said, I wasn't expecting you to disrupt one of my recruitment meetings in such a bloody way. That was your own fault."

"God—everything out of your mouth really pisses me off."

"Do we have a deal or not?"

Saffron bit down on his tongue, not wanting to answer right away, knowing the words would ride the wave of emotions churning in his gut, in his chest. He tempered the fires of annoyance, shoveling mud on them until they suffocated enough for him to breathe in the fresh nighttime air around him. Grounding him back in reality, instead of his emotions. Just like he always tried to do when he tasted blood rising up the back of his throat, to drip from his nose. But not that time. He would keep control of himself.

"Fine," he finally said. "But on the solstice, whether you help me or not—you'll have a meeting with the kings. And with Prince Cylvan. And you'll talk to them like equals, instead of doing all of this recruitment in the shadows. I think they can be far more compromising than you give them credit for."

Ryder chuckled a little laugh drenched in something he didn't say, making Saffron puff out his chest a little more.

"And you have to stop recruiting humans from Avren."

"Absolutely not. Not when so many are suffering *right now*. I know you have lots of ideals and fantasies about making a better world for humans once you become king, Saffron, but there are people being mistreated *now*, and I'm not about to abandon them."

Saffron deflated. He opened his mouth to argue, but—there was nothing for him to say. Ryder wasn't wrong.

"Then," he went on, though his voice had lost some of its intensity. "At least stop sacrificing owls to prove a point."

"I'm not going to do that either."

"Ryder—!"

"I'm not going to make myself smaller, or quieter, or more easily swallowed for the people who want me dead." Ryder's voice claimed the intensity Saffron's had lost. "Especially if you expect me to kneel in front of the high fey kings and beg for mercy, I'm going to make sure they know who I am and what I can do, first. Maybe you think they will be willing to make changes out of the goodness of their hearts—but if that were true, they would have done it already. God knows even if King Ailir *wanted* to do something to improve the lives of humans, he wouldn't. Not when he barely earned his throne in the first place. There's a reason he's so scared to do anything that might stir ire amongst the courtiers, the other Sídhe families—he has to maintain his 'Day King' image above all else, or the rest of them might conveniently remember he's the bastard son of King Elanyl and a common whore. It's a miracle he developed Sídhe powers at all, seeing as that's the biggest indicator of one's right to rule in Alfidel. I'm sure many of those in power are chomping at the bit for a chance to oust him at the first breath of disrupting their way of life, especially by showing mercy to the humans who give it to them."

"That's—"

"Instead of waiting for these kings, or anyone else, to find the courage to stand up for us who make their lives so grand, I'm going to show them what might happen if they *don't* turn those pointy ears to listen."

"You're putting all of those humans in danger," Saffron hardly let a moment pass before interjecting. "I'm sure you know as well as I do what will happen to them if they're found abandoning their contracts—let alone practicing arid magic!"

"I think what you're trying to do is commendable, Saffron. Let me make that very clear," Ryder said. "I think the opportunity you have to sit on the throne as one of the most powerful beings in this world has the potential to save lives and make genuine change. But—humans have been forced to wait too long. Humans who aren't going to get an anti-aging ring like you. People will live and die a dozen times over before you ever even kneel for your coronation. I'm thinking about *them*. I'm thinking about *now*, while you have the privilege to consider eternity. Right now, I only ask that you consider how things can change with the both of us. Together. You influencing who and what you can on the inside, and me rescuing as many suffering humans as I can on the outside. Getting them out of danger while you try to put an end to the danger for good."

Saffron stared at him. Unblinking, unmoving, speechless. He felt like he'd been kicked in the chest—or perhaps shoved naked in front of a laughing crowd. Something about Ryder's pleas opened a floodgate of memories he'd hidden away, decades of his own mistreatment and abuse at Morrígan, in Amber Valley, even in his time growing up with Luvon. Memories blurred and softened with weaverthistle tea to make every day a little easier to carry on; but memories that would never leave him entirely. He didn't hide them away because he believed everything would be fine since he could finally be with Cylvan—but he couldn't pretend like there wasn't a part of him that had pushed them down in all his efforts to put on a believable act of being a high fey, either. A proper fey lord who had never lived a beantighe life, scrubbing floors on his knees, knowing more than anyone how it felt to have his finger-nails peeled off or to be kicked in the ribs until one broke. To have his hand crushed beneath a heeled shoe.

Selfish, the word rang in his head like bells. Selfish, to push those memories away so he could enjoy his new life as a high fey with the person he loved, while people like him still suffered. While people he cared about were administered weaverthistle tea to forget his face so that he might safely live a new, indulgent life as a fey lord. So that one day, in another few centuries, he might make some changes once he eventually rose to the throne.

It might not have been true—but Saffron couldn't fault Ryder for thinking as much. And that twisted his heart between clawed hands.

"I..." He didn't know what to say. He could hardly think. Any composure he still clung to crumpled like a pile of snow in the sun, and he felt the familiar drip of hot blood from his nose. Ryder stepped forward, using the bottom of his shirt to wipe it away with a gentle touch.

"I'm sorry," he whispered, before smirking. "Ah, bet you haven't heard those words in a while, huh? It's a human thing. We say it when we mess up. Like when we verbally dig into someone who doesn't deserve it. Erm..."

He shifted on his feet.

"The thing I was going to tell you about—the suggestion I have for you—it's called a witch's mark. Or a rowan mark, an arid mark, sometimes even a veil mark. It's usually given to both bridge partners when they make a veil oath together, and it's supposed to act as a ward against magical overwhelm..." he pressed a hand to Saffron's chest, palm flush against the ugly scar Saffron had there. "Because you don't have a bridge partner, the veil didn't give you a witch's mark, so your body is trying to harbor all that magic on its own. And since you weren't formally trained in arid magic, not even as a spring witch, it's just going to keep growing more and more wild until it eats you alive... or eats the people you care about, considering what it did to one of my own at Ériu's shrine. There's a reason old witches made veil oaths on equinoxes, then rested on solstices. The veil attunes with the days—an equinox means a balanced veil; a solstice harbors an unbalanced one, where magic can run even wilder than normal. And since you especially don't have a bridge partner to help you out... well, I worry what might happen the closer we get to the solstice, how you might accidentally hurt someone, if you're not careful... worse than you already have."

Saffron thought he might cry. The backs of his eyes burned, but he didn't know why. Too much, all at once. He could no longer stand up straight or square his shoulders. The confidence that puffed out his chest had already deflated.

"How is any of that supposed to help me?" he asked, weaker than he expected. Ryder's hand lingered on his chest, before finally stepping back.

"If we can figure out how to communicate with the veil, you may be able to ask it for one. Or maybe there's some other spell we can perform to create a temporary one, or something, until you can find a partner to bridge with one day. You said you don't remember what Sunbeam's veil circle looked like, right?"

Saffron's heart sank. He shook his head. Ryder's gentle smile remained.

"That's alright. Might have been something unique if you didn't even see any knock-knots on it. I'll do some digging while you peck around your high fey libraries for now. Don't be too disappointed when you don't find anything useful, though, heh."

All Ryder ever did was tease. Worse, Saffron couldn't even curse at him before a torrent of wind suddenly crashed from the sky, and his prince did indeed plummet from the darkness like a meteorite. Whatever that was.

"Your highness," Ryder greeted with a flourished bow as Cylvan shoved hair from his eyes, whirling on the man with a bloodthirsty smile splitting his face.

"I'll have you skinned and gutted, you human maggot," he hissed. "I'll eat you flambé with a honey glaze."

"Huh—maggots? That a specialty in the royal family? I'm honored."

Cylvan practically snarled, stepping forward to carry out his threat—but Saffron grabbed the back of his tunic, first. He couldn't meet Cylvan's eyes, just shaking his head.

"I want to go home," he whispered. "Please. I want to go back home."

Cylvan turned his back on Ryder as if those words reduced his rage to dust in an instant. He took Saffron's face, briefly glancing him over, searching for anything that would give him reason to ignore the request and eviscerate Ryder on the spot after all—but when Saffron was fine, with not even a scratch or a hair out of place, Cylvan let out a breath and nodded. He didn't offer Ryder a second glance, scooping Saffron into his arms and taking off into the sky.

17

———————

THE CALM

Snow and ice crunched beneath his boots, but Saffron felt it in his teeth. Like biting down on hard candy, shattering it into splinters. Sticky sweetness lingered in the air, one that reminded him of Luvon's frost-fruits that grew in the iciest, coldest temperatures of the Winter Court's true season. But the fruity tinge filling his nose wasn't of oranges or grapes or apples or plums—it was something different. Something Saffron was sure he'd never tasted before.

So why did it also ring so familiar, like a perfume he'd smelled since childhood without ever knowing who wore it?

Making his way down the path, the dusting of familiarity remained. The way was clear between thick pine trees and snow-laden bushes, silent in the way only the Winter Court could be. Too cold for songbirds, for insects, even for frost pixies who only came out during the warmth of winter's full moon. Blanketed in a thick layer of snow that nearly reached his knees, while more still fell. Pieces of cloud cotton, floating to the earth where it would cling, unmovable, until spring came along to prick at it. Even then, depending on how far north he wandered, the white covering might still not budge except during the hottest week of the middle of summer during the week of Beltane. Even then, the ice would stay.

At the end of the snowed-over road, something emerged from the snowy mist. Saffron stopped, touching a hand to his heart as it suddenly thundered, making the healed wound in his chest ache. It pounded against his ribcage, as if trying to warn him of something —and then he heard it. Approaching from behind. He turned—but felt terror before seeing it, lancing his already-aching heart and erupting through his body sharply enough that he jolted instantly out of sleep.

Gasping, Saffron lurched upward. A mistake, as blood spilled from his nose and filled his mouth, choking him. Coughing, he buckled forward, throwing his hand over the bottom half of his face as his instinct was to smear it away—but it was too late. Despite the blackness of Cylvan's blankets, Saffron could see the dark ruby stains where his blood had splattered. His first morning waking up in Cylvan's bed—and even then, there was no peace allotted to him.

"Saffron?" Cylvan's voice emerged from his fog of sleep, but Saffron was busy trying to kick the blankets away so he could hurry to the bathroom. He didn't want Cylvan to see, he didn't want Cylvan to worry—but Cylvan grabbed his arm, pulling him back. His eyes bulged, mouth dropping open as Saffron looked at him timidly.

"I'll call the healer—" Cylvan attempted, but Saffron quickly pulled him back.

"Don't," he said, voice hoarse. "You don't have to, I promise. I'm alright, this isn't... it happens all the time, really—"

"What?" Cylvan gaped at him. "What do you mean, *all the time?* This is not... Is it because of...?"

"It's got something to do with my magic," Saffron tried to explain, tried to smile in reassurance. A fresh line of blood dripped from his nose, and he lifted his hand quickly to catch it, before finally managing to detangle himself from the blankets and hurry for the door to the attached bathroom suite. Cylvan followed, naked with long hair flowing behind him like a cape. He met Saffron at the sink, where Saffron bent over the faucet and drenched the lower half of his face in cold water. God, it felt nice. He didn't realize how clammy and sweaty his skin was until he went to wash the blood off.

"It's alright, I'm alright," he repeated, then swished water around in his mouth. The bright red color he spit into the drain made Cylvan grab the edge of the counter like he was about to faint. "It happens when I get overwhelmed, especially when I'm angry or upset..." He tried to recall exactly what was so intense about that dream, but it was only a blur. A blur of snow and trees. Still, a part of him thought he knew. He didn't have to see it directly to know the beast that approached him from behind, stark against the white road beneath it...

"Why haven't you ever told me?" Cylvan asked. A hand found the nape of Saffron's neck, fingers tucking up through his hair. He nudged Saffron's face upward toward the mirror, as if he really wanted a better view of what remained.

"I didn't want you to worry." Saffron shook his head, mustering another attempt at a reassuring smile. "Baba Yaga told me it wasn't unusual, since... well, since I'm holding all the magic of two people, when it's normally shared between them... But she said—she said it should even out, eventually, once my body finds equi—... equir—... oh, damnit! I can never remember that damn word..." His smile turned into something more of a grimace. Cylvan didn't look convinced. He ran a thumb under Saffron's nose, though Saffron had wiped away any remnants of the staining blood.

"What can I..." Cylvan spoke softly. "How can I...?"

"I sent a letter to Baba a few days ago," Saffron said, before realizing he'd never told Cylvan about Fiachra. "In it I asked if she or Adelard had found anything to help. I know she and the professor are doing what they can to learn what they can, but I know it's also difficult since they don't have a lot of resources and don't want to catch any of the wrong kind of attention, but hopefully it's only a matter of time..." he thought back to Ryder's offered suggestion the night before—something about a *witch's mark*. He scowled, shaking his head, pushing the thought away. He would wait to hear from Baba. He wouldn't give that man the time of day. Not any more than he absolutely had to, at least.

"What about that spell we did once outside the Kyteler Ruins? In that old henge," Cylvan said immediately, ideas churning behind his worried eyes. Saffron's heart thumped painfully. He hated how the color drained slightly from Cylvan's face when he shook his head.

"I actually asked Baba about that once, already. But it's not the same as becoming bridge partners for the first time. It was confusing how she explained it, but I think that's more for when someone is already veil-oathed, loses their bridge partner, and wants to join with someone else instead... I don't know... there's still so much even Baba Yaga doesn't know. Apparently she was never supposed to have that spell in her grimoire, anyway, she copied it down in secret... You should have heard how she scolded me when I told her I tried it, I think they could hear her shouting all the way in Cottage Monaghan..."

Cylvan remained unsatisfied with all of Saffron's reassurances, silently searching every inch of his face with worry in his indigo eyes. Saffron didn't know what else to say, what else to offer, since he'd only ever planned on hiding it from the prince until he had it under control. He settled on taking Cylvan's face in both hands, kissing his cheeks before pinching his bare shoulder.

"Good morning, your highness," he cooed playfully. "You know, I like waking up with you. The first thing I get to hear all morning is your voice. It's nice. All I could ever ask for, really."

Cylvan's demeanor didn't soften right away like Saffron wanted, but he at least sighed and pulled Saffron in to kiss him on the forehead.

"Good morning, your highness," he mumbled in reply, lips brushing Saffron's skin. "Let's run away together today, how does that sound?"

"Hmm." Saffron smiled, wrapping his arms around Cylvan's

waist. "I can't. I was invited to go to breakfast in Avren with someone I met at the gala last night."

Cylvan narrowed his eyes, sharp enough that Saffron choked on a laugh.

"Who?" He asked tightly. "Was it Lord Sneml? I saw you two dancing together. You should know the rest of his family is as silly as their name."

"No, I don't think it was him," Saffron teased, turning and stretching his arms over his head and making a show of elongating his back, his waist, his legs, letting Cylvan's borrowed nightshirt lift to reveal the bottom curve of his ass. "I don't remember his whole name, it was such a long one."

Cylvan put hands on either side of Saffron's waist, caging him against the edge of the counter. His eyes never changed.

"Long names don't imply anything."

"I thought the longer name meant the more power their family had?"

"No, Saffron! You're so—Did he tell you that, too? What else did he say?"

"He said he's from one of the most powerful families in all of Alfidel. And he has at least one-hundred beach houses all along the coast."

"Surely he only said that because you told him you like the view of the sea."

"Maybe. I thought high fey can't lie?"

"You and I both know that's bullshit."

Saffron laughed, crossing his arms around the back of Cylvan's neck.

"Are you jealous?"

"The court will be thinner by morning."

"What do you mean?"

"I will execute every fey lord who so much as looked at you last night. There will be only ladies and gentles left."

"Plenty of ladies and gentles spoke to me, too."

"Then it will be a bloodbath."

Saffron laughed again, though Cylvan remained serious as ever.

"I'm talking about *you*, your highness. *You* are taking me to breakfast today. Your prince demands it. Come shower with me first, though. You can slaughter your courtiers later this afternoon."

"O-oh," Cylvan's tight expression loosened in an instant, watching as Saffron pulled the sleep shirt off over his head, throwing it at Cylvan and tangling it in his horns. Cylvan scrambled free, throwing it to the floor and hurrying after Saffron toward the shower. "Really? That was only a joke? You can't joke with me like that, Saffron, I might actually have people killed."

"I can assure you, Prince Cylvan, not a single high fey of any family or stature or length-of-name had anything of interest to say to me all night long. It was actually a miserable experience all around, if I dare to admit it."

"Gods above, I almost resorted to genocide."

"Do you really think any of them would interest me like that?"

"I think... I think they're all very lucky to be as vapid and dull as they are. Oh, Lugh forgive me for the vile thoughts I just had. Danu bless me with thine head turned, for I was not trying to manifest..."

Saffron couldn't stop giggling, teasing Cylvan's mouth with his own while his fingers trailed over the bare skin over his navel, all while luring him a little further.

"Why don't you remind me why you're the one I'm choosing?" he asked, hardly separating their mouths, laughing sharply as Cylvan immediately lifted him off the floor, carrying him into the shower without ever parting their mouths for more than a moment.

Saffron washed Cylvan's hair with velvety shampoos that smelled like honey and flowers, and Cylvan washed Saffron's in return, before pinning him against the wall to smear a dozen expensive serums all over his face. He whined as Cylvan washed between his legs, huffing as every inch of him was warm and sore from the long night on his feet at the party—but he got his revenge by clawing marks down Cylvan's back as washing soon turned to massaging, and Saffron could hardly keep himself upright.

He leapt into Cylvan's arms, crossing ankles around Cylvan's waist, biting down on his shoulder as he was thrust into with a sharp moan. He clawed at Cylvan's back, his shoulders, all while Cylvan decorated him with bite marks and hickies down his neck and across his collarbones, whispering about how they would have to see if Saffron's glamour would cover them up, too. How he hoped it didn't; he hoped everyone would be able to see, the Flower of Alvénya had already been claimed by a demanding lover in Alfidel. Saffron bit back every smiling moan, obsessed with the thought of being left with ownership marks once they were done.

Finally escaping the shower after a second round of washing each other clean, Saffron dressed in one of Cylvan's tunics and leggings before braiding and pinning up Cylvan's hair for the morning of breakfast, then shopping, then maybe even walking the beach. Cylvan chose to glamour himself again, that time as a fey lord instead of a human, and Saffron loved seeing all the ways he could change the appearance of his hair, the color, the length, the style, like draping a veil over his head, into anything at all he wanted. All the while, he answered all the questions Saffron had never been able to ask. Like how most glamours were only visual, not tangible, but not because there was no such thing—because it was physically more exhausting. It was why high fey developed glamouring charms like the one Saffron used, though they were mostly only visual as well. Charms for physical and visual glamours could cost as much as a private island. All the while, Saffron nodded along, arms crossed over the back of the couch while he watched Cylvan dress then demonstrate more of his tricks. When he asked Cylvan *how* he did it, smoke practically spilled from the prince's ears as he tried to figure out a way to explain something that, according to him, came naturally. Without thought.

"It's like how you're able to draw from memory," he eventually said. "You can just... do it, without thinking. After much practice, of course. Like, I could easily perform a physical glamour but Asche can't, yet. But if you, the beautiful, talented artist you are, tried to explain how to draw to someone else, well, there are ways to teach, but it's mostly a learned skill. A mental, visual, psychological one."

"Intangible and tangible, opulent and arid," Saffron said, chuckling when Cylvan smirked at him. "What does that make my charm, then?"

"Both. Neither."

Asche always answered the same way whenever Saffron asked them to explain the soul of what wild charms were, too. Both. Neither. Wild charms were, in essence, a perfect marriage of tangible and intangible magic that could be manipulated to benefit one or the other by practiced hands...

"Like oracles and memory threading," Cylvan went on thoughtfully, pulling on a pair of boots while seated on the couch alongside Saffron. "Oracles are half-human, half-fey. And—now, don't tell anyone I told you this, it's extremely taboo information —which I know you have never, ever dabbled in a day in your life —but many scholars claim memory threads are equally opulent as they are arid, too. Because a memory is intangible, but a thread is not. And threads, in themselves, aren't physical things that can be touched except by threadweavers—"

"Unless they're knotted in a specific way," Saffron finished for him. Cylvan beamed like he always did when Saffron caught him off guard like that. "I think I mentioned in the crow book how on my first day of class, the professor talked about celtic knots a little bit. I, um, proceeded to embarrass myself by saying too much about memory knots, of course, but... it was interesting to learn that those knots aren't unlike arid-ogham circles. Just a different sort. Something to do with the language of the veil."

"Exactly right. Your arid-ogham circles are just a means of communicating with the veil—especially since your magic isn't natural here on this side. The opulent side, I mean. Just like how fey magic works differently on the human side—because we have to, theoretically, communicate with the veil what sort of magic we want to use from the side we came from. Like sending a messenger bird and asking for a favor."

"And the veil is the bird."

"That's right. And the marks on the circle are the letter asking for what we want from the other side."

"Then circles for veil magic must let the messenger-bird-veil know, 'hey, wait, it's *me* they want something from'..." Saffron grinned, though admittedly his head spun a little bit. "Because oracles are half-fey and half-human, are they able to perform both human and fey magic?" He recalled something he'd learned from the beannighe outside the Kyteler Ruins, heart skipping. "You once said oracles are the only ones allowed to perform arid magic without getting in trouble, like when they charm patron rings. I know they give true names, too, which are like arid steles..." he trailed off, touching his chest while gazing at Cylvan's in the same place. Recalling how he'd once witnessed true names glowing from the sternum of every high fey at the Ostara fete. Meanwhile, Cylvan gazed at him like he'd said something shocking, and Saffron realized perhaps he didn't actually know that about true names, himself.

"You grow more dangerous by the day, beantighe," the prince finally said threateningly. "I've said it before. Far too clever for your own good. You're going to get us both in trouble, eventually."

"Good thing I have a very scary Night Prince to whisk me away when that happens. Maybe straight to Alvénya, since the king there seems to have taken an interest in me. He sent me the most beautiful fur-lined cloak, you know."

"Oh, gods, do not send anything back. Not even a thank-you.

Let King Tross handle that. The Danae of Alvénya has at least a dozen sons who I *know* would go mad over you."

"Oh, I know. They've already offered their sons to me. Perhaps I am destined to start wars in more than one country."

"You joke."

"Didn't you literally just consider committing genocide over the thought of someone else catching my eye?"

Cylvan went to argue, but in the process stepped straight through his clothes piled on the floor from the night before. Whatever he kicked jingled like bells on a wind chime, and he smiled wickedly, bending over to pick it up. He revealed a thin chain weighed down heavily by at least two-dozen silver pendants, holding it up like a trophy.

"These are all of the courting lockets I received last night alone," Cylvan announced, jangling the handful of charms again in emphasis before tossing them at Saffron. Saffron fumbled the chain, and it clattered to the floor with a deafening sound. Several of them opened once they hit the floor, and Saffron bent over the back of the couch to sweep them back up and look. Inside, minia-ture painted portraits of different high fey gazed back up at him, all beautiful and flawlessly depicted. Perhaps it wasn't Cylvan's point, but Saffron found himself more interested in the minute details of the brushstrokes over the threat it was supposed to pose.

"What's a courting locket?" he asked, holding one of the tiny portraits closer to his face, the rest of the cluster clattering against his stomach with the movement. Cylvan joined him on the couch, sitting cross-legged and opening a few more of the offer-ings. He wrinkled his nose at every single one. Saffron took them to see for himself, though couldn't quite understand what the prince found so ugly about them. Every single one was beautifully crafted, down to the fine details carved into the outer locket faces, or the little jewel charms that dangled from the loops for an added sparkle.

"A high fey tradition. The interested party offers a self-portrait to the person they wish to court," Cylvan explained, inspiring the exact reaction he originally hoped for when Saffron suddenly pouted in annoyance at how many there were. "Should the intended agree, they remove the initiator's portrait, have their own added to the second locket face, and send it back via messenger bird. A sign of mutual interest. Feeling threatened now, beantighe?"

"No," Saffron mumbled stubbornly, though it was a lie. Of course he felt threatened. He didn't need a handful of so many courting lockets demonstrating true interest in his beloved to be threatened. Not when he was just a glamoured beantighe in a room crowded to the brim with high fey. "I actually think they're all rather ugly. And boring. And forgettable."

"I think you're right," Cylvan agreed. Saffron looked at him, still frowning, but Cylvan was all smiles. Annoyed, Saffron tossed the lockets back to the floor.

"I don't like joking about this," he said.

"Oh, so you can joke about the King of Alvénya's twelve sons sharing you at once?"

"Yes. Because that's not actually going to happen. Not like..." Saffron waved at the puddle of necklaces on the floor. He furrowed his brows. "Not like how... any of this could happen."

"None of this is going to happen," Cylvan chuckled, returning to his feet and kicking the chained lockets away declaratively, scraping along the wood floor all the way under the dresser. Saffron kept frowning up at him.

"I don't like any of them thinking they might be able to have you. When you're already mine," he went on stubbornly. "You're mine, right?"

Cylvan pushed hair from Saffron's eyes, then wrapped an arm around his waist and pulled him from the couch. Lifting Saffron until his feet dangled off the floor, making him laugh as he wrapped his arms around Cylvan's neck, where Cylvan nibbled at the curve of his neck and made him blush.

"I'm yours," he promised. "No one else will ever compare, Saffron dé Tuatha dé Danann."

Saffron pursed his lips again, but wrapped his arms possessively around Cylvan in return. "How long until you and I can fall in love?"

"Ohhh," Cylvan groaned, rolling his head back and gazing at the ceiling as he thought about it. "Perhaps another month. Perhaps only a few weeks, if we play our cards right. Danu knows I only have so many more suitor parties in me. Danu knows how close I came to wiping out my entire court at the mere thought of someone else showing interest in you." He tugged Saffron closer, bending down to bite at the curve of his ear, then cupping the back of his neck and making Saffron giggle. "I want everyone to know you're mine, and only mine, and they will rue the day their eyes linger immorally on you for longer than a moment."

Saffron finally smiled at him again, hopping up and down on his toes before kissing him. The tiniest reassurance—but one that still made his heart flutter in relief.

18

THE HUNTERS

Leaving the palace side by side on horseback was like something out of a dream. Crossing the long bridge over the ravine, they exited through the palace gate on the opposite side and took their time heading into the city. Arriving on the outskirts, Cylvan motioned Saffron to a carriage house, where they tied the animals off and Cylvan paid for them to be moved to the road that would lead to Mairwen. So they wouldn't have to walk the whole way after breakfast. So they wouldn't have to lead horses through the crowded streets all morning, either.

By the way no one in Avren turned to give them a second look, Saffron wanted to ask why Cylvan didn't run away like that more often, but decided it must be as complicated an answer as everything else. Surely Cylvan couldn't run away often, or for long, without being noticed. Perhaps it was more trouble than it was worth, most of the time. He wouldn't squander the rare opportunity to enjoy royal trickery that morning.

Hand-in-hand, Cylvan walked slowly so as to not rush. He gently pulled Saffron out of the way when the crowd was too rough around cramped corners, or hooked a hand around Saffron's waist and pulled him close whenever a rush of bodies hurried by, or whenever Saffron startled at a loud noise. No one turned a second glance at all. Saffron even stopped and pecked a kiss on Cylvan's cheek at one point, and no one even blinked. He felt like he could fly. He knew it wouldn't last, especially as he made himself better known at Cylvan's galas—but those little moments made him weightless. That was how he'd wanted it when they visited Connacht while Saffron wore the black veil, it was all he could think about—and he finally had it. Ériu bless him, he finally had it, even if it was only a brief taste.

Before breakfast, Cylvan purchased Saffron the most beautiful doublet he'd ever seen, cream-colored wool decorated with pastel-embroidered flowers down the front lapels and sprawling like fireworks around the waist and up the back. Even the sleeves were adorned with colorful blooms and mushrooms, Saffron losing himself in the detail any time he got the chance. Cylvan took the opportunity to shop for himself, as well, purchasing a long coat in black with similar floral embroidery snaking like vines up the back and the sides. Saffron complimented him the whole time, telling him in a whisper how absolutely stunning it would be with his dark hair and purple eyes. Cylvan grinned smugly as if the accolades refilled his arrogance-reserves.

They eventually settled for breakfast at a little bistro where they could sit outside and watch people as they passed by, which Saffron quickly realized was something he enjoyed. Those crowded streets were filled with so many people of all walks of life, from all places around Alfidel and beyond, wearing such unique clothes and speaking such different languages, passing to and fro beneath banners and other Beltane decorations placed on lanterns and between buildings in preparation for celebrations coming in another few weeks. It reminded him of King Tross' request for him to participate in the opening ceremony of the Midsummer Games on the solstice, asking Cylvan if he knew anything about it —all the while pushing away any reminders of Ryder in the process. The deal he and the man had made. The things Ryder said about Saffron's magic as the solstice came closer.

Cylvan groaned and rolled his eyes in a way that made Saffron laugh, asking to not be reminded for a little bit longer. As if Tross had already traumatized him over requested favors of his own. Saffron teased him while they shared coffees, only relenting when Cylvan bought him a pastry to keep him distracted.

Cylvan changed the subject by asking how humans celebrated Beltane, and Saffron told him all about the dancing, the bonfires, how in Beantighe Village they had to scrounge and save their alcohol for special events like those. It reminded him to ask if Cylvan had heard anything from Morrígan's new headmistress about the village and how repairs were going, surprised when Cylvan pulled out a bound notebook and handed over a letter from Elding, herself, itemizing everything done in the past week alone. As Saffron read it, Cylvan continued scribbling additional notes as if reminded of something he wanted to follow up on. He even paused before writing something else, mumbling about *'perhaps I should see if that is common practice with palace beantighes as well...'* It made Saffron smile, like knowing Cylvan cared enough to check in even without Saffron asking first was the most romantic thing someone could do for him.

Before making their way to the beach, they made one last stop at a stationery shop where Saffron made sure to *ooh* and *aah* over every little thing that caught his attention, knowing it was like a secret thrill of Cylvan's to snatch objects of interest off the shelf behind his back to purchase, later. He made sure to ogle at a few things he knew his prince would like, too—fine quills and silky inks, black paper, fancy glass inkwells—so he wouldn't end up as the only one with treasures to return to school with.

While helping himself to the shelves of special paper and inks, he paused at the sight of blank silver lockets dangling from chains on a hook, tilting his head in curiosity and unable to resist trailing his fingers through them. They tinkled like little bells, and he realized they were courting lockets like the ones Cylvan showed off in his room. It only took Saffron so long to recognize them because of how plain they were in comparison to the ones he'd rifled through, though the thought of even common, lower fey partici-pating in such a charming tradition made him smile to himself.

"Have someone special in mind?" the gentle voice of a shop attendant surprised him, making Saffron jump and turn to her. A human girl, hardly older than a teenager with acne spots and crooked teeth. Her apron was well-pressed, hair braided down her back, nails scrubbed and shirt perfectly wrinkle-free. He noticed she didn't have a name embroidered into the apron like the cashier clerk had. Something about that needled him. He made sure to return a warm, friendly smile.

"Are these courting lockets?" He asked. "I'm not from Alfidel, but I've heard of them. Do I have to commission an artist to paint the portrait for me? Or can I paint my own?"

"You can certainly paint your own portrait." she smiled, hands remaining clasped over her stomach, polite as ever. She was careful not to meet Saffron's eyes too often, or for too long, either. It pricked him deeper, reminding him of how that beantighe in Mairwen's library politely refused to utter a single word. As much as he understood, he hated feeling like someone untrustworthy.

"I think most have their portraits done by an artisan, but if you're an artist yourself, I'm sure that would be far more charming for your intended partner," she continued.

"What do the people who can't paint and can't afford an artist do? Or are they cursed to a life alone?" he went on, secretly pleased with himself when her standard-polite smile cracked into something slightly more genuine.

"I've heard of people printing their initials, instead," she said thoughtfully. "Or sometimes they press flowers into them."

Saffron smiled. "What would someone like you prefer?"

"Oh—I would never exchange a courting locket." Her smile turned awkward as she put her hands up. "That's a tradition reserved for high fey, of course."

Saffron bit his lip. "Well—how would you do it, then?"

"My lord?"

"To show someone you wanted to be courted by them. Or vice-versa. How would you do it?"

She must have thought Saffron was teasing her, because her face flushed in confusion, mouth opening and closing like she genuinely wasn't sure how to respond. No one had ever asked her that before. Saffron knew exactly how she felt, suddenly kicking himself and scrambling for a way to relieve the discomfort. He had to get better at pushing his own selfishness away, to stop making other humans so uncomfortable in the face of him.

"Do you sell paints here as well? What kind do you recommend?" He asked, relieved when she instantly relaxed and invited him to follow. He didn't originally intend on getting all of the extra things, but once he pinched the blank locket between his fingers, he couldn't stop thinking about it. If he was to be courted by a high fey lord, why not do it the way Cylvan would find meaningful? Even if their relationship was wholly unorthodox, all things considered, even if the lockets for sale in that shop weren't anything close to as expensive as the ones he was given by fellow courtiers—even if he already wore a courting ring from the fey he intended to court—Saffron felt the urge to show Cylvan he wanted to participate in those little traditions, too. Fey traditions. And, if anything else—it might just make Cylvan happy.

He was in the middle of discussing the best kind of paints to use on a metal locket face when the bells over the shop door jingled. Saffron thought nothing of it, until Cylvan was suddenly there behind him, grabbing his arm and whispering his name. Saffron barely managed a sound in reply, huffing in surprise and annoyance when Cylvan rudely pulled him away from the human girl before he could even thank her for her help—but then Cylvan came to a sudden halt against the opposite wall, staring toward the door. Saffron's heart was racing long before he ever took the slight step forward to see for himself.

Black veils. Simple black gowns. Three androgynous shadows standing at the same height, build, anonymity. Veil weights dangled from the back of the opaque chiffon draping their faces, donning silver sun motifs. Around their waists, belts with loops weighed heavily with more silver suns, bells, jingling charms, and —a variety of glass bottles clacking against one another, filled with varying levels of silver liquid. In the center of their chests, another silver emblem that sent chills rocketing through Saffron's entire body, plummeting him straight into the walls of Danann House. Into the streets of Connacht. A silver triangle, tipped with rings. The same mark he once saw in Kaelar's bedroom; the sign of Queen Proserpina's human witchhunters.

The memory of cold silver hands found his throat, slowly compressing his windpipe until no words could escape. A silver choker, hands folded over a knife, instantly silencing every sound he could possibly make. The bitter taste of a silver half-moon flooded his mouth, drying his tongue and making the back of his throat swell. The weight of it pulled against the roof of his mouth, chain reaching over the center crown of his head, dangling heavy from the sun on the chain at his lower back.

"It will only be a moment, my lords," one of the witchhunters said, directed at Cylvan and Saffron in the corner. Speaking clearly despite the weight in their mouth. As if practiced with it.

They remained where they were, blocking the way of the door, as the other two proceeded into the shop to speak with the clerk. Saffron barely heard them. The world spun beneath his feet, turning and breaking and attempting to suck him through the worn floorboards. Back into Danann House. Back into that attic he was never meant to leave.

The scars on his forearm burned. He pressed his palm into them before lifting it to his throat, rubbing up and down against his windpipe. He didn't know if he felt the silver choker or not. He swore that cold silver slid beneath his fingers.

"Do you have any humans in your employ? I would like to speak with her, please."

"Ah, hello there. You have nothing to worry about."

"Have you recently been contacted by the Red Adage humans passing out cards on the street?"

"You can be honest."

No—*no*, Saffron wanted to scream. *Don't tell them anything. Don't say anything at all.* He wanted to scream, he wanted to tear free from the bones that kept him rooted against the floor—but he couldn't move. He never took his eyes from the one veiled figure in the doorway. Seeing without seeing. Hearing without hearing. Smelling the humid rot of Danann House's attic. The acrid stench of burning flesh searing into a cobblestone street. He rubbed his neck; he clawed at his throat. He raked fingernails down the length of his windpipe, searching for the silver hands that choked and silenced him, that tightened every time he attempted to inhale. Colors rimmed his vision as he slowly suffocated—until the shadow at the door glowed with a faint pink light. His forearm burned hotter. He tried to blink the glow away, but it only intensified. Like the red glow of a true name given to a high fey; like the red glow of those arid-magic summoned rowan vines that nearly strangled Fiachra at the foot of Ériu's shrine. He thought of tearing that veiled hunter into pieces like he did those vines. Tearing apart the dangerous thing that reached for something innocent, wishing to squeeze the life out of it—

The witchhunter at the door stiffened. Their hands folded over their stomach fidgeted, before one lifted to press into their chest. They inhaled a breath deep enough that Saffron saw their shoulders move. He wished they'd choked on it. He wished they would drop dead. He wished their lungs would rent apart in their body and they would cease living in an instant—

Blood spilled from both nostrils. He heard it bubbling up in his ears. He tasted it in his mouth. The scars on his arm screamed —and had a gentle, familiar hand not touched his shoulder at that very moment, the beast may have torn free and slaughtered every living being in that shop. Cylvan's hand was the only thing to temper it enough to keep it down—only because Saffron feared hurting Cylvan more than anything.

A dark handkerchief touched his face, next. Saffron still didn't move or speak, still hardly took in a breath. Cylvan silently wiped the blood from his nose, his mouth. He dragged the cloth over the streams of crimson pooling in his ears and dripping to his shoulders. Only when he realized he couldn't keep up with the deluge of overwhelm did he resort to taking Saffron by the shoulders and slowly turning him away. Putting Saffron's back to the witch-hunter at the door. Only another moment passed before the witchhunters interrogating the human girl thanked the shopkeeper for his time, and excused themselves without trouble.

The bottom half of Saffron's face was sticky and wet with blood; the front of his tunic was soaked through. He couldn't breathe. He was still being choked by the silver hands. Only when he heard the hollowed-out, far-off reassurance from Cylvan that everything was alright, they'd finally left—did Saffron's tightened muscles relax, exhaling a long held breath, before his eyes rolled back into his head and he crumpled to the floor.

SAFFRON WOKE IN A ROOM THAT WASN'T HIS. HE WAS getting used to that.

Every inch of his body was stiff, like he'd frozen solid in a Winter Court squall before being tucked into whatever bed it was in which he lay. Stiff, sore, aching all over, enough that he closed his eyes again and waited for the sensation to pass. Or perhaps to kill him. God, he was exhausted. He was so tired of feeling worn down to dust.

When he finally sat up, it was with a quiet groan, dragging a hand down his face, then his throat, until it slumped into his lap with the other one. He ran heavy fingers over the thick black duvet covering him, turning to observe the matching black sheets, then matching black pillows, and he knew where he was. At least, he knew it was some place belonging to Prince Cylvan.

It wasn't nearly large or ornate enough to be any bedroom at the palace, which gave Saffron his only other most likely option: the prince's private suite at Mairwen. Glancing around the floor scattered with random articles of clothing, uniform shoes kicked off at the door, and the mountains of books lining the walls when they weren't partially toppled and kicked out of the way, it reassured his assumption was correct. In his search of the room, he spotted a handwritten card on the table alongside the bed, reaching for it before curling back up under the blankets.

YOU'RE SAFE BACK AT MAIRWEN. PLEASE DON'T LEAVE THIS ROOM ON YOUR OWN WHILE I'M AWAY. YOU'RE WELCOME TO SNOOP THROUGH ANY AND ALL OF MY THINGS IN THE MEANTIME. I WILL BE DONE WITH CLASS AT LUNCHTIME AND WILL COME BACK TO YOU IN AN INSTANT. UNTIL THEN, GET SOME REST.

YOU'RE SAFE, PÚCA.

Saffron sighed through his nose. That reassurance given to him—twice—was almost embarrassing. Closing his eyes, it reminded him too much of Connacht. Again, a reminder of Connacht. *You're safe, you're safe, you're...*

Saffron opened his mouth to whisper the promise out loud, but the words wouldn't come. His throat tightened before he could make a sound.

19

THE COLLAR

Try as he might to forget what happened earlier that morning, he still couldn't utter a word even as Cylvan came back to the room to gather him at lunchtime. Saffron could sometimes manage a whisper, but only while constantly rubbing at his throat in frustration. Cylvan watched him with agony in his eyes, constantly taking Saffron's hand when his nails clawed a little too roughly and threatened to break skin. Cylvan would pull Saffron's hand to his mouth, kiss his knuckles; pull him into a protective embrace, kissing the side of his neck. Never once telling Saffron to *stop*, or trying to reassure him there was no silver collar there—only trying to ease the anxiety when it flared a little too high. Smiling at him and kissing him and going about the day as if it was just another one. Saffron wished he could stay in the prince's private suite forever. To be his beantighe pet that only existed to eat cakes and dress nicely and kiss him. But it was only his first week, and he'd already missed classes. He couldn't hide away forever.

God—it was *only his first week*.

Sneaking from Cylvan's suite, Saffron hurried to his dorm room. When Copper greeted him with a loud, booming voice, Saffron smiled awkwardly and touched his throat once the shock wore off. *I lost my voice*, he passed off. *Too much fun at my first gala last night, I guess...*

Copper, at least, didn't push it. He teased Saffron endlessly, though, which made Saffron laugh, which lifted his spirit a little bit more.

Throughout the rest of the day, and then the rest of the week, he continuously failed to find his voice again, sometimes even choking on an inhale if he did so too deeply, or something startled him from behind. More than once, Cylvan found him crouched behind a building trying to catch his breath, where Saffron would smile weakly and shake his head, trying to assure him he was fine. It was fine. He was, unfortunately—used to that feeling.

After a few days, every now and then something akin to words might emerge, especially if he was alone and spoke in a whisper. The worst came in his *Ashen States and History of the Veil* class when the instructor unexpectedly called his name, and Saffron could only open his mouth before pathetically sitting back down again in silence. Staring at his hands in his lap as the instructor scoffed and said something about him being *rude*. Saffron kept his head bowed, rubbing his hand up and down his throat in frustration. There was nothing there. There was no silver there to silence him. He should be able to speak. It had been almost a week since he saw those witchhunters in the stationery shop. Nothing had changed. He wasn't in trouble. He wasn't in Danann House. He wasn't in trouble.

At the very least, classes made for good distractions from what happened. His new friends didn't push too much to ask what was wrong or when he would get better, though Sionnach gently nudged more than once that maybe he should go visit the healer. That only made Saffron more anxious—because he didn't know if the healer knew his situation. He didn't know how he would explain what was wrong with him. How could he, when he couldn't even say anything out loud?

No—he would just focus on school. On being a normal fey lord. Not one who got nosebleeds whenever he was a little overwhelmed; not one whose voice had inexplicably vanished, whose throat tightened and made a horrible clicking sound whenever he opened his mouth to try, anyway. One whose emotions would never summon a vicious wolf from nothing and nearly slaughter a group of humans. Not one who was sought by Ryder Kyteler to act as something those same humans could look to for hope of liberation, or whatever it was he'd said the night of the gala. Not one who, apparently—had to rely on something called a *witch's mark* if he ever wished to exist normally, peacefully, ever again.

God above—Saffron had only wanted his romantic summer with Cylvan. Ryder had promised him that. Was it really so much to ask? When he wasn't rubbing and clawing at his throat, he was massaging the scars on his forearm. Constantly whispering commands for the animal to stay where it was. Forever. He never wished to see it ever again. He blamed that beast for bringing Ryder Kyteler back to him in the first place; he may have had his perfect summer if it hadn't emerged and made everyone know who he was, where he was.

In his mythology and literature class, he learned about high fey theology and religion, including gods and historical figures the likes of whom Prince Cylvan worshiped. Saffron took copious notes, though the frustration grew every time he didn't know how to spell something, or didn't understand one concept or another on account of growing up very differently from everyone else in that class. He dreaded the day he would have to take courses he really had no interest in, which was the curse of being a Danann House student. Expected to take and excel at every single course offered over all three other houses, the other three academic tracts—but Saffron just wanted to learn about romantic stories. And pixies. And what mushrooms were edible in the woods. Classes where he could do his own thing, mind his own business, sit and listen without ever having to speak aloud at all.

. . .

Sɪᴏɴɴᴀᴄʜ sᴜʀᴘʀɪsᴇᴅ Sᴀꜰꜰʀᴏɴ ᴏɴᴇ ᴇᴠᴇɴɪɴɢ ᴡʜᴇɴ they knocked on the door to the dorm, standing on the other side with a disheveled looking Fiachra. Saffron cried out her name in surprise—though it was quickly cut off again—swallowing and putting out a hand to flatten some of the messy feathers on the owl's chest. Her messenger token was missing, as well as the letter he'd sent off for Baba Yaga, which made his heart sink in disappointment. He'd been praying for that letter to come. But disappointment was quickly overtaken by relief when he realized how glad he should be that she returned safely at all, sick at the thought of Ryder's people catching her all over again. Making an example out of her, nailing her to the palace gates without him ever knowing.

"I guess she's not a messenger bird after all," Sionnach said with an awkward laugh, like they weren't sure if it was something Saffron would be comfortable to joke about. But Saffron, despite being unable to summon the words, smiled, then sighed, then put out his arm for the owl to grumpily scuttle onto. Sionnach hovered in the doorway a little longer, before asking: "Since I work part-time in the paddock, um, I also help Madame Arva with flight-training classes. Do you want to do something like that? I'm free right now, if you don't have anything else..."

Saffron was surprised at the offer, but managed to whisper a small *"Alright,"* before his throat closed up in protest. He didn't know if it was the ghostly hands of silver that did it—or the realization he would have to wait a little bit longer to get an answer from Baba Yaga. Ryder's voice echoed in the back of his mind, reminding him of the solstice. Those things he said about Saffron's magic only growing worse.

He pushed them away. He smiled at Sionnach. He pet his bird's soft feathers. He didn't want to think about Ryder fucking Kyteler.

After stopping by the paddock for a few supplies, he and Sionnach wandered into the woods on the outer edge of campus. Sionnach gave Saffron something called a *recall ring,* bronze with a secondary ring inside of it, before clipping a matching circlet to one of Fiachra's legs. When he spun the secondary ring, it would vibrate on Fiachra's in tandem, endlessly buzzing until the bird returned to his hand. Thankfully, Fiachra didn't have much problem with return and recall, as she was quickly proving herself to be the laziest bird alive, preferring to sit on Saffron's shoulder and chew his hair, or chase things in the grass by foot with wings extended to make herself appear bigger. Sionnach commented that it must have been why she never managed to deliver his message, especially if it was supposed to travel all the way back to Alvénya—and Saffron smiled awkwardly, glad he had no voice that would force him to lie.

When the lessons devolved against Fiachra's preference for chasing mice and bugs through the undergrowth, he and Sionnach sat in the grass with opened sketchbooks. Saffron appreciated Sionnach's work with paints, particularly watercolors; he himself didn't have much to show in his own book as it was brand new from the shop in Fullam. What a relief, as he wasn't sure how he would ever explain to his friend why there were so many drawings of Prince Cylvan in his old one.

Sketching each other's portraits for practice, Saffron disappeared into his friend's delicate features, the texture of their horns, the velvety softness of their doe-like ears. He may have accidentally drawn them a little too pretty, though, with fluttery lashes and sparkling eyes, making Sionnach blush and stammer out a *thank you.*

As he sat gazing off introspectively into the distance for Sionnach to draw him in return, Sionnach stumbled over a few more sentence starters, before finally asking: "Did something happen at the prince's gala?"

He knew better than to turn his whole head, else risk messing up Sionnach's study, but his eyes flickered to the side. Sionnach kept their eyes on the paper, as if meeting Saffron's eyes would only embarrass them more. Still, they continued:

"When I found out you were going, I was so worried, especially after what happened on your first day... Prince Cylvan is a truly horrible fey lord, I've never met anyone more cruel in my life... he's bullied me for years, too, so when you came back and couldn't speak, I thought... I was worried something had happened, and I just... I just want you to know, you're safe with me! I won't even push you to talk about it. Or talk at all, if you want. I just want you to know—you're not alone, and I'm here for you, and I want you to feel like you can confide in me, if you ever want to..."

Saffron's attention turned to them as they spoke, rambling, voice growing shriller as they scribbled frantically on the page, like they wanted to stop talking but the words refused to obey. Growing more and more and more agitated and embarrassed the longer they went—until Saffron interrupted them when he laughed, then shook his head in apology.

"It's alright," he said softly. That time, his throat only tensed. The words croaked out of him. Perhaps because of Sionnach's reassurance. Perhaps because of their naturally quiet disposition. As if the squeezing choker he no longer wore considered them nothing more than a ghost he was safe to speak to. "It—wasn't anything—because of P-Prince Cylvan."

Saffron pressed his hand to his throat, forcing the words out. Dragging his palm up and down his windpipe, actively proving to himself yet again there were no silver hands choking him. It was only a bad memory. It was only a nightmare creeping back into his life. Still, despite managing the words, his heart raced faster than ever with fear of someone overhearing and coming through the trees to punish him. Someone he couldn't even imagine, someone he didn't know, someone who didn't exist. Or perhaps just—someone who he knew to be far away. Taran mac Delbaith was far, far away. He would never know Saffron spoke at all.

Sionnach looked relieved at the reassurance, finally meeting Saffron's eyes with a gentle smile.

"That's good," they said. "It wasn't Copper, then, was it?"

Saffron laughed under his breath again. "No."

"That's good."

Saffron swallowed against the tightness on his windpipe. "Copper—also bullies you?"

Sionnach returned to their sketch, starting a new one since Saffron moved from his original position. Saffron readjusted how he sat, trying to make his new pose a little more natural.

"Yes," they whispered. "Lots of high fey at this school do, actually. But I'm used to it by now."

"I'm sorry," Saffron said, throat collapsing in on itself with a new rush of shame and embarrassment for speaking those human words again. Still, he gulped harder against the tightness. He wanted to speak, damnit. "Is it be-because you're part satyr?"

"Yes," Sionnach repeated quietly. "Mostly, at least. Some people are more creative, but..."

"I'm sorry," Saffron said again, that time forcing himself to not feel embarrassed. He meant it. He cleared his throat to continue. "I've—been—bullied by high fey, too. All—my l-life."

"Why?" Sionnach appeared genuinely surprised, leaning over their sketchbook with wide eyes. "Even in Alvénya? People aren't already bullying you here, are they?"

Saffron grimaced. Sionnach had no idea exactly how much had happened in only his first few days, though ironically not because of any high fey. He rubbed his hand down his throat again, watching as Fiachra burst through some bushes on the other side of the small clearing, chasing down a squeaking mouse with her beak wide open and hungry. He couldn't help but think of the things Ryder said, about wanting the high fey to know humans were unhappy. They were done being mistreated. How if they wanted to change how humans were treated, they would have a long time ago. Sionnach's words highlighted a bigger issue, one Saffron had never considered any deeper than annoyance when witnessing how students treated pixies at Morrígan—high fey were cruel to anything, anyone who wasn't exactly like them. Humans, half-fey, wild fey. And what about high fey who weren't courtiers? Who didn't come from wealth, from powerful family lines? Where did the mistreatment stop? They weren't even shy about how they spoke of and treated the crown prince, like he was a scourge on their way of life, a threat to their very being.

Saffron clenched his jaw. He closed his hands into fists on his legs.

Maybe that's all Ryder really wanted to show them—the same thing Saffron had wanted to show high fey for a long time, too. There were worse things than a Night Court.

MORE DAYS PASSED. SAFFRON FOCUSED ON HIS CLASSES. He focused on his homework, though it continually piled up no matter how hard he tried to keep on top of it all. There was too much back-reading he had to do, too many words he had to look up, too many times he sat in spinning anxiety because he worried his poor grammar and spelling would be mentioned to the entire class and he would be laughed at again. Cylvan helped when he could, mostly through scribbled conversations in the crow book, but otherwise, they were trapped in keeping a distance from one another. Occasionally they would cross paths on campus and Cylvan would smile and wish him good morning, or they would catch each other's eye in the dining hall while Saffron ate lunch with Copper, sometimes nodding at each other while he studied late with Sionnach in the library—but Saffron was forced to spend most of his hours out of reach of his prince. When he did get a chance, the last thing he wanted was to spend it complaining about homework, asking for Cylvan's help, begging for his prince to read over his hand-written essays to check for spelling errors. Slowly, he stopped asking Cylvan to help him at all, not wanting to worry him. Saffron could figure it out. He'd dreamed of attending school for his entire life, he'd taught himself how to read, how to draw, how to get by—he could figure out how to study and catch up on homework and even get passing grades.

At least with the small outing with Sionnach, he'd worked through the thing inhibiting his voice. It was another few days before he could speak completely normally again, for him to go an entire conversation without choking once, but he still found himself touching his throat occasionally without thinking. He started tucking the chair under the knob of his bedroom door before going to sleep, at first without realizing what he was doing. Even after realizing, he continued like it was normal. It was a comforting action, even if it was strange. Even if he didn't know how he would explain to Copper or anyone else if they ever saw it.

All the while, Fiachra refused to don another messenger token. She only ever left Saffron's room when he went with her. He hardly needed to use the recall ring on their walks, as she rarely flew out of sight, no matter how high she swooped in and out overhead. If he ever lost sight of her, he could practically count down to when she would come sweeping back again to skim the top of his head, mess up his hair, then flap away again. Like she was the one keeping track of him, instead of the other way around. When asking Cylvan if that was normal or not, Cylvan talked about his own experience training Balor to deliver messages, mostly about how the raven was eager to get far away from his perch at any given opportunity, sometimes even dropping parchment and pens into Cylvan's lap to request something to fly off and deliver.

When Fiachra soon even refused to nest in the paddock with other student birds, bringing her own trinkets and treasures, branches and leaves, cotton fluff and fur to build a home in the clock on Saffron's mantle, Saffron knew it had to be something more than laziness or stubbornness. His owl was restless. She cleaned her nest just like Saffron cleaned his room and the rest of the dormitory. Obsessively. Especially when he couldn't sleep, when his mind scrambled with anxiety over one homework assignment or another, or as robins came from Letty telling him how more palace beantighes were talking about leaving, or how Saffron himself swore the staff at Mairwen looked a little thinner. He couldn't seem to escape signs of Ryder anywhere.

He tried not to think about it too much. He didn't want to

think about how Fiachra's near-death experience at Ériu's shrine might have traumatized her in the same way Saffron's experience in Danann House had. He tried not to think about it—but couldn't deny the bond they formed while passing gifts back and forth, walking silently in the woods together, checking up on one another between classes. A messenger bird who couldn't fly, a high fey lord who wasn't a fey at all. Even if she couldn't deliver letters for him—Saffron was happy to have a friend to keep him company while he cried over homework at midnight, or screamed into his pillow from the stress of it all.

Copper sat on the couch in the common room one evening, distracting Fiachra with pieces of jerky by tossing them into the air for her to hop and catch, while Saffron dug through her increasingly-cluttered hovel in the mantle clock in his room. He knew he had to work fast, else she notice and squabble at him for stealing her treasures, feeling exactly like he used to digging through the pixie hollow in search of stolen trinkets from Beantighe Village. Especially as he uncovered various access tokens from around campus, he smiled wistfully to himself, tucking them into his pocket to see if they were worth trying to return, later. Access tokens, the shiny nibs of quills, hair clips, a thin makeup brush, an earring, a dozen black feathers of every size stolen from messenger crows she chased down in the sky, Saffron left as much of Fiachra's treasure where he found them, only purging what he knew should be returned—only for the world to slow to a ringing halt when his fingers trailed over something unexpected. He stared at it, heart pounding in his ears in confusion.

A golden access ring from Morrígan Academy.

20

———

THE BONFIRE

Saffron sent another letter to Baba Yaga the following morning, that time using Cylvan's bird to do it. Cylvan was even thrilled at the request, since Balor had resorted to pulling out his hair while he slept in protest for being kept inside for too long. With Saffron joining him in Avren, he simply had no one else to send messages or gifts to regularly, and the poor bird was going stir crazy. Saffron hoped it meant the message would be delivered even sooner. Clearly, by the ring in her nest, Fiachra had made it all the way to Morrígan at some point after all—and Saffron could only wonder exactly when and where the letter was lost. He didn't know which unsettled him more, the thought of someone having the one he sent, or reading the one Baba Yaga replied with.

SAFFRON DIDN'T REALIZE BELTANE HAD COME UNTIL Copper was pounding on his door a few nights later, asking if he wanted to go to Avren for the festival. It came at the exact worst moment, as Saffron's mouth was indisposed on Cylvan's anatomy for the first time in two weeks. He only barely lurched upright and smothering his prince beneath the blankets when Copper threw the door open to ask again.

"A-a festival? It's tonight? God, I didn't realize," he wheezed, fighting to sound like he didn't just have something hard pressed into the back of his throat. "Um—yeah, sure, of course. I'll meet you outside, alright? Oh, who else are you inviting?"

Copper narrowed his eyes. Saffron frowned, narrowing them back.

"I know who you're going to ask about."

"Who? There are at least two names on my mind."

"Two?" Copper scowled, crossing his arms. "I didn't invite the goat. Either of them."

"Wh—'either' of them?"

"Yeah—the goat with the legs. And the goat on the throne."

The body crushed beneath Saffron squirmed slightly, releasing a muted grunt when Saffron elbowed him in the stomach. "Who is the goat on the throne, exactly?"

"The prince."

"Why is he a goat?"

"He has horns too, you know? Dunno why he thinks he's in any place to bully Sionnach for theirs."

Saffron bit back a smile. "And what makes you think Prince Cylvan was the other person I was thinking of? I barely know him."

"Considering the way you sigh every time he walks in and out of a room, or the way you light up when he's mentioned, or how you keep checking the mail for another gala invite, I'm assuming you meant him. But I already told you once, we're not friends, and I'm not going to formally introduce you anywhere outside of his stupid galas. Including tonight. At the festival."

"Well, I don't really need you to introduce me, since I already got my second invitation to the gala next week, so..."

Beneath him, Cylvan mumbled something about being *'descended from dragons'* before calling Copper a dirty name, but

Saffron smothered him further. "Give me twenty minutes and I'll get dressed, alright? I'm going to invite Sionnach, though."

"C'mon, Saff, Sionnach is—"

"Sionnach's my friend. And if you want to be my friend, too, you have to be nice to them. You know that. I intend on telling Prince Cylvan the same thing, one day."

Copper groaned—and Cylvan groaned mutedly in tandem—and the fey lord in the doorway threw his head back and collapsed against the frame in the most dramatic way possible. Saffron told him to get out and finish getting ready. He waited a few extra moments after the door closed before releasing Cylvan from his blanket prison, laughing when Cylvan gasped from nearly suffocating.

"He dares call me a goat when he's a genuine, dirty little mongrel! Of course a fox would compare a dragon to a goat, that *prick!*"

"Are you really descended from dragons, my lord?" Saffron asked with a sigh, slipping back into a seductive tone and pushing Cylvan down into the pillows again. He flattened himself between Cylvan's legs, taking the prince's cock back into his mouth to finish what he started. It met the back of Saffron's throat as Cylvan exhaled a satisfied sound, grasping Saffron's hair and gently rolling his hips in and out.

"You'll have to—ask my mother about it, one day. I get my horns and dragonesque lineage—*mmh*—from them," he said through clenched teeth, grinning all the while. Saffron rolled his eyes before teasing Cylvan with a few searching fingers between his legs, giggling as the prince bucked and nearly choked him. "Are you really—going to subject yourself to Avren's silly festival? You wouldn't rather—spend the rest of the night with me, beantighe? Even after we've been apart for so long?"

Saffron smirked, pulling back until his lips curved over the end of Cylvan's length, leaving him wanting.

"Perhaps I'll wait for you to come find me in the city, to finish what we started in an alleyway or some other dirty place. Maybe a temple to some fey god like you once offered. How about that?"

"You wouldn't dare. Hey—Saffron! Godsdamnit, Saffron, no, don't leave me like this—!" he agonized as Saffron wiped his mouth, laughing and scrambling away when Cylvan lunged and grappled for his arm. Yanking him back, Saffron let out a sharp laugh, only for it to be cut off again by Cylvan's mouth. Their lips pressed into one another, like two pieces made to fit in place, before Saffron finally pulled away with a content smile.

"Will you really not go with me?" he asked. "To my first Avren festival? You're really going to let Copper be my first for something else? You got so upset last time."

"I really would rather not," Cylvan answered, mumbling it and kissing Saffron again. "Why would I, when you're all the entertainment I could ever want right here?"

Saffron smirked. He kissed Cylvan again, hands returning to the prince's erection and stroking until he melted, then using his mouth again to devour every inch and leave nothing behind. Only once Cylvan was satisfied did Saffron finally push away, wiping his mouth on his hand and hopping to his feet. "Then you're welcome to lie here in bed and wait for me to come back. But I think it's important for me to take part in high fey celebrations. You know, to act the part and all that."

"Am I not celebration enough?" Cylvan draped himself over the bed as dramatically as Copper had against the doorframe. "Am I truly not enough to keep you satisfied?"

"Of course you are, your highness," Saffron fluttered his eyelashes, before stripping off his shirt to change into something else. "But I have royal duties too, you know. You can join me or stay here."

"Are you really going to invite the goat?"

"Sionnach. And yes."

Cylvan collapsed back into the pillows, rolling back and forth and complaining a moment longer before finally sighing in defeat and sitting up again. "Fine," he grumbled. "I will wait and rot in my own loneliness while you go enjoy yourself with your poor choice in company."

"Fine," Saffron whispered, kissing him on the forehead. "But if you insist on being so stubborn, at least promise me you'll come back later tonight so we can finish what we started. Even if I'm too drunk to move. Just do whatever you please with me."

"You've given your consent, I will do exactly that," Cylvan sighed, taking his time as he pulled his pants up and went to the window. He leaned against it for a minute, looking as sad and dejected as possible, but Saffron turned and went about choosing a top to wear. Cylvan pursed his lips before sitting on the edge of the windowsill, tipping backward and falling out of it in finality. Like a man leaping to his death. Copper could never hold a candle to the Prince of Alfidel's dramatics.

SAFFRON DRESSED IN A SOFT PINK BLOUSE AND BROWN pants, running fingers through his hair to try and comb down the mess left behind by Cylvan's hands. A part of him regretted kicking the prince out—there was a lingering desire in the pit of his stomach that had also gone unsatisfied—but the thought of going somewhere new, seeing something new, with new friends he was still trying to get to know better, was exciting. He hoped Cylvan would still change his mind and surprise him.

Knocking on Sionnach's door across the hall, it didn't take much convincing for them to agree to join him—until Saffron mentioned Copper waiting outside, having to shove himself between the door and the doorjamb before Sionnach could slam it in refusal. Saffron promised Copper wouldn't give them any trouble, and if he did, Saffron would gladly shove him into the Beltane fire as sacrifice. Sionnach's resolve eventually broke, silently changing their clothes all while Saffron repeated reassurances.

"I really like your outfit," he said as they descended the stairs for the front door. Sionnach flushed in embarrassment, flattening the front of their skirt and button-down blouse cinched up to the collar. Their slender legs and tail were distracting, even to him, and Saffron couldn't stop staring. It was the first time he'd seen their bare arms as well, finding them as smooth as his own and covered in freckles. The soft downy fur only extended to their legs. Would that be strange to comment on? Saffron had to resist touching them, constantly wondering if even their bare skin was as soft as their fur.

"I was wonderin' what was taking you so long," Copper scoffed when they met him in the dorm courtyard, arms crossed and looking Sionnach up and down with an impish smirk on his face. Like he was preparing an insult, like he was about to say something terribly rude—but his eyes skimmed up and down Sionnach again, then again, before he scoffed once more and turned suddenly, declaring they were going to miss all the good food. Sionnach was pale as a ghost when Saffron finally looked back at them, chuckling under his breath and taking their hand to head for the horse stables. Apparently even Copper couldn't find anything to insult when Sionnach looked so cute.

Beltane in Beantighe Village was all about dancing, bonfires, and finally being able to drown oneself in alcohol scrounged and saved for celebrations like those. As they made their way toward Avren, the distant sights and sounds of a high fey festival made Saffron wonder how those in the village were doing. How they were celebrating. If the improvements all around meant they'd been given more food and drink and supplies to celebrate with as well. Closing his eyes, he made a tiny prayer to Ériu, asking that she bless them with endless alcohol and the foresight to keep the bonfire at a manageable level. God knew the cottages didn't need to be burned down for a second time.

Avren smelled of burning spiced logs before they even made it off the road from Mairwen. Saffron could hear the music, the cheering and laughing; he could smell the decadent treats and practically tasted hot sugar and bread on the air. His heart swelled in anticipation, biting back too big of a smile all while nudging his horse, Boann, to pick up the pace. He wanted to see it. He wanted to be in it. He wanted a night of pure indulgent fun, where he wouldn't have to think about anything except keeping his friends accounted for and drinking until the world tumbled all around him. God, what a relief. He was going to get absolutely fucked up.

Leaving Boann at the stables with the others, Saffron didn't hesitate to find something to eat and drink like he wished, and Copper was close on his heels. He scoured vendor tables selling bundles of flowers and herbs, eyes sparkling at fertility totems carved from rose quartz and garnet. He held a piece of phallic quartz the size of his arm in one hand and a pint of ale in the other when Sionnach finally flushed so hot they were the color of apples, snatching the crystal away and steering Saffron off in the opposite direction.

He showed his friends how to weave crowns from ferns and flowers and grass, making an extra one from purple wildflowers and irises just in case they ran into a certain royal stranger later in the evening. Both Sionnach and Copper watched in rapt attention, but neither asked who the extra crown was for. Perhaps neither of them really wanted to know the answer. Saffron donned both on his head and acted like it was a drunken accident.

They danced around one of the dozen bonfires in the courtyard between city blocks, spilling more ale as Copper spun Saffron in circles then grabbed him by the waist to lift and throw him. Saffron never stopped laughing, not knowing the dance or its steps, standing no chance as it was clearly something from the Fall Court where Copper was from. Saffron gladly let it happen to him, until his drink was empty and he had a free hand to pull Sionnach in, instead, stumbling back and clapping with the crowd while his two friends awkwardly found their step with one another. Sionnach was back to blushing beet-red while Copper struggled to keep pace with a shorter, lighter partner, but soon found a rhythm and spun and threw and pulled Sionnach just as much as he had Saffron. Sionnach lacked the same hesitation with the movements as Saffron did, from the Fall Court themself, and Saffron's heart lifted as he watched how effortlessly they moved with one another. Without meaning to. Even if Copper frowned like he hated every second, even if Sionnach was apprehensive the entire time, Saffron was glad Copper at least wasn't so cruel to knock Sionnach off their feet or, god forbid, trip them into the fire in front of the rest of the city. Even Sionnach eventually cracked a smile, though they never met Copper's eyes.

"A little drink and suddenly they're as wild as humans, don't you think?"

Saffron jumped and whirled around, before frowning at the last person he expected—or wished—to see. His mood instantly soured at the sight of Ryder grinning at him, features slightly changed from what Saffron remembered, realizing why when he spotted a pair of pointed ears. He was wearing a glamour, not unlike Saffron's, in order to blend in. Saffron didn't care to question why, and Ryder laughed when he turned his nose up and away. The man nudged Saffron in the back, leaning closer to be heard over the surrounding cheers and merrymaking.

"I saw you dancing with that big ginger one. Did you used to dance with Hollow like that back in the Spring Court?"

"It's none of your business, but yes," Saffron snapped. He focused on clapping with the music, watching his friends circle the flames like Ryder wasn't there. Trying to appear too busy to chat. Or, at the very least, not interested. But the man was persistent.

"It's a little different how they do it here, isn't it? In the Winter Court, you know, they—"

"I'm from the Winter Court," Saffron grumbled, hoping no one else heard, but growing more irritated the more Ryder talked like he knew everything. "I know how they dance on Beltane. In every part."

"Me, too."

Saffron glanced back at him, surprised that he was surprised. Ryder smirked.

"From the Winter Court, that is."

"Forgive me for not believing you."

"Why not?"

"Because I think you're someone who says whatever you think the other person wants to hear. But it won't work on me."

"And here I thought we'd finally gotten past all this the last time we were together. You think I'd lie about something like that? Maybe you should have a little more to drink, to soften you up again. I liked you better when you were clinging to me for balance. Much cuter."

"We didn't... get past anything," Saffron said, but felt instantly embarrassed. He glanced down at the drink in his hand, wondering if throwing back the entire thing really would make that interaction easier to manage.

"Ah... well, come on, then." Ryder claimed Saffron's hand, making Saffron yelp. He nearly tripped over his own feet, digging in his heels as Ryder took Saffron's drink and handed it off, then led him toward the dancing circle in the middle. Saffron was a little too buzzed to put up a real fight, instead tripping on a piece of cobblestone and tumbling into Ryder's chest. Ryder caught him easily.

"Stop it!" Saffron hissed, clawing at Ryder's hand, but Ryder positioned his feet in a way Saffron hadn't seen in a long, long time. It made his heart thump, before sighing and closing his eyes. Accepting defeat, wishing for it to all be over with quickly, he matched the position—and with all the ease of two Winter Court-born humans, they slipped into the steps of northern Beltane dance.

There was no *start of the harvest* in the Winter Court, at least not like in warmer courts. In places farthest north, the snow never even fully melted, though the middle of summer would be warm enough to strip off heavy coats and scarves in favor of lightweight tartan sweaters and linen pants. It was always during those warm weeks that Beltane was celebrated, always during different weeks depending on where the town was located, making it one of the longest-running holidays celebrated across the coldest court in Alfidel. A traveling festival. Before Saffron worked at Morrígan, he would always spend a month at a time traveling with Luvon to every Winter Court town to sell wines and watch Winter Court fey celebrate, all in ways that were exactly the same, but different. The same foods but different spices. The same candies but different flavors. The same bonfires but with different spiced logs.

That was how he knew exactly where Ryder had learned his way of dancing. The same but different. He wasn't from Amber Valley, or the Ambegun Academy area. His steps originated from as far north as Saffron ever joined Luvon to sell his wares, a place called Fjornar, where they never spent the night because Saffron's patron-master was too afraid of freezing to death. A place they needed special permission to enter the gates of, and even then only into the small town on the outskirts, because it was considered sacred to the high fey. Luvon never explained why, and Saffron never asked a lot of questions. He never thought about it at all, until that moment. Until he was drawn in by Ryder's steps, hands on Saffron's waist, moving and turning as a bead of sweat dripped down the side of his face from the effort. Until Saffron even smiled every time Ryder met his hands and matched his steps perfectly. Knowing what Saffron would do, how he would step, where to meet him. Saffron had rarely been able to dance with anyone like that in Beantighe Village, since most of the others working there came from Spring or Summer Court families. He'd learned all of their steps, instead, and loved every moment of it. But to be able to dance something from home, from a place he always missed, it was enchanting. It gripped him in warm, comfortable hands, allowing them to twist his heart up in excitement and glee.

They danced until the music swelled, turning and stepping faster and faster until it crescendoed in a final turn and step. Around them, the crowd cheered and applauded—though the sound of it all fell away as Saffron stared at the man standing at arm's length from him, fingertips barely touching in the final step of the dance. Both of them breathing heavily, smiling at one another like they each had something they wished to say. But Saffron didn't know. Saffron didn't know if there was anything to say. Just like the other handful of times he'd crossed paths with Ryder Kyteler, no matter how brief—he was always left a little speechless afterward, for better or worse. Speechless, and just a little bit more curious as to who the man really was.

He wasn't sure how he ended up fast asleep and woozy at a tavern table on the street, but it was Sionnach's voice that woke him, and Copper's hand on his back that pulled him to sit up. Saffron giggled, trying to speak full sentences, but he felt drunker than ever, thoughts a swampy mess and memories even blurrier. He remembered dancing. He danced so much. He vaguely remembered sitting and chatting with Ryder outside the tavern, even laughing with him. How Ryder said lots of things like *'I'm glad we bumped into each other again; I always have fun with you, you know.' 'Have you had any other frights with your magic, lately?' 'That's good to hear... remember what I said about the solstice, though. It's only getting closer. Please, come see me soon...'*

God, he drank so much. He got exactly as drunk as he wanted to. Enough to apparently flop lifelessly against the tavern table, where not even Ryder could resuscitate him.

They rode back to Mairwen with Boann leashed to the back of Copper's horse, Saffron slumped in the saddle behind his giant roommate with arms secured tightly around his thick middle. Trying to keep his eyes open as even Copper struggled to keep the horse on the road, constantly steering them into the bushes and once into a low-hanging branch that smacked both of them from the saddle. Laughing and talking way too loud and constantly getting shushed by Sionnach who was the soberest of all of them. Saffron kept trying to add in on the conversation, too, feeling like it was rude not to, but he couldn't find any words to piece together. It felt like his brain had been squished around in by searching fingers that left trails behind. Maybe only because of how hard he clawed at his own mind to summon memory of how to speak proper words. Rolling his tongue over in his mouth, he licked his lips, but couldn't follow any threads that weren't draped in inebriated darkness.

Arriving back at Muirín dorm, Sionnach stood no chance hauling both Saffron and Copper up the stairs, and it took four times as long as if they'd been able to walk upright. Once through the door to their room, Copper collapsed facedown on the couch and snored in an instant, leaving Saffron on his own to stumble toward his bedroom. He accidentally crashed through the door a little too hard, startling the absolute shit out of the wild shadowy thing waiting impatiently on his bed. Already naked, hair spread over the pillows, a glass of wine in his hand and a book on his lap barely covering his modesty.

"Ohhhh, shit, what's this? What's come into room—into my room—while was I—away?" Saffron slurred a little too loud, smiling like on the verge of tears with restrained laughter. Cylvan stared at him a moment longer, before quickly setting his wine glass on the bedside table. Saffron managed to slam the door behind him, though nearly faceplanted into the floor in the process. Cylvan caught him before he could fall, and Saffron grinned up at him like a drunk in love. Ah—that was exactly what he was. He pawed at the flower crowns still, by some miracle, in his hair, smashing the wildflower and purple iris circlet onto Cylvan's head, looping it under his horns.

"Beautiful," he grinned, pressing hands to Cylvan's cheeks enough to make the prince's mouth pucker. "You're so beautiful. Beautiful dragon princess. My king of the forest. I'm your

Mayday queen, please, do with me as you wish. I danced a lot. I drank so much. And I touched so many crystal penises."

Cylvan burst out laughing, having to bite it back so as to not alarm the man slumped on the couch in the front room. He asked Saffron to tell him more, to tell him everything, tilting his head up and kissing him before tossing him onto the bed. Saffron kissed him back like he'd never tasted anything sweeter.

21

THE IMPOLITE

It was a new sort of overwhelm Saffron felt while preparing for his second gala, that time without Luvon there to join him. Luvon, who had returned to the Winter Court weeks earlier, leaving his townhouse empty except for the beantighes who made sure it remained upkept in case of any future surprise visits. And—to help Saffron dress for his fetes. Just like they did that night.

All the while, Saffron couldn't help but wonder what Luvon and his family were doing that same night. Luvon, whose life had essentially gone back to normal the moment he was back north, while Saffron continued to have his own split into a thousand directions with every new morning. Saffron envied him. A part of Saffron even wished he'd gone with him. That night was the first time he was dressed by beantighe-hands only, without his patron father there to compliment him and tell him everything would be alright. It would be his first time traveling and arriving at the palace by himself, without Luvon there to walk him arm-in-arm like a comfort.

While Saffron knew he could do it, he knew how to do it— the loneliness was tangible. Despite being surrounded by beantighes who helped him get ready—Saffron suddenly felt more alone than ever.

WORD OF SAFFRON'S STRANGE BEHAVIOR FROM THE first gala had spread through the other courtiers, it being the first thing he heard as he arrived at the palace. Whispers of how he'd been so rude to Lady Callan and forced Prince Cylvan to *show deference* to a beantighe. He grabbed and chugged down the first glass of wine he could find to keep his annoyance under the surface.

Just like the first time, Saffron sought out Cylvan in the crowd the moment he arrived. Like a moth to flame, it took almost no effort at all, as the prince was as handsome and perfect as always, and stood out like he knew it. That night, Cylvan wore a stiff high-collared tunic in black with emerald-green accents, a keyhole opening in the front showing a peek of pale skin, and dripping with gold beads like a waterfall down his chest and back. The tunic cinched tightly at his waist, emphasizing the silhouette of his shoulders and chest, tapering to his stomach, his hips, to those slender legs Saffron knew were stronger than they looked. He had to look away again when he thought about it, immediately rocketed back to the blurry, euphoric memories he'd managed to keep from the night he returned from the Beltane festival. Cylvan had done such nasty, terrible things to him, and he would always regret not being sober enough to remember every moment whenever he wanted. Ah—did anyone else see how he blushed right away?

Oh—Sionnach definitely did. Sionnach, who attended that gala after an unexpected invitation formally arrived in their mail slot, who looked pale and ghostlike for a myriad of reasons, a stark contrast from the fitted lilac blouse and long skirt they wore. Their look of veiled horror directed at Saffron was one of many, like they couldn't believe someone they considered a friend would find such a nasty daemon so attractive, how he could ever let his eyes linger across the room on the personification of evil for so long. Saffron only shrugged like he couldn't help it. They really had no idea. If only they knew the fuzzy memories Saffron worked tirelessly to uncover from the night of Beltane.

Saffron's own outfit was a visual opposite from the prince, dressed in a soft blue blouse embroidered with green vines and leaves cascading down his arms and dangling off his shoulders. His high-waisted slacks were a darker shade of blue and embroidered with pastel flowers around the waist, disappearing into tall boots that came all the way up to his knees. He tried to focus on how much he liked the design instead of letting his eyes linger on the dark, evil daemon prince across the ballroom any longer. He focused on how delicate the little flowers and leaves stitched into the airy fabric were. How their color matched to the emerald stone in his courting ring. How, that time, he definitely, most definitely, was not going to make a fool out of himself while looking prettier than he ever thought possible. He stood out, but that time for all the right reasons. Not because he forced the prince to *show deference* to a beantighe, or whatever those gossip columns said. He would be on his best behavior. He would act like someone worthy of marrying the prince, becoming a prince, then one day King of Alfidel...

But then someone slapped a hand on Saffron's back, and Sionnach paled further as a loud exclamation of greeting skipped across the ballroom floor, turning heads with wrinkled noses. Saffron knew who it was without having to look—he'd grown accustomed to the sound of Copper's laughter. He was surprised the lord had been invited at all—but perhaps even more surprised at how well he cleaned up, red hair pulled back into a small ponytail and littered with shiny clips, donning a forest green tunic that admittedly made him look like a palace beantighe at first glance. Saffron couldn't help but wonder if that was done on purpose, like the dress code was shared incorrectly on Cylvan's behalf, and he and Sionnach could only bite back bouts of laughter as Copper pretended like he hadn't been made a fool of.

"Look at you, swooning over dark lord spindle-legs over there. Careful, I think they prefer not to let this part of the stairs get wet," the fey lord said, doing a poor job of hiding his annoyance as he went on.

Saffron punched Copper in the stomach in a rush of embarrassment, making him grunt, then wheeze out an apology. Behind him, Sionnach stifled a laugh, though it was a little shrill.

"What are you doing here?" Saffron asked. "You're not… You're not here because you want to…? Are you…?"

"Fuck no," Copper groaned, straightening back up again and plucking a glass of wine from a passing beantighe's tray. "My old man heard there hadn't been any dé Bricriu representation at any of these suitor galas and thought it'd look bad for the family name and all. Like the royal family had no interest in even some friendly intrigue, y'know?"

"I guess," Saffron muttered, though it made him glance at Sionnach, too. Sionnach, after Cylvan offered his initial informal gala invitation—never knowing it first happened at Saffron's request—told him they'd never received an invite to any galas, either, and wished to keep it that way. Saffron narrowed his eyes back to the dark spot on the dance floor, wondering if Cylvan was really so keen on keeping in Saffron's good graces by extending basic formalities to the people he'd made friends with. Copper, meanwhile, downed the whole glass in his hand in one go, before wiping his mouth and appraising Sionnach. Up and down. Up and down. Even a third time. It was a little too close to how he looked Sionnach up and down before the Beltane festival, and Saffron wondered if they'd end up dancing together that night, too.

"How about you, goat?" he mumbled. "Didn't know they were doing a countryside theme tonight."

Saffron smacked Copper on the chest again, making him huff.

"I—I'm not here for that, either," Sionnach insisted. "I'm here to support Saffron, of course. As his friend. He's still not used to Alvish galas, after all, and I didn't want him to feel self-conscious. And obviously I know better than to refuse an invite from the kings, no matter what the occasion, so... at least I was invited on my own merit... and not because my father insisted, or whatever..." they trailed off into a self-conscious mumble, like the attempt at insult lost steam the longer it went on. Or perhaps because of some other reason, as Sionnach quickly averted their eyes as a sarcastic smile formed over Copper's mouth.

"Right. Your father. Do satyrs even know how to hold a pen? I always thought the hoof would get in the wa—" he grunted as Saffron elbowed him once more, hissing threats for him to check his behavior. Copper wheezed, rubbing his stomach before offering Saffron an apologetic smile. "Right—no wonder you didn't like that countryside comment, *Lord* Saff, I forgot you're from there."

"I'm not—!" Saffron started, but didn't know what exactly he was trying to defend. Huffing again, he snatched his own drink from a passing tray and gulped half of it down.

"Don't tell me... You're not gonna seek prince fancy-foot's hand in marriage either, right?" Copper went on, nudging Saffron in the side as all of them turned back to where Cylvan left the ballroom hand-in-hand with someone Saffron didn't know. Another suitor in an endless line, proven by the number of people who followed right on his heels. Saffron bit his lip, swirling the drink in his glass.

"I... don't know," he mumbled. "Why not?"

"I should have known. Look, I know it's easy to get all oogly over him on campus, but you gotta make sure you know who you're crushing on before attending their suitor galas willy-nilly. I don't know how things work in Alvénya, but here, you have to be more careful than that. God, you're so lucky I'm here and willing to tell you everything, as a friend. Where should I start?"

"Everyone here is ogling him as much as the next fey," Saffron argued, though tried not to. He had to bite back everything else he wished to say, reminding himself he was just a 'country fey'.

Just a country fey from Alvénya. Why would he know any of the worst rumors about Prince Cylvan?

"Sure, but only because marrying into royalty will outweigh any threats of a Night Court. Not 'cause they actually like the guy."

"He's been nice to me," Saffron insisted. Copper laughed, and Saffron had to resist punching him again. "It's true! He's been nothing but nice to me, actually—"

"Didn't he kick you into the mud on your first day on campus?"

"He was technically kicking me," Sionnach muttered. "Saffron was simply standing in the wrong place."

"That's..." But Saffron couldn't think of a way to defend it, especially without revealing he and Cylvan had definitely shared more than a few words with one another in passing. He didn't even really want to, especially since Cylvan actually did deserve all of the shit-talking for that stunt in particular, but any less-than-positive talk about his raven behind his back always made Saffron's nerves fizzle like he was about to catch flame. "I mean... maybe he's just misunderstood, is all..."

Sionnach and Copper glanced at one another—before Copper erupted into laughter, and even Sionnach laughed behind their hand. Saffron commanded them both to *quit it*, he was being serious! But Sionnach shook their head, placing a hand on Saffron's shoulder like Saffron was the sweetest, more innocent, naive little fawn in the forest.

"It's alright, Saffron. You don't have to defend him. You can think he's handsome and nice, too. Just... take your feelings slowly, don't jump into anything too quickly, especially if he approaches you for anything. I mean, you're cute, so I doubt he's going to bully you to your face. He usually doesn't act out where most people can see, either, like in the middle of campus. He's sneakier than that."

"Yeah, Saff. All his worst tricks are done by the cover of night," Copper said with threat, wiggling his fingers for emphasis.

"Or under his breath when he wants to embarrass you," Sionnach added on. "Like when he acts shocked I'm not wearing uniform-assigned shoes... then gasps and apologizes because he 'forgot they don't make shoes for feet like mine'..."

Copper laughed louder than he should have at that, slapping a hand on Sionnach's narrow shoulder and nearly sending them to the floor. Saffron steamed in silence, swallowing back the rest of his drink. He nearly shoved his way back into the conversation with more veiled defenses of his rude-and-callous-but-genuinely-misunderstood-prince-of-darkness, but then Lady Maeve suddenly appeared, looking like a goddess in a silver dress that clung to every inch of her. Saffron smirked, expecting her to scold the others for being so noisy at a formal event—disappointed when instead, she wrinkled her nose.

"You guys talking about Cylvan? He really insists on dressing like it's his own funeral for every event. Yet he gets so angry when you imply he's anything other than a ray of sunshine straight out of Lugh's ass. Gods—every time I'm forced to attend one of these galas I'm reminded of how close I came to being the one to take that walking piece of darkness' hand. Every day I thank my parents for shuffling me away to the Summer Court before it could go any further. Even though everyone here keeps asking when I'm gonna dance with him... *Please.* Maybe when my head's lopped off from my body and I stumble into him chasing after it."

Saffron gaped at her, never expecting such crude language to come out of the mouth of the same person who kept herself so pristine and flawless even while beating down Copper's bedroom door, but then saw how clear it was that Maeve was drunker than all three of them combined. Her words never slurred, her posture never sagged, she never even wavered on her heels, but it was obvious the second she met Saffron's eyes and smiled lazily, before patting his hair then pinching one of his cheeks.

"You clean up well, country-boy. Like a little bunny rabbit. I just want to put you in a basket with a bunch of fruits and flowers, and carry you on my arm through town..." She glanced at

Sionnach, next, who stiffened in anticipation. But then her eyes flickered to Copper, before taking a long, slow drink of wine. "Seems we have the whole farm in attendance. Appropriate that the prince only received courting-lockets from forest creatures, when he's the nastiest demon-of-the-wood of all."

Saffron gave up on trying to defend anyone, knowing it was futile, knowing there was nothing he could say to any of them when—for one, they weren't entirely wrong. For two, it would look strange for him to go on and on about how Cylvan was actually tender, and polite, and kind, and all of those things, especially if Saffron really was the only person he had ever been *those things* with. His heart squeezed at the thought, fighting the urge to snatch another drink from a passing beantighe, reminding himself he needed to be on his best behavior. He wrung his hands together, instead, searching the ballroom once more as the others went on about how miserable Cylvan was as a classmate.

Cylvan danced with Lady Callan when Saffron spotted him again, their hands pressed flat together, circling one another, smiling politely as flute and string music guided their steps. Could nobody else see how Cylvan's expression was empty? How his smile was just an act? It was so lifeless. It never changed. It never twitched or widened, it didn't even lift the bottoms of his eyes like it always did when he smiled at Saffron. Was Saffron the only one in that entire room who knew Cylvan's bottom lashes creased whenever he genuinely smiled?

Behind him, Sionnach, emboldened by their own inebriation, went on a long tangent about how if they were all wild animals, then Cylvan was no different considering his horns. Their hands waved around in emphasis as they rambled on about something called 'the zodiac' that was popular in the human world, which assigned Cylvan something about an ox, only for Copper to interrupt and ask if there was anything about a fox. Sionnach grinned like it was the most cutting insult they could utter, to tell him, no, humans didn't give a shit about foxes.

All the while—Saffron watched Cylvan. He just watched

Cylvan, as if there was no one else in the room at all. He heard what people said about him, in every direction, even as they stood mingling in the ballroom while he minded his business out on the garden terrace.

"Where is Daurae Asche? Their presence would certainly help lighten the mood."

"Did you see that scuff on Prince Cylvan's boot? So embarrassing."

"A scuff? Darling, did you see the hickey on his neck? Clearly he's doing more than just dancing with each of these suitors. How unbecoming of him."

"Well—his harmonious partner will only exist to please him carnally, we all know. There will be no harmony to offer in any other way."

"You misunderstand—having a harmonious hole to fuck all of his aggression into may be exactly what we need to keep the Night King from sinking us all the way into a Court of the Mounds."

"If my only job is to be fucked by him, then perhaps I will get my own locket portrait painted after all."

"You're naughty."

Saffron couldn't fucking take it anymore. If he heard it, Cylvan certainly did as well.

There wasn't much he could do—except, perhaps, remind the prince there was at least one person there at that gala who still thought kindly of him. He was just drunk enough to have the guts.

Saffron handed his drink off to Sionnach without warning, without a word. He weaved his way through the crowded ballroom toward the terrace entrance, where he had to pause and reorient himself before spotting his dark, shadowy, demon-of-the-wood amongst the courtiers who watched him dance. Whispering amongst themselves, smirking to one another, all of them with Cylvan's name on their tongues, but no propriety to color the words. The meager wine in Saffron's stomach boiled. He knew it wasn't appropriate, it wasn't the right time, but—he couldn't stand the thought of being there, standing there, hearing what people said where Cylvan couldn't hear, without doing something to insist the opposite could be true, too. There could be a single person at that suitor's gala who didn't only pursue the prince because a royal marriage would always be worth a Night Court.

Moving like a beantighe through the outside crowd, like water between river stones, he waited only as long as it took for the music to dwindle before rising, again. Other fey swapped partners, though Cylvan seemed fine to put on another show with Lady Callan. Perhaps because he felt like he had to, or because sticking with her meant he wouldn't have to start new platitudes all over again with someone else. Saffron was going to give him a break from it all.

Approaching where they began another dance, Lady Callan bumped into Saffron first, and Cylvan looked at him in surprise.

"Pardon my intrusion, your highness," he said with a newly-mastered, handsome fey-lord smile. Lady Callan scoffed, clearly recognizing him from the previous gala, and Saffron felt a sharp heel slam into the toe of his shoe. He flinched, but never took his eyes from Cylvan. He even side-stepped, putting himself directly between his prince and the lady. "I simply couldn't resist complimenting you on your appearance tonight. You truly are as breathtaking as everyone claims."

"What's the meaning of this?" Lady Callan snapped, grabbing Saffron by the arm and attempting to yank him away, but Saffron grabbed Cylvan's arm in turn, wrapping his hands around it flirtily. Cylvan only stared at him in confusion, a bit of disbelief, eyes searching every inch of Saffron's face for an explanation. As if he expected the only reason Saffron would approach without planning ahead of time was because something was *wrong*, never anticipating Saffron was simply a little buzzed, a little annoyed, jealous, possessive.

"I'm... aware, thank you, Lord Saffron," Cylvan finally answered, putting on a polite, yet still confused look. The words of someone trying not to fan any flames, an aloof prince who, in any other case, would respond the same way to exactly anyone else who so rudely interrupted. "I see you are wearing one of my father's designs, again. I appreciate the chance to see it up close. Perhaps later I can get a better look once I tire of dancing."

"I hoped you'd accept a dance with me, your highness," Saffron said, maintaining his pretty smile and fluttering his lashes. "I don't know the customs of such a thing in Alfidel, so excuse me if I am being rude."

"You're excused," Lady Callan growled, grabbing the back of Saffron's blouse to yank him away, but Cylvan put his hands out to steady him. His eyes shone with a strike of understanding, then a sparkle of rebellious thrill, and the uncertain smile on his face twitched into something a little more deviant.

"I believe you've once again indulged in plenty of Alvish wine, my lord," he said, hands sliding down Saffron's forearms to settle on his wrists. "It seems you still aren't used to how we drink in Avren. Perhaps I should escort you back to the ballroom, so you do not get lost."

"Will you dance with me there, your highness?" Saffron smiled. He saw the urge to misbehave flicker stronger behind Cylvan's eyes, like it was truly the most difficult choice he'd ever made. The naughtiness grew the more Saffron kept smiling at him, the more he teased under the cuffs of Cylvan's long sleeves with the tips of his fingers.

Cylvan's smile finally gave in fully to mischief, leaning in slightly to whisper a threat into Saffron's ear.

"You really should be taught some manners, Lord Saffron," he said. "I will be sure to do so later, out of sight of my esteemed guests. Until then, I want you to continue watching me dance with everyone except you, until the jealousy eats you alive."

Saffron smirked, though goosebumps traced down his arms.

"Perhaps I will find my own dance partners in the meantime," he whispered. Cylvan interrupted before he could continue:

"Only if you wish for this night to end in a bloodbath, Danu curse it."

Saffron bit back another smile, a little nervous giggle, stepping back as Cylvan removed his hands and turned back to Lady Callan. He said something about how 'Lord Saffron simply doesn't know any better, let us not hold it against him, he's still learning how to be a polite member of Alvish court...' and Lady Callan grinned, turning her nose up and tightening her hands on Cylvan's arm. Saffron was clearly meant to be embarrassed—but he stood there flushed, warm, wanting. He had to clench his fists in and out a few times while watching Cylvan and the fey lady walk away arm-in-arm back toward the ballroom, worried he might faint at the injection of pure heat Cylvan had left in him. The jealousy would certainly eat him alive.

But as Saffron followed Cylvan and the lady back toward the palace ballroom, fully intending on behaving as Cylvan suggested for the rest of the night—he saw the moment Cylvan's entire body stiffened. How he paused for a step at the mouth of the ballroom doors, before casting the quickest, briefest glance over his shoulder, as if to see if Saffron remained behind him. Saffron smiled playfully, wishing to tease him more —but then he saw what Cylvan did. He felt the sudden tension emanating from the ballroom, how the volume of string music and chatter had died down. His feet halted, rooted to the spot, only stumbling forward again when a wave of people from the terrace suddenly rushed the doors to see what was going on inside.

Black tunics. Black dresses. Black veils hiding faces. Silver, triangular pins on their chests and chains of silver charms and bells and glass vials of matching liquid around their waists. Jingling with every step as they made their way through the crowded ballroom, bodies moving quickly to step out of their way, as if it was a sin to be touched.

"Are those witchhunters? I thought they retired a century ago."
Saffron's ears rang as voices cascaded around him in an

instant, growing louder and softer with every slam of his heart against his ribs.

"This is my first time seeing any in person as well—"

"They have been surveying Avren more often recently. Perhaps because of the witch who attacked Lord Taran on Ostara?"

"Gods bless them, then."

"Is there a plague of them returned to Alfidel?"

"I hear they gather to revel naked in the woods. Trying to resurrect Ériu as a crimson witch. Forming a coven with only fellow changeling babies..."

"Why are they searching here instead of the beantighe dorms?"

"You don't think there are iron witch apologists here in the court, do you?"

"I mean... this is a gala of the seelie prince, don't forget."

A rush of cold adrenaline compelled his hand outward, grabbing a fistful of the back of Cylvan's tunic without thinking who might see. Cold, silver hands tightened around his throat. A tearing heat erupted in his forearm, the same hand clutching Cylvan's tunic as Saffron's mind raced and made it impossible to think straight. To consider what to do next. He should run—he should run, but everyone would see. They would question it. Why run? What was there to be afraid of? No high fey lord had anything to be afraid of—

Cylvan threw him another look over his shoulder, before turning forward again—but his hand bent behind his back. Saffron swiftly grabbed it, stepping in slightly more, blaming the closeness on the rambunctious crowd pushing behind him. He clung to Cylvan's hand with a tight, trembling fist, staring at the gold chains dangling from his back instead of the scene in the ballroom ahead of them. He didn't want to see. He didn't want anyone to see him. He wished to be a ghost. He wished—to be hidden beneath a veil.

The kings were away in the Fall Court; without them present to intervene, Cylvan would have to say something himself. Perhaps that was why he hesitated so long—even he was apprehensive. Saffron could feel it in the way his grip trembled in Saffron's just as much. God—Saffron wished he could say something. Do something. To do something more reassuring than simply holding his hand.

Ah—he reached down his shirt, pulling out the amethyst pendant. He closed his eyes, squeezing it tightly, knowing Cylvan always wore his as well. He would feel it. A flicker of reassurance. *It's fine. This is fine. I'm scared, but—it's going to be fine.*

As soon as Saffron did, Cylvan straightened slightly. He squeezed Saffron's hand once, twice, three times, before releasing him and pulling free from Lady Callan's grasp. He didn't glance back again, but instead, with a subtlety only Saffron could see, motioned to the inner wall of the ballroom with a finger. A lump formed in Saffron's throat, knowing what he meant. *Sneak out through the beantighe passage once you get a chance.* A part of Saffron wished he could protest, wanting to grab Cylvan by the back of the tunic again and hiss every argument he could think of —but then Cylvan stepped into the crowd, announcing his presence by asking, "What's the meaning of this? You were not invited here. And, with all due respect, I have no interest in courting an old witchhunter."

An uncomfortable chuckle rang out through the guests, though it admittedly eased the growing tension slightly. Saffron's ears rang too loudly to hear if there was any reply from the black-veiled visitors, taking the opportunity to side-step through the crowd that bustled further with want to hear everything. Maybe they wouldn't notice him slipping away after all. He might still know how to pass as a ghost when he needed to.

As much as Saffron hated leaving his seelie prince there to deal with it on his own, how he hated that there was nothing he could do—his eyes lingered on the silver potions dangling from the witchhunters' waists, and his instincts won out. He had no choice. He wouldn't stand a chance, he wouldn't have any excuse if for whatever reason, they made him take even the smallest sip. And he knew, as much as he hated to abandon Cylvan to deal with it alone, the prince would have a much better chance at doing so with all the finesse and elegance of someone like him if he knew Saffron was long gone and out of danger. If that was all Saffron could do to help, he would.

Finding the crease in the wall, moving silently, not a single head turning to see what he was doing, Saffron unlatched one of the wainscoting panels behind a massive bouquet of flowers. Hunching down, he stepped backward into the passageway, never taking his eyes from Cylvan who continued to monopolize everyone's attention in the center of the ballroom. Saffron barely released the breath he was holding once he thought he was safe, but then unexpectedly bumped into someone, turning quickly to find four pale-faced beantighes staring at him with wide, terrified eyes. They wore uniforms of the serving staff, and Saffron's heart pounded with relief that they'd had enough foresight to sneak away and hide, too, before any of the witchhunters spotted them and demanded an interrogation.

"Alright?" he asked. The one in the front nodded silently, before gulping back a lump in their throat.

"You're—you're one of us, aren't you?" they asked. Saffron's blood ran cold, staring at them, making them put their hands up slightly in defense. "I'm sorry—we've only heard rumors. That's all..."

Saffron didn't have to ask to know from whom, exactly, palace beantighes were hearing rumors. And it wasn't any of Saffron's own friends.

Knowing there was no use in trying to deny it, he nodded stiffly, then attempted to shimmy through the narrow opening to the side of them to escape. But the one who spoke grabbed his arm before he could get far.

"Th—the others," they said. "There were others gathered at the beantighe dorms, to be taken to the ruins tonight. You don't think...? Could someone have told them...?"

Saffron stared at them. The ringing in his ears grew to a fever pitch, until not a single thought formed before shattering like brittle ice. Wet, crimson magic dripped warmly from his nose. Blood, overwhelmed and bubbling in the back of his throat.

His body moved on its own. No longer needing his thoughts to direct it. Knowing without knowing.

He shoved past the beantighes hiding in the wall. He dragged himself as fast as he could through the narrow passageway, then shoved his way through the portal at the end. He rushed into the main hallway on the other side. He took only a moment to reorient himself, then took off running. All without a thought. Not a single full thought—only images. Broken fragments of panic.

His friends. Ryder. The dorms.

Could someone have told them?

"Fuck!" he gasped, clutching his chest as he ran, as his weak heart ached and pounded as hard as it could to keep up. As blood rushed up the back of his throat, filling his nose and mouth, though he never stopped to spit. His friends. Ryder. The dorms.

Could someone have told them?

22

THE NIGHTMARE

Blood spilled freely from Saffron's nose, coating his tongue and dripping from the corners of his mouth. It reminded him too much of Ostara. How wild he must have looked then, even with a veil on. How grateful he was for all other courtiers to be gathered in the ballroom to witness the drama unfolding there, so as to not cross paths with him. Would they think he was a ghost? Would they think the rowan witch who cursed Taran mac Delbaith had torn free of their silver and yew tomb, only to come and wreak havoc on them and their grandiose party all over again? Despite everything, he smirked. Bitterly. It tasted like rust and copper.

Doing his best to recall the way to the dorms from the first time he visited, he cursed himself for being so drunk that time, too. He had to stop following the lead of all the fey around him at every party—it was going to get him killed. It was going to result in nothing but foggy memories of his entire first year of school. Still, he managed to hurry with an unbalanced gait through the expansive palace gardens, constantly wiping blood from his nose and mouth on his sleeve, growing more and more unsteady with every step as the wooziness kicked in. Dizziness from earlier glasses of wine, from the amount of blood spilling out of him, the adrenaline inebriating him worse than any fairy wine ever could.

The gardens were dark, silent, empty in every direction. God, he hoped Cylvan was alright. He knew Cylvan, of all people, could handle such a delicate situation with all the grace and aplomb of a prince—but he couldn't silence the worries that they would do something horrible to him. All those people in that room, not a single ally once Saffron left. God, he prayed they would not choose that night to turn on him. He prayed, even with how much they disliked him, at least Copper, or Maeve, or Sionnach would do something, anything, to step in, if things took a turn for the worst. He would never forgive them, otherwise. Maybe he should have told them that before he left.

He pressed a hand to his chest when it wouldn't stop throbbing in pain. His vision grew fuzzier the harder he pushed himself, a combination of every faculty breaking down at once beneath the weight of crushing, frantic worry. His friends. His friends. He had to know if they were safe. He had to make sure they were safe, first, then he could collapse and die. Even more than Letty, Hollow, and Nimue—Saffron worried for every human there in the dorms. He even worried about Ryder, if it was true he was there to take more beantighes back to the Finnian Ruins. He worried there were other arid magic users unprepared for their things to be rifled through, either, not given enough warning to hide taboo belongings. He worried he would arrive to people bursting into flames on their knees, moments after cursed silver was poured into their mouths from a glass bottle.

The mental image made him stumble, flooded with the memory of smoke and burning flesh, the sound of cruel chanting ringing in his ears louder than his own gasping breaths. He tripped off the garden path into a tree, propping himself against it and hunching, fighting to catch his breath.

He thought he heard the crunching of boots approaching from behind, but saw nothing when he turned to look. Moving too quickly, he stumbled over an upturned root, throwing his hands out to catch himself—but he fell into a pair of outstretched, waiting arms, as if anticipating it. Saffron didn't recognize them at first, eyes blurry from the pain in his chest and the panic in his blood, but the sound of their voice was plenty enough to identify him. Saffron groaned audibly, and Ryder Kyteler chuckled. They really had to stop meeting like that.

"Easy there, your highness," he said in a low, gentle, teasing voice. "You don't look so good."

"What are you still doing here?" Saffron asked, attempting to push out of Ryder's arms, but Ryder held him in place.

"Same thing I was doing the last time," he said, unexpectedly pushing hair from Saffron's face with a frown, feeling the clammy sweat on his forehead. He wiped the blood from Saffron's nose with a thumb, frown only growing deeper. "What happened to you?"

Saffron was too disoriented, too worried about his friends to think straight, to shove Ryder away and command he keep his hands to himself—so he slumped against the man, secretly grateful for the extra support on his feet. Even if it was the very last person he'd hoped for. He caught his breath before answering.

"W-witchhunters in the ballroom. I have to make sure my friends are safe."

"You don't have to do that," Ryder answered. "You should find somewhere to go until they leave, Saffron, it isn't safe for you, either."

Saffron shook his head. Still clutching his chest, fighting to catch his breath, he memorized every inch of Ryder's face in the low light. That man that wasn't supposed to be there. Who Saffron knew, deep down, couldn't be trusted. That man who kept insisting he was Saffron's salvation, the only one who could teach him how to properly learn and control his wild rowan magic. He couldn't help but smile bitterly at the thought, especially in that moment, as that very magic was fighting to tear out of him, setting his forearm on fire, bursting from his nose and mouth like cotton from the split seams of a doll. God help him if the wolf emerged from his arm once more, tearing apart anyone who got in the way. Didn't Ryder know that? Didn't he know how dangerous Saffron was while blood spilled down his face?

"If you're going to insist on helping me—then help me to the dorms," he finally commanded. Ryder chuckled airily again, and it grated on Saffron's nerves like needles.

"I like when you use your royal voice on me. Alright, your highness, come on. Keep quiet, I'll take you where you need to go."

Saffron knew he still couldn't trust the man—he knew he shouldn't, at least, without question—but that was an emergency. He needed the help, and he would admit it. He only wished he wasn't so pathetic while asking for it. A part of him had hoped to go his entire life without ever asking Ryder Kyteler for anything at all; perhaps Ériu was punishing him for something. Perhaps for spilling human blood at the base of her abandoned shrine. Perhaps for dancing amongst high fey on Beltane. Either way, he groaned in defeat, slumping heavier against the man and accepting he had no choice but to rely on his help. Just for a little bit. Ryder seemed to enjoy the submission of the beantighe prince as much as Saffron hated it, smiling to himself the whole time he dragged Saffron's sorry, dizzy ass through the trees, keeping clear of the garden paths.

"Stop smiling like that," Saffron grumbled. "It's really pissing me off."

"I'm sorry. I can't help it. I've been waiting for another chance to prove I'm not a bad guy. This seems right up your alley, too, what with how much you love all those old romantic myths. Isn't this, objectively, sorta romantic?"

"How do you know any of that?" Saffron huffed. "I hate that you know things."

"I'm getting to know your friends better, that's all. They talk about you sometimes. Nothing suspicious, I promise."

Saffron wasn't convinced. He stared straight ahead, constantly wiping his nose, flexing his hand when his forearm flared up again with want to let the wolf free. That beast would race directly to the dorms and tear apart anything or anyone that posed a threat—or so Saffron imagined. He wasn't about to risk it to find out.

But then a rush of guilt and shame rattled through him like a beating drum. What if he'd accepted Ryder's help sooner? What if—he'd actually learned how to control the manifestation, so that it really could race ahead and help people in trouble? Instead, Saffron had avoided it, ignored it, worried more about being seen with defecting humans and how it would make him look. Perhaps Saffron had fallen victim to the words carved into his back all over again. Without ever realizing until what he cared about was put at risk.

He turned his eyes downward, watching his feet as they paced in rhythm with Ryder's. He tried not to lean on him so much for support. He removed his hand from his throbbing, aching chest, as if it no longer hurt. But it did—it hurt worse than it ever had before, almost as badly as the first time the bolt punctured him.

"Could you really help me?" he asked. So softly, it hardly existed. It might as well have been the breeze. He wasn't sure why he did, or if he should have kept his mouth pressed tightly shut—but it didn't matter. Ryder never got the chance to answer as someone suddenly hurtled through the trees, crashing into the both of them.

Ryder's hands flew out to grab Saffron again, holding him securely as the other person pitched backward and hit the earth. Ryder barked at them to stay back—but then Saffron shoved out of his arms, already exclaiming her name.

"Nimue!" he cried, stumbling to where she was on the ground. She clawed at him in an instant, eyes wide like she was shocked to find him there—or perhaps to have found him so easily. There was already a plea on her lips, one of which was split and bleeding dark undine blood.

"Saffron, you have to do something!" she screamed in response—and Saffron wasted no time, grabbing her by the arms and wrenching her back to her feet, racing forward without having to ask what she meant. He already knew. He already knew —and it struck him with a new rush of adrenaline that kept him upright, no longer needing Ryder's help. He ran hand-in-hand with her through the trees, over fallen logs, through bushes and low-hanging branches that scratched his face and tore at his hair. On their heels, Ryder followed.

He would have run straight through the edge of the trees had Ryder not snapped his name and grabbed the back of his blouse, fine fabric tearing at the shoulder from the sudden stop. But Saffron felt nothing, heard nothing, only watched as a huddle of three black-clad witchhunters stood in the center of the dormitory buildings—while two others pulled a shrieking, thrashing, fighting blonde woman from the door of one of them. Letty, her hair wild, bleeding from her nose. Clawing at the hands that gripped her, dragging her through the door toward those in the center.

The scars erupted with devouring heat. He slammed his opposite hand against them with a gasp and a cry of alarm, but the sound was cut off as a rush of blood surged up the back of his throat and spilled from his mouth. Choking him instantly, making him cough and gasp as he accidentally inhaled it into his lungs. He pressed harder and harder against the scars, pleading the beast inside to stay where it was, it didn't need to be summoned, not with Nimue right next to him, right there—he didn't know if he could control it. No—he knew he couldn't. He knew nothing about it, except that it might tear his friends apart in an instant while trying to help—

Something flashed out of the corner of his eye, and he barely inhaled a breath before Ryder launched himself through the bushes, sword drawn and moving faster than any human should have been able to. In one swift raise of his blade, he drove it through one of the three dark figures, slamming them face-down into the dirt. The other two scrambled backward with cries of alarm, those clinging to Letty doing the same and giving Nimue a chance to rush into the fray, too. It left Saffron in the trees, alone, bleeding from his nose, choking on the blood in his lungs, pressing a palm into his forearm with all the desperation of someone pinning a bloodthirsty animal to the road.

Was there really nothing he could do? Was he really so helpless, made so dangerous by his own rowan magic that he could only sit and watch as Ryder cut the witchhunters apart, as Nimue raked claws through the veiled faces of others to shove them away from Letty pinned on her knees? He wanted to scream—he wanted to cry and scream and rip his skin off in shame and guilt and regret and pure self-hatred for being so powerful but so useless. The most powerful witch in centuries—the most useless person left on their knees in the bushes.

He couldn't stomach doing nothing. He couldn't stomach the thought of being so useless. Even if he couldn't trust the wolf in his arm, even if he didn't know the full extent of his rowan magic—he still had magic. He was still an arid witch, damnit.

Using a stick from the nearby grass, he drove it into the dirt and drew a wide circle. He paused for only a moment before deciding which spell to carve into it—*radiate; opulent, petrify.*

A rush of magic burst from the circle, nearly knocking him backward, his thundering adrenaline delivering it with the same intensity as ocean waves crashing against the cliffside.

Blinking through the nervous sweat and low light, he watched as the shockwave ricocheted off everything within reach, witnessing the exact moment the spell caught the witchhunters in its web, paralyzing them in an instant. One by one, they went still as statues, locked in their own bodies. *Opulence, petrified.*

Barely catching his breath, Saffron leapt to his feet and lunged for his friend. Letty shrieked his name the moment she saw him, jumping into his arms. Saffron clung to her with a ferocious protectiveness, clutching the fabric of her shirt, burrowing fingers into her back, as if to prove she was real. She was real, she was there, she was safe. He still had her. She wasn't lost.

"I'm so sorry," he whispered. "I'm sorry—it's alright. It's alright, it's going to be alright. Where's Hollow?"

"I don't know," she croaked. Saffron grit his teeth, but forced the new rush of terror away. He shook his head, holding Letty's face for a second before turning as someone else rushed up to them. Nimue crashed into Letty, tearing her from Saffron's arms, frightened and protective and feral.

"It's fine—go with Nimue! Go, go!" He commanded, pushing both of them back to their feet where they raced for the dark trees. Somewhere to hide. Somewhere safe, where no one would find them, even once Saffron's spell wore off. His breath caught when he then spotted Ryder lying prone, motionless, on his back in the middle of the others.

"H-hey! Ryder!" Saffron gasped, racing to him, dropping to his knees and grabbing the front of Ryder's shirt. The panic thinned in an instant once he laid eyes on Ryder's stupid, grinning face, allowing him to *fwump* heavily back to the ground. Ryder wheezed, before letting out a breathy chuckle.

"Dunno what you did to them," he said wearily. "But that one got me, first. Compelled me onto my back. I should be thanking you, I guess. Kinda liked the way you called out for me too just now. Were you worried for a second?"

"Shut up," Saffron muttered. He bent down to slide an arm under Ryder's back, straining his muscles to heave the man upright. "I should leave you here until the enchantment wears off, just for saying th—"

"Saffron!" Ryder exclaimed, and Saffron turned, but not fast enough. One of the witchhunters had recovered enough to lunge and tackle him, slamming him to the earth beneath a crushing weight. Saffron snarled for them to *get off, get the fuck away from me!* but they clawed at his face, gripping under his jaw. A flash caught Saffron's eye, screaming as they grappled for the bottle of silver liquid on their belt, uncorking it, fighting to lift it to his mouth—

The fire in Saffron's arm blistered, sweltering with impossible heat that snapped like a piece of leather stretched too long. It cascaded through the rest of his body, filling him with hot fury, filling his mouth with the taste of iron—and his vision with a glowing halo of magic. Surrounding the person on top of him; pink, like the veil. Like mixing red and white watercolors; mixing aridity and opulence. The witchhunter was half-fey, half-human—just like an oracle.

Saffron thrust his hands out, slamming them against his attacker's chest. Gritting his teeth, he summoned the same wild rage he'd once felt when tearing those rowan vines from strangling Fiachra—beneath his fingertips, the person's rosy magic shuddered, before shifting darker. Sinking into a deep crimson, like blood, like smoldering embers. Whether he dredged the opulence from their body, or buried them in aridity, he didn't know—only that the deep, menacing shade of red soon devoured every inch of them, and then blood splattered across Saffron's chest. That time, not from his own nose or mouth—but from the witchhunter pinned on top of him.

Saffron shouldn't have looked. He shouldn't have turned his eyes up to see for himself—because the eyes staring back at him branded themselves into his mind. Glazed over, inflamed, blood-shot as if every capillary burst and flooded their irises. He gasped, reeling his hands back, stealing their magic glow with the move-ment—and the witchhunter collapsed on top of him, motionless. Dead.

Saffron didn't move—he couldn't.

He'd just—

Had he really just—

A scream tore up the back of his throat, thrashing and kick-ing, attempting to shove the heavy weight off of him. Ryder was suddenly there, pulling the body from Saffron's legs before grab-bing him before he could claw back to his feet and race into the trees in his panic. No—Ryder sank to his knees, meeting Saffron where he was in the grass. He pulled Saffron into his body, embracing him tightly, hand cupped against the back of his head as Saffron swore at him, clawing and hitting and fighting, wishing to be let free, wishing to run, about to tear apart from the inside out—!

"It's alright, Saffron!" Ryder told him, tightening his arms until Saffron only had enough freedom to breathe. Cutting off his screams, his thrashing. Forcing him to—breathe. Still, Saffron's hands gripped Ryder's tunic, trembling, white-knuckled, terrified.

"I—" he stammered. "I didn't—I didn't mean to—!"

"It's alright," Ryder whispered again. "You were only defending yourself. You were defending your friends. It was your life or theirs. You understand that, right? You would have died if they forced you to drink that silver. You would have burst into flames. You only did what you had to. They were eager to kill you. You did nothing wrong."

Ryder's reassurances came quickly, one after another, flattening any protests Saffron tried to make in reply. Until Saffron had no more words to utter, no more pleas for forgiveness or cries of apology. Until he was nothing but a shaking, hyperventilating mess, and all he could do was fight to keep the tears at bay.

"Let me, Ryder," Hollow's voice appeared from the darkness. Saffron's eyes bulged, straining to search for him, a pathetic whimper escaping his trembling lips the moment he saw him. Blood waterfalled down the side of Hollow's head, as if he'd been hit from behind. There was a small line of silver smeared away from the corner of his mouth, and Saffron knew in an instant, they made him drink it.

He shoved free of Ryder to grapple for Hollow instead, pulling him close, closer, closer, closer, until his nails drew blood through his friend's shirt. Thank god, thank god, thank god, Hollow wasn't eating rowan berries and practicing magic. Thank god he hadn't burst into flames. Thank god—Saffron hadn't lost him.

"C'mon, Saff," Hollow encouraged gently. "Back on your feet. Good. Letty and Nimue are this way, I saw where they went. Can you walk? Alright, yeah, good... come on..."

They were within a few yards of the tree line when a blade of wind sliced the gap between Saffron's heels and where Ryder followed behind them. Saffron threw his hands up in surprise, only to be swept into another pair of protective arms that immediately yanked him away from Hollow and Ryder, both. With one hand firmly around Saffron's waist, Cylvan brandished a golden sword with the other, pointing it at Ryder with Hollow at Saffron's back. His amethyst eyes bulged in fury, nostrils flaring as if it took every ounce of willpower not to flay the man where he stood.

"Cylvan!" Saffron exclaimed, leaping forward and shoving the blade down. Cylvan's attention snapped to him, taking in the state of Saffron's face for the first time in the darkness. His grip on the sword trembled, a muscle straining in his cheek, his neck, as he lifted the hand around Saffron's waist to brush the back of his knuckles through the drying blood on Saffron's chin.

"What happened here?" he asked, voice harsh as he readjusted the weapon in his hand. He kept it locked on Ryder, and Saffron swore in frustration, wriggling free of Cylvan's arm and pushing the blade down a second time.

"We're not alone here—!" he started, but then saw the small cluster of royal guards slipping into view between the dorm buildings. Saffron almost called out for them to stop, but bit down on his tongue. They grouped around the motionless veiled bodies, gathering them up to be carried off. As if they thought they could pretend like nothing happened. But Saffron knew—and he knew Cylvan knew—that was no longer possible. Not when Saffron had proven to those of them still alive—there was at least one arid witch amidst the prince's gala and the beantighes that served it. There was an arid witch who had paralyzed some, and brutally murdered another, through the use of their magic alone.

He turned over his shoulder, searching for Letty. He found her clutched in Nimue's arms, just on the other side of the trees. Barely illuminated by the lanterns held by the guards searching the buildings for any other witchhunters who might be hiding.

Saffron faintly heard every time they offered reassurances to the humans inside, though it did nothing to quell his nerves.

When Letty's wet, frightened eyes flickered to meet him, his heart sank. He wished he could reach out to her, to hug her, to tell her it was alright, she was going to be safe—but he didn't know that. Not anymore. He couldn't promise her that. He was the one who put her in danger by making her a beantighe in the king's court in the first place.

"This is my fault," he whispered. "Letty, I'm so sorry—"

"It's not your fault, Saffron," Ryder interjected, stepping forward, though his balance was still a little wobbly from being compelled. Cylvan responded by grabbing Saffron's arm again, pulling him back. He returned his sword upright, and Ryder put his hands up in defense.

"You're going to tell me exactly who you are and what you want with Saffron," Cylvan demanded. "I will only ask kindly, once. The next word out of my mouth will be an enchantment, so do not test my patience."

"Can you help them?" Saffron interjected before Ryder said something sarcastic in reply. He pushed Cylvan's blade down for a third time. His voice cracked as he spoke, practically begging. "Ryder, please—can you help them? Can you take them somewhere safe? They can't stay here, not anymore."

"Saffron, your friends..." Cylvan started, but trailed off. He knew as well as Saffron did, there was little he could do to shield them if rumors spread. He'd once said as much to Saffron, upon first witnessing the arid circles drawn in Saffron's sketchbook. Not even the crown prince of Alfidel could protect someone discovered to be practicing arid magic in secret.

"Aye," Ryder said, speaking directly to Saffron. His eyes were intense, even in the low light. "I can take you somewhere safe as well, Saffron, if you wish." The implication of those words was deafening, and Saffron knew he wasn't the only person to hear it. *Prince Cylvan can't protect you like I can.*

"I can't," Saffron answered before Cylvan could interject again. He reached down to take Cylvan's hand, a silent promise that he had no intention of leaving. "Just—just, please, take care of my friends for now." He looked at Hollow, then to Letty and Nimue. "I'll come and find you soon, I promise. I'm so sorry— I'm sorry for putting you in this position."

"It's not your fault," Letty whispered. "Thank you for coming, Saffron. Erm—you as well, Prince Cylvan..."

"I'm glad you're alright," Cylvan answered, equally sincere, before squaring his shoulders. "I swear to all of you, I had no knowledge of this happening. I apologize for not coming sooner." Silence rang in their circle—as if not one of them could comprehend receiving an apology from a high fey, let alone the prince of Alfidel. "Letty—whatever you need, please let me know. You can send a bird from wherever—"

"Very generous, your highness, but we can take care of anything she needs just fine." Ryder was the one to interrupt that time. Cylvan's hand tightened around Saffron's, once again fighting the urge to snarl and tear Ryder apart with his bare hands.

Ryder turned back to Saffron, just as Saoirse appeared from the darkness carrying a lantern of her own. She looked tired, the front of her silver and gold armor smeared with blood, likely from the witchhunter Ryder had impaled with his sword—or perhaps the one Saffron had crushed from the inside out with his magic. His stomach rolled nauseatingly every time he was reminded.

"Everything is taken care of here, your highness," she said, offering a bow. "Please, I'll escort you and Lord Saffron back to the palace."

"In that case, we'll head out before any other guards come sniffing around," Ryder went on, still with his eyes on Saffron. He paused for another moment, before approaching where he stood still tucked into Cylvan's side. Cylvan stiffened, but that time kept his sword down, even as Ryder reached into his back pocket for a handkerchief and offered it. "Before, you asked if I really could help you. I think we both know, it's time to come find out for yourself, your highness. There's no more time to waste, and things are only going to keep getting worse."

Saffron silently took the offered handkerchief, using it to wipe the blood from his nose. He only briefly met Ryder's eyes before turning away again, knowing he was right.

Ryder continued: "In the meantime, whatever you choose, I will take care of your friends."

"Thank you," Saffron whispered. Ryder stepped back, offered a nod to Cylvan, then turned to motion for the others to follow him.

"Your highness," Saoirse whispered, leaning forward slightly over Cylvan's shoulder. "Those beantighes are property of—"

"Saoirse," Cylvan interrupted. His grasp on Saffron's hand tightened again, protective and reassuring, like his insides coiled up in defense. A muscle clenched in his jaw. "Humans are not property. Let them go."

Those words echoed in Saffron's mind, all while he watched his friends disappear into the darkness. Led by Ryder Kyteler, who, in one night, Saffron had lost all his privilege of doubting.

He walked with Cylvan and Saoirse down the main path. Between the palace and the beantighe dorms, where they slipped through a side-entrance into a back corridor. All the way up to Cylvan's room, never once crossing paths with any other living soul. All the while, Saffron gazed down at the blood-stained handkerchief in his hand, edged with cotton lace trim that reminded him of the intricate work Baba Yaga used to make before her hands hurt too much to continue. He listened as Saoirse assured Cylvan the fete had been peacefully broken up once he excused himself from the initial encounter, all guests escorted back to their carriages without trouble. Cylvan asked her to send a bird to Luvon in the Winter Court right away, just in case he heard gossip of what had happened, to assure him Saffron was safe and sound. She nodded, then excused herself once they reached the door to Cylvan's bedroom.

Inside, Cylvan kept his hand in Saffron's. He squeezed it tightly, never letting go even as he dropped his sword to the marble floor with a loud clang that made Saffron jump. Before Saffron could say anything, Cylvan was already pulling him into the bathroom suite, lifting Saffron onto the edge of the counter without a word. He soaked a soft towel with hot water, proceeding to wipe the blood from Saffron's nose, his mouth, the front of his throat, off his torn blouse where it stained. His jaw clenched the entire time, until the muscles in his cheeks trembled. He never met Saffron's eyes. Never said anything, never made a sound, just focused on wiping Saffron clean.

"Cylvan," Saffron finally croaked, unable to take the silence any longer. He touched Cylvan's hand clutching the towel, but it overpowered him. It continued sweeping over his skin, even when he was clean. Even when there was no more blood to wash away. "Cylvan—Cylvan, it's alright!"

Saffron took Cylvan's face, forcing their eyes to meet. Cylvan's features twisted in distress. His hands flattened against the counter on either side of Saffron's hips, pressing himself into Saffron's body, burying his face into the crook of Saffron's neck. Saffron slowly wrapped one hand around Cylvan's back and pet his hair with the other. Only then did he realize how tightly Cylvan clenched every muscle, every inch of him shaking.

"I have never been more terrified," he whispered. "I have never felt—so terrified, seeing them, knowing you were right behind me. I don't know how I managed to remain standing at all. I don't recall what I said, even once you left. Oh, gods—I have never been so afraid, Saffron."

Saffron pulled him closer, as close as he could, as Cylvan shuddered and sank heavily into him. Saffron didn't know what to say, didn't know what to do—all he could do was pet his prince's hair and whisper:

"I'm safe. I'm right here. With you. You haven't lost me."

Cylvan clung to him. He repeated those words like promises. As if it was all he could bear to do.

23

THE GOSSIP

Snow and ice crunched beneath his boots, but Saffron felt it in his teeth. Pulling his cloak closer, his fingers were stiff as old branches, pink in the cold. What happened to his gloves? His scarf? His hat? He knew better than to wander the Winter Court wildlands without dressing warmly. He'd watched enough of Luvon's other beantighes lose fingers, toes, ears to the bitter cold growing up. He knew better.

At the end of the pathway, a building of stone and glass and metal waited for him. One he'd never seen before—one that was strangely familiar.

Behind him, something crunched, and he turned—finding a massive black wolf hunched low in the snow. But it was impossible to hide in such a pure-white blanket of fresh snow in every direction around them. Familiar, but unfamiliar.

"Hello?" He called. The animal's ears perked up, as if not expecting Saffron to call out. When it otherwise didn't react, Saffron continued. He pointed behind himself. "Do you know what this building is?"

After a long moment, the beast nodded. Saffron nodded back.

"Will you come here?"

The animal hesitated again, then shook its head. Saffron put his hand out, anyway.

"Come."

Something tugged on the underside of Saffron's wrist, but when he looked, there was nothing. Only the gnarled scar of an ogham stele. It glowed a low crimson, but every time he tried to read it, to recall what the lines said, they blurred. As if drenched in water; cloaked in fog.

When he lifted his eyes again, he jumped. The wolf had come within reach, red eyes bright and glowing. Its body shuddered with heavy breaths, steam puffing from its nose.

"What are you doing here?"

The animal's mouth didn't move, but Saffron heard its voice. In his head, in his ears. Inside of him, but all around him. It should have frightened him, but Saffron smiled slightly in curiosity.

"What are you doing here?" He repeated. "Do you belong here?"

The wolf's nose wrinkled in annoyance. It showed its teeth, trying once more to intimidate him, but something told Saffron it was all an act. That animal couldn't hurt him, even if it wanted to.

"No," *the ghostly voice echoed in a growl.* "And neither do you. Leave, beantighe."

"Beantighe," Saffron repeated, raising his eyebrows. A flicker of familiarity found him, tingling in the back of his head. His lips parted, mouth hanging open slightly as a name crawled to the forefront. It took longer than he expected, but when it finally came, his arm burned as he uttered it.

"Taran?"

CYLVAN HAD WRAPPED HIM IN TIGHT, PROTECTIVE arms after collapsing into bed with one another. Saffron whispered reassurances that everything was alright, he was safe, he was always safe when Cylvan was with him—until soon, Saffron wondered if they were as much reassurances for him as they were for his prince. He only wanted to forget. Just like the first time, at the shrine, then when Ryder first showed him the ruins—Saffron just wanted to forget. His friends were safe, there was nothing else for him to do. He wanted to sleep. He wanted to close his eyes and sink into the safest place he knew, which was held in Cylvan's arms beneath dark, warm blankets.

Waking gently the next morning, the unsettling dream trailed on his thoughts, leaving him disoriented. He groggily lifted his arm out from under the blankets, running his fingers up and down the scars on his forearm, feeling Taran's name on his lips as if he'd uttered it out loud. Perhaps it was his magic telling him it was disappointed to be held back the night before; the beast in his arm had wished to leap free and taste blood. It envied how Saffron had taken it into his own hands. It wanted the blood for itself.

"Fuck," he groaned, pressing his palms into his eyes, smashing hard enough to see a flutter of colors. Blinking up at the dark ceiling when he opened them again, he scowled, pounded on his chest a few times to force his sore heart to relax, then finally sat up in frustration. He was supposed to forget. Just like every other time, damnit. He knew what he had to do, he knew there was no more denying or avoiding it—he knew he had to go see Ryder Kyteler in the Finnian Ruins. He had to accept Ryder's help, especially with the previous night's developments. He knew that, damnit. His body no longer had to clench as if in danger.

Saffron gazed down at his hands again. Hands that killed that witchhunter who meant to kill him, first. Perhaps flooding them with aridity, perhaps draining them of opulence, he still didn't know—and he hated the thought that Ryder might actually be the one to be able to tell him. Especially as his magic grew wilder, just like Ryder warned. Especially as Baba Yaga still had not sent a reply letter, which Saffron had used as an excuse to keep waiting.

He had no more choice. Those witchhunters had forced his hand, placing his friends in Ryder's ruins. Saffron would no longer deny it—he would no longer avoid the man and his promises, his suggestions of witch's marks and veil circles.

Glancing down to the pillow next to him, Cylvan remained

fast asleep, hair still littered with ornaments from the gala the night before. A nest of knotted black hair, which Saffron knew was caused by the restlessness of his sleep. He knew, because he'd hardly slept right alongside him. They sank in and out of sleep and wakefulness in tune with one another, all night long. God— Saffron's raven must have been as exhausted as he was.

Sighing to himself, wishing to treat it like any other soft, gentle, romantic morning he'd always dreamed about, Saffron bent to kiss Cylvan on the cheek. He giggled when Cylvan groaned and mumbled something before turning the opposite way, and Saffron reveled in knowing how none of the other suitors would ever know the prince just like that—sleepy and grouchy in the morning after a restless night of holding one another.

Sliding beneath the blankets, Saffron coaxed Cylvan to return to his back. The prince slumped into the mantle of cushions, a halo of tangled hair spreading around him on the pillows. Crossing his arms, Saffron plucked a few of the biggest ornamental pins from the raven strands, flicking them away with small *clinks* when they hit the hardwood floor. He excavated at least a dozen of them before his interest waned, instead tracing a whispering finger across Cylvan's brow, down the slight bump in his nose, appreciating the perfect shape of his lips. He placed a soft kiss to that mouth, unable to resist. Fantasizing over a soft, gentle morning for himself. Where nothing haunted them, where nothing awful had happened the night before.

When Cylvan still didn't respond, Saffron returned to trailing a finger over every one of his prince's perfect features. His touch soon walked the sharp square of Cylvan's jaw, then the pointed lobe of his ear, back down again to his neck, then the wrinkled collar of his fancy tunic. Both of them, too exhausted to undress before collapsing into the bed.

Saffron pressed a kiss to Cylvan's neck, tugging the collar out of the way. Trailing down, he pushed the blankets away until sunlight cast itself over the rest of the sleeping prince, and Saffron bit his lip before letting his hands tug on the undershirt still tucked into Cylvan's waistband, pulling it free. His hands undid the buttons down the front of Cylvan's pants, next, pulling the fabric free of his skin and bending forward to press his nose to the base of his navel. He trailed kisses over the curve of one of Cylvan's hips, smiling to himself but still not lifting away when Cylvan let out a long breath.

Saffron's mouth found the base of his cock, softly kissing, then sliding his tongue up as it hardened beneath his touch. Cylvan stirred, the muscles of his stomach clenching and loosening, before a heavy hand emerged from the depths of sleep to gently rest against Saffron's hair. Saffron slid his tongue down the thick shaft again, then took it into his mouth. Tasting Cylvan all the way to the back of his throat.

Cylvan's fingers combed through Saffron's hair, as if unsure whether it was only a dream or the reality he would wake up to—and Saffron was in no hurry. He reveled in the way Cylvan's muscles tightened with every roll of pleasure, the way his perfect, handsome face flinched in tandem, lips parting slightly to inhale sharp breaths and whisper sounds that weren't yet words.

Saffron knew Cylvan was fully awake and aware the moment the hand in his hair tightened, hips flexing upward to thrust into his mouth. He choked against it, but didn't pull away, meeting Cylvan's eyes as they finally fluttered open and searched for him. Bright amethyst gemstones gazed down at him, half-lidded and flushed, jaw clenched as if he could hardly resist doing worse to Saffron's throat. Saffron teased him further, silently offering permission—and Cylvan finally snapped, sitting up and dragging Saffron closer. He grunted as Saffron's hands pressed into his inner thighs, his stomach for balance, forced to breathe through his nose as Cylvan moaned his name and combed fingers through his hair in encouragement.

"Look at me, your highness," the raven prince requested, and Saffron obeyed, meeting Cylvan's gentle but devouring gaze. A thumb brushed against Saffron's cheek, before wiping the corner of his wet mouth. Caged against his stomach, between his legs, Saffron sighed at the way Cylvan's eyes alone made his insides light up, sliding a hand between his stomach and the bed to touch himself—but Cylvan grabbed his wrist before he could get far. He smiled wickedly, shaking his head.

"I don't think so. I want all of your attention on me, first."

Saffron whined, rutting against the blankets bundled between his legs for even the smallest amount of relief. Cylvan watched with a satisfied smile, hand spreading over the back of Saffron's head, before trailing down to split his fingers over the bare skin of Saffron's nape. They slid under the back of Saffron's collar, sharp nails dragging up the top of his spine and making him shiver.

"If you wish to use your hands so much," Cylvan went on in a low voice. "Then take this off. But don't dare pull your mouth from me."

Saffron did his best, undoing the laces down the front of his blouse and shrugging it off his shoulders, all while stroking his lips and tongue over Cylvan's cock. Cylvan watched him with whispered encouragement, occasionally bucking his hips deeper into Saffron's mouth, or tugging on his hair when he pulled away too far, before caressing him gently again. By the time Saffron managed to free himself of his blouse, he was on the verge of begging.

Saffron kept his mouth in place even as Cylvan tightened, holding the back of Saffron's head as Saffron sucked on him greedily, wishing to take it all on his tongue, down his throat— and only once he had it, did he relent, pulling away and wiping his mouth and chin with a satisfied smile. Before he could say or do anything else, Cylvan grabbed him by the shoulder, shoving him back to return the favor. It took only a few strokes of Cylvan's mouth, soft and wet and warm devouring him, before Saffron's boiling, pent-up frustration released in return—but Cylvan insisted he be given more. He was still hungry, starving, and Saffron could only whimper and moan as he was brought to climax again and again by the mouth of the dark prince on top of him. Again and again, until there was nothing to think of except how euphoric it was to keep Cylvan's mouth on him.

NEWS OF THE SEARCH AT THE PALACE MADE ITS WAY TO Mairwen long before Saffron ever returned later than morning, though Saffron felt like he shouldn't have been so surprised. It had likely traveled all the way to the Winter Court already, as well, and he silently thanked Cylvan for thinking to send Luvon a letter before the night was even over. Still—he was not prepared for how it felt to overhear every word of the gossip as it evolved, inevitably taking on grotesque, stomach-churningly false lies he was forced to bear while walking to class, sitting in class, fighting to focus on homework while seated in the library with his head in one hand and the tip of his quill dripping ink onto parchment on the table.

Only he knew the 'beantighe servant girl' who was almost arrested—who only Saffron knew to be one of his closest friends —was not harboring dark, evil magic to use against the kings. She was not plotting an assassination attempt. She was not plotting with other human defectors to 'spirit-away' all of Avren, whatever that meant. But Saffron could say nothing. He could say nothing, do nothing, to defend his friend's reputation against such rumors, only glad they didn't know her real name, her face. They didn't know anything about her at all—they didn't know it was *her*, who Saffron held so dear. The least Saffron could do was not engage with it, ignore it, smile awkwardly whenever he was inadvertently pulled into conversation by the nature of simply sitting too close, even though his teeth grit the whole time.

Little did he know, his own disinterest in the gossip was on display. He never considered how people watched him while chatting, how not engaging with them might spotlight rather than hide him—and then it tumbled faster than he knew how to stop it. Quietly, at first, but undeniable once he overheard it the first time.

Whispers of his own affections for beantighes became a secondary scandal for his peers to feast on. Saffron, the flower of Alvénya, who defended a beantighe against a high fey lady at his first royal gala; who was said to even tell them "please" and "thank you"; who never asked them for a thing on campus, who had been seen chatting with them as casually as anyone else.

In turn came whispers about Cylvan's potential interest in him—the flower of Alvénya and the seelie prince, who together coddled the beantighe who got in Lady Callan's way, then who together embarrassed her again by chatting in the middle of a suitor dance. Seelie Prince Cylvan, who had a history of showing affection to beantighes where everyone could see. Whispers passed of his growing benefaction to the beantighes of Morrígan Academy—followed by renewed scrutiny of his vicious behavior in Connacht months prior, when he nearly suffocated an entire fete to protect one mistreated, pretty moon-ear that kissed him on his lap. Saffron was haunted by those words—Cylvan's *lovelier choice.* Those words that drove Taran over the edge, words that reduced Saffron to rubbing his throat in class and fighting to keep his voice.

He wouldn't engage. He wouldn't acknowledge. That was what Catrín taught him during his two weeks in the Winter Court, learning how to be a proper high fey. And he would do his best. He only hoped the intrigue would die out quicker than his depleting patience.

He only had to wait a little bit longer. Then he would be able to visit the ruins, to visit his friends. To make sure they were safe. To begin the process of making *himself* safe, for everyone around him. He wouldn't ignore what he should do any longer, he wouldn't waste any more time, he wouldn't be selfish or impertinent or arrogant any longer.

Despite the way it went against everything he'd done until that point—he forced himself to think of nothing but Ryder Kyteler and the Finnian Ruins, waiting for Saffron's arrival.

24

THE CALLER

Guilt chewed on him some, but not enough to change his mind. Saffron knew Cylvan intended on visiting the palace that morning to speak to the kings, who had finally returned from Fall Court, about the sudden influx of witchhunters in Avren. Specifically the chaos they caused at his most recent suitor gala—but also how he and Saffron had crossed paths with them so casually in the stationery shop a week before that. Wanting to know who oversaw them, why they'd suddenly emerged from the woodwork without any warning. Reassuring Saffron the kings would never have anything to do with something so cruel, Saffron promising he never even thought of that.

All the while, Saffron didn't want to mislead him—but he also knew if Cylvan joined him to the ruins that day, it likely wouldn't result in anything productive. He imagined Cylvan and Ryder as little more than two feral cats wishing to skin one another alive. He knew Cylvan wouldn't deny it, either. It was for his own good not to be invited that first time, really.

Sharing Boann's saddle, Saffron followed Asche's directions through the city, rain clouds crept across the sky as they made their way up the overgrown path. Saffron's heart pounded as it reminded him too much of the same road leading to the iron gates of the Kyteler School outside of Morrígan. He couldn't help but constantly glance in each direction the moment they left the furthest edges of the city in favor of the woods, blanketed in a thick mist. Bracing for a red-veiled beannighe to lunge from the fog and sink her teeth into him.

According to the daurae, the Finnian Ruins sat just outside the edge of Avren, past poorer neighborhoods that lacked the same shine and glamour as the main parts of the city. Neighborhoods decorated in less gold ornamentation, less harp music teasing the air, fewer smells of rich breads and pastries. Fewer people running up and down the streets with all the liveliness of the city, smiling with candy in one hand and a shopping bag in the other.

Even without the clouds blocking out the light, the streets would still be grayer than the main thoroughfares. Less polished, with patches in the road where the packed dirt underneath showed through unkept cobblestones. Saffron never knew there were parts of Avren like that; it was never anything Cylvan or anyone else mentioned. It made him think of Beantighe Village before Elluin was ousted and replaced. Crumbling buildings and ruined roads.

Asche soon pointed him down a dark alleyway between two long abandoned buildings, emerging on the other side to another overgrown street, unmarked, untouched for decades. Practically hidden behind a wall of thick foliage.

They wandered between foggy trees for what felt like an eternity, until Saffron no longer knew where the road ended and the forest began, But Asche didn't seem bothered, so he stayed quiet. If there was anything Saffron could trust implicitly, it was the daurae's ability to find secret places in the woods. Perhaps that was the biggest thing they had in common with one another.

At the end of the barely-remaining path, Saffron pulled Boann to a halt as a staircase emerged from the mist. Bookended on either side by a pair of stone statues, the steps were moss-and-vine devoured, cracking and crumbling as they stretched over a tall knoll into the trees. Forming an archway over the bottom steps, the statues held a golden ring adorned with spikes between them—like rays of the sun. Saffron's mouth went dry, ears ringing as he stared at it, reminded of a similar motif he'd seen all over Proserpina's abandoned chapel in the Kyteler Ruins. Beneath him, Boann shuddered and rumbled back and forth on his feet, wishing to leave. Wishing to turn in the other direction, as if he, too, could sense the change in the air. Saffron swore it was a taste of rust and iron—like blood. Like the blood he'd tasted the night he killed the witchhunter, flooding his mouth in exchange for magic.

He didn't want to ask, but he had to. He knew he had to, because otherwise walking into it would only make it more difficult to stomach once he was too far to turn back.

"Asche," he said quietly. "Are these ruins... related to Queen Proserpina?"

Asche's delayed response was an answer in itself. They shifted in the saddle behind him, absentmindedly picking a leaf from the back of Saffron's cloak while mulling over an answer. Saffron waited until they responded, though the silence already told him what he wanted to know.

"Yes," they said softly. "I'm just realizing, perhaps I should have mentioned it sooner..."

"No, it's..." Saffron started on instinct, but he didn't know how to explain it. How to explain, *no, it's fine, don't worry about it*—when the thought of crossing the threshold of anything related to the queen made ghostly silver hands squeeze his throat. He closed his eyes, cleared his airway, and re-centered himself. He was safe. He scratched at his throat, his wrists. He was safe. There were humans living in secret in those ruins, according to Asche and Ryder and everything else Saffron knew, which meant they no longer belonged to the queen. Humans had taken them for themselves. Saffron could find some sort of pleasure in that thought.

He just wanted to know if Letty had made it there safely. If

Nimue was still with her, if Hollow was still with her. He just wanted to know his friends were safe.

His boots splashed in the mud of the road after hopping from the saddle, offering Asche a hand and pulling them down with him. Finding a low branch, Saffron tied Boann's reins securely, then used the toe of his boot to draw a large circle around the beast and hatch the edges with a spell that would not only keep him put, but keep others out. Ever since he'd performed that spell outside the beantighe dorms, he found himself impulsively drawing more and more whenever he needed the convenience, which was both anxiety-inducing and liberating after so many weeks forcing those urges down. Knowing if anyone caught even the slightest hint that he was not only not ashen, but in fact arid, it would spell catastrophe. To be able to do even those menial little spells was... rebellious, in a sweet sort of way.

He spun Fiachra's recall ring next, smiling when she responded and swooped down to meet him in an instant, though clacked her talons playfully on Asche's horns, first, making them whine. Saffron scratched under her chin, then shifted her to his shoulder, glancing back to the staircase. Perhaps she could sense his apprehension, because she adjusted her stance, then pecked gently on the glamoured curve of his ear. He scratched her one more time under the chin.

"I tried to come back and visit a few weeks ago, but it was... different from what I remembered," Asche whispered, joining Saffron at the base of the stairs. "It changed a lot, even just in the few months I stayed at Morrígan with you guys..."

They took Saffron's hand, squeezing it, furrowing their brows in frustration before whispering: "I hate thinking they're the same people causing problems around the city. I just... The humans who lived here when I used to visit... they weren't like that. They wouldn't do that. At least... I never thought they would..." they glanced at Fiachra. Asche, who was more than familiar with the dead barn owls being nailed to the palace gates and left on Lugh's altar. They turned their eyes away again quickly, like even the healthy bird on Saffron's shoulder summoned bad memories.

Saffron squeezed their hand, but didn't know if it was in reassurance or just... comfort. He didn't know the answer to that question, either. It was one of the many reasons he'd avoided obeying Ryder's siren call for so long, knowing it would be equally dangerous to be spotted with the defecting humans as much as if someone spotted him performing taboo magic. It was only because he had no choice that he finally stood at the base of those stairs. Those witchhunters had taken his choice from him. He wondered if Ryder considered it a blessing in disguise.

Saffron inhaled a deep breath, steeled his nerves, then began the ascent with Asche right beside him.

Perhaps it was because Saffron absentmindedly rubbed the scar on his forearm while they walked, perhaps it was because Asche was equally on edge, especially with the thickness of the fog in every direction, but the daurae's anxiety rode an all-time high, and they couldn't seem to stop talking.

"If anything, I might be able to get a yew branch to make a new bracelet for you, today. Since I haven't been able to find any others growing in the woods around the school. I think it's because they empower opulence, sort of like how rowan words for arid magic—so oracles and school admins are always out there cutting down yew trees so students don't take them for themselves to strengthen their magic during exams..."

"Hm..." Saffron hummed, trying to listen, but his mind wandered as much as Asche's chatter did. He watched his feet on the cracked, mossy steps as they neared the top of another incline, trying to listen beneath the daurae's words to make sure nothing snuck up on them. "You said there were iron gates around the ruins—do you feel alright so far? With your own rowan bracelet."

"Oh, yeah, I feel alright." Asche fondled the wristlet to prove it.

"Does this place suppress your sídhe magic like the Kyteler Ruins, too?"

"Yes, but I'm used to it by now. Um, you know, it's ironic, because Sunbeam once told me that ancient human monasteries had rowan trees in their courtyards to repel evil spirits, or something. Er, Proserpina also called these places monasteries, I mean, which is why it's ironic. Don't say that in front of Cylvan, though, or he'll go off on a whole tangent about the real usage of that word on the human side and how great-grandmother only borrowed it for her own use."

Saffron chuckled despite himself. "Right. I've learned to be careful with what words I use in front of Cylvan, too, if I don't have the strength for an entomology lecture."

"... I think you mean etymology, but, yeah. He's really the most insufferable person I've ever met, always acting like he knows everything about everything... really never shuts up, does he... You know, there are actually five of the queen's monasteries all around Alfidel, one in each court, including Mid Court, or this one here in Avren. This one was her favorite, though, back when it was the Queen's Keep. There's a similar one up north for the king, too. They were meant to house her priestesses, as well as to train oracles, and... and, well... um... well, you know about... witchhunters, and all that... They're considered sacred places in the other courts, but this one fell into disrepair once the Holts formally de-sanctioned it at the end of the war... King Elanyl even prohibited access to it, though we both know how short his reign was before my father was coronated as a baby... I always wondered when humans started taking refuge here..."

"Delightful, as always," Saffron smirked. "Do you think the humans living here know all of that history?"

"I think so, yes." Asche nodded, before adding in a whisper: "I think that's part of the reason they chose it."

Saffron almost asked why the other monasteries were made sacred places, but something distracted him from deep in the fog, and the words died on his lips. He turned, but didn't disrupt his pace.

Every bird had fallen silent, and he'd only just noticed. Just like outside Morrígan's ruins. Fiachra on his shoulder shifted uneasily between her feet, wings fluffing and jittering in agitation like she itched all over. Saffron searched the opaque fog steadily, once again expecting the old beannighe's shadow to wander by—but then Asche stopped short, tugging Saffron's hand and pulling him to a halt.

Fiachra clacked her beak, nearly tumbling from her perch in surprise, eyes focused on something else far up ahead. It was only another moment before Saffron saw what they saw—a humanesque shadow leaning out from one of the silhouetted trees on the side of the path.

"Saffron..." Asche whispered, and Saffron turned slowly, goosebumps rising up his arms when he realized there wasn't only one. Blending in with the trees, the undergrowth, the foliage—there had to be at least a dozen others leaning out enough to watch them, all while going unnoticed—until they didn't. Saffron turned with a chill down his spine, realizing even more shadows shifted in the mist behind them. He hadn't noticed, and they'd been surrounded.

The moment the shadows knew they were spotted, they raced from the trees. Saffron attempted to keep Asche behind him, but with every additional threat rushing from another direction, his efforts were quickly made in vain. When one came a little too close, Saffron moved on instinct, hand flying out to grab the pommel of the attacker's sword from their belt, while simultaneously slamming his shoulder into their chest. Fiachra screeched as she was knocked off balance, but used the momentum to flare her talons and claw at the attacker's face before swooping straight into the sky.

Saffron didn't know anything about using a blade, except from occasional sparring matches with Hollow and sharpened tree branches—but he knew how to cut with a sharp edge, and that was all it took to be a threat.

He circled where they stood, Asche clinging to him from behind, their nervous silence proving that was definitely not the welcome the daurae normally received when coming to visit. Saffron's stress built higher in his chest, filling the back of his throat, and he felt the rush of blood coming—but moved before it ever dripped, deciding to take advantage of it.

Spinning on heel, he tore the blade through the dirt in a circle around them. Using the tip of the blade, he carved hatchmarks into the edge of the ring, hissing and whipping the blade out whenever someone tried to interrupt—and the moment he clawed the last one, a wall of red light and forceful magic rushed outward like a ripple in water, flattening every assailant before they could step closer, disturbing the thick fog like a wind through smoke.

"I'm here to see Ryder Kyteler!" he called out into the chorus of groans as his victims rolled onto their backs, sat up on their knees, held their heads. He raised the blade to the attacker closest to him, meeting their eyes as blood finally dripped freely from his nose, staining the collar of his black tunic. He grabbed the amethyst pendant and yanked it off over his head, revealing his moon ears underneath. "He should be expecting me."

"Alright," someone else said, making Saffron whirl around. They had their hands up, clearly apprehensive, expression visible as they'd pulled down the cover that masked the bottom half of their face. "We're not going to hurt you. You're Saffron, aren't you?"

"You can't really blame us, considering how many witch-hunters are wandering every corner of the city lately. Look how you're fuckin' dressed," someone else said. Saffron's heart thumped in regret, lowering the sword.

"You're right," he agreed, though still didn't offer the weapon back. "You have every right to treat unwelcome guests like this. Especially if you think they're witchhunters."

"Hasn't done us wrong yet," the first one said with a slightly-less uncomfortable laugh. "You must be Saffron, right? Oh—Christ, yeah, that's Birdie behind you, isn't it? I should have known. Been a while, kid."

"Aschewing!" Asche snapped, still clinging to Saffron's arm. "You look as ugly as ever, Breton."

"And you haven't aged a bit. Dunno what I'd do with a fey fountain of youth like yours, Birdie. C'mon then, both of you. We gotta leave the road, it's barricaded up ahead. You know, to keep *unwelcome visitors* from getting too close."

Saffron nodded, spinning the recall ring and summoning Fiachra back down to earth. It took her a few moments longer than normal, that time, but she eventually descended like a dart, swift and cutting. Straight back to Saffron's shoulder, where she pressed her wing into the side of his head. He felt how tense she held herself, how her wings and talons twitched every time someone stepped too close or spoke a little too loudly. He pulled open the front of Cylvan's tunic, which was too big for him anyway, motioning for her to nestle inside if she wished. She did, burrowing into the wide chest, though leaving her head visible so she could continue to watch. Still, every time someone moved past, she flared up and coiled back like a snake. Saffron brushed the back of her head in reassurance. He wasn't going to let any of them hurt her. Not again.

No matter how far they walked, the fog never lifted, just like around the Kyteler Ruins. Saffron kept the stolen sword for himself, and the woman who'd owned it previously said nothing to ask for it back. He almost mentioned it, but instead found himself wrapped up in listening to them all chatter amongst themselves, instead. All of them, suddenly so at ease, as if the realization Saffron was one of them relaxed all of their nerves back to being casual friends on a walk. Despite still being a total stranger. It encapsulated the exact reason Saffron struggled so much with trusting, distrusting, trusting Ryder Kyteler—it was hard for humans not to inherently trust one another, especially in a world where they were each others' only allies.

He never expected how the things they talked about so normally would make him feel wistful, almost sad, as things he'd somehow forgotten about. Things he never realized he missed. They didn't talk of fancy parties or fine fabrics or jewelry, they discussed how someone's recent attempt at baking bread had failed, and how it was because they only used half the required amount of yeast. They argued about which branches were best for carving practice swords and which bird feathers were best for fletching arrows. They got excited when a fat chipmunk scurried across their path, laughing and reminiscing about a time one had broken into the cellar and drank its weight in wine, how someone tried nursing it back to health in a box stuffed with cotton, only for the creature to chew its way out again.

But not only that—they talked about magic. They talked about arid magic, right there in front of both Saffron and Asche, as if it was something as innocuous as what they had for breakfast. As the chipmunk who drank their wine.

When one of them asked what spell Saffron used on the road, Saffron hesitated, internally asking if it was some kind of trick, if it was really safe to answer.

"'*Red, burst, wall, expand.* Uh, *red* because I wanted to be able to see it, and I thought it might be a little intimidating... *burst* because I wanted it to be sudden... *wall* because I wanted it to be as tall as all of you, and *expand* because, well... you were all circled a few feet away from me...'"

"You did it so fast!"

"Did you eat rowan berries before passing through the gate?"

"Do you speak Gaeilge fluently?" Someone else hurried a little too close, and Fiachra clacked her beak at them in threat. Saffron patted her on the head while replying.

"I'm definitely not fluent, but I'm at least spring witch level, according to my henmother. Self-taught, though, so my craft definitely isn't perfect..."

"But you have the whole feda alphabet memorized?"

"Of course—that should be the first thing you do."

"Really? Breton says you should learn the language first."

"Only so you don't misspell something and accidentally blow us all sky-high," Breton answered from ahead of them, and Saffron laughed, making the man's tawny cheeks flush like he was embarrassed. They mumbled, *"Am I wrong?"* under their breath.

"I think that makes perfect sense," Saffron answered. "Especially if there are a lot of people learning at once, I guess, and you can't keep track of what they're all scribbling down. Erm... are there...? A lot of people?"

"I think about fifty right now? Who can be called spring witches like you, at least," Breton said, scratching his neck as he thought about it. "Lots more non-witches in the ruins, though. Lots who are curious but not ready to commit, you know. Too scared right now."

"Yeah," Saffron whispered. "I can't blame them. What level are you, Breton?"

"Just Arid," he answered. "Mostly self-taught, too, actually. I had a mentor for a few months, but the hunters got her and burned her about a year ago."

"Oh," Saffron's voice went quiet. "I... I'm sorry."

Breton shrugged, eyes flickering to Asche, then to Saffron, then back down again.

"So... is it true? That you're a... a rowan witch. First one in centuries, or whatever."

Everyone else went quiet, like only in that moment did they realize exactly who Saffron was. The one who'd asked whether or not he'd eaten rowan berries before arriving made a sound of realization.

"Ryder never shuts up about you," someone else muttered, but Saffron couldn't tell who when he turned to look. His face went hot.

"What else does Ryder say about me?" He asked, suddenly nervous.

"Said you didn't mean to hurt Sav," Breton said. "And you only did because you don't know how to use your magic yet."

"Is that so?" Saffron said with a rush of annoyance, before chomping down on his tongue before he said anything else. Tamping the emotion back down, he added. "Ryder thinks rather highly of himself, I think. He says he can help me with my magic, yet arid witch is the highest all of you have gotten?"

"Dunno how to make an oath," Breton answered with a hint of defensiveness. "That's the only reason."

"Not even Ryder can tell you? He who talks like he knows everything."

"Veil won't talk to Ryder," someone else said, but Breton shushed them. Saffron wanted to ask why—but the Finnian Ruins came into view through the mist ahead of them before he could. Perhaps he would just have to ask Ryder, himself.

25

THE COVEN

Not unlike the mist surrounding them, those ruins were so similar to the ones of Morrígan's Kyteler School of Arid Magic. Same in the way moss and vines claimed stone walls and kept many of them from collapsing entirely; how some had been reduced to only crumpled foundations while others maintained their original structure. Saffron could only wonder. He could only imagine what it had once looked like, both when occupied by the Night Queen, then after being claimed by the humans during the war. Different from the Kyteler Ruins in how their state of decay wasn't so heavy; it didn't bear the scars of burning from the inside out, but rather like it'd simply been left to rot in emptiness. Crumbling beneath the weight of neglect rather than violence. Even the atmosphere was lighter, fresher than that of the other ruins, and he somehow knew there couldn't be nearly as many ghosts roaming around in that place in comparison.

Heading toward one of the largest standing structures, Saffron had to swallow back the lump in his throat when he recognized the colorful rose window centered in the peaked stone facade. A massive, ornate stone building, far larger than Morrígan's Grand Library, mimicked by that church that had crushed him and his leg back in the Kyteler Ruins. A true church, a cathedral, built to worship the Night Queen who killed, maimed, displaced so many people. Saffron tried once again to find the lovely irony in it being reclaimed by humans in her death—but instead, he habitually reached to rub at his neck. Fiachra nibbled his hand before he could. He scratched the top of her head, instead.

"You'll have to wait outside, Birdie," the woman whose sword Saffron had stolen said, motioning to Asche.

"Oh, Diana!" Asche groaned on cue, throwing their head back. "Why didn't you say anything sooner? I walked all the way here!"

"And why are you always trying to get in trouble?" Diana growled in return. She grabbed Asche by one of their horns, shaking them back and forth like Baba Yaga would grab her orange cat by the head and wobble him to and fro when he clawed at Wicklow's couch cushions. "You know better than to come down the main entryway, dumbass! Even if it's with an invited guest. *You* aren't invited, and you know that."

"That was my fault—" Saffron attempted, but Asche whined first, swatting at the woman's hands as they were tugged away, stumbling over their feet. Saffron instinctively reached for them, but Breton put a hand out and placed it gently on his shoulder. Saffron met his eyes, and for some reason, in that moment, seeing the man's face up close—it was human. It was so human.

He glanced around the rest of the group as they finally pulled their face coverings down while in the safety of the ruins, and something about it was different from the faces he knew from Beantighe Village. Even from the ones he didn't know that worked at the palace. Faces that were round and soft and inherently friendly, even when wrinkled in annoyance or apprehension. Faces scarred and worn down by the sun, showing their age by wrinkles and pockmarks and acne. They weren't perfectly sculpted like the high fey, or even perfectly washed or plucked like beantighes who worked in the palace.

"Ryder is this way, in his study." Breton motioned with his hand. "Daurae Asche will be alright. We all know they aren't a threat, but Ryder banned them from visiting a long time ago. Diana will keep an eye on them until you're ready to leave."

Saffron nodded, grateful for the reassurance, memorizing the man's features since the tension had died down and he finally stood close enough to be properly seen. Breton's cheeks were round, with warm brown skin and dark brown eyes. His black hair was woven into long locs, pulled back into a thick plait hanging between his shoulder blades. He matched Saffron in height, but something about him naturally commanded respect—perhaps the way he never seemed to relax the square shape of his shoulders. Or maybe it was the ornate crossbow clipped to his belt, which Saffron knew with a glance, was likely stolen from some Avren guard. He regarded his own stolen sword at the thought, examining the design and realizing it, too, was definitely snatched from the same.

Following Breton to the cathedral entrance, Saffron paused at the sight of a massive arid stele carved down the center of the double doors that stood three times as tall as he did, hatchmarks extending from the seam between them. He barely had a chance to skim and read them, mouthing the words *only iron entry* before they were pushed open. Breton smiled to himself, like it was his favorite part to watch people see something so menacing for the first time. At least, menacing to those who didn't know any better. Saffron's own heart fluttered in awe.

Inside, Saffron's mouth dropped open for a different reason. Crowding the extravagant marble mosaics on the floor, more humans than he anticipated milled about, relaxed in rows of cots, made conversation with one another. But more than the crowd—there were books. There were large, sprawling parchments hanging from the walls; scrolls both ancient and new scattered around on shelves and stone sills; tables and desks sat cluttered with writing materials and other preservation tools for making sense of old writings probably once destroyed during Proserpina's Night Court. Amongst them, ogham markings were painted on the walls, the floors, carved into wooden beams, chiseled into stone tympanums stretching over the center walkway. Out in the open for anyone and everyone to see. For humans practicing arid magic—or simply finding sanctuary in it.

Iron warning; repel charms; opulent near, glow; warning buzz; Saffron's eyes skimmed over each and every protective circle and stele they passed. His heart thumped in continued appreciation and elation as they made their way down the length of the nave and he skimmed more, overheard more conversations, caught sight of more humans helping other humans. Laughing with one another, teaching each other how to read, sharing meals, watching over others as they slept with bandaged injuries or dirty faces from working outside. He wondered if that was even the slightest reflection of what the inside of the Kyteler School of Arid Magic once looked like.

"This is all..." Saffron couldn't find the words. There were no human words in any human language to describe how that beautiful, maddening, torturous sight made him feel. He felt all of it. He felt everything all at once, until it was nothing but a swirling, cottony, thorny tempest in his chest.

"This way," Breton continued, and Saffron had to quicken his pace to keep up. He stared at the people as he passed, and they stared right back. Could they tell his clothes were high fey? Could they see the details on his cloak, borrowed from Cylvan? Could they tell that Fiachra tucked down in his tunic was a barn owl, or even one they'd already tried to sacrifice? Oh, god—did any of them recognize him from the scene he caused at Ériu's shrine? The thought made him jump, hurrying to keep up on Breton's heels, suddenly self-conscious. Even though, at least by the conversation with Breton in the woods, people knew Saffron was coming. Even if they knew he was the one who caused a scene at the shrine—they likely also knew he was the first rowan witch in centuries, and his arrival was to be anticipated. He wondered what else Ryder had told them. If he'd made any promises in Saffron's stead. God, he hoped not—but a part of him already knew he was going to be disappointed.

Walking the length of the cathedral's nave, he followed close behind as Breton reached, then climbed an endless set of narrow, winding stone steps at the opposite end. The rest of Saffron's entourage fell back as they did, but Saffron never lost the sense that he was surrounded by people. It was impossible to feel isolated even when walking with only one other person, as the congregation of humans below had voices that bounced off the walls and high ceilings like a chorus. Like the cathedral was built for singing, even if just in the form of humans sharing in magic with one another.

By the time they reached the top of the stairs, Saffron had to ask Breton to wait a moment so he could catch his breath. Leaning against the stone wall, he pressed a hand to his chest as his heart pounded with the effort. Breton didn't make a fuss, gazing to where Saffron's hand hovered. As if there was something he wished to ask, but kept at the back of his throat. Saffron then wondered exactly how many others knew *exactly* how he came to be the most recent rowan witch, specifically around his involvement in the Ostara engagement party that did away with Taran mac Delbaith—and then whether they knew about his engagement to Cylvan right afterward. He wondered again how Ryder had ever learned about it, himself. He wondered exactly what kind of tales that man had spun that Saffron would be expected to uphold. He hoped to finally get some answers, so he never had to wonder anything ever again.

Walking down the length of the clerestory, Saffron couldn't help but gaze out the tall, decorated windows over the ruins below, though most remained hidden beneath a layer of fog. Rain had picked up since entering the cathedral, tapping against the window and further warping his view. He almost asked where Diana had gone with Asche, but Breton stopped before a nondescript door, then stepped to the side until Saffron made it within reach. From there, he knocked once, twice, three times, before unlatching the handle. Saffron bit his lip, offering a quiet nod of thanks before pushing the door inward.

Upon sliding his head inside, he first saw the thousands of books on shelves along every wall, then the arid tapestries filling in the gaps, the thin branches of a rowan tree that climbed between cracks in the stone wall and sprouted red berries. Overhead, the high-vaulted ceiling was painted like a crimson night sky, and Saffron stepped in with his mouth hanging open in awe. Only once he was satisfied with every detail did he finally lay eyes on two people hovering around an oak desk at the head of the room, beneath the tall lancet windows that nearly pierced the rose window overhead.

One of them, his dirty blonde hair pulled back into a ponytail, lifted his eyes and called out Saffron's name with a smile. The other Saffron recognized in an instant, and he sighed with a smile of relief.

Saffron raced straight for Hollow, who dropped the book in his hand to squeeze Saffron in a hug. Ryder made a sound of mock insult, like he was shocked to not be met with the same enthusiasm, but Saffron was fine to ignore him. He pulled away from his friend, grabbing Hollow's face before checking over the rest of him for signs of mistreatment, even if it had been barely a week since they last saw one another. There were none, to his relief. Hollow even wore surprisingly nice clothes, though they were surely also stolen from some high fey lord in the city.

"Your highness has finally come to pay me a visit," Ryder interrupted. Hollow elbowed him in the side, but Ryder pressed forward, putting an arm around Saffron's shoulders in greeting. Fiachra in Saffron's tunic screeched in protest, wriggling like she wanted to bite his fingernails off, only quieting again when Saffron calmly pet the top of her head. "I was wondering if you would really come like you promised."

"Of course I would," Saffron huffed, also elbowing Ryder

until he finally stepped back. "I had to make sure *you* kept *your* promise."

"For you I would do much more than that."

Saffron didn't bother asking what that was supposed to mean, throwing a look back to Hollow before letting his eyes regard the rest of the room for a second time. The number of books on the walls made his insides twist and flip in excited anticipation, and he was on the verge of asking if he could look around when Ryder wrapped his arm around his shoulders again and pulled him away.

"I'm so glad you found your way to us safely," he said, shepherding Saffron toward the center of the room. "I know you haven't seen much, yet, especially with the fog outside, but what do you think so far? Surprised? I wish I had been able to see your face the first time you stepped inside the cathedral."

"Breton and the others gave me a very warm welcome," Saffron answered, forcing himself to relax. He offered a brief smile to Breton, who nodded when Ryder did the same. "Is Letty nearby?"

"I have her set up in one of the private cottages a little deeper in the woods, in case we get an unexpected raid. No one will be able to find her. Why don't I take you?" he offered, steering Saffron toward the door. "It's not too long of a walk. Wish you'd be able to see more of the landscape, though, it's really something."

Saffron glanced back to Hollow, but Hollow's attention was out the window. It put Saffron's nerves on edge, like he could sense something was off. Hollow wasn't acting like himself; he seemed far too quiet. He was normally so sarcastic, always had something to say, especially when Ryder was involved. Even with so few words exchanged, even with only his body language, it was clear Hollow wasn't fully accustomed to all of the recent upheavals, yet. Saffron wished he had more time to speak with him, first, but the promise of checking on Letty was too overwhelming.

"Let's go," Saffron agreed, turning back to Ryder. "I'd like to see her."

Ryder grabbed a cloak from the back of a couch, sweeping it over his shoulders before looking Saffron up and down with a cocked eyebrow. He met Fiachra's eyes and held them for a moment, both narrowing their gazes at one another in distrust.

"Who's thi—" Ryder attempted to pet her, but she scraped her beak over his knuckles before he could even get close, breaking skin and drawing blood. Saffron bit back a laugh, scratching under her chin as a means of both calming her down and showing off, just a little bit.

"Sorry about her," he said. "She's a little touchy."

"Damn, you could have said something first," Ryder answered flatly, before licking the blood off the back of his hand and shaking it out. "Come on then, bring your little monster. Let me show you to Letty. We'll take the side passage."

He tugged on the curve of Saffron's hood before Saffron could reach for the latch of the main door, making him stumble backward. Saffron had to bite back the urge to swat his hand away. He followed in silence.

"Hollow and I go way back, you know," Ryder reiterated as they made their way down a narrow, spiraling staircase separate from the one he'd first climbed with Breton. As if he saw how Saffron's attention had lingered on Hollow by the window, as if Ryder knew Saffron could tell things were tense and wanted to try and smooth it over. By then it was the third or fourth thing he'd said to try and start a conversation, though Saffron hardly engaged in the previous attempts. "The last time we saw each other it ended on less-than-ideal terms, but I was so happy to see him at the palace dorms alive and well a few weeks ago. Happy and surprised, honestly. Surprised he didn't end up in a cell somewhere with his attitude. It's a relief to have him back where I can keep an eye on him. You know his real name is—"

"No," Saffron interjected. Ryder threw him a look, and

Saffron shook his head. "I don't want to know. If he wanted to tell me, he would have already."

They found the bottom of the back passageway, where he used a key from under his shirt to undo the lock and step aside for Saffron to pass through. Saffron paused on the other side long enough for Ryder to close the door behind them, before starting his own string of accusations. He kept them honeyed and soft, though, like any high fey lord at a party would.

"I'm starting to think you've already told everyone here about me," he said. Ryder didn't answer right away, too busy hiding the door behind a curtain of vines. "I want to know what you told them I was going to do. Since I didn't agree to anything like that the first time we talked."

The man clucked his tongue like he was disappointed with Saffron's tone, or maybe his eagerness to get to the point. He tucked the key back down his shirt, then a hand suddenly found the curve of Saffron's waist, pulling him to walk. Saffron stumbled at first, holding his breath as Ryder held him close down the narrow trail they found and broached. The moment they entered the verdant corridor, Fiachra wriggled free of Saffron's tunic and shot into the sky like an arrow.

"Let's talk somewhere a little more private, shall we?" Ryder went on under his breath, tone shifting from lighthearted to something more serious. "All of this isn't for anyone to overhear."

Saffron didn't want that. Saffron didn't want to be taken somewhere *more private* when the entirety of the ruins were already deserted enough. But he didn't know how to decline, he didn't know what else to do or say. Even if he did, he wasn't sure he would. He wasn't sure he had the option anymore, just like he no longer had the option to avoid Ryder at all. He rubbed his throat at the thought, flattening that itchy feeling of having no choice. He scratched his wrists in habit, next, then hurried to keep up with Ryder's pace as they reached the top of a set of stone steps and immediately took a sharp turn into a thicket of trees.

Ryder's voice, his smile, even the way he glanced over his shoulder was annoyingly handsome as they went—but he clearly knew it. He clearly did it on purpose, as if thinking he could still woo Saffron into trusting him. Unfortunately, that hadn't even worked with Prince Cylvan in the beginning, who was the most beautiful person, fey or otherwise, to walk the earth. Ryder really stood no chance.

"Who are you?" Saffron asked instead, not wanting to play along with the man's insufferable games. "I mean—who are you *really*, because I still don't believe I'm being told the entire truth. I think everything out of your mouth is half a lie. And I don't think you're actually any kind of descendant from the Kyteler family."

"You wound me." Ryder's arrogant smile remained, though he paused his walk. He turned partially to face Saffron, but Saffron leaned away. "Perhaps it's only fair that I ask you that question as well. Who are *you*, Saffron, changeling-beantighe and soon-to-be Crown Harmonious Prince of Alfidel? Or are you the flower of Alvénya today? I would like to know exactly who I'm speaking to before I reveal all of my sexiest, most scandalous secrets."

Despite the playful tone in his voice, the more he spoke, the more Ryder's words edged into accusatory. Saffron's hands clenched into frustrated fists at his sides. But instead of breaking the man's nose, he ground out: "You seem to know plenty enough about me, already."

"Not as much as I would like to. Clearly."

Saffron remained frowning; Ryder looked more than pleased with himself. He must have known Saffron was three words away from turning on heel and storming away, because he motioned with his hand for Saffron to continue walking with him.

"I'm not leading you away for nothing. Before we check on your friend, I have a gift for you, if you'll take it. To make up for all the trouble I've caused you so far. Come on."

Saffron grumbled in annoyance, but followed all the same. He kept his hand on the stolen rapier on his belt the entire time, hoping he looked at least a little bit threatening in the process.

The overgrown path confused Saffron the longer they walked, with its piecemeal stonework, the occasional column arcading in different states of crumbling, the occasional peeks through the trees across distant landscapes of grassy plains only visible through brief windows in the fog. He wasn't sure how far they walked, only that there was a slight incline on the path that soon made the backs of his legs ache with effort. When he had to stop and catch his breath, clutching the ache in his chest, any sense of pride he had left went straight out the window. At least Ryder didn't say anything snarky, didn't offer to carry Saffron on his back or anything more humiliating than that—he just stood and waited, patiently, though kept his eyes on Saffron the entire time. He only spoke again when a handful of humans suddenly appeared at the head of the path, carrying buckets of water and a basket of lake fish between them. They were laughing, smiling, jovially sharing in a conversation, all four of them pausing to nod and wave and say good morning to Ryder, who smiled and returned it. Something about it was surreal. Something about it—was far too normal. It twisted Saffron's insides into a knot. It reminded him too much of Beantighe Village.

"Why do you look so surprised?" Ryder asked. Saffron scowled, finally straightening up again but keeping his hand pressed to his chest. Ryder's eyes flicked down to it, before back to Saffron's face. "Your prince did that to you, didn't he?" He asked, motioning to it. "At his engagement party. On Ostara."

Saffron didn't want to answer, like always, but once again he found himself more curious as to how Ryder knew any of that at all. Again, and again, he wanted to know how Ryder knew everything he did. Knowing that asking outright never led to straightforward answers, however, he decided to play along. Perhaps he could learn some of the information he wanted without ever giving Ryder the thrill of thinking Saffron was curious.

"Not on purpose," he answered, touching his fingers back to

his chest with one hand, opposite hand returning to the pommel of his sword. "He was compelled to do it."

"Everyone thinks that's the shot that killed the rogue arid witch."

Saffron recalled what Cylvan told him in the royal infirmary right after he woke up. *They think I killed you. When I fired that bolt into your chest... they all assumed you died, and that's the pervading rumor in Avren..."*

"Probably for the best." He forced himself to smile, albeit in annoyance. Playing along might be harder than he expected. He used to be so good at it, smiling and nodding and playing along with someone's bullshit, especially when he was trying to get something out of them—but maybe his time at Mairwen had slowly eroded that ability away. Had left him too exhausted to ever put up with any bullshit. He really should re-learn how to be a good beantighe, again. "Otherwise they would all be on the hunt for me. And it would be a lot harder for me to blend in at Mairwen."

"Aren't they? Considering the recent influx of witchhunters in Avren... that's not thanks to your prince, is it?"

"What? Of course not," Saffron practically growled.

A little seed of information, to see if Ryder took the bait and revealed more of what he knew. Instead, Ryder watched him for a long time, before motioning to Saffron's ears.

"Glad to see you've already removed that ugly glamour," he said, before stepping closer and catching Saffron off guard. "I much prefer you as you are, your highness." He pulled Saffron's hood up as new rain sprinkled from the clouds. "Like this, I mean. You're much prettier as yourself. A shame those fey can't see it."

Saffron's mouth dropped open to tell him off, but it caught in his throat. He never expected the weight of those few words, even from someone who had no reason to tell the truth, who clearly was trying to impress Saffron in any way he could. But not because no one had ever said such a thing to him—Ryder seemingly knew everything, except how often and prayerfully Cylvan reiterated how Saffron's real face was his favorite, how beautiful he thought Saffron was.

No—perhaps the surprise stemmed from how Saffron forgot he'd already removed it at all. He squeezed the pendant in his pocket at the thought. His heart thrummed nervously when he considered—the fey lord who gazed back at him in the mirror every morning was no longer a stranger. Would there come a time when he wouldn't even recognize his own human face any longer?

26

THE COTTAGE

"How much farther?" Saffron asked with as demanding a tone as he could muster. Ryder smiled that uneven, arrogant smile once more, finally motioning up ahead. Saffron glanced around him to see the encroaching end of the path, blocked off by a pair of golden wrought-metal gates. On the other side, they climbed yet another set of mossy, broken stone steps until, at the very top, a modest stone building waited for them.

Its thatched roof blended with the thick trees in every direction, and Saffron inhaled a long, deep breath of air. It was crisp, fresh, lacking any of the warm, buttery scents of Avren he'd grown so used to, leaving only the fresh mountains and the sound of birds. A breeze through the trees. A distant trickle of water. His heart fluttered as he couldn't help but be reminded of the Agate Wood, where he once found so much solace and peace during his miserable time at Morrígan. How could he have forgotten that sweet feeling so easily, once swept off his feet and brought to Avren? As if, in an instant, every worry and pressure and tension he felt in his new life was stripped away as easily as the glamour fell as soon as he pulled the amethyst from around his neck.

Behind him, Ryder undid a padlock on the door of the little

cottage, glancing back at Saffron and nodding with his head to follow. Saffron bit his lip, but did, though clutched the pommel of the rapier again. Fiachra, meanwhile, fluttered back down again to perch on the lantern rod outside the door, though it was clear she had no intention of joining him inside. Saffron couldn't blame her. He himself stopped at the threshold, unsure if he was confident in following the man farther inside, too.

The inside was dark and cluttered, but not in the way of a place that had been abandoned. It reminded him more of Baba Yaga's bedroom closet, or perhaps Cottage Wicklow's pantry, or maybe the attic where they stored extra moth-eaten blankets, pillows, veils and uniforms, broken furniture that could be used for firewood, other contraband that would get all the cottage residents in trouble if discovered. Cluttered, but intentional. No dust on the floor or tables or anywhere else, implying someone came and visited regularly enough to tidy up.

Ryder disappeared into a closet door at the end of a long work table scattered with old herbs and leaves, while dried bundles of other wild plants hung from a series of strings across the width of the house. The air smelled spicy and bitter, and Saffron found himself creeping inside slightly more as his curiosity got the better of him.

Dragging his fingers down the length of the table, he went past where Ryder had disappeared, ducking beneath a low-hanging valance of bundled herbs and stepping into the next room, strangely enamored by the small bed in the corner, the wash basin, the little window that gazed out over foggy rolling fields at the base of the hill. There was another study table against the wall that reminded Saffron too much of the one in his attic room in Danann House, swallowing back the lump forming in his throat and approaching to see what book was spread open on it. But then the lump grew, lurching upward in the form of a gasp. *Intro to Aridity: A Beginner's Guide to Magical Terms, Crafting, Spells, and Concepts for Spring Witches.* He'd seen that book once before, scouring his memory, before realizing it was one of the few

Pimbry Scott had offered him before she was tried and killed in the street. Before Cylvan and Asche were forced to burn down the bookshop, and everything inside of it...

Grabbing it, he flipped madly through the pages. His heart pounded until it ached when he realized there were handwritten notes inside. Down the margins, between lines of printed text, in the blank gaps between chapters. But it wasn't just one set of handwritten words—it was many. Many readers, many note-takers. A whole group of them, maybe even across time.

"Our little secret, right?" Ryder asked. Saffron jumped, slamming the book shut and whirling around in surprise. Ryder smiled at him, leaning against the entryway. "This is exactly like the one where we'll go see your friend in a little bit. I've already given her all the books I have about arid plants and plant magic, too, so she has plenty to do and learn while hiding out. There's even a little lake next to hers so her undine girlfriend can stick close by."

He shrugged from the doorway and approached. Holding out a closed hand, he waited for a moment before sighing and claiming one of Saffron's to open his palm and take what was being offered. A small, black stone ring plunked into his grasp, and Saffron raised his eyebrows in confusion.

"This stone is called hematite. It's made from the blood of deceased rowan witche—"

Saffron jerked backward in alarm, but Ryder grabbed his wrist before he could make it far. "Whoa, hey! It's alright, listen—it's not like Proserpina's Silver, alright? This stuff won't give you any extra powers—it just helps to localize them. It attracts the iron magic in your blood, helps you learn how to narrow the control and visualize it and all that. We use them when teaching Spring Witches their first arid circles. It helps with deliverance, too, so you don't wear yourself out too quickly. Think of it like one of the daurae's yew bracelets, except this won't just keep you from feeling sick. It'll actually help you."

Still, Saffron's ears rang at the mere idea of wearing anything made from the parts of a once-living being. He squeezed his eyes closed, forcing himself to just—just breathe. Just breathe.

He closed his hand around the stone ring. Inhaling through his nose, he forced himself to look down at it. Ryder's own hands hovered around his, as if anticipating Saffron dropping or throwing it.

"I know they've done terrible things to you with their own magic; with their opulent silver, and more," Ryder whispered, and Saffron's eyes snapped up to meet his. Those words cut like knives into Saffron's back. "But you don't have to carry that burden alone any longer, Saffron. There are people here who have gone through as much as you have, and you can teach each other what you know. You, especially, can teach us all things we'd never know without you." His eyes were intense, holding Saffron's in a vice. "Ériu never wished us to live this way. You know that, too."

"What do you want from me?" Saffron asked weakly. His hand in Ryder's trembled. He could only watch as the man pressed the ring more firmly into the center of his palm.

"Nothing more than what I've already asked—I only want your help," Ryder beseeched softly, stepping closer until they stood a foot apart. Until Saffron could see each of his dark eyelashes, the freckles on his cheeks from the sun, the fine scars on his jaw and over the bridge of his nose. So small, so thin, as if they'd been painted on. "I want you to trust me until the solstice. I want you to take on the mantle of someone these people can look up to, as a symbol of hope. You, the first rowan witch in centuries. Who will not abandon them when others have. Who won't vanish when things get hard, or complicated. Morale around here is lower than ever, ever since Sunbeam left, and the people just want... someone to look up to."

"I don't want to fight in any wars—"

"Who said anything about a war?" Ryder frowned. "I'm not building an army to fight with them. I'm teaching them the magic they have every right to know, and they can choose what to do with it on their own."

Saffron bit down on his tongue, embarrassed. He stared down at where their hands were entangled. Ryder's breath disrupted his hair.

"Why don't you do it yourself?" he asked next, voice quiet. "You're their leader and all."

"I may be their leader, but I cannot be their inspiration. Not like you can. I can inspire them to rebel, maybe, but I cannot show them all the wonders of arid magic like you. You, the rowan spirit, who could be so stunning. Who could be so bright, and visible, and terrifying, if you wanted to. It's like I said the first time—together, we can do wonderful things for these people who wish for a better lot in life. We can do wonderful things to reclaim our place in society, as equals to these fey who have subjugated us. If you only agree to be the rowan spirit for these people to look to for hope like you once did for the beantighes of Morrígan."

"I... I won't let you hurt him," Saffron replied pathetically, despite knowing it was a terribly selfish thing to say after everything Ryder spoke leading up to it. But Saffron couldn't help but think of Cylvan any time talk of beantighe wellbeing was mentioned, especially after all he'd done for Beantighe Village when it was destroyed. He remembered how it sounded for Cylvan to command Saoirse to allow Hollow, Letty, and Nimue leave the night of the witchhunters at the palace. *Humans are not property.*

Saffron believed Cylvan would help. He believed Cylvan would be an invaluable asset to whatever Ryder had planned. He was even at the palace that very afternoon to speak with the kings about what could be done about the witchhunters in Avren. Did Ryder really not care to know? Was he really so embittered toward even the prince that he would refuse to listen, until Saffron forced him to talk to the kings on the solstice like they once agreed?

"I will have no need to do anything to your prince if he agrees to play his part."

"Which is?" Saffron asked, jumping when he realized exactly how close their faces were. He held his breath when Ryder's hand found the center of Saffron's chest, right where Cylvan had shot him. Saffron bit down on his tongue as the fingers applied enough pressure to make him flinch.

"I only wish for an equal world," he whispered. "Like Ériu intended. Like Acacia Kyteler intended. Like Verity and Virtue Holt intended. Everything has gone so wrong since Queen Proserpina's Night Court—I only wish to set things right again, for all humans' sake, on this side of the veil and the other. We deserve to live and practice our magic as freely as these opulent fey, don't you think? Even your prince should be able to recognize that."

"He does," Saffron started, before slowly closing his mouth. Knowing it didn't matter what he said, as he could tell by Ryder's expression exactly how little the man would believe anything good he said about the prince of the next Night Court. Instead, Saffron pressed his lips together, not wanting to talk about it any longer. He knew what he needed to know. Ryder knew what he needed to know, too.

"How does this ring work?" he asked to change the subject, pinching the black stone ring between his fingers. "Does it have anything to do with the witch's mark you promised to tell me about if I came to visit?"

Ryder chuckled, claiming Saffron's hand back and snatching the ring to tuck it onto a finger, opposite Saffron's emerald courting ring.

"For you, specifically, rowan witch, I have a special request to see how it works. The next time you have a chance to practice some arid-ogham circles or steles... instead of physically putting them down, like carving them into the dirt, try drawing them with this finger, here." He touched the tip of the finger donning the ring. "Use this finger as your wand."

"My what?"

Ryder smiled like his most favorite thing in the world was when Saffron asked questions, giving him the opportunity to go on and on about how smart he was. "Like I said before, wands are used by spring and iron witches when learning to focus their magic, usually in the form of the utensils used to carve hatch-marks in their arid-ogham spells. Using any knife, stick," Ryder wiggled Saffron's stolen rapier. "Or *sword* you find lying around is actually considered crude—but those are all technically wands, too."

Saffron's thoughts ran wild. He gazed down at the ring again, before thinking back to how he'd used Elluin's silver needle to carve the arid marks into Taran's back. Had it counted as a wand then, too, despite being an opulent tool? He could already imagine the heated debate such a thing would spark between him and Professor Adelard, if he ever got the chance to ask.

Ryder watched Saffron's face the entire time Saffron considered it, and he worried he'd given something away simply by not asking any further questions. He snatched his hand away again and held it behind his back.

"You still haven't told me anything about a witch's mark," he said. He used his most polite-but-demanding prince voice to do it. "You promised me information the last time we were together."

"Ooooh, look who's suddenly making demands," Ryder crossed his arms, leaning back against the desk. "Actually, your highness, I prompted *you* to try and find that information on your own, first. Remember?"

Saffron ground his teeth together in annoyance, then turned back to him.

"You and I both know there won't be any information about something like that in a high fey library."

"Then what have you been doing in all our time apart? Other than attending fancy parties and enjoying all your little classes."

Saffron thought he might pop, though didn't know if it was more out of irritation or embarrassment.

"Give me unrestricted access to that library I saw in the cathedral," he insisted. "That one in your study."

"There are no books on witch's marks in my study, first of all. Secondly—I don't let just anyone read what's in my library whenever they want," Ryder answered, tapping a finger to the book on the desk behind him. "Especially not wild valley witches who are engaged to the current high fey Crown Prince of Alfidel. Like I said before, how am I supposed to know you won't turn around and tell him everything you read? There are some very dangerous secrets in there."

"What, your sexiest and most scandalous ones?" Saffron mocked.

"Some of them, yes."

Saffron pressed his lips together, not sure how else to argue. Ryder loved every second of it.

"If you intend on being prince, and then king, you really should learn how to make your demands harder to refuse," Ryder smiled. "Come on, be a little brattier. Maybe I'll fold and give you anything you like. Do to me whatever you did to wrangle your prince."

"Oh, bratty works for you?"

"It would from you."

Saffron narrowed his eyes. Ryder kept smiling.

"I can help you, but I can't give you every answer about a witch's mark right away. Why don't we practice some other things together, first? I think your overall craft could stand to improve a little bit," Ryder went on.

"Can you try and be a little more condescending? That comment didn't annoy me as much."

"Apologies, your highness. I assumed you'd be used to being talked down to by now, what with the Night Prince as your fiancé and everything." Ryder finally stood, mouth still tilted in that infuriating, uneven smile. "You promised me until the solstice. I'm going to take that time and put it to good use, teaching you everything you need to know. So that when we do manage to get you your witch's mark, it won't be for naught. You really will be the most powerful, wonderful, amazing rowan witch to walk in Alfidel."

Saffron held his breath with how closely Ryder approached again. Staring up at him, he didn't know how to respond. He could hardly find his feet to finally turn away, breaking their gaze.

"I... I'd like to see my friend now," he said, before hurrying toward the door. Ryder laughed under his breath, following Saffron out.

To Saffron's relief—and slight surprise—Ryder obeyed as he promised. Still, the entire way back down the path, turning to continue deeper into the woods, Saffron's heart pounded. His thoughts raced. He gazed down at the shiny, black stone ring, then farther up his arm to where Taran's name was carved beneath his sleeve. He wondered if something so small could truly be such a blessing. Akin to a yew bracelet. A means of tightening his control, even the smallest bit. Focusing it. It wasn't a witch's mark —but with it, Ryder better proved his knowledge, his potential to help, just a bit more. Saffron should have been thrilled—so why did he only feel more anxious?

THE FOG WAS THICKER IN THE WOODS, BUT RYDER seemed to know the way as if it was the path back to his own home. Saffron kept close, kept on his guard, kept one hand on his sword while they walked, all while Fiachra swooped in and out of the sky overhead. Occasionally he asked about ruined stone buildings they passed, always a little surprised at how much Ryder knew about each one. He talked of them as if he'd been there when they were fully intact, but the youth on his face betrayed any question of his age. He couldn't have been any older than Cylvan, if Cylvan were judged in human years. Twenty-five. Maybe twenty-six, twenty-seven. Perhaps he was as passionate about those buildings as Saffron was about pausing every time he thought he heard something wild crunching through the fog where he couldn't see. He wished he'd brought his sketchbook.

The trees finally thinned before opening wide into an endless meadow of long grass waving in the wind, and Saffron's heart leapt at the sudden release from the crowded trees. The thick fog remained, but he could hear the lapping of lake water, could smell the grass and the fresh air, as well as—bread. Fresh bread, made with cinnamon and rosemary, just like Baba Yaga used to make. His stomach flipped, hurrying his pace, nearly bypassing Ryder entirely, had the man not reached out to grab him by the sleeve.

"Slow down, Saffron. This clearing's a lot bigger than it looks. Wouldn't want you to get lost. I promise, I'm taking you the quickest way to Letty."

Saffron didn't say anything. He also flushed slightly in embarrassment, nodding and turning away. Glad the fog was so thick, hoping it did something to cover the color in his cheeks.

"I'm surprised your prince allowed you to even come see me, today," Ryder went on. Saffron scoffed.

"I'm free to come and go as I please."

"He just seems like someone who... struggles to relinquish control. Especially on someone as wild as you are."

"I'm not wild," Saffron muttered.

"Please, you don't have to lie to me. I mean it as a compliment."

"You can keep your compliments to yourself from here on out."

"Oooooh," Ryder chuckled. "Hard to believe you still don't care for me, despite everything I've offered to do for you."

"I haven't asked for anything," Saffron insisted, despite knowing it was an exaggeration. He hurried his pace when he realized how childish he sounded. "And you're right, I don't care for you. I don't like you, either. I'm only here to make sure my friend is alright, that's all."

"You're welcome to want more from me," Ryder repeated for a hundredth time. "I'm not about to stop offering."

"I wish you would."

"Why?"

"Because it implies I don't know what I want." Saffron didn't expect his tone to come out so firmly. "Or that I don't know what's best for me. If I need something specific from you, mister

Kyteler, I will be sure to ask. I appreciate your offer to help me learn magic, and I can assure you I will take advantage of what you have to offer when I think I need it—"

"You're welcome to take advantage of me in any way you like."

"—but you should know you're not my only source of information!" Saffron's voice cracked. "So until I actually ask for something again, just—shut up, already!"

Ryder laughed. He laughed at everything Saffron said, as if every word was the last one he expected to hear. Saffron huffed in another wave of embarrassment, hurrying faster with confidence when he spotted the dark shape of a cottage appearing through the mist, sitting right on the edge of the water.

Without waiting for Ryder to catch up, Saffron raced up the rickety steps of the wooden porch, straight to the front door, where he knocked twice before grabbing the knob when he recognized two voices arguing on the other side. His heart leapt into his throat the moment he laid eyes on his freckle-faced friend, arguing with Hollow who was backed meekly into the wall with his hands up in defense. The moment Saffron burst inside, Letty turned to him, face lighting up as she exclaimed his name and nearly tackled him to the ground with a hug.

Saffron hugged her back. God, he hugged her back, knotting his arms around her like cinching a bow around a prized possession.

"I was so worried about you," he croaked. "I'm sorry, I'm so sorry this happened, I'm so glad you're alright."

"Me, too," Letty pressed her face against Saffron's shoulder. "I was worried they'd find you, next. I was so glad when Hollow told me you'd come."

"I wouldn't let anyone take his highness that easily," Ryder said like a promise from the entrance. Saffron pulled away from his friend, frowning at the man leaning with arms crossed against the doorway. Ryder narrowed his eyes back with a sarcastic smile, before putting a hand up and announcing he'd give them some privacy. He must have sensed how Saffron was five seconds away from cursing him to stone.

According to Letty, the night the witchhunters were at the palace, there was no initial indication of them suspecting her or anyone else in the beantighe dorms. They simply passed through without so much as a second glance at everyone and their things, they didn't even pause longer in front of Letty than anyone else. Perhaps because they wanted to catch her off guard, later. Perhaps they wanted to give her a false sense of security, to see what sort of conversation would pass around between the human servants right after no one was arrested. And despite still not knowing how or when, someone must have overheard something. Seen something. Said something.

"Nimue is out in the lake," Letty went on as Saffron poured tea for her and Hollow at the worn table between them. The cottage wasn't much different from the one Ryder had offered for his own use, a single room with a narrow bed in the corner, a cooking pot dangling in the fireplace, a washbasin and towels hanging on the opposite wall, a table that doubled as a place to eat as well as read. "She likes it much better here, I think. Less requirement for legs and all."

"Yeah, I bet," Saffron mumbled. While Letty spoke, Saffron held accusatory eyes with Hollow, wanting to know what had him acting so strangely that morning. He purposefully swirled the teapot and pouring half the grainy leaves into the man's cup as a warning. Hollow groaned quietly, clearly debating his options, only saved at the last moment when a face suddenly pressed against the window and made all three of them scream.

Daurae Asche knocked on the glass, demanding to be let inside. Sighing, Saffron pulled open the window, and Hollow reached out to hook the daurae under the arms to pull them through like a cat lifted out of a kitchen drawer. Inside, they brushed themself off, commenting on the smell of tea and bread and inviting themself into Saffron's seat to sip at the cup he'd poured for himself. Saffron sighed, perhaps relieved the daurae had found him again at all.

"Don't let Ryder see you here, Asche," Hollow grunted. "Who knows how he'll react."

"As if I don't already know that," Asche sneered. Saffron smacked them on the shoulder, hissing about manners while they whined and whimpered at him.

"I'm surprised Cylvan let either of you come here at all," Letty laughed, finishing her tea and pouring another to replace Saffron's stolen cup.

"Cylvan definitely doesn't need to know about any of this," Asche replied before Saffron could say anything. Saffron thought about how Ryder had said something similar as they approached the lake. "And he doesn't need to. Gods know he would throw a bitch fit for the ages, maybe chain us both up in the dungeons..."

The words warbled off as anxiety filled Saffron to the brim. Anxiety mixed with guilt, forcing him to close his eyes and sip his tea. He didn't like keeping secrets from Cylvan. He didn't want to keep secrets from Cylvan. They'd once sworn to one another they never would, ever again.

Saffron would not keep any more secrets from his prince, whether Asche—or Ryder—liked it or not. And, whether Ryder liked it or not—Saffron was sure Cylvan would provide everything in his power under the sun—or the moon of a Night Court —to help Saffron with any request he made. No games, no tricks. Perhaps Ryder could learn a thing or two about wooing the first rowan witch in centuries from the Night Prince, himself.

27

THE LIBRARY

Saffron waited in Cylvan's Mairwen suite for the prince to return, indulging in rifling through every one of his things like he was once invited to do. He couldn't help backsliding into a few beantighe habits in the process, knowing Cylvan likely prohibited Mairwen servants from entering his room to tidy up just like back at Morrígan. Just like at the palace. Saffron was the room's only hope for sustained livability.

He gathered clothes off the floor, threw some down the laundry chute, hung up others, made the bed, wiped down the bathroom counter and eating table—and while it felt strange to spot his high fey reflection in the mirror every time he passed it, heavy-laden with his raven's clutter, the routine movements were cathartic. Familiar, safe, comforting, a series of tasks he knew how to do. Things he didn't have to question or ask for someone else's input on. He might have been the most well-versed fey lord out of everyone on Mairwen's campus when it came to pressing sheets and organizing even Prince Cylvan's disastrous habits.

He was on his hands and knees scrubbing the bathtub when the door to the suite opened and slammed shut, joined by angry mumblings and the sound of a bag and shoes hitting the floor. When the newcomer suddenly paused, going completely silent,

Saffron could practically see the shock on Cylvan's face at the sight of his newly-tidied suite. He scrambled over the edge of the tub and hurried back out into the main room.

"Cylvan!" He exclaimed, making Cylvan jump and turn. The prince's annoyance immediately melted, throwing his head back with a groan of relief and stalking over to collapse into Saffron's arms with all the dramatics Saffron had come to expect from him.

"Did it... go poorly?" He asked, wrapping his arms around Cylvan's back. "With the kings?"

"Ugh. Essentially a non-starter until after the solstice. They worry too much about stirring scandal right before so many members of the court are going to be in Avren for the Midsummer Games. Please say you have something good to tell me."

"What?"

"I assume you're here to give me good news, since you couldn't wait to see me," Cylvan murmured into the side of Saffron's neck, before suddenly picking him up in his arms and carrying him to the nearby chaise lounge, where he dumped Saffron before collapsing on top of him. "I'd like to hear good news."

"Oh... well... ah—" Saffron chuckled nervously as Cylvan's mouth kissed up the side of his throat, hot and distracting. "I have more of a confession than... news... good or bad..."

"A confession?" Cylvan asked in a low, dangerous voice. His teeth scraped lightly down Saffron's skin, making Saffron shiver. He put his hands on Cylvan's shoulders, though there was no effort to push him away. "Go on, then. Tell me. Since I have you vulnerable, anyway, I'll decide if you deserve to face consequences."

"Oh, that actually makes me very nervous."

Cylvan pulled away. He narrowed his eyes, but Saffron kept smiling innocently.

"What did you do, beantighe?"

"Nothing! Nothing, really. Nothing that should come as a surprise, anyway—"

Cylvan's hands found Saffron's wrists, binding them together and bending his arms behind his head. It made Saffron's breath catch, wriggling slightly beneath Cylvan's straddling hips.

"I'm—I'm sure you remember what happened the night the witchhunters were at the palace?"

"Saffron."

"It's just—!" He wriggled, but Cylvan was relentless. "I had to go check on Letty! And Nimue and Hollow. And while I was there, I decided I might as well hear what Ryder Kyteler had to say."

"Saffron."

"You should rest assured he didn't actually have anything new to tell me. I wasn't particularly impressed by anything he had to say at all. I mean, I am curious about some of the books he offered me, as well as what the other humans have going on th—*ah, Cylvan!*" Saffron squirmed, gasping as a hand slid between his legs, curving down and pressing fingers against him through his pants.

"You're in serious trouble."

"Nooooo," Saffron whined, attempting to squeeze his thighs together but Cylvan sat in the way. "Cylvan—!"

"You did all of that today?"

"Yes!" Saffron confessed. "Asche said I should keep it a secret—"

"Asche was with you?" Cylvan's voice turned venomous. Saffron fluttered his eyelashes, smiling as best he could as Cylvan's hand between his legs firmed.

"Asche—was just there to show me the way."

"You are definitely in trouble."

"I know how I want to make it—up—up to you," Saffron panted as Cylvan's mouth returned to his neck, opposite hand undoing the top button of his shirt as the other continued groping him. He couldn't resist rolling his hips, lying his head back over the armrest to try and keep his thoughts intact as Cylvan exacted his punishment. "I want—I need—someone who can get me—into the National Library."

"Hmmmm," Cylvan hummed, tongue trailing a line down the center of Saffron's throat before biting at his collarbone. "And how is that making it up to me?"

"Because you're the only one with enough influence... and power... and prestige... to get me in after-hours. So I can rifle through—their restricted section, in my search of taboo magic. You're the only one who can help me, your highness. It would impress me so much... I would be so grateful."

"Are you sure your new favorite human doesn't have what you need in his dirty old ruins?" Cylvan frowned.

"Oh... maybe you're right," Saffron sighed. "I'll go see him again first thing in the morning, perhaps he really can give me everything I—"

He laughed sharply as Cylvan's mouth smashed against him, silencing him, biting at his lower lip and making Saffron's back arch as the fondling hand between his thighs found its way down his pants. Saffron's hands broke free from Cylvan's grasp, pulling him closer—and shrieking with laughter when Cylvan lost his balance and they both tumbled to the floor.

THE NEXT DAY, PRINCE CYLVAN WAS MORE THAN HAPPY to assert his authority as the Crown Prince of Alfidel in order to get a special access token for the National Library. Saffron kissed him until he couldn't breathe.

Once night fell, he then begged Sionnach to join them, going on and on about how he'd *'asked Prince Cylvan for help getting into the library'* and *'he agreed to help me, isn't he so nice?'* then *'Please, I want to give him a chance. He's been nicer to you lately hasn't he? Come on, don't leave me all by myself with him in an empty library in the middle of the night...'* *'I'm just really... really*

*trying to find some very specific information about, um, Gaeilge,
like I mentioned a while ago...'*

A hard-won battle, but won all the same. Sionnach was terrified of a myriad of things with the entire request, even once
promised that Cylvan wouldn't bother them if Saffron was there.
Mainly—getting caught being there after hours and subsequently
arrested. Getting expelled from school. Losing access to every
restricted library in Alfidel. Losing any opportunity to ever get
grants or research mentorships for the rest of their life. Saffron
just tilted his head, pursing his lips before whispering "I hadn't
thought of that." Sionnach looked like they might faint.

Still, even with a panicked flush in their cheeks and movements stiffer than a corpse bobbing under the surface of a frozen
lake, they joined Saffron outside Muirín Dorm once the sun went
down. Saffron barely had a chance to warn them of one more
change of plans, right as Copper burst through the door on their
heels and threw Saffron in a headlock.

Copper's motivations for joining them, compared to Sionnach's, were slightly less noble: he was jealous of not being invited on
the secret, illegal trip to trespass in the library at midnight. He even
threatened to tell Maeve, which told Saffron his feelings really were
hurt, and Saffron had no choice but to invite him along. Copper
might at least come in handy—he would be the perfect distraction if
they got caught. He could lead the guards in the opposite direction,
then outrun them in an instant. At least, that was what Copper told
him. Almost verbatim. It took a lot more convincing of Cylvan as
they huddled around Mairwen's front gate in the dark, but the
moment Saffron reiterated Copper's threat of telling Maeve, Cylvan
was almost eager to invite his enemy to join them.

"Like you said, Lord Saffron—he will be a perfect sacrifice to
our cause, should something go awry."

"You wearing your noisiest shoes for a reason, Cylvan? I heard
you coming from a mile away. Thought you were a kelpie at first."

Cylvan seethed, instantly on the verge of giving the bitchiest dis-invitation ever, had Saffron not clapped his hands together and declared it time to go.

They didn't take horses because they would be too hard to hide while in the library, and even harder to manage if they needed to make a quick getaway in the late-night streets. It meant the walk was farther than Saffron preferred, and it wasn't long until his chest ached and his lungs complained, eventually having to climb onto Copper's back to be carried. It would have been strange to be seen on Cylvan's, what with their brand-new burgeoning friendship and all Saffron was grateful for the chance to rest without forcing everyone else to stop—though the looks Cylvan kept throwing at Copper made him nervous for Copper's life. He made sure to smile at Cylvan every time they met eyes, though Cylvan always turned away with a small huff to pretend he hadn't been looking at all.

They took a roundabout way to the library, waiting for the street to clear of pedestrians and other potential wandering eyes before approaching. Cylvan was ready with the access token the moment they reached the door, hardly pausing before pushing it open and stepping aside for the others to trail in behind him. It was only when the door closed on their heels that Copper finally let Saffron back down again, but the moment Saffron entered the building, he was left breathless like every other time a library unfurled in front of him.

The Avren National Library was easily five times the size of both Mairwen and Morrígan's libraries, with just as many levels climbing the circular perimeter of that main atrium. A massive overhead dome curved into the sky, painted with charmed gold paint that shimmered even without light on a velvety blue background, exhibiting a map of the stars and constellations Saffron was sure existed in perfect alignment right on the other side of the ceiling. False clouds even collected near the apex, and despite knowing it was all made of stone, kept tricking him into thinking he gazed up at the sky itself. Especially once he realized the starscape traveled gradually across the curve, he might have stood there for an eternity, captivated by the sight. It was only Cylvan's gentle nudge against the small of his back and a soft chuckle that brought him back to earth.

"How does it compare to Derdriu, beantighe?" he asked in a low voice, making Saffron's heart flutter. He grinned at Cylvan over his shoulder, wishing he could exclaim how stunning and miraculous and amazing it was—but that would never be Derdriu, whose face he'd once caressed while wrapped in Cylvan's arms.

Cylvan had already determined where Saffron should begin searching, handing Saffron a scrap of paper with locations and reference numbers, adding a sarcastic whisper of *'remember what I taught you about library navigation?'* Saffron elbowed him, before hurrying off to find Sionnach and take them by the hand to join him.

Unlike other libraries Saffron knew, there were no rows of long study tables, cushioned chairs, candles or desk lamps with warm-bulbed electric light there. That library wasn't a place for sitting and studying, for making oneself comfortable, sharing in light conversations; a part of him didn't believe it was even meant as a place for people to peruse for research or general information-gathering. Something about its unwelcome interior painted to look so beautiful told Saffron it was more of an archive, a prison of information rather than somewhere to openly share what it held in its walls and on its shelves. But rather than depress him—it encouraged him. His heart twirled. He might actually have a chance of finding something, for once.

However, it also meant all the library tomes were harder to read. It meant the collections were stuffed full of anything and everything, an eclectic mix that was instantly overwhelming. Once Saffron found the first section Cylvan suggested—*'History of Magic'*—he stood paralyzed by exactly how far every shelf spread, how tall they climbed. There was simply—so much.

He didn't know where to start—settling on grabbing the first book within reach and cracking it open. Then the next. Then the next—but even two hours into his efforts, he only grew more frustrated. He was supposed to find something new and forbidden—yet, still, there were hardly more than a few sentences that meant anything to him despite the number of promising books he opened. His agitation steadily grew, before snapping and shoving the book in his hand back onto the shelf. He wanted to push it over and watch the entire library bury itself beneath its stupid, useless books.

But as he considered the ways to proceed with his destructive plan, even expressing to Sionnach exactly how he wished to go through with it, something familiar—something nauseating and excitingly familiar—showed itself. The symbol for iron carved into the edge of one of the shelves. Stopping short, he stepped away from Sionnach mid-sentence, captured in an instant.

"Hold on," he said in a breath, partially in disbelief. "I'll... be right back. Just a second."

Sionnach said his name in question, but didn't follow. Saffron thought of only one thing as he wandered away—the symbol was tilted, slightly. He knew right away what that meant. His feet even moved before he fully registered understanding. Recalling how he'd once trailed the same markings around the corner of a bookstore in Connacht.

Another, barely visible in the mosaic tiles on the floor. Saffron would have missed it, had a mouse not scurried past his feet in the light of his lamp. He followed where it pointed, finding another carved faintly in the corner of a study table. He trailed fingers over it as he passed, and his vision suddenly flickered, making him flinch. Shaking his head, he tried to blink away the sudden faint auras ringing his eyes, before realizing—there were tiny, crimson spots scattered around the atrium. It brought him to another halt, blinking a few more times before glancing over his shoulder, realizing what was happening as his companions all shimmered with faint halos of white. His hand immediately went to his forearm—but there was no burning sensation that time. It left him breathless, gazing down at the glamoured scars in confusion, before searching the area again. He didn't want to think about what usually happened after the auras appeared, he *really* didn't want to think about what it meant for them to appear without any blood trickling from his nose or the wolf attempting to tear out of his arm. He just followed the spotted trail of red around the room. Pushing out Ryder's voice that once warned how Saffron's magic would only grow more unpredictable the closer they got to the solstice.

Along the trail of his hunt, a horned daemon suddenly appeared from behind the corner of a shelf, snatching Saffron's hand and tugging him into a cramped, shadowy corridor between books. Saffron barely whispered his name before Cylvan kissed him, gently pressing him into the shelves and smiling between their mouths. Saffron kissed him back for a moment, before snapping out of it and hitting him on the shoulder.

"Stop that!" he hissed. "You're distracting me. I'm actually very busy."

"Hm," Cylvan purred mischievously, ruffling Saffron's hair before nodding in the direction Saffron had been headed. "Go on, then. I'll come with you. Maybe we'll find someplace else even more private."

"Hm," Saffron mocked. He raised his oil lamp in the direction of the nearest glowing mark. "Perhaps I'll be a little more easily convinced if you help me find something impressive. I'm disappointed so far. Nothing you suggested led to anything helpful."

"Oooh, a challenge," Cylvan grinned. "And if I do?"

"You can do whatever you want to me."

"Perfect. That's my preferred reward. I'll follow your lead."

Saffron rolled his eyes, but smiled in exasperation all the same. Cylvan kept on his heels for the next symbol, then through a dim passageway that was so far out of the way of the main library, Saffron never would have found it had he not been shown exactly where to go. Even Cylvan made a sound of genuine curiosity as they passed through a door in the wall, descending a set of stone steps that reminded Saffron a little too much of those leading down to the archives below the Kyteler Ruins.

At the bottom, there was no dust-blanketed floor or wandering spirits—but it was clear that place hadn't been regularly visited in some time, either. Books sat untouched on shelves, many where they belonged, many more stacked around on the floor as if someone had rifled through two-dozen titles before deciding it wasn't worth it to put them all back. As much as it bothered him, Saffron focused back on searching for any more markings around the room.

No more iron symbols revealed themselves—but Saffron stumbled across something else that stopped him dead in his tracks. Around the bend behind a particularly tall and disorganized shelf, a painted portrait on the wall stole his breath away. Cylvan said his name in question, wandering over to see what grabbed him so instantly—and his own breath hitched in surprise.

"That's..." Cylvan trailed off. Saffron forced his attention downward, reading the placard beneath the old frame out loud.

"Dame Acacia Kyteler... Founder of Modern Oralcry and Schools of Arid Magic..." His eyes returned to the woman's face, heart racing for a different reason. By the name he introduced himself with, Ryder implied Acacia Kyteler was his ancestor—but gazing at the woman right in front of him, Saffron knew he'd been right all along to question the man's relation to the Kyteler family.

Acacia Kyteler—looked almost exactly like Sunbeam.

28

THE HISTORY

The woman's features were striking, with dark skin and silver eyes like coins. Her ears were hidden beneath long waves of silvery hair blowing in the wind, so Saffron couldn't tell at first if she was human or fey—but he didn't have to. Anyone who knew better wouldn't have to check the woman's ears or read her title on the placard to know. Her name gave it away.

It was only because he couldn't stop gazing at her, running fingers over the details of her portrait, trying to digest the certainty of her resemblance to Sunbeam, that he noticed the strange posing of her hand. Fingers pinched as if meant to be holding something—and only when he brushed his own fingers over the surface did he sense the slight difference in brush strokes. Pigments added later. Had she been holding a sprig of rowan berries? Maybe an iron cross? A stele with ogham hatchmarks?

His hand traveled to touch her face, as gently as he once touched Derdriu's on the ceiling. Their posing was so similar—and a tiny voice in the back of his head wondered if that was on purpose.

"You don't think... Sunbeam is..." Cylvan said, clearly

attempting to make sense of it as much as Saffron was. Saffron finally pulled his hand away, shaking his head.

"I have no idea," he breathed. "Only that... something told me Ryder was lying about who he was from the beginning. And seeing her, I know for sure. Not to mention all those things he said about Sunbeam, once..."

Cylvan gazed at him in question. Saffron closed his eyes, pinching the bridge of his nose as his thoughts swirled in an agitated tidal wave.

"Sunbeam was originally to Ryder and the humans what Ryder now wants from me. He called it an 'inspiration,' a symbol of hope for the people living in the ruins. But then Sunbeam left, and refused to go back, and Ryder didn't know where to find her."

Cylvan was quiet, gazing at Madame Acacia in thought.

"Perhaps he only wanted her back because he stole her namesake," he muttered. "Perhaps she meant nothing special to him at all. He just didn't want to be caught in a lie."

Saffron's stomach twisted. He'd had that thought, too, but not in such clear terms.

"I think he went there to take her place," Saffron added in a whisper. "According to Asche... she was the caretaker of the refugees in the ruins long before Ryder showed up and took them from her..."

"And took her name in the process. Perhaps to make himself appear more trustworthy. Any human who knows anything about arid magic knows the Kyteler name."

"Like what?" Saffron asked. Cylvan pretended to be insulted, like he himself would never be so foolish to be versed in arid history—but then Saffron nudged him in the ribs, and he laughed under his breath.

"Obviously, even with all my influence, I too have only been able to scrape together things that—well, still exist. Saved from great-grandmother Aryadne's purge. But Acacia Kyteler was the great-great-grandmother of Harper Kyteler—who was Verity

Holt's lover. She helped the Holts win in the War of the Veil. She was also King Elanyl's main advisor even once Verity passed."

"King Elanyl was only king for a few seasons, right? Where did she go after?"

"She was very old by then... I believe she returned to the human world, where she passed away peacefully. Just before she went, though, she gave my father, King Ailir, his true name."

"Did she ever have any children?"

"Not that I know of."

Saffron listened in rapt attention, all the while gazing at Madame Acacia in front of him. All of that felt exactly right, even peaceful, reassuring—but he couldn't shake the feeling there was something he wasn't considering. It was too simple. Nothing was ever so simple. He'd learned that a long time ago.

He gazed at the woman's name on the placard, her title, her accomplishments, planting them like seeds in the back of his mind to blossom again when all the pieces finally fit together. Until then, he had to maintain focus on the task at hand.

SAFFRON HAD NO WAY OF KNOWING HOW MUCH TIME passed, deciding he would simply try to get as much done as he could before Sionnach or Copper came looking for them. Unless they couldn't find where Cylvan and Saffron had gone at all, in which case Saffron hoped they would know it was alright to leave before anyone arrived in the morning and spotted them.

Surrounded by a half-moon of books where he sat on the floor, he scribbled notes into his sketchbook as he went, not sure what would be useful information in the future or not. He wrote down everything. Anything even tangentially related to any useful word he'd ever learned.

The book that captivated his attention most was titled *Hopkins' Discovery of Witches: How Human Witch Hunters Lead to the Demise of Arid Magic in Alfidel; translated and annotated by Fleur de l'Authier.* Saffron's attention was first grabbed by the name of the author, recalling them as the one who wrote the book he once skimmed through in the Aon-adharcach suite, his first introduction to the concept of knocks or 'handshakes' in relation to the veil. The second thing came from the title itself—the words 'human witch hunters.' He couldn't comprehend how or why *humans* would be called witchhunters—and the reality of it made his stomach turn with nauseating disbelief. Still, he fought through the discomfort, scribbling down anything that seemed relevant.

Alice <u>Kyteler</u> documented as the first human to bring arid magic through the veil; said she escaped persercution in the human world for magic in the "early 1300s" (? I think this references a calander date?). While originally coming to Alfidel, ancient writings hint that she settled with the druids of Ptelea (country east of Alfidel across the eastern sea), as they were the first ones to ever write about arid magic. No clear Alvish dates because of a fire that burned the Avren capital centuries ago. Because of course!

While Mme Kyteler (alegedley) found refuge in Ptelea, a witch hunt started in the human world. Religious basis but scholars beleive some people accused were ancient arid witches. Many other victims were completly innocent. Many trials were held based on instructions from ~~Melleus~~ Malleus Maleficarum. "Hammer of Witches".

Mid "1600s": 'Discovery of Witches' published and influenced more witch trials in a place called "New England Colonies."

Queen Aryadne

Saffron's pencil halted. His heart drummed against his ribcage at the mention of the old Night Queen. He swallowed the thorny lump in his throat, forcing himself to keep reading, to continue writing, even though his hand shook.

Queen Aryadne (Proserpina) resided on human side in New England Colonies in mid "1600s". Said this is where she learned

witchhunting tactics later used during War of the Veil during her
Night Court. Similar tactics include:
> *Sleep deprivation*
> *Ducking stools ("swimming tests")*
> *Existence of an animal familiar*
> *Cutting the skin to check for blood*
> *Pricking witch's marks*

Saffron jolted forward. He read faster, skimming so rapidly he didn't bother scribbling any notes.

"*'Witch's marks in the human world were hardly more than moles or dark freckles said to indicate communion with 'the devil,'*'" he mumbled in concentration, "*'...though the name was appropriated during Alvish witch hunts when referring to marks left by the veil when making oaths, i.e. 'rowan marks', 'oath marks', 'witch's marks'—!'* Cy—Cylvan!"

Saffron practically shrieked, eyes bulging as he skimmed further down the page. He called Cylvan's name again, leaping to his feet as he read a minuscule footnote at the bottom. Hardly more than a few lines of text, hardly larger than a pixie's hands. Cylvan snapped the book in his hand closed across the room, hurrying over to lean in and skim where Saffron pointed. Unable to read it aloud, himself, too instantly overwhelmed. Cylvan took the initiative, speaking in a low whisper.

"*'Oracles were traditionally trained under Mme Kyteler's methods to open dialogue with the spirit of the veil, including in rituals to beseech the formation of an oath, the building of a bridge, and the bestowing a veil or 'witch's' mark; because of this, oracles were greatly utilized as witchhunters during Q. Aryadne's Court due to their familiarity with arid magic, specifically rowan magic...'*"

Saffron snapped to look at Cylvan with wide eyes. His entire body swirled, insides twisting the opposite direction and nearly pulling him into two pieces.

"An oracle!" Saffron exclaimed. "It says—they used to open

the veil for people who were trying to make an oath, so maybe we just need to find—!"

"An oracle," Cylvan breathed. His mouth dangled open slightly, first in disbelief, before shifting into something like the one wreaking havoc in Saffron's body. Saffron tugged on his sleeve excitedly.

"The Tuatha dé Danann have family oracles, don't they? The royal family oversees all oracles and oralcry, don't they?"

"Well... yes, but..." Cylvan's voice lowered slightly more. Saffron forced himself to swallow back the thrill. To return his heels to the floor from where his spirit nearly hit the ceiling in excitement.

"But?" He asked softly.

"But... are there any I could trust with a secret like yours?" Cylvan turned back to Saffron, eyes suddenly full of worry. Saffron could see a thousand scenarios playing in his prince's mind, none of them good. All of them ending in catastrophe.

"Oh..." Saffron trailed off. He turned his eyes back down to the book, suddenly embarrassed for getting so excited—but then Cylvan hooked an arm around Saffron's middle, tugging him closer until both their noses were back in the book.

"What's this part above it? Here, about a 'witch's familiar'?"

Saffron searched, before reading out loud: "'An animal 'familiar' was said to help the witch commune with the devil or provide energy for casting spells; it's thought this term was appropriated at some point into the human world from the use of similar companions amongst oath-made witches or mancers. Familiars in regard to arid and opulent bridges were used to ease the transference of magic through the veil...' ah, I wonder if *mancer* is the opulent alternative to *witch?*"

"Focus, beantighe."

"Right..." Saffron thought back to how one of his arid trials forced by Elluin involved 'summoning a familiar'—and how Saffron had used it as a means of trapping Taran right where he wanted him. He smirked at the memory, gazing down at the scars on his forearm as if to curse him all over again.

"Fiachra," Cylvan suggested, breaking through Saffron's distraction. "What about that nasty bird of yours? Since she can't even deliver a letter properly, perhaps she can be useful some other way."

"She's exactly as useful as she needs to be now!" Saffron huffed. "Moreso than your old bird that can't stand the sight of you."

"That's not fair. Balor loves me. He's been with me since I was a child. I was the one who knocked out his eye and even then he stuck around."

"And yet he's been with Baba Yaga for weeks with no reply," Saffron grumbled—but Cylvan might have had a point. Perhaps he could find a way to make Fiachra his familiar, in a real way, in an attempt to ease the burden as much as he could until they could find a single oracle they could trust with his secret.

"Hey," Cylvan whispered, touching under Saffron's chin to nudge it toward him. "This is something impressive, right? Are you impressed?"

"Oh," Saffron chuckled, recalling what he'd said a few hours earlier. "You're right. Very impressive. I was the one who technically found it, though."

"But I'm the one who pointed out that bit about an animal familiar, so..."

"... Fine. Alright," he sighed again dramatically. "Shall we start over, then? I'll be more enthusiastic and impressed with you this time."

"Yes, let's."

"Alright," Saffron repeated, turning back to the book. He cleared his throat, then put on a theatrical look of shock and awe. "Oh, Cylvan, you're incredible! Truly the smartest person I've ever met, no wonder you're in the top three of your class! Just look at what you've found for me, this says all I have to do is—!"

He giggled sharply as Cylvan suddenly kissed him, knocking

the book from his hands as he stumbled backward into the shelf. Cylvan smiled into their pressed lips, kissing Saffron like he was the most magnificent thing in the world.

"You're the smartest, cleverest person I've ever met," Cylvan told him in return, hardly breaking their mouths apart. "You said I could do anything I liked—and I think I want to reward you for all your hard work."

"And what do you have in mind, your highness?" Saffron asked, then inhaled sharply when Cylvan hooked hands under his thighs and lifted him, pressing him back against the shelves again.

"I don't think I can hold myself back," Cylvan told him, clawing at the back of Saffron's shirt. "Will you open my pants for me, Lord Saffron?"

Saffron shivered, but obeyed, moving his hands to where Cylvan pressed into him, grinding his hips between Saffron's thighs and making Saffron's blood boil in anticipation.

"I'm still—ready from last night," Saffron breathed between battling tongues, undoing his own and pulling the waistband down, which Cylvan hooked a hand over and yanked up Saffron's thighs between them. Opening Saffron up to be penetrated, skin against skin as Cylvan's hard length slid and teased between the soft skin of Saffron's thighs flattened between their chests, knees parted over Cylvan's shoulders.

"Still spread open from the size of me?" Cylvan asked. "From how much I fucked you last night?"

"Y-yes," Saffron panted. "But I want more—please, give me more, Cylvan, hurry. Before anyone comes—*mmh!*"

Cylvan pressed Saffron's thighs together, thrusting between them until his cock throbbed and dribbled with wetness, before fingers buried into Saffron's mouth. Saffron instinctively sucked on them, gazing at Cylvan through heavy-lidded eyes, curling his tongue over the bumps of the invading fingers. Biting on them, he gasped silently as Cylvan pressed his swollen length into Saffron's entrance, pushing inside with a warm tightness of something previously well-used and eager for more. With his thighs pressed into his stomach, crushed beneath Cylvan's weight, it was impossible to breathe easily—only made more difficult as Cylvan thrust deep inside, shoving him harder against the shelves at his back. Saffron's legs clenched tighter over Cylvan's shoulders, toes curling in his shoes as he fought against moaning out loud. Cylvan knew how hard Saffron tried to stay quiet, enjoying every moment of it, smiling viciously and slamming inside again while pressing a hand over Saffron's mouth to smother the cries of pleasure.

"Did you spend all day wishing I was back inside of you? Aching for me?"

Saffron nodded pathetically, pressing his hand to Cylvan's still covering his mouth, unsure if he'd be able to keep quiet much longer. He gasped through his nose as Cylvan slammed up into him from below, sometimes rolling his hips with slow indulgence, other times ramming so hard and fast it made the old bookshelves at Saffron's back clatter against the wall. Saffron moaned sharply each time behind Cylvan's hand, barely able to open his eyes, vision blurring and spinning with how it instantly overwhelmed him. He hooked one hand over the edge of one of the shelves, opposite gripping a tight handful of Cylvan's tunic; trembling, white-knuckled, unable to relax for even a moment else he fall to the floor. Else he lose his balance and sink further onto Cylvan's cock piercing him, which would surely split him in half. The thought made him tighten, and Cylvan purred in appreciation, thrusting long and slow before surprising him with another weighty slam of his hips.

Saffron came in an instant, spilling up the front of Cylvan's tunic. His breath hitched, body tightening further, which summoned more demanding thrusts from the wicked prince having his way with him. Folding Saffron over himself until there was nothing in the way of every collision of Cylvan's body against his, stretching his insides until Saffron thought his blood had been replaced with champagne.

"You feel so good, Saffron," Cylvan whispered, pushing hair

from Saffron's eyes that struggled to stay open, struggled not to cross in delight. "Every time I get a taste of you—I swear, you're sweeter than the last. I'll never tire of it—every bite of cake you give me."

Saffron groaned, parting his lips beneath Cylvan's crushing hand. He slid his tongue along the crease between his fingers, before turning his head slightly and inviting them back inside. Sucking on Cylvan's fingers like they were coated in sweet honey, until spit collected in the corners of his mouth. Cylvan praised him the entire time, pressing against the flat of Saffron's tongue, teasing him, tickling the sharp ends of his nails against the back of Saffron's throat. It made Saffron tighten again as his gag reflex flinched, and Cylvan praised him even more.

"You're so beautiful," he went on, removing his fingers to cup the side of Saffron's face with sudden gentleness, kissing him, licking the wetness from Saffron's lips. His thrusts slowed, drawing in and out in long strokes, driving Saffron absolutely mad. Cylvan pressed his face into the crook of Saffron's neck, whispering more compliments and kissing below his ear, nibbling on the curve of it, before his own grasp firmed and he came, inserted as deep as he could between Saffron's legs. Saffron cursed him weakly, but was too hollowed out to actually scold him. He just claimed his mouth and desperately kissed him more, instead.

Saffron's legs wobbled beneath him as they returned to the upper floor of the library, and he couldn't tell if they'd been overheard or if Sionnach and Copper had had their own uncomfortable interaction with the way they were awkward all the way back to campus. Saffron chatted the entire time like he was two coffees into his morning, invigorated and refreshed and experiencing every emotion a human being could all at once. The fresh nighttime air was so crisp, it wasn't too hot or too chilly; he could smell the ocean despite being in the middle of the city; did anyone want to stop for drinks on their way back...?

Arriving back to Mairwen, Saffron wasn't sure how he would manage to naturally break away from Sionnach and Copper in favor of Cylvan's dorm, but Cylvan took care of it, clearing his throat and putting on the practiced voice of *selfish prince who will not be refused.*

"Walk me to my dorm, Lord Saffron? I have that book I offered you earlier in my private library."

Saffron bit back a smile. Copper looked at Cylvan with narrowed, suspicious eyes, while Sionnach looked at Saffron with a flicker of worry—like they thought Saffron was in some sort of trouble. But Saffron brushed off both, yawning and pretending like he was tired, commenting that it was getting late, but he was grateful for Cylvan's offer if it wasn't too much trouble.

"No trouble at all. Come, this way."

Saffron wished Copper and Sionnach goodnight, hurrying to catch up with the dark prince who feigned aloofness and walked away without him. After catching up, he was careful not to be too flirty right away, even waiting to say anything at all until Copper and Sionnach were out of range.

"Will you walk *me* back to *my* dorm tomorrow night? It's very romantic," he whispered with a tiny smile.

Cylvan laughed lightly, shaking his head like Saffron was making a joke. "Of course I will."

"Is something funny about that?"

"Not at all. I was a little stunned by how adorable it was."

"O-oh..." Saffron blushed. "Well, stop it. I really only want to commandeer your bathtub, since you made such a mess..."

"Of course," Cylvan sighed, surprising Saffron by suddenly taking his hand and squeezing it. Saffron's face went hotter, instantly embarrassed, shy, heart racing like it was the first time anything so sweet had ever happened to him—as if proof of their romp in the library archive wasn't already on the verge of dripping down his legs. "Something about studying in secret together in the library is familiar, you know. Couldn't tell you why, though. Hmmm."

Saffron laughed, bumping their shoulders together. "I know one thing that's different from last time."

"Oh?" Cylvan smirked, tucking a finger under the collar of Saffron's shirt to peek at the hickies like rose petals on his pale skin. "Enlighten me."

"You never would have walked me all the way back to Beantighe Village, before."

Cylvan gasped, insulted. "How dare you. I may not have walked, but I distinctly remember carrying you at least once."

Saffron laughed again. "Well, from now on I want to walk. It doesn't go as fast that way."

"Let's take the long way around. We'll take the path along the edge of the shore. Come on, over here."

Saffron followed behind him, giggling as he was pulled along to keep up. They took a sharp left onto a worn path into the trees, soon reaching the end of the foliage for a fenced-off path on the edge of the drop-off into the sea. Saffron had to stop and appreciate it for a moment, mesmerized as always by how bafflingly far it stretched to the horizon. Had the moon not been so bright, it would have been only blackness, except for the occasional flickering light of a sailboat. He closed his eyes, breathing it in deep, tempted to jump and take a late night swim.

"Is it all you ever hoped for?" Cylvan asked, crossing his arms on the fence and leaning against where Saffron stood.

"What, the ocean?"

Cylvan chuckled again. "School."

"Oh. Hmm," Saffron exhaled, leaning back and swaying as he gazed up at the stars. He thought about his classes, the good and the bad ones, the weight of trying to balance all of it while also navigating the unpredictable maze that was Ryder Kyteler and his promises. He thought about the lecture he shared with Cylvan, and then the class with Copper where all they did was scurry around in the underbrush in search of wild creatures. How a week earlier, they'd used that class to search for a new hollow-home for the rainbow pixies living in the vents in their dorm. He smiled at the thought of joining Sionnach for art classes one day, and all the times they'd studied in the library together like any other students did. He reached out to put his hand on Cylvan's holding the railing. "I like some parts of it better than others."

"What parts don't you like?" Cylvan asked cooly. "You mean Copper? You can tell me, I'll be sure to keep it a secret. For the record, I don't care for him, either—"

"No, not Copper," Saffron laughed. "Copper is really nice. He's funny, too, and a good roommate." He thought about it a little more, biting his lip as he wasn't sure exactly how much he wanted to talk about. He didn't want Cylvan to worry, especially with everything else going on around them. "I... I don't like that I have to share you with other people, even on campus. They all look at you like something to eat, especially in that class you're an assistant for. God, I've never heard so many tedious opinions spoken by the most vapid people to exist... *it's said Cú Chulainn batted the sliotar into the hound's mouth with such force it died instantly—was that meant to be taken literally or as a political metaphor? I can't imagine a beast would die in such a way'—* Listen! They absolutely can, and I have the scars to prove it! Rich, coming from a high fey who's probably never held a hurling stick or even seen a dog in the wild before..."

Cylvan held back his amusement all the way until Saffron finished, where he burst out laughing, hanging over the railing and howling into the sea far below. "Gods above, I wish you would have said that in front of the whole class! I'd love for every single one of them to fear Lord Saffron, the flower of Alvénya, defeater of wild hounds."

Saffron laughed, too. "Maybe next time, if you promise to praise and compliment me a lot. Make them all believe you think I'm the smartest, cleverest, most interesting person in the room. They should know they don't stand a chance. It would really make our public engagement that much sweeter."

"Our engagement? I thought you had a fiancé back home,"

Cylvan teased, pinching at Saffron's courting ring. "What was his name we gave him, again? Lord Rockmuncher?"

"It was... oh, god, I actually don't remember. I guess my time in Alfidel has changed me. I can't even picture his face anymore... there's someone else that comes to mind when I want to feel my heart race."

Cylvan grinned. "Unfortunately, I worry I must break your heart, flower... I have far different preferences for who makes my heart race."

"Oh?"

Cylvan smirked, eyes mischievous. "There's this beantighe I met back at Morrígan. I simply cannot get them off my mind."

Saffron barked a laugh, shaking his head, though it was mostly to hide the blush on his cheeks. "I suppose I should expect nothing less from the seelie Prince of Alfidel."

"What can I say? Humans are much more preferable than fey. Softer, warmer, more polite, submissive... which makes them far more fun in bed."

"Oh?" Saffron feigned shock. "I wouldn't know. I've only ever slept with my high, noble, extremely opulent Alvényan lord fiancé. I suppose that's to say I really don't have any chance of seducing you as well, my lord."

"I wouldn't say that. I feel like you have a secret. There is something... soft and human about you."

"There's nothing soft about me. How dare you imply I'm anything other than a flawless and perfect high lord carved from marble sourced from the deepest reaches of Lugh's—ah!" He yelped when a hand suddenly cuffed the back of his neck, laughing when Cylvan squeezed and almost made his legs buckle.

"Definitely human," he whispered. "No high fey would show off the bare skin of their neck like this, let alone whimper so pathetically when grabbed by it. Not when they know how it makes high fey like me think horrible, disrespectful things."

Saffron turned, grabbing one of Cylvan's horns and yanking him down, smiling at the grunt of surprise it elicited. "I could say the same thing about these," he said in a low voice. "Something to hold onto, I think."

"Be careful who you grab so roughly." Cylvan smiled darkly, stepping closer, backing Saffron against the railing. "Especially if you're unprepared for what might happen."

"What might happen?" Saffron tugged again, heart racing at the deep sound that came from the back of Cylvan's throat. "Should I be frightened?"

"Oh—terrified."

Arms locked around Saffron's waist, and the ground vanished beneath them. Saffron shrieked a laugh, throwing his arms around Cylvan's shoulders and flailing his legs. Cylvan laughed with him, pulling him close and angling their embrace toward his dorm on the lake, all while accusing Saffron of hiding something, lying about his fiancé, his name, where he came from. Even once they returned to solid earth, Cylvan refused to silence the accusations, pulling Saffron toward his dorm as Saffron attempted to cover his mouth and silence him. Up the stone path, through the front doors, they couldn't stop laughing and whispering for the other to *be quiet, someone would hear them, they had to be more careful.* Saffron couldn't stop laughing even as they stumbled into Cylvan's suite, reduced to hardly more than wheezes and having to prop himself against the wall to try and catch his breath.

Even as their mouths found one another again, stripping naked piece by piece while stumbling lip-locked to the bathroom, hands groping one another while drawing a bath, hissing for the other to be quiet again, to be careful, giggling and fighting for dominance all the while. Even as Saffron perched on the edge of the tub and Cylvan opened his legs, sucking on him while using his fingers to clean Saffron out, Saffron couldn't stop smiling. Tugging on Cylvan's horn, he laughed every time the prince growled playfully in response.

Even as they washed one another in the bath, then fell into Cylvan's bed naked and barely toweled dry, Saffron couldn't stop smiling. He collapsed against Cylvan as his heart swelled and spun in pure elation, climbing on top of him and kissing him all over again. Unable to get enough. Never satisfied, not even once he was fully devoured all over again, sinking heavily into sleep draped over Cylvan's chest.

Perhaps there was at least one simple truth in the world: Saffron would forever be madly in love with Cylvan dé Tuatha dé Danann.

29

THE PRACTICE

It was another quiet few days of attending classes while Saffron scrambled to figure out a way they could find and get in the good graces of an oracle. Scouring the limited offerings of books in the campus library, even attempting to meet his *High Fey Theology and Opulence* professor outside of normal lecture hours to, as casually as possible, ask if she would be any more willing than the first time to discuss oracles and veil magic— only to be reprimanded about how *'people in Alfidel know better than to ask such taboo questions so blatantly'*; how Saffron should be more focused on his piling late assignments and failing test grades than bothering her with such impertinent questions. He rubbed at his tightening throat the entire time she scolded him, before finally gathering his things and leaving in the middle as soon as he tasted blood pooling in the back of his throat. Cylvan, channeling his frustrations from the lack of progress with the kings over witchhunters in Avren, already had his hand on the door to the headmaster's office to complain when Saffron finally caught up to him and begged him to let it go. They went into Fullam with Sionnach and Copper for dinner instead, where they bought Saffron an endless line of drinks and entertained him so much and for so long he finally burst into tears because he couldn't stop laughing.

He and Cylvan wrote endlessly back and forth about what was common knowledge about oracles amongst high fey, including how wealthy families generally had their own; how many towns and cities had a few on hand for the welfare of the people living there; how most practiced standard oralcry while others specialized in things like divination, trauma healing, altar and temple priesthood, historical religious study and advocation, mentorship to new oracles, and so on; they also discussed how not every half-human, half-fey was expected to become an oracle, but since their opulence was naturally diluted, and they had no reason to perform aridity outside of oralcry practices, they were rarely given opportunities elsewhere. There were even fully-fey oracles as well, though their responsibilities differed greatly. Many courtiers, politicians, religious leaders, and oracles who practiced most traditionally claimed only half-humans should be allowed to train and practice; others believed anyone half-human should be purged from the practice entirely—and Saffron couldn't believe how much contention existed in every facet of fey politics, no matter where he turned. Perhaps he shouldn't have been so surprised.

Only when they finally broached the topic of memory threading did Saffron remember he once knew someone studying to be an oracle to specialize in just that. A half-human, half-fey little shit who had tangled fingers around in Saffron's mind at the demand of Taran Mac Delbaith. But Saffron wasn't sure Eias Lam was meant to be their savior, even if they'd apologized for what they'd done with Saffron's memories. Saffron wasn't sure they'd ever even be able to find them, since they and Magnin had both gone as silent as Taran since Ostara.

All the while, Saffron grew more and more aware of how Balor had not yet returned with a letter from Baba Yaga. Cylvan even wrote to Headmistress Elding using another palace crow, and was assured nothing had happened to the old henmother in the previous weeks. Perhaps Balor was just enjoying his time with her.

Perhaps he'd gotten distracted on his way to or from campus. Perhaps it was nothing more than poor timing victimizing his anxiety. But Saffron's nerves refused to temper. If there was any time he needed wise words from his arid henmother, it was then. He wasn't about to send a third attempt at a letter, either—and he felt more trapped, more suffocated, every time the bird still failed to return.

When the conversation around oracles simmered, Saffron focused on familiars. Witch's familiars, how they were used in the human world or within arid magic. He snuck nights in the campus library with Cylvan like they once did at Morrígan, growing bolder in how they were seen together more and more as time went on. But as he already knew, the campus library didn't provide anything useful for him. Even Sionnach, who searched the restricted section by Saffron's request, had nothing to offer. Cylvan's access to the National Library had expired, and he wasn't sure he'd be able to request another without raising questions. Saffron was—stuck.

When a robin eventually arrived donning a scroll on its leg, Saffron knew who sent it before having to look. A note from Ryder, asking when Saffron would be back to visit again. Saffron wanted nothing more than to write back 'I don't need your help any longer, Mr. Kyteler, I've found everything I need already"— but instead sighed and bitterly scribbled back: *I'll come see you again in a few days.*

Perhaps there was a half-human person living in the ruins who he could ask. Perhaps Ryder, despite being so unbearable, could provide an iota of help with the lead Saffron had gained. Even if he still didn't have any ideas about a witch's mark, the man may be able to, at minimum, shine some light on how to perform a familiarizing spell with Fiachra.

If not that—then Saffron might at least get his chance to ask why Sunbeam resembled Acacia Kyteler more than Ryder ever did.

. . .

Saffron scribbled into the crow book after turning the words over and over in his head, making sure they were perfectly innocent and clear and brief so as to not alarm his prince with the sudden request.

I am leaving to do some additional taboo research away from the school today, with a particular maggot I know you greatly dislike. I promise I will be home in time for the gala tonight. I will be wearing my pendant, too, and I will respond if goes warm. I love you.

It took a few minutes for a reply to come, and Saffron braced for what words would appear in answer. They were a relief, and Saffron fell a little more in love with his raven as he read them.

Be safe. I look forward to hearing all you've learned when we see each other again. Even if that maggot has nothing to give you, don't get discouraged, our own search is far from over. If you feel inspired, don't hesitate to rub it into that man's face how much I impress you and how well I satisfy every one of your needs.

I look forward to seeing you tonight. Try to be back in time for me to ravish you before the party ever starts.

I love you.

Saffron's amethyst glowed warm a moment after the words finished, and he smiled to himself, holding it in return. *Thank you. I'll be back soon.*

Despite never telling Ryder exactly when he would be visiting, the man was there waiting for Saffron at the cottage that morning. He frowned at the sight, a part of him having hoped to scour the cottage's minimal offering of books without Ryder ever knowing he'd come by at all. He considered turning right back around and going to visit Letty's cottage first, instead, but then sighed and accepted his fate. Fiachra was all too displeased with the decision, taking every opportunity to nip at Saffron's ear in protest before finally flying off to sit stubbornly on the thatch of the cottage roof.

Ryder sat outside the front door, leaning over a long, bowed branch with a carving knife in one hand. Tiny sounds of blade on wood lured Saffron closer, stepping from Boann's back in order to get a closer look. Ryder glanced up the moment his boots hit the earth, and Saffron smiled before thinking. Ah—perhaps he still held on to some beantighe habits, after all. He cursed himself.

Ryder smiled back, sunny and cheerful, actually catching Saffron off guard with how genuine it was.

"Good morning, your highness," he said, getting to his feet and putting out a hand for Saffron's doublet. Saffron shrugged it off after a moment of hesitation, then question, since it was still cool enough to not get overheated. But he hated asking Ryder questions, so he obeyed. More beantighe behavior.

But then Ryder frowned upon looking Saffron up and down, and Saffron frowned right back.

"Your prince sure does like dressing you like a fancy little pet, doesn't he? I suppose to show you off before anyone even knows you're his."

"What's wrong with how I dress?" Saffron asked, glancing down at himself. Napped leather leggings; a light blue, high-collared tunic that cinched at the waist; polished leather boots with metal leaf lace pins. Oh, maybe he knew what Ryder meant after all. "I don't... have anything more casual," he grumbled. Why would he? Considering what he was *supposed* to be doing day-to-day, things that very much were not *meeting human rebels in the woods.*

"I'll grab some things for you next time," Ryder promised. "So you can be more comfortable while you're here. And so you stop freaking everyone out when they see you. God, the rumors I had to address last time because you didn't take your glamour off until after you'd attacked Breton's entire group on the road."

"I'm just used to wearing it," Saffron huffed. At the thought, he patted around on his chest, hating the thought of pulling the amethyst off—but he didn't want to keep wearing it if Ryder was going to continue giving him grief. "Also, stop calling me *your highness*. Just call me by my name."

"Then I'll grab some more comfortable clothes for you next time, *Saffron*. So you don't look like such a prissy thing out here in the woods."

"I'm not—!" But then Ryder held the carved branch toward him. Saffron nearly snatched it, wanting to snap it in half in annoyance, or maybe smack him with it—but then he realized what it was, and the urge clamped behind his teeth. A curved longbow, oiled and polished to shine, though he could tell by the layers of carved designs that it wasn't a brand-new branch Ryder had cut himself. It resembled the same markings as on Breton's stolen crossbow, or the sword he himself had snatched from Diana.

"This is...?" He trailed off, feeling how lightweight it was in his hand, made of oak, or maybe maple. It was hard to tell with the reddish-brown stain on the outside, though the leaf design carved into the grip definitely resembled oak. It was ornate down to the smallest details, with even the eyelets at the top and bottom tip shaped like leaves where the string would be looped and pulled.

"I heard you were asked to perform the opening shot at the Midsummer Games. But you don't know a damn thing about archery, do you?"

Saffron frowned. He bypassed asking 'and how exactly did you hear that?' knowing it was futile.

"What makes you say that? I know plenty about archery."

Ryder cocked an eyebrow, then motioned to the bow. "Go on, then."

Saffron's frown deepened. He waved the bow in annoyance. "There's no string. How can I prove anything with a broken bow?"

"Gods above. Just as I thought," Ryder laughed, approaching him. "Let me just show you, alright? You don't have to be so stubborn all the time. Must be exhausting. Take a break from the fey act for one morning. It might be a nice break for you."

Saffron grumbled under his breath, hating how his cheeks went hot in embarrassment.

"Seems they've taught you to forget *thank you* so quickly, too."

"Th-thank you!" he exclaimed on instinct, before scowling. Ryder couldn't bite back his satisfied smile, removing a coiled cord from a little pouch on his belt. He unraveled it with a flick of his fingers, searching out a loop on one of the ends.

"The handle there is old as hell, found it in the armory; this bowstring is brand new, though, so it might be a little tight to start with. Here, I'll show you how to string it."

Reclaiming the handle, Saffron watched Ryder loop one end of the string through the ornately carved tip, then rotated and tucked the wooden beam into the inner curve of his boot. Pulling down on the flexible wood, the muscles in his forearms strained as he bent it enough to slide the second loop over the opposite tip and notch it into place. He moved with such ease, Saffron was unintentionally hypnotized by it.

"Easy," he said. "Were you paying attention?"

"There wasn't a lot to see."

Ryder smirked, then to Saffron's frustration, popped the string off and handed it and the bow handle to him. Saffron gaped in disbelief, holding both, before huffing and proceeding to do the same steps for himself. It was harder than Ryder made it look, especially since he struggled to find exactly the right angle to bend it in order to notch the opposite end, more than once pulling wrong and launching the bow shaft a hundred feet into the bushes. He wasn't even completely unpracticed with using one, especially since they'd occasionally have them in Beantighe Village for hunting when food offerings were particularly low—but he'd never been made to string one, himself. He'd never even had to shoot anything with accuracy. But he wasn't about to use those excuses on Ryder, who would just laugh that stupid laugh and claim it had something to do with pretending to be a high fey for so long.

Saffron finally gave up when the bow snapped and smacked him in the face, splitting his lip and sending Saffron into a rage. He would have thrown it into the woods had Ryder not grabbed his hand and yanked it back, laughing so hard he bent over his knees to catch his breath. Instead of insisting Saffron keep trying, he finally strung it, himself, then grabbed Saffron's hand before Saffron could avoid it.

Licking the blood from his lip, he followed the man around to the back of the cottage, where a handful of wooden slabs dangled from tree branches around the edge of the little clearing.

"Oh," Saffron said in surprise. "You... really put a lot of thought into this."

Ryder pulled him into place, handing over the bow and an arrow fletched with owl feathers. Behind them, Fiachra made a little noise of disapproval.

"Get into position," Ryder instructed.

"Alright. You win. I don't know what that is."

"Then get into what you *think* is position and I'll nudge you in the right direction."

Taking the bow in one hand and hooking a finger over the string with the other, Saffron barely pulled it back a few inches before Ryder *hmmm*'d, patting around on his belt.

"Almost forgot," he said, before taking Saffron's hand to slip a leather thumb glove and wrist brace over it. Saffron watched in continued, embarrassed silence as Ryder cinched up the strings below his elbow, then motioned for Saffron to continue.

Saffron focused on the closest plate of wood hanging in the trees, holding his breath as knowing hands suddenly slipped in, tapping his bowstring elbow higher, straightening his grasp on the handle, adjusting where his hand sat on the grip, then indicating exactly where he should place the target in the view of the tip of the arrow. Saffron did everything as Ryder said, shaking it out before pulling back again, only to still miss when he loosed it.

Ryder said nothing, handing over another arrow to try again. Then again, and again, as each and every time Saffron launched it into the woods. On the fourth try, Ryder finally let out a clearly restrained laugh, and Saffron smacked him with the carved bow.

"You're not helping!" he insisted. "You don't know anything about archery at all, do you!"

"I do!" he insisted with a grin, putting his hands up. "Why'd you think you'd master it in one go? It's alright to be bad at things when you first start."

"Not for me." Saffron put his hand out for another arrow, but there weren't any left.

"We'll have to go get the ones you shot into the ether," Ryder said with a nod toward the trees. Saffron grumbled, setting the bow down in the grass and tromping ahead to do just that.

They spent another two hours shooting, gathering, shooting, gathering, until finally Saffron's patience grew so thin it snapped, and he cheated by drawing an ogham circle on the target with his finger donning the hematite ring, then a companion stele down the length of the arrow, all while Ryder cooed at him about how cheating was wrong. Saffron ignored him, more curious to see if it would work at all. When the arrow slammed dead-center in the target's circle, he barked a laugh, grinning arrogantly back at Ryder who chuckled and shook his head. Saffron carved more steles, more arid circles, thunking arrow after arrow into each piece of wood with growing confidence.

"You act like they'll let you do that at the opening ceremony, too," Ryder said, pulling out a lunch offering from his satchel in the grass. "You're not learning anything at all like this."

"They might let me," Saffron argued, setting the bow against the side of the house and collapsing into the grass with a sigh.

Breaking to eat, Saffron was amused by Ryder's repeated attempts to befriend Fiachra who sat on Saffron's shoulder, though she couldn't be swayed even by the offerings of treats. He just ate his lunch in silence, letting Ryder suffer rejection over and over again while definitely not encouraging the owl's behavior by offering her bits of dried meat whenever she snapped at the man's hand.

When Saffron wasn't teasing either of them, he was gazing off into the line of trees. Listening to the birds, the breeze, the chittering of squirrels and magpies, he couldn't help but sigh at the innate peace it brought him. Mairwen was right on the woods, too; he could hear similar things through his dormitory window, too—but something about it was... different. Something about it was almost unsettling, rather than comforting. Perhaps because, when he heard those sounds alongside Mairwen, it was always as Lord Saffron, the high fey, the visitor from Alvénya. But there, sitting in the shade of the secret cottage housing books about arid magic, seated alongside a human man who preferred Saffron without his glamour, who exhumed an old bow from the ruins' armory, cleaned it up, and spent all morning showing Saffron how to use it, Saffron felt... normal, again. For the first time in longer than he could remember, he felt like everything was back to normal, again. Almost like he was back in Beantighe Village, surrounded by likeminded people he didn't have to worry so much about hiding from while right amongst them.

"You're sighing a lot," Ryder commented. Saffron sighed again. He didn't want to talk about it. Especially not with that man, specifically. He took another bite of his sandwich, searching for any other reason to explain himself.

"I don't get a lot of chances to sit in the grass and listen to the birds, anymore," he said, skirting the line between truth and not saying too much. "Back when I was just a beantighe at Morrígan, though... this is how I spent all of my free time. Wandering around in the woods, drawing the wild fey I found, memorizing paths through the trees that only I knew about. I never realize how much I miss it, until... well, until I do, I guess."

"You have a lot on your plate, I imagine." Ryder nodded. It was the first time he'd said anything sympathetic to Saffron's situation, not painted with sarcasm or something else. "How do you never feel like a caged bird when you're with him?"

"I won't discuss Prince Cylvan," Saffron reiterated. And he would keep reiterating the same thing, no matter how many times Ryder tried to bait him into it.

"Like a caged bird with *them*, then. The high fey," Ryder said, rolling his eyes and laying back in the grass. He bent arms behind his head, closing his eyes as the sun warmed his face. "They put on such a big show of *tradition* and *honoring the roots of their wild ancestors* and their *connection to the elements,* especially those Sídhe with elemental magic they all laud so much... but how often do any of them just...?"

"Walk around in the actual wilds?" Saffron chuckled. He couldn't help it. "Not often, unless there's a paved path. So their shoes don't get dirty."

"And only if they have a picnic basket and a bottle of wine in tow."

"And they have to be wearing their most florally-embroidered clothing, so they feel one with the natural surroundings. But as soon as a bug or a leaf ends up in their hair..."

Ryder laughed, and then Saffron laughed. A part of him felt bad, but—there was a special kind of relief that came with speaking so openly, so plainly, with another human like that. He'd always been able to do that with his friends back in Beantighe Village. Maybe he didn't realize how desperate he was for that kind of easy chatter until it was in front of him.

"Thanks for taking care of Letty," he went on, deciding to offer a speck of vulnerability. "I... don't think I properly said so, last time. Thank you as well for providing her things to do, like books to study. I think she really has a knack for plant magic."

"Letty is a doll," Ryder sighed. "Her undine girlfriend, however, is a bucket of trouble."

"Nimue's harmless so long as you are."

"I am most certainly harmless. I'm practically a fluffy little dandelion compared to the company you keep on the other side of these trees."

Saffron shook his head again. He was running out of food to bite into to buy some time to think of a response, so he chewed a little slower.

"Not all high fey are so wicked." It wasn't what his instincts told him to say, but the words escaped nonetheless. There was nothing in the way to stop them.

"Let me guess—"

"I'm not only talking about Prince Cylvan," Saffron interrupted. He was also talking about Sionnach, Copper, and Luvon —even the kings, to an extent.

"But you are also talking about him."

Saffron pressed his lips together. But he couldn't bite it back. "Yes, I am. And I'll keep defending him every time you say something like that, no matter how many times you try to get me to speak poorly of him."

"Why?"

"Because I think it would be unfair of me not to."

"What kind thing has your prince ever done? No, let me finish." Ryder propped himself up on his elbows as Saffron attempted to argue. "What kind thing has he ever done for beantighes *other than you?*"

Saffron scoffed. "He's the only reason Beantighe Village was rebuilt so quickly, and so well, back at Morrígan since it was burned down. Which vastly improved the lives of the people who live there. He also allowed Letty, Hollow, and Nimue to leave the palace on their own free will, when he was technically their patron-master and could have demanded they stay. He also knows where this place is, in case you've forgotten, yet he lets you all stay here freely."

"Sure. And what of the beantighes who live in the palace?"

"What about them? He—"

"What is he doing to improve their lives?"

Saffron frowned. "I don't know exactly what he's doing when I'm not—"

"Exactly. Because he knows you don't see it. So he doesn't. You know as well as I do, because you were there when they left—there are plenty of humans seeking refuge here, as we speak, who escaped miserable lives in your prince's own palace. There are humans who've escaped miserable lives on Mairwen Academy's campus, too, where, need I remind you, he's been back to attending for months. Where is his grace for those beantighes? Or is it reserved only for the ones you know personally?"

"What is he supposed to do all by himself?" Saffron said tightly.

"He's the Prince of Alfidel, Saffron. Who else has any power to do anything?"

"He can't just wave his hand and make grand, sweeping changes. Even if he did, it doesn't mean the cruelty would stop. You can't just write a new law that says 'humans don't have to be beantighes anymore'!" The words tumbled out of him, unhindered, unstoppable. "Because then what would they do? Where would they go? They have no connections outside of their patron families. High fey have no reason to house or employ them honestly. If anything, it would only leave them all like foundlings without anywhere to go, and they would all be forced to live as refugees in ruins just like these ones. It's not as simple as Prince Cylvan walking into the palace and making beantighehood illegal. Plenty of cruel, illegal things happened on Morrígan's campus—but they never faced any consequences because just making things *illegal* doesn't mean anything if there's no system in place to enforce it."

It left him breathless. He didn't know where it came from, those frustrations he'd clung to for years—decades—perhaps even his entire life without ever putting them into words. Stringing those words together. Let alone uttering them out loud. But it was the first time he'd been able to truly vocalize why everything Ryder said, everything he was doing, frustrated him so much when on the surface the man's intentions were good. They were things Saffron agreed with, things Saffron found inspiring. Things he wanted to be part of. But something about the way Ryder spoke about it like it was as easy as 'removing humans from their contracts' made him wonder if the man had ever been a beantighe in Fjornar at all. If he'd ever actually been a foundling with nowhere to land on his feet.

His heart thudded when thinking of the portrait in the basement of the National Library, and how that implied Ryder actually did lie about most things when it regarded where he came from. Saffron's mouth opened to accuse the man in an instant—before he slowly closed it again. He remembered how intent Ryder was on finding Sunbeam, and how intent Sunbeam had been to get far away from Ryder. Too scared to speak a single thing about him, simply wishing to disappear through the veil and never speak to anyone ever again if she could help it. It was the only thing to keep Saffron from tearing Ryder apart with accusations right then and there.

Still—Saffron couldn't just say nothing.

"You keep accusing Prince Cylvan of being unhelpful, and cruel, and mean, but he's actually been far more helpful than you have." Saffron hoped those words stung, just a little bit. "He was able to get me into the National Library of Avren just the other night, where we found books on veil magic and oath making. I even have an idea of where to go, now, in terms of getting my witch's mark."

Ryder surprised Saffron with silence in return. Saffron was suddenly apprehensive at the thought of meeting his eyes, so he didn't, just drawing circles in the grass.

"Is that so?" Ryder finally asked. Saffron nodded. "And what, exactly, did you learn?"

Saffron told him about how oracles were supposed to be able

to speak to the veil, open communication with it, even how they were traditionally the ones who opened the veil in the first place with the intention of making oaths. Ryder remained silent, but Saffron felt his eyes on him. Growing heavier, sharper, until Saffron thought his lungs were being squeezed from the inside.

"So what will you do now?" Ryder asked, next. Perhaps because Saffron wasn't caught up in his handsome smile, he sensed how the man fought to keep the sharpness out of his tone.

"I want to learn how to familiarize with an animal," he answered, turning to seek out Fiachra at the thought, who was busy attacking a wild blackberry bush near the corner of the cottage.

"What, to familiarize with a bird who doesn't even like to fly?" Ryder asked.

"And whose fault is it she's afraid to fly?" Saffron snapped back, before forcing his mouth closed. He took a deep breath. "Why are you so angry? You should be thrilled. You're the one who once said I should find some information on my own. Well, I'm finally able to contribute."

"Yes, something you found in a high fey library, on the heels of your dear prince—"

"I know what restricted archives look like!" Saffron practically snarled at him. "I spent weeks in one beneath the Kyteler Ruins! I know how to tell if a book is genuine or fake. You're only angry because Cylvan was a real help to me—without all of the same games you keep playing."

"Don't test me, Saffron," Ryder growled. "I am the last person you want to—"

"You don't scare me, Ryder Kyteler," Saffron hissed. "Sunbeam made an enemy of you long ago, and she made it out just fine, from what I saw. She spent an entire year scrubbing floors at Morrígan Academy without ever being found by the likes of you."

Ryder moved fast. Saffron flinched backward, but it wasn't enough. Ryder grabbed him by the front of his tunic, tearing the fabric and yanking Saffron closer to his face.

"They have you thinking like this!" He shouted. His fist burrowed into Saffron's pocket, grabbing his amethyst. Saffron attempted to snatch it back, but Ryder yanked it away, snapping the chain. Saffron threw his hands out for it again, but Ryder clamped fingers around his wrists and slammed them into the grass over his head. "They have you wearing fine clothes and a glamour that hides who you really are—they have you at their galas and in their classes, and now you think you're one of them! Smarter and better than the rest of us, is that it! While you've been sleeping on silk sheets and eating four meals a day, the humans you were meant to protect are starving and sick! Yet you accuse me of something as petty as jealousy? You think I'm jealous of that Night Prince—that evil fey lord who will destroy any progress we make the moment you do something to upset him? Look me in the eye and tell me who is more likely to be *petty* and *jealous*, Saffron! Why else are you so terrified of making a single mistake! Of being imperfect!"

Fiachra screeched, talons flaring as she crashed into Ryder and tore at his hair, shrieking and slashing until Ryder threw an arm back, knocking her into the grass. Saffron cursed at him, throwing himself back and forth in further attempts to break free, but Ryder said nothing. He watched as the owl righted herself again, shaking out displaced feathers—before grabbing the amethyst in her beak and taking off into the sky. Saffron watched her go in disbelief, heartbroken tears burning in the backs of his eyes.

"Get off of me—!" He commanded, writhing beneath Ryder's weight. The tightness in his throat returned; he was pinned by the wrists. By hands, or by cuffs, he didn't know, but he couldn't move. Restrained. His heart pounded harder, faster, kicking his legs and thrashing his upper body. "Get off of me, Ryder! Let me go!"

"Where will your prince be when your magic tears free and slaughters everyone in sight?" Ryder asked in a low voice, pressing a thumb into the scars on Saffron's forearm until Saffron's eyes watered. "When one day you get too overwhelmed trying to bow to his whims, and you hurt someone who doesn't deserve it? Think about Daurae Asche. Think about those friends you're making at Mairwen. What then?" He pressed harder into Saffron's wrists, and frustrated tears finally spilled from Saffron's eyes. Blood choked at the back of his throat, dripping from both nostrils as he pitifully begged for Ryder to let him go. "We both know you can't control that beast. Not yet. Has your prince even seen it? Would he trust you to control it? Or would he be afraid of you? You and your wolf that resembles Taran mac Delbaith so much, who tortured and abused Prince Cylvan for years—do you really think he will still trust and love you once he realizes the horrific thing you're hiding from him?"

"Stop it!" Saffron screamed. Heat swelled in his forearm. As if Ryder could sense it, he pressed a thumb into the scars again, making the pain swell to a fever pitch. Saffron begged him to get off, get away, he could sense the magic rising in his body, flooding his arm, overwhelm spilling from his nose and into the back of his mouth, but Ryder remained right where he was. Breathing heavily, face hardly a foot from Saffron's. Crushing him.

"I'm the only one who isn't afraid of you, Saffron," he said. "I know you can learn to control this beast. I know you can learn to control your magic. That's all this is—it's just your magic running wild, out of control inside of you, anchored to your emotions because that's how you first beseeched it. Full of emotion, full of fear and horror and uncertainty. But I know you're strong enough to hold it back. I can see it on your face right now—you're fighting against it, aren't you? Because you don't want to hurt me. Because you know I'm right. You know I can help you. I can tame you. You know that, one day, when it's revealed you're completely imperfect, and flawed, and unique, and *special*, unlike anyone else who has ever existed—I will be all you have left."

"P-please," Saffron's pleas sputtered out like a candle flame with only a fingernail of wax left to burn. How that man could claw down into Saffron's being and dredge up every fear Saffron had always carried, but could never put into words—he was being hollowed out and put on display for the last person he ever wished to see him so vulnerable.

"He wouldn't—he won't..." Saffron sobbed, shaking his head.

Ryder's hands finally released Saffron's wrists, and Saffron stiffly bent his arms to pull his hands into his chest. Shielding himself from Ryder's digging hands, though one still found Saffron's cheek, thumb smearing away the thick blood pooling under his nose.

"I know you think that," Ryder whispered. "But you barely know him, Saffron—and he knows that, too. He may only be taking advantage of that naïve part of you that wants nothing but a love straight out of a myth. But you fell in love with him when he was trapped, when he was desperate for anything to distract him from his own suffering. He used you as a way to amuse himself, until he could escape from Taran. Then he used you as a means to do just that for him."

Saffron's lips quivered. He tried to shove them back, but he was reminded of Cylvan's first betrayal. Tricking Saffron into learning about arid magic, so that Saffron might be able to charm the fern ring to protect his true name from Taran. With the intention of leaving Saffron to the wolves if they were ever found out; to abandon him to execution while claiming innocence...

"Ground yourself, beantighe."

Saffron's heart skipped. He lurched, throwing his head back, in every direction, searching for the owner of that voice. The owner of that horrible voice. Why did he hear Taran's voice? His arm burned. It burned, throbbing with his racing heart as he squeezed his palm against it.

Saffron's fingers bent in on themselves. They fondled the hematite ring he wore, the one Ryder gave him. His eyes cracked open, blurry with tears, seeking out Ryder who remained hovering over him. Caressing the side of his face, wiping the blood from his mouth.

"There," Ryder whispered. "Just breathe, Saffron. Relax. Good. You're safe here with me. You don't have to go back, you can stay here with me. Where you belong. Where you know you belong."

"No," Saffron whispered. Cylvan was expecting him back in time for the gala. Saffron was going to be late. He'd wasted another day away with Ryder, learning nothing, gaining nothing, as the solstice crept even closer. "No—let me go—"

"Back to him?" Ryder asked. His voice was flat. "Despite everything, you still wish to return to him? What will you do when he decides to keep you from ever coming back?"

"He won't have to," Saffron's voice cracked, a frustrated, overwhelmed sobbed escaping him. "I'm never coming back here again. I don't need you, you haven't done a thing for me. You just keep—wasting my time."

Ryder was silent. His hand remained cupped under Saffron's jaw.

"I'm wasting *your* time?" he asked, low and accusatory. "You blame me for wasting time—when it took you a whole month to finally come see me? Had I not brought Letty here to keep her safe—you never would have come to me at all. Yet I'm wasting *your* time? When you know as well as I do what a walking danger you are?"

"Get off of me—I have to go—"

"No," Ryder growled. He grabbed Saffron's arm again. "No, Saffron—I can't let you go. You're not going anywhere. Not when I'm the only one who knows exactly what you're capable of. I'm not going to let you leave this place again, when you're going to hurt people. Try and deny it all you like, but you're going to kill people!"

"No!" Saffron begged, throwing his hand out, smashing it against Ryder's face, fighting again to kick him off. "Get the fuck —off of me, goddamnit!"

He couldn't stop it—magic surged through his body, vibrating his bones, compounding in his arm, and bursting from the seams. The rotten smell of the beast filled his nose before the sound of heavy paws colliding with the earth ever hit Saffron's ears. Ryder leapt off of him in an instant, stumbling backward, away from where the wolf hovered protectively over Saffron still on his back. Saffron rolled onto his side, gasping and crying, fighting to regain any composure he could scrape together. For the first time—he found relief in the smell of that animal. The way it shadowed his vision. The feeling of it nearby, shielding him.

"Saffron," Ryder attempted once more, answered by the low growl of Saffron's beast. A clawed foot pawed at the ground alongside Saffron in threat, head low with ears back, never taking its eyes from Ryder. "Saffron, do you see? You can't deny it any longer—if you summon it even to threaten me, the only person who has ever offered you—"

"Shut up," Saffron begged, finally pushing himself upright. The wolf stepped aside, just enough to give him room, before stepping forward again. Placing a foot over Saffron's middle, guarding him as his back was to Ryder. "God, just—shut the fuck up, already. I never want to hear your fucking voice again."

He pushed himself to his feet.

"I'll find somewhere else for my friends to go," he said, finally turning back to Ryder. He knew his face was red, splotchy, eyes swollen with tears, but he didn't care. Ryder stared at him in reply, looking a little frantic, like he knew he was watching Saffron slip through his fingers. And there was nothing he could do to stop it. Not unless he wanted to be torn apart by the teeth standing between him and the rowan spirit he wanted so badly.

The rowan veil belonged to Saffron; he never stopped being the rowan spirit. Ryder never had any right to offer it to him at all. And Saffron would prove it to him, to his human coven, in due time. Saffron didn't need Ryder, didn't need his promises of a witch's mark. If the wolf that protected him was truly the incarnation of his wildest, most violent magic—then so be it. He would find his own means of taming it without Ryder Kyteler's help.

"You need me, Saffron!" Ryder shouted as Saffron turned to Boann in the trees. "You know your prince has a breaking point— you know there will come a time where he won't protect you any longer! You're really going to turn your back on the people who need you most—to be some high fey's beantighe whore instead?!"

Saffron ignored him. He heard the wolf's body shift as if Ryder attempted to follow. Saffron ignored him. He pushed out everything Ryder said, every insult, every accusation of Saffron's betrayal. He grabbed Boann's reins, kicking his leg over the saddle. The wolf vanished the moment he steered the animal into the woods, rushing into it without a trail to follow.

Only when he was far enough away that Ryder's angry shouts no longer found him—did Saffron finally allow himself to break, hunching forward and sinking into gasping sobs.

30

THE DANCE

Saffron eventually found Avren again on the other side of the woods, but didn't realize how much time had passed in the process. He didn't realize much at all. Even once back on the streets, Saffron hardly registered the thought of steering Boann in the right direction—just staring at his hands clutching the reins, only vaguely considering which way. Staring at his hands, his wrists, a constant reminder that there were no silver cuffs there to restrain him. Staring at his hands, his forearm, a constant reminder that—there was something dangerous living inside of there. His wild magic, manifested. An eruption of violence that fed on his emotions, one that would continue to feed until he figured out how to stop it. Whether it be a familiar spell or a witch's mark, he wasn't sure any longer. He wasn't sure what mattered. He could only hear Ryder's words, even as they cut him. Even as a part of him screamed to ignore them, because Ryder was not someone to trust.

But then how did he know exactly how to speak every one of Saffron's deepest fears aloud? Fears Saffron had avoided, pushed away; others he hadn't even yet discovered, but knew to be true the instant they struck him. Digging and digging deep enough that soon that wolf in his arm was more of a comfort than the man himself. Pushing Saffron over the edge. Until he was danger-ous. Until he could have hurt someone.

He pressed a hand to his face, squeezing his eyes closed. He couldn't think. He couldn't think. It was all he had to keep from crying again, from allowing himself to feel anything that might summon the blood back to his nose. It was all he could do to not cause a scene when people already turned to look, to gaze in question at the human covered in dirt, wearing a torn tunic and riding on the back of a fey lord's horse. He didn't look at them, either. He stared down at his hands. Bare. Unrestrained.

He didn't know how long he wandered on the back of the horse, except the sun had set. Avren was illuminated with street lanterns and cheerful voices in taverns and in the streets. Saffron was exhausted. His head spun. His eyes kept filling with frustrated tears before drying again, never once allowing them to drip over his cheeks. He barely noticed when a barn owl suddenly descended from the sky and landed on his shoulder. When another black horse suddenly trotted up alongside him, and a brunette fey lord reached out to gently claim Saffron's reins from him. He didn't protest. He let the stranger take them. In his foggy mind, he was just glad to be able to close his eyes and let his head hang forward, heavy with an invisible weight on the back of his neck.

The stranger pulled Boann off the road into the trees. In the darkness, Saffron wavered on his balance, collapsing gladly into the arms of the person who gently took his hands and pulled him from the saddle.

"It's alright, Saffron," Cylvan whispered. "You're alright. You're safe, now. I've got you."

The tears he'd been holding back dripped over his cheeks. Saffron lifted his hands to shakily touch Cylvan's face, finding him back to normal, the glamour shirked. His chin quivered, touching the prince's face all over as Ryder's words bombarded him—until he could no longer hold it back, bursting into tears. Cylvan wrapped Saffron in strong arms, pulling him in close and petting the back of his head. Whispering reassurances, promises of safety. *You're safe. You're safe. I've got you.*

Saffron clung to Cylvan as a terrified, inexplicable part of him worried his chances to hold tightly to his raven might soon come to an end.

SAFFRON COULDN'T REMEMBER HOW THEY MADE IT back to the palace. He didn't know how long it took, when they got there, how he ended up in that room where beantighes puttered around him, dressing and preparing him for the gala with the rushed atmosphere of someone running late. Saffron could faintly hear the sound of a party happening through the windows, telling him he really was late. He was going to miss it, if they didn't hurry. But—he couldn't find the strength to help. He couldn't find the strength to do anything except gaze at his own reflection in the mirror. Wearing his glamour again, returned by Cylvan, who complimented Fiachra the entire way back to the palace. *She brought your pendant to me. She took me right to you. She was so insistent, she flew so fast. She attacked me more than once when I couldn't keep up. What a good girl, the best girl.*

Fiachra perched on the mirror Saffron stared at himself in, preening the feathers of her wings and purring occasionally in satisfaction. Whenever she noticed him looking, she paused to give him her full attention, adjusting her stance as if preparing for him to spin the recall ring and give her a task. Every time, it made him emotional all over again.

"Good girl," he whispered, voice cracking. "Good girl. Thank you for bringing him to me."

AS ALWAYS, SAFFRON'S PRINCE OF DARKNESS WAS stunning in the palace's brightly-lit ballroom, garden windows open wide for guests to come and go with the warm nighttime air. Cylvan was the most beautiful person in the room, as always. That time, Saffron didn't bother pretending like he didn't look. He wasn't sure how he'd made it to the ballroom at all. He couldn't even recall what his outfit looked like. His ears rang endlessly, his head hurt, his chest hurt. No—his heart hurt. Beaten down by everything Ryder had shouted at him, all of Saffron's deeply-buried fears and insecurities dredged up by that man's hands without any care for how they would leave him feeling like a ghost in his own body.

The only comfort he could bring himself was the repeating thought—that he never had to see Ryder again. He would never have to ever see Ryder again. He could find somewhere else to send his friends so they would be safe; he could find what he needed with Cylvan's help in Avren. Saffron didn't need Ryder Kyteler, he'd never needed Ryder Kyteler, and Saffron never had to lay eyes on him ever again.

"Good evening, beautiful," Copper's flirty voice came from behind, and Saffron turned with a habitual smile, though it took a few extra moments for him to feel the positivity reach the rest of his body. Copper complimented him again, pinching the pretty fabric bunched between ribbons on Saffron's sleeves, then offering him another drink. "One of King Tross' designs again? He sure knows how to doll you up. What kinda favors are you giving him for the gifts?"

"It's not like that," Saffron laughed weakly. A flicker of life returned to him, allowing his heart to beat differently. Copper was like an immediate splash of color in the blurry, overcast place Saffron floated. Saffron chased that offering of vibrant distraction, explaining how Luvon and King Tross were old friends. How it meant Saffron had connections.

"Ah, so King Tross is sorta like your patron-fey while Master Luvon is gone. Since you're a beantighe and all with that name of yours. Wish I had my own patron-fey to watch over me, *sighh*," Copper went on, clinking their glasses together before throwing his back. Saffron followed his lead, feeling even better as the first mouthful of alcohol hit his stomach. He sighed at the sensation, hoping it would smooth out all the wrinkles in his demeanor. The last thing he wanted was for someone to ask him what was wrong, anyway. "Ohhhh, the ice queen's got her grips on your favorite prince. Does that drive you crazy or what? I think you could take her, though."

Saffron followed Copper's indication, smiling to himself at the sight of Cylvan and Lady Maeve dancing in the center of the crowd. Courtiers swooned and fanned themselves as Cylvan pulled Maeve closer, turning her with the music, hair and skirts and sparkling jewelry making them look like dolls plucked straight from Tír na nÓg. Everyone smiled at one another like they clearly thought it was a perfect match even after all those years. Cylvan and Maeve, who were once expected to court one another when they were only children. Had Saffron not known any better, he might have actually felt jealousy—but he could see how tight Cylvan's smile was, how bloodthirsty Maeve's was in reply. Staring at one another without blinking, like it was a challenge to see who would break, first. Saffron swore Maeve's fingers were even slowly freezing Cylvan's as their palms were pressed to one another, sure he could see the slightest blue discoloration on Cylvan's skin. It made Saffron laugh, the sound of it surprising himself.

Saffron claimed another glass of wine, liking the way it helped his mood. How it helped blur away his most recent memory. He claimed a second drink before asking Copper to dance, and Copper agreed with a massive grin, leaving his own half-empty glass right there on the edge of the buffet table. He scooped Saffron completely off his feet, making Saffron laugh as he was hauled out onto the dance floor. Copper, at the very least, knew better than to be too rambunctious in the middle of everyone else, sliding into the steps of the dance with ease, guiding Saffron through them whenever Saffron lost track of where to go.

"Is Sionnach not here tonight?" Copper asked as they circled the room for the third time, the question making Saffron dizzier than the steps did. He had to ask Copper to repeat himself, unsure if he'd heard correctly. For some reason, it made Copper flush and avert his eyes. "I asked if... if Sionnach was coming tonight or not. What's so weird about that, huh?"

"Oh, nothing," Saffron grinned. "I just don't think I've ever heard you say their name before."

Copper scoffed. "I absolutely have... What are you talking about... You're the one who always gets all mad whenever I call them *goat...*"

Saffron kept smiling, making Copper scoff again, shaking his head and declaring *'nevermind!'* in a clear rush of embarrassment. As much as he hated to be the bearer of bad news, Saffron told him Sionnach had already declared they would never attend another of Cylvan's suitor galas ever again since the previous one, and Copper put on a smug act as he agreed, saying it made sense, such events of propriety weren't places for hooves and tails. But Saffron saw right through it. The fact Copper brought up Sionnach at all meant he'd been looking for them in the crowd. Meant he was curious. Meant he was thinking about them. Oh, Saffron couldn't wait to tell Sionnach, later. He could already picture how red their face would go, how they would blabber and stammer over their words before declaring Copper a beastly embarrassment of a Sídhe lord.

The music softened, before swelling again into the next dance, and Saffron was more than happy to keep his hands in Copper's for the rest of the night—had a shadow not suddenly appeared at their side, nearly stampeded by Copper's giant body. But Cylvan politely shoved Copper away, breaking his hand from Saffron's and leaving Saffron in a state of shock. Staring at Cylvan with one hand still extended, mouth hanging open slightly in confusion. Petrified, wondering if he'd done something wrong, if there was something wrong, if he hadn't noticed more witchhunters or something else entering the ballroom—

But then Cylvan took his hand, gentle as ever. He offered

Saffron a shallow bow, one foot extended ahead of him, the first step of a dance Saffron knew. Saffron's face went hot, his heart pounded in his chest.

"What..." he rasped. Cylvan bit his tongue like it took everything in him not to burst out laughing. Like the surprise on Saffron's face was enough to tide him over for another eternity.

"Will you dance with me, Lord Saffron?"

Saffron's mind raced, his heart raced; his eyes flickered down to his hand still held in Cylvan's, for the first time worried the prince's sharp nails were dangerous to the touch. But then he carefully stretched his hand out slightly more, inserting himself into the cup of Cylvan's palm fully, where it belonged. Where it was always meant to be, dancing or otherwise. He couldn't help the smile that crossed his face, perhaps brighter and more excited than it should have been. Cylvan smiled back at him, enough that the bottom line of his lashes creased.

"Y-yes, your highness," Saffron said. "Of course. I would be flattered."

Swept onto the dance floor before any nerves could change his mind, hand in hand with his prince, the rest of the room fell away. The watching, whispering, gossiping crowd fell away, and it was only Cylvan. Cylvan, who moved with grace and elegance, who held Saffron's hand both gently and firmly, who pulled Saffron into steps with the music as if he already knew Saffron wasn't familiar with that specific footwork. He smelled of verdant greens and patchouli, hair pulled out of his eyes so they could pierce Saffron straight through. Saffron couldn't look away from him, could hardly blink as he was carried through each movement without thinking, led in every step by the leanan sídhe lord who'd stolen him away.

"I didn't mean to surprise you," Cylvan said under his breath. He never stopped smiling that impish grin, as if still reveling in the surprise on Saffron's face. "I couldn't stand the sight of you dancing with Copper dé Bricriu before I ever got my chance. He's already been your first for too many other things. It wasn't fair."

"I apologize," Saffron laughed, but trying to maintain the facade of meek flower of Alvénya was harder than he expected with such overflowing joy spilling out of him. He had to bite his lip to keep the constant smile at bay. He had to constantly blink his eyes to keep happy tears from dripping and ruining his makeup. Soon he could hardly meet Cylvan's eyes as they turned and stepped in perfect rhythm with one another, because every time he did—he lost any sense of where he was. Who he was supposed to be.

"We're dancing," he finally whispered, unable to keep the growing pressure of pure elation from escaping. The way Cylvan smiled back at him as he said it—Saffron really had to fight back tears.

"I hope you're prepared to dance endlessly with me every day from now on."

"Really?"

"Something tells me I won't be interested in any other partners, ever again."

Saffron laughed. His heart soared. He wanted to cry. He wanted to leap into Cylvan's arms and kiss him. But until he could, he would just express how happy he was, how the golden joy in his chest made every inch of him buzz with warmth, in the way of perfect steps back and forth, around, turning and gliding, never again taking his eyes away from the dark perfection moving in perfect tandem right in front of him.

Saffron's waking reverie cracked the moment someone suddenly grabbed him, yanking him back into reality. Nearly pulling him off his feet, breaking his connection with Cylvan's hand. He turned quickly, heart exploding in a flood of fear—but it was the wide-eyed, pale face of a palace beantighe he found. Their cheeks were red and splotchy, eyes wet in clear panic. Saffron's breath caught, simultaneously grabbed by Cylvan and pulled back again, protectively. Saffron put a hand on Cylvan's chest as a silent request to *wait*, as the beantighe suddenly spoke low and fast.

"Please, Saffron—please help. Please help, they're—some of the other fey—they took the others, said they were going to moonhunt them. They told me to come find you, please—"

"I—" Saffron started, but the words cut short when he realized everyone was still staring. Every high fey courtier watched, standing near and far, like a flock of wolves licking their lips wondering if the masked creature in the middle of them was truly wolf or lamb. Saffron's response would be an answer. Saffron's response, in front of all those bloodthirsty people—would not be forgotten, for centuries to come. Even Cylvan behind him realized the sudden danger, gently taking Saffron's hand and squeezing it.

"I will have guards search the grounds," he said. It was humiliating that he was able to speak before Saffron could. But Saffron had forgotten how to talk at all. He heard Ryder's voice in his head, asking if he was human or fey. If he would appease human liberation from fey frivolity.

"Did Ryder ask you to do this?" he said under his breath. He didn't know why; he regretted it the moment he did. His heart broke when the beantighe's expression crumbled in clear discouragement.

"What?" they asked weakly. Saffron's heart pounded, swelling into the back of his throat and choking him. Why did he say that? Why would he have said something like that? He attempted to say something else, but hardly a choked exhale escaped him. The beantighe took another step back, before hiding their face and hurrying away. Back into the crowd of fey, who watched them go, a few even giggling and nudging them, trying to trip them. They whispered more, then laughed on the human's heels. No longer paying attention to Saffron—as if he'd responded correctly. He'd reacted like he was supposed to. He'd turned the beantighe away in tears—just like any other high fey would have. A wolf, after all.

He stared where the beantighe had shoved their way back through the crowd, ears ringing, even as Cylvan put up a hand and called Saorise over. As he explained what the beantighe had said, asking her to gather some guards and go search. To arrest anyone engaging in moonhunting, no matter who they were. Saoirse replied with a breath of hesitation, as if even she knew the potential fallout of something like that—but Cylvan insisted. Cylvan, the crown prince, the highest of all high fey, who Ryder insisted was no friend to humans that weren't already friends with Saffron—who, in an instant, did more than Saffron was able.

You're really going to turn your back on the people who need you most—to be some high fey's beantighe whore instead?

His knees went weak. Cylvan grabbed him, as if sensing it. Saffron clung to him. He stared off to where that beantighe had left.

Perhaps Saffron really was the wolf. Perhaps he'd slowly grown fangs and claws, too—perhaps he'd done worse to blend in, to be one of them. Perhaps he'd become the thing he'd always feared most. Perhaps he and Taran mac Delbaith weren't all that different—both of them willing to do anything, hurt even the most vulnerable, just to keep their dark prince safe.

Saffron pushed from Cylvan's arms. He hurried through the crowd, guests stumbling out of his way. He followed that beantighe's path, searching for them, following them all the way through the garden doors, until he stood alone on the terrace outside. As music returned to the ballroom, as gossipy chatter filled his ears and made them ring all over again.

You're really going to turn your back on the people who need you most—

Saffron fought to shove those words away. He clawed at them, wishing to tear them into shreds. That wasn't it. It was more complicated than that, that wasn't the truth at all—

His vision spun. He stumbled to a stone bench out of view of the rest of the party, hidden in the shadows between an overflowing pot of flowers and pristine bushes. Carved and arranged by beantighe hands, he knew. He thought he heard whispering, giggling from the dark trees on the other side, making his heart race. Filling the back of his throat with bile.

Why would he do that? Why would he say that to someone

begging for his help? Why would he force Cylvan to take it into his own hands, even if it meant more rumors? More gossip? The seelie prince who favored beantighes, how strange of him to give such a rude interruption any attention at all—

He clawed at the markings in his forearm until his nails broke skin and blood bubbled out. Hating them, hating what they were doing to him—hating what the fey were doing to him—hating who, what he was becoming while simultaneously abandoning for a single scrap of joy in that world that wanted nothing more than to chew him up and spit him out. He raked at the splitting skin until his fingers smeared through crimson like oil paint—until a clawed hand suddenly appeared, grasping his wrist and pulling it away. A shadow knelt in front of him, and even in his over-whelmed haze, Saffron knew it shouldn't have. Cylvan shouldn't be kneeling in front of him when he looked so beautiful, when Saffron felt so ugly. In every way he could.

"Saffron," Cylvan said softly. He touched Saffron's face, summoning Saffron's eyes upward.

"They're going to call you seelie prince again," Saffron whis-pered. His heart thumped. Cylvan didn't flinch. He pulled a dark handkerchief from down in his shirt and gently wiped the blood away from Saffron's forearm. It injected Saffron with a burst of anger, wrenching his hand away before taking the piece of cloth and tearing at it. "Stop it!" he cried. "Stop it, I can't take it anymore! I can't take it—I can't do this anymore, I can't do it! I can't do it, Cylvan—I feel like I'm going mad, everything is falling apart and there's nothing I can do to stop it—!"

He screamed into the bloody rag, hunching forward as the emotions claimed every inch of his body, summoning blood to drip from his nose, to mix with his spit and drip from his mouth. The weight of everything he'd done, every mistake he'd made, every time a beantighe looked at him with apprehension, how the crowded gala smiled at him like he'd won their favor by brushing off the human seeking his help. Everything Ryder had said, every reiteration he made of how dangerous and monstrous Saffron was, how foolish he was for letting it go for so long, how he would eventually kill everyone he loved. His failed classes, his wild magic, how he kept apologizing and apologizing and apologizing even though fey didn't do that, because that was all he knew, all he'd ever known was apologizing for every mistake he made because apologizing was all he ever had in a world designed to suffocate him—

Cylvan pulled him into his arms, until Saffron sank off the bench and they knelt on the stone together. Saffron clawed at Cylvan's tunic, desperately seeking the comfort he'd found so many times already when wrapped up in him, but it wouldn't come. It only made Saffron feel worse. A disappointment. A failure. He couldn't do anything right; from the first moment he stepped off the ship in Avren, he hadn't done a single thing right. Suddenly he was back in Danann House, silenced, restrained, imprisoned, failing again and again to find or do anything that would help the people he wanted to protect, only putting them in more harm's way, fighting against systems of cruelty older than he was, older than Cylvan, Luvon, King Ailir, even older than Queen Proserpina—when he was only a beantighe. A stupid, silly beantighe, a changeling baby traded through the veil by human parents who didn't want him. He could be offered kingdoms and thrones and all the power in the world—but he would always be a stupid, silly beantighe first, and every person surrounding him would be put in harm's way by result of his own stupid fucking hubris. And the Crown Prince of Alfidel who once made the mistake of falling in love with him—would be the first harmed in every way Saffron failed.

But despite all of that—the Crown Prince of Alfidel held Saffron like he was something precious. Again. Just like he always did. Holding him like something precious and fragile and littered with cracks in the ceramic armor he'd masked himself with. He held Saffron close, until Saffron couldn't fight, until he couldn't speak, until his only option was to sob into Cylvan's beautiful tunic as months of pressure finally released through miserable gasps and pleas for relief. Cylvan held the back of Saffron's head in one hand, as the other trailed up and down his back in comfort.

"We were finally dancing," Saffron sobbed. "I was finally able to dance with you—and it was all ruined, god, why can't I have anything, just a single thing..."

"I know this is not easy for you," Cylvan whispered after a few moments. His hand continued up and down Saffron's back, silently summoning peace back into his body. Saffron shuddered, barely keeping the sound of his weeping at bay to hear it. "Perhaps it was selfish of me to ask you to come and endure all of this—"

"No, Cylvan—"

"There is nothing I can say or do to make it go away," Cylvan went on, hardly more than a whisper. "I can only reassure you— that I will be here to hold you every time it all feels like too much. Just like you once held me when I thought I would finally buckle beneath the weight of it all. I'll hold you until you can breathe again; until you feel strong enough to carry it, again. You've held enough for now, Saffron—let me take some of the weight until you catch your breath."

Saffron clung to him, pressing his face harder into Cylvan's tunic, trying to hold his breath, trying to silence himself, to find his composure, but those gentle words undid every messy stitch he'd sewn into his skin in quiet moments of self-punishment. Every wound, hairline or cutting, split open and bled, and he clung to Cylvan like his only anchor in reality. Something to hold on to, something to hold as a promise that the crushing weight on his back would pass, and he would have the blessing of opening his eyes to find his raven gazing at him with all the gentleness in the world. For the first time—for the first time, when Saffron felt so crushed and hopeless, Cylvan would be there when he opened his eyes. Cylvan, whose hands would undo the clasp of the queen's silver around his throat; the bracelets on his wrists; who would pull away the black veil meant to silence and hide him.

Saffron cried until he had nothing left. He cried while tucked safely in the comfort and protection of Cylvan's arms. Cylvan, who didn't care if anyone saw; who sat back to cross his legs on the ground and pull Saffron into his lap so he didn't touch the stone at all. Giving him all the time he needed in a perfectly safe place to just—feel all of it, all at once.

When his body slumped heavily, breaths finally slowing, Cylvan made a small sound of reassurance and brushed hair from Saffron's eyes.

"I am so lucky to hold you," Cylvan whispered. "To have the blessing of holding someone as brave and inimitable as you—I am so blessed to be allowed to protect you. I am so blessed to be able to comfort you like you once comforted me. I will comfort you every day of your life, for as long as you need it. Please let me."

Saffron pressed himself closer into Cylvan's body, pressing his face into the crook of Cylvan's neck and holding his breath. Holding it until his lungs burned, until all he could think and feel was how badly he wished to inhale.

"I know being a member of court is miserable," Cylvan went on softly. "I know it is mundane, and insufferable, and terrifying... but as a selfish creature, I must admit, having you here with me makes it so much more bearable. I've never had someone like you to hold and be held by, until now. It makes it all so much easier to swallow."

He kissed the side of Saffron's head, and Saffron finally inhaled the breath his chest begged for.

"We will dance again," he went on in promise. "We will dance a thousand more times, at least."

"But this was our first time," Saffron whispered pathetically. Cylvan chuckled, squeezing him and nudging under his chin.

"It wasn't, actually."

Saffron lifted his head slightly in question. Cylvan never stopped smiling, taking Saffron's hand and pressing their palms together, before intertwining their fingers.

"Don't you remember? That night in the Aon-adharcach suite. I taught you the Waltz... the Allemande.. the Minuet..."

Saffron's eyes flooded with emotion all over again. He

nodded, before pressing his face back into Cylvan's chest. Cylvan laughed lightly again under his breath, kissing Saffron's hair and humming the same song he'd played on his violin that night. The first time they danced together, barefoot and drunk.

"Let me purge the ballroom of these courtiers for you," he went on. "Then you and I can continue our dance alone."

Saffron nodded against Cylvan's chest, before forcing himself to sit up again. Cylvan kissed the tears from his cheeks, petting the back of his hair, before gazing at him with all the intensity of a lord appreciating his most treasured gift.

"I love you, Saffron," he said. "And while I cannot shield you from every one of these burdens... I will always hide away with you when you need it. I can promise that much. So please— whenever you need to catch your breath, let me know, and I will sweep you away."

"I love you," Saffron whispered, pressing their foreheads together and closing his eyes. "Thank you."

Cylvan pressed back, then placed a hand to the back of Saffron's neck, holding him there. Somehow knowing exactly when Saffron's heart finally stopped racing, sinking him into a semblance of peace.

Saffron promised to wait right where Cylvan left him, shrouded by the bushes and bouquets and other garden growth as he broke up the party inside. Saffron took the time alone to close his eyes and focus on breathing, pressing his hand into his chest as his weak heart pounded hard against the inside of his ribs. He wiped at his nose last, expecting it to be gushing blood like every other time emotions gripped him so tightly—only to be surprised when it was dry to the touch. As he thought about it, the scars on his arm never burned or ached with want to let the wolf loose, either. He dragged his thumb up his forearm in silent question, wondering if he was finally regaining control of himself—or if, perhaps, Cylvan was capable of even smoothing the nerves of Saffron's wild rowan magic as much as the rest of him.

Hearing Cylvan's return approach from behind him, Saffron

straightened up, wiping his eyes one last time in an attempt to compose himself. Knowing his makeup was destroyed, that the only thing keeping him even mildly together was the glamour. But Cylvan didn't care. He wouldn't care. Saffron knew that, and he was impatient to put his hand back into his raven's once again.

He saw the darkness before he felt hands grabbing him. Ripping him off the bench, shoving him to the stone ground. He tasted the sackcloth yanked over his head and between his teeth before he felt it scratch his cheeks. Cutting him off from the rest of the world, gagging him, making it impossible to speak or scream.

His body reacted first, reeling backward, throwing out his arms and slamming his boots against the ground, but more hands found him. More and more and more—and then something nauseatingly sweet permeated the fibers of the sack, filling it, flooding him with every panicked gasp—and no matter how hard he fought to keep his eyes open, he soon sank heavily, vision blurring. Like air made of glue, pinning his lashes together, making the inside of his throat sticky like sap between cracks in old bark, until he could no longer fight against it.

31

THE BURIAL

Saffron woke like the sun rose. Only a crack of light at first, hardly realizing the sky changed at all, hardly realizing he was a consciousness in a body until his fingers twitched and sent a shockwave of cognizance through his bones. A rush of sensations buried him in an instant—the chill of nighttime air, fresh with the smell of the forest. Summer crickets and the scuttling of creatures through the undergrowth. Scratchy dirt, grass, pine needles beneath his cheek, in his hair, sticking to him with sap. The crunch and slide of dirt being shoveled somewhere nearby. His arms bent stiffly behind him—his wrists bound together with scratchy rope tight enough to make his fingers tingle.

His bones felt like they were made of lead, pinning him where he lay. On his side, crushing one arm beneath his weight. Even trying to open his eyes made him nauseous, vision spinning, blurring with darkness and only a few pricks of orange light. His heart beat a little too slow, blood that had already settled under his skin groaning as it was forced to flow again. His skin prickled with ice, then warmth, then sweat as a light breeze turned it sharp.

"Don't move."

Saffron couldn't, even if he wanted to.

Where am I? His thoughts wandered through the thick sludge of his mind, not meaning to respond to the voice that first woke him. But the voice answered. Taran's voice answered, as if beckoned to.

"I couldn't tell you," it said, low and rumbling. *"But I sense the danger nearby."*

Yeah... fuck, Saffron mentally grumbled back.

He tried opening his eyes again, but still only saw orange specks in the darkness. Like glittering pixies dancing in drunken circles. He might have thought they were, had there been more shrill laughter. But there were only hushed voices. The sound of shoveled dirt. He blinked a few times, fighting the lead in his bones and the thick syrup of his brain, clearing enough away to realize the light came from lanterns dangling from long sticks in the ground.

"Saffron—don't worry. Relax. I'm going to get you out of here."

Saffron frowned. He blinked a few more times, furrowing his brows in confusion. That time—the voice didn't come from inside his head. It definitely hit his ears. It didn't belong to Taran. No, that voice belonged to—

"Sun... beam?" he rasped, attempting to turn his head as something tugged on his bindings. He saw only the faceless shadow of a black veil, but he was too deep beneath the tide of whatever they used to drug him to panic. The lanterns cast the slightest glow on the chiffon, and he swore he knew that face beneath it.

Sunbeam shushed him, glancing to the group of other veiled witchhunters shoveling dirt a hundred feet away. "Don't call me by that name here."

"I thought you were gone," Saffron mumbled, tongue fat and heavy in his mouth. He slumped back to the grass when holding his head up grew too tiring. "... again. Why do you... keep doing that. Why did you... leave again? I have so much... to tell you."

He could picture her face at the sound of a breathy chuckle

through her nose. How it smiled, slightly, like what he said was funny.

"Because idiots like you and Asche would have certainly caused me another mountain of trouble," she whispered, before swearing under her breath as the knots around Saffron's wrists gave her more trouble than she anticipated. "Instead—it looks like you got yourself into a mountain of trouble on your own, huh? Moron..."

Saffron tried to laugh, but it was too hard to make his lungs hiccup for the sound. "Why are you... hunting human witches?"

"I'm not," she hissed. Like he'd just called her a dirty name. "What the fuck are you saying!"

"You're the one wearing the veil..."

"But I don't participate in hunts," she growled. "I'm only hiding with them because they can teach me about oralcry. And veil magic. And because... well... it's right under his nose. He would never think to look for me here. No one ever expects to see your face."

There were a thousand things Saffron could have asked—should have asked—but instead, he turned his tongue over in his mouth and mumbled: "Whose nose?"

"Nothing for you to worry about," she insisted. Saffron would have rolled his eyes if he had the strength to even open them all the way.

"You really should stop being so coy... when I have secrets to tell you, too..."

"What?" she snapped. "God, you really can't keep your ass out of trouble wherever you go, can you?"

"Why did Ryder take your name from you?"

Sunbeam's hands halted on the knots. She made a sound like she wanted to say something, but it caught in her throat.

"What?" she asked quietly. "Why would you say that? He didn't... I'm not..."

"You resemble someone... named Acacia Kyteler," Saffron whispered. He couldn't resist smiling to himself, recalling that beautiful woman he stumbled across in the National Library. How he might have never seen her had Cylvan not given him a way inside. "The founder of modern oralcry... and Kyteler Schools of Arid Magic..."

"No..." Sunbeam mumbled. Her hands returned to the knots, quick and annoyed. "Shut up. You don't know what you're talking about. You shouldn't have anything to do with Ryder Kyteler at all, by the way, if you've thought about it. He's nothing but trouble. Stay the fuck away from him, Saffron, I mean it."

"Wish you would've warned me sooner," Saffron smiled drunkenly, shaking his head, drawing more sap-sticky pine needles into his hair. "He is definitely... nothing but trouble. A real... fucking... asshole. But I had no choice... he's the only one keeping my friends safe... from *these* assholes..."

Sunbeam suddenly grabbed Saffron's face, turning his head and staring at him with wide eyes. "He what?" she asked sharply. "He has your friends? Don't tell me—don't tell me, Letty? Hollow?"

"And Nimue," Saffron sighed. "But not for much longer. I'm gonna... send them to live with Luvon, maybe..."

Sunbeam dropped him. She returned to the knots, nodding again and again. "Good. Good, Saffron. Do that. Do that very first thing once I get you out of this mess. Don't leave anyone you care about with him. Don't trust Ryder Kyteler with anything you care about. I made that mistake once—I don't want you to make it, too."

"How?"

Sunbeam bit her tongue. "Chandry," she whispered. "He... was the one who took Chandry from me."

"Oh..." Saffron trailed off, before licking his dry lips. "But Chandry got away. She's waiting for you in the human world."

"No, damnit—!" Sunbeam started, before gritting her teeth. "Saffron, Ryder put Chandry in the human world! He trapped her over there! He has people on both sides of the veil—and they're holding Chandry hostage on the other side. He did it to try and get me to stay. She got away for a little bit, that's why I was in such a hurry to finish that veil circle in the ruins—but then she... but then she..."

"Stopped answering," Saffron recalled. Quietly. Like something he wasn't sure he should say out loud. Sunbeam exhaled through her nose, but nodded.

"Stopped answering," she repeated. "Probably because... his people found her again. Took her back. That's why I'm here with the witchhunters, though—because they know about veil magic. They're constantly moving back and forth through it. I'm going to learn everything I can from them, and then the second an excuse to pop through the veil opens up—I'm gonna volunteer. I'm gonna get to the other side, where I can find Chandry and get her as far the fuck away from Ryder Kyteler as I possibly can."

"Ryder told me... he doesn't have Chandry anymore," Saffron said. He didn't know if he was trying to offer comfort, or—if he vocalized it like a question, without asking directly. Sunbeam scoffed, and that was answer enough.

"You gotta stop believing everything you're told. Especially if you're going to be king one day. God help us. Ériu and Christ and the devil and everyone in-fucking-between."

"That's not nice," he groaned. "But... I hope you do. I hope you get your chance and find her. If you do... send that bird back through so I know you're safe, at least... Yama, I mean, that little blue guy... As your friend, I wanna know you're safe..."

"... Alright," she muttered. "I'll remember to do that."

Before Saffron could say anything else, Sunbeam suddenly clamped a hand over his mouth. She held her breath, and Saffron strained his ears, heart thudding nervously as he realized what she did. The shoveling had stopped. There was the sound of crunching wood, then the kiss of fire on Saffron's skin. The smell of yew. One of them scoffed in disgust.

"As we thought," they growled. "There's no rowan witch in here. Not any longer, at least."

"If there ever was at all."

"Go get him. Let's get this done with."

Sunbeam's hand on his mouth trembled. Her breath hitched, then skipped. She made a small noise of uncertainty, before slowly pulling her hand away.

"Saffron, I..." she said, voice tight. "I'm—I'm sorry. I'm so sorry, I can't... Christ, I'm just so sorry, please understand!"

She vanished into the bushes at Saffron's back, but Saffron didn't turn to look. He scoured his muddy vision, watching as two other witchhunters approached. Blocking out the pricks of lantern light with their bodies.

Hands grabbed him, lifting him from the earth. Saffron attempted to thrash, but his limbs were too heavy. His muscles were numb. He still wasn't in control of his limbs, he couldn't even inhale as much as he needed to fill his lungs—

Do something! He begged the wolf that lived in his arm, recalling how it had emerged the last time he was with Ryder, when he felt threatened, trapped, even back then. *Help me—!*

"I can't while you're drugged this way," the voice growled back. *"I cannot do anything while your magic is subdued like this. It's your fear that summons me, witch."*

I'm fucking scared—! Saffron screamed internally, gritting his teeth as he was carried to where they dug. Attempting to fight. Attempting to break free of their grasp on his shoulders, his legs. But the witchhunters dropped him heavily into the hole they dug, six feet down. He grunted as the air rushed from his lungs, unable to inhale another as the excruciating stench of yew filled his nose and drowned him as easily as water. His throat closed up, making his eyes burn as he clawed at it internally for desperate breath.

"Wait!" he managed to croak. Someone joined him in the hole, the heel of a boot smashing into the side of his head and making his world spin.

"Be quiet," they muttered. "I don't know how you got out of this box in the first place, but it's not going to happen again."

Do something! Saffron shrieked in his mind, writhing in a panic and attempting to kick the person who grabbed the lid of the silver coffin to cover him. He summoned the wolf to his mind, clawed at his forearm where his wrists were bound together beneath him—he did everything he could think of, even biting down on his tongue, trying to make himself bleed. But the drugs in his body, the yew in the air, the terror that clutched his heart in a vice grip, for the first time, his magic wouldn't come. It didn't boil or bubble under his skin at all.

"Do something! *Do something!*" he begged, commands tearing out of his tight throat, tasting like blood as the yew incense scraped the inside of his mouth. The scars on his arm burned like fire, like hot metal pressed into his skin. He clawed at them further with his opposite hand, straining against the ropes and screaming until his throat closed up. Tearing his nails through the marks until blood spilled from the scabs he'd already clawed at the gala. "Do something you useless—fucking—! *Icarus, do something!*"

Cold electricity raced through his veins, igniting under his skin before detaching like a spirit unhooking from his bones. It elicited another scream from his mouth, as if a part of his soul tore away at the seams, from the rough stitching he'd sewn himself together with in the months since Ostara.

More cries cascaded between the trees—but that time, not from him. From those on the surface above him. From the witch-hunter whose feet straddled him in his coffin, whose heel was stained with blood from where it slammed into his head. Saffron strained to see, still weighing heavily beneath the weight of the drugs—but he saw the pale fear on the person's face. The hunter who stood over him, how his mouth dangled open in shock, staring at something Saffron couldn't see. Something Saffron couldn't smell over the stench of yew, couldn't sense from beneath the vibrating agony of the silver coffin embracing him. But he didn't have to see it; to smell it, or sense it—to know the wolf tore its paws into the soil and buried teeth into the first person within reach.

The witchhunter standing over him scrambled from the

grave, crushing Saffron's chest in the process. Saffron groaned, blinking back tears and fighting to breathe again, only lifting his head when another veiled person threw themself into the hole and clamored for him.

"Come on, come on!" Sunbeam commanded, pulling Saffron up, then heaving him over her shoulder. She threw him from the grave before scrambling out after him, that time grabbing a nearby knife from the dirt to slice the ropes around his wrists. As she did, Saffron had gone still—watching as his wolf, his violent magic, tore every witchhunter apart with its teeth and claws. Until blood pooled thick in the grass, flooding the soil and splattering the trees. He opened his mouth to cry out, to command it to stop —but the words didn't come. He couldn't blame it on the yew incense, the silver coffin, even the fear in his chest—

The words simply didn't come. He just watched, mouth hanging open as he battled every urge he had. As Ryder's voice rang out in his skull, calling him dangerous, violent, a threat to everyone he held dear—as Saffron watched the beast rip through the same people who threatened those he'd only ever wished to protect. At his own command. Compelled by the same name he'd once given Taran mac Delbaith.

He gazed down at the markings on his arm. Drenched in blood, warped from where his nails raked over them. Bleeding as freshly as they had the day he first carved them in place. *Icarus.*

"Why is he here?" Sunbeam asked weakly from behind him. Saffron lifted his eyes, gazing across the open grave to where the wolf hunched, heaving with breath, drenched in blood as the woods fell silent around them. No more screams. No more running feet or tearing teeth. The beast turned its head, ears back, spit and blood dripping from its mouth. Its eyes were red as rubies, as bright and vivid as the fresh blood coating Saffron's arm.

He didn't have to ask who Sunbeam meant, that time. *Why is he here?*

Saffron got slowly to his feet. The world still tilted this way and that beneath him, but he found balance in holding the wolf's gaze. The beast turned to face him directly. Saffron found himself breathing heavily in tandem with it—sharing the exhaustion. The taste of blood filled the back of his mouth, just like that which dripped between the wolf's teeth in front of him. But when he parted his own lips to speak, his mouth was free of bubbling, crimson overwhelm. There was only a rush of understanding.

"Icarus," he said. The wolf's ears perked upward. Saffron's heart thumped. "I gave you that name on Ostara."

The beast lowered its head slightly. Its exhausted breaths slowed. It nodded. Just once. Chills raced down Saffron's spine.

"You cursed me on Ostara," it answered. Saffron watched its mouth twitch as it did. Spoken out loud, that time, even Sunbeam hearing it. Saffron's heart raced faster. *"With more than just a name, beantighe."*

Saffron's breath hitched, but he still didn't move. Neither did the wolf across from him. A memory sparked in the back of his mind, but not one of his own. A moment he recalled, but seen through eyes that weren't his. Eyes that stood where Taran mac Delbaith had at the bonfire. Gazing at the rowan-veiled witch in front of him, heaving with breath, blood and bile flooding the back of his mouth, body writhing and wracked with pain as that given name bled from his back. *Icarus.*

Hearing his own voice, giving that first command—*"Do as I say—and reveal yourself."*

"Taran," the word escaped him in a breath. His heart had gone still. Everything, all around him, went still, except the throbbing of the feda marks carved into his arm. *Icarus, Icarus.* The wolf wasn't only a manifestation of his nightmares—he'd been summoning Taran mac Delbaith since the beginning. He suddenly understood that he didn't have to worry about learning how to make a familiar—the veil had already given him one.

"He's here," Sunbeam suddenly said, voice rushed. "Saffron, I have to go—!"

"It's alright—" Saffron attempted to comfort her, turning

quickly, but she was already gone. The sound of the forest crashed back to life around him, pounding in his ears. Trying to find where she vanished so quickly, he wished to explain as much as he could—but then something emerged from the bushes behind him.

Saffron turned to look, barely catching sight of Ryder Kyteler —before one hand grabbed the back of his hair, the other pressing a finger to his forehead. The world unraveled in an instant, and Saffron sank into darkness.

32

THE FAMILIAR

Saffron dreamt of that cold, colorless place in the Winter Court again. That time, the black wolf walked alongside him instead of up ahead, joining him rather than leading him. Any time Saffron lost his balance on the slippery ground, he threw out his hand for balance, and the animal was there. The beast's thick, dark fur was warm and protective against his skin.

"Wipe the blood from your face, witch. It's unbecoming."

Saffron smeared his arm over his nose, his mouth. It smeared across his creamy white sleeve like a corpse dragged over a sandy beach.

"You look terrible."

"I feel terrible," Saffron muttered, but the words indicated more than the blood dripping from him. He couldn't recall why. He didn't know what they referred to. His mind was nothing but a blur, a fog, as thick as the wild clouds filling the wilderness all around them. Saffron focused on the building up ahead, though kept his hand buried in the wolf's thick fur as he walked. Something about the support was nice. Welcoming. A gracious gift on such unsteady ground.

"Does it ever snow like this in the Mid Court?" he asked. The beast snorted through his nose.

"Not like this. Aryadne hated the cold in Fjornar, so her king built her a Keep in Avren. This is—"

"The King's Keep," Saffron whispered. He didn't reiterate that final detail—in Fjornar. The dog released another sharp exhale in agreement. "What do you know of this place?"

The wolf's pursuit of the building came to a sudden halt. Its head remained tilted downward, nose nearly pressed into the snow.

"This is where I became what I am. This is where they trained the oracles who turned my bones to silver."

Saffron stared at the ceiling for a long, long time. Naked rafters. Cobwebs that were no older than a week. Painted with natural pigments, once colorful but faded over time. Decades, maybe centuries. Beams carved with arid steles. Sunlight illuminating dust motes that danced along the edges like drunken pixies. A fresh morning breeze through lace curtains, the smell of it telling him as much as he already knew just by what he saw overhead. The cottage Ryder offered him. His cottage on the outskirts of the Finnian Ruins.

Saffron jolted upward at the sound of something scraping the floor. His breath lodged in his throat, searching the cramped bedroom in search of Ryder Kyteler or another human face—baffled by the fucking *relief* he felt upon seeing only the massive black wolf lying on its stomach in the corner of the room. Ears perked up, snout resting on crossed paws. Only because it didn't wave its tail back and forth, Saffron knew it wasn't just any dog.

"Oh, fuck off," he groaned. The beast frowned, lifting its head and narrowing its eyes.

"Good morning to you too, bint."

Saffron stared at it—not expecting to hear it reply. Not like that. Not so casually, as if it understood what he said, the tone he said it in. More than just a warped projection of Saffron's magic, his personality—and then he recalled flashes of the night before.

Staring into its crimson eyes across the open grave between them. *You cursed me on Ostara.*

"B-be... be gone." Saffron pointed at his forearm like it would suck the animal right back in again—but then he realized, there was no more blood caked on his skin. His arm had been fully washed, bandages peeking out from under the quarter-sleeves of the tunic that wasn't his. Running his hands all over himself, he realized every inch of himself had been scrubbed while he slept, even his hair feeling soft and clean as he ran fingers back through it. Staring down at his bare feet, he swore even his toenails had been trimmed.

"What the..." he muttered in disbelief. He turned back to the wolf, who remained on its stomach, watching him with what Saffron swore was a smirk. "What are you looking at?"

"I forgot how stupid you look when you're confused. Your mouth hangs open like a gaping fish on the beach."

"Oh, fuck off—!" Saffron attempted again, leaping to his feet —but the words caught in his throat. Thorny and tangling, forcing him to close his mouth again. "You... 'forgot'?"

"There it is again. That stupid face."

"Sh-shut up." Saffron put his hands up. He turned from the animal, raking fingers back through his hair again, trying to find his thoughts, trying to string images and memories together, hating how they felt so piecemeal. Remembering only bits and scraps from the night before, most of it going blurry after Sunbeam pulled him back out of the grave. His hands trailed from his hair down his face, pressing fingers into his lips and staring silently out the window over the cottage lawn. His ears rang. He tasted rust and salty blood on his tongue, though none bubbled from the back of his throat. No, it was a memory. He'd tasted it, too, while staring directly into the wolf's crimson eyes.

He turned back to the beast, who by then had straightened up. Who still looked a little too *domestic pet* with how it sat, despite the top of its head reaching the same height as Saffron's, fully standing. Nothing close to domestic pet, and yet—

"I... I felt your rage last night. For what I... for what I did to you. You... I know who you are, right? You're..."

"You know who I am," the wolf replied. Saffron finally pulled his hands from his face. They clutched the front of his shirt, instead, dangling there as if he thought he might collapse.

"No, that's... you can't be..." His throat tightened. He forced it back open again. Every single inch of his nerves flared like sparking candles, burning against every horrible memory he had given to him by the person whose name he was too frightened to speak. As if saying it out loud would bring him. As if it would unlock the door in the back of his mind where he hid everything he still couldn't fathom had happened to him, else he wake shrieking from a dead sleep with blood spilling from his nose and mouth. Danann House. The attic. The black veil. The queen's silver.

But the beast in front of him just kept staring at him. And Saffron knew. Saffron knew, perhaps, simply by the way it never blinked. By the way there was so much life and cognizance behind those eyes that, the last time he saw them, had been golden yellow. Perhaps turned crimson by Saffron's own magic laying claim to him and his magic. Owning him.

"T—" he attempted. It took another few tries before he managed to utter the name out loud. "Taran?"

The wolf exhaled sharply through its snout.

"You're... Taran mac Delbaith?" Saffron emphasized.

"Yes. I don't know how you've done this, beantighe, but it's me, alright."

Saffron stared at him. His hands clutching the front of his unfamiliar tunic trembled, palms clammy as nervous sweat built on his forehead.

"Really?" he asked again. He thought he might keep asking, again and again, until the thing finally admitted it was lying and disappeared into a cloud of black smoke. But it didn't—it just kept eyeing him. And despite the wrong color of the irises—the longer Saffron stared back, the more he knew it was the truth. As horrible, terrifying, stomach-churning as it was—Saffron had been summoning Taran mac Delbaith since the beginning.

"Prove it," he whispered, voice cracking. "Tell me something only Taran would say."

The wolf closed its eyes. It let out a sound like a sigh of exasperation.

"The fern ring in the back of my throat was fucking unnecessary."

Saffron jumped back. A partial shriek of laughter burst from his mouth, before he quickly smothered it behind his hands. He didn't know why—there was nothing funny about it—perhaps just from the pure shock of it all. He had to be dreaming. It wasn't the first time he'd had nightmares about Taran or the wolf coming to find him, to tear him apart—but the reality of it was far stranger.

Finding the confidence to step closer, Saffron examined the animal all over, even reaching out to pat it on the head, then flattening his hand hesitantly to its snout. It wrinkled beneath his touch in annoyance, but Saffron didn't pull away. He pet between its eyes, then scratched between its ears. The wolf didn't react. Just glared at him, as if to ask what the fuck he thought he was doing.

"Sorry," Saffron whispered. "I think I'm just... in shock. It's just—it's you! It's you, you—! You asshole—And you have to do whatever I say, don't you? You came when I called last night. Oh my god—how long have you known?"

"Not very," Taran growled, clearly growing more impatient as Saffron teased him. "I think it took some time for my opulence to fully meld with yours. The first few times you summoned me, I barely remember. I acted on instinct. All I know is I was minding my business—before suddenly appearing in the fucking woods outside of Avren. Overcome with the urge to..." he trailed off. His eyes flashed in the sunlight, head tilting slightly as if he couldn't resist his own burning curiosity. Clearly not having all the answers despite pretending like he did. "The urge to protect something. I didn't even realize it was you, until recently. Imagine my disgust."

"I don't have to. I'm feeling it right now."

Taran's ears flattened. Saffron pet Taran's head again, giggling when Taran growled.

"Also, *whose* opulence, exactly? From what I remember, I took that for myself, too—"

Taran snapped his teeth, making Saffron jerk his hand away.

"Well—if you're really the manifestation of my rowan magic..." Saffron managed an awkward smile, clinging to the single reassurance that Taran could not actually hurt him, even if he wanted to. He probably did. "I suppose Ryder can't claim it to be *wild* anymore, can he?"

"I don't know if I would go that far," Taran said. Saffron almost made another sarcastic comment about how he *definitely* had full control over him as a wolf, but Taran huffed and shook his head. "*I mean*, I hesitate to believe I am the full extent of your rowan magic. It's irresponsible for you to think as much for even a second, either. Nothing this easy would make sense."

"Speak for yourself. None of this has been *easy*." But Saffron knew Taran was right. God—what an absolutely surreal thought to have. And to think it so casually, too. Saffron might still be dreaming. Perhaps he really had gone mad. Perhaps those witch-hunters really had buried him and he was drunk on yew incense and silver.

Frowning, he returned his hand to his hair and turned. He glanced around the cottage, before down to his bandaged forearm.

"Do you remember how we got here?" he asked. Taran shook his head.

"My memories are yours. The ones we made while bonded, at least."

"Huh..." Saffron muttered. He didn't have the strength to dig any deeper into that sentiment.

Instead, he tried to recall anything he could from the moments following Ryder's appearance at the gravesite. At least—Saffron thought it had been Ryder. It was such a blur, everything felt so choppy—was it possible he'd only imagined it? Perhaps a dream? Like trying to find his reflection on the surface of a frozen pond, ice cracked and warping the view. Some edges of his memory were fuzzy, others sharp and precise. Like shearing a bolt of fabric with new scissors, claiming a piece before sewing opposing ends back together.

He dragged his hand back down his face.

"I'm... going back to Avren," he said, deciding there was no point in waiting any longer—but then something else made him pause. He turned back toward the window, gazing through it to the trees on the other side. Something Sunbeam had said stuck with him, haunting him. Sharp and certain.

Don't leave anyone you care about with him. Don't trust Ryder Kyteler with anything you care about.

Saffron would go to Letty's cabin first. He would gather her, Nimue, and Hollow, first. He would take them back to Avren with him. He would send them to live with Luvon, just like he'd said to Sunbeam. Away from the witchhunters, away from Ryder.

"You," he said, turning back to Taran. "You, um... go home. Erm, go back. Back inside. Come on." He pointed at his bandaged forearm. Taran's nose wrinkled in insult, though Saffron persisted. "Please! Go away."

The beast snorted, following as Saffron rolled his eyes and gave up, proceeding into the adjoining room, toward the front door. Taran mocked him as they went, laughing like a forest coyote and making goosebumps flush Saffron's skin. Saffron turned to tell him off, to command him to never make that noise again—but then Taran suddenly perked up, ears bolting upright, petrifying in an instant. Saffron stared at him, going still only because the beast did, jumping when Taran suddenly reanimated and looked at him with wide eyes.

"Open the door. Hurry," he commanded. Saffron rolled his eyes, feeling like he was being teased again—but then he did as Taran said, and his stomach dropped into his ass. On the other side, hand raised as if to knock—Daurae Asche looked as surprised to see Saffron, Fiachra perched on their shoulder. Around her neck dangled Saffron's amethyst pendant, like a messenger token. Asche nearly greeted him—before spotting the wolf over Saffron's shoulder. Saffron barely threw a hand over the daurae's mouth before they could release a blood-curdling shriek.

It took compelling Taran to roll around on the floor like a sheepdog to convince Asche that Saffron had full control over him, but even then, the daurae still clung to Saffron's hand as they hurried up the trail toward the lake. They constantly glanced over their shoulder to the beast on their heels, as if expecting him to suddenly lunge and sink teeth into their backs. Every time, Saffron just pulled Asche to hurry, to watch where they were going. They would have more time to talk about it, later. He would explain better, later. He was in a hurry. Ryder had been the one to bring him back to the ruins, after all—he knew Saffron was there. And Saffron knew he wasn't likely to leave Saffron alone for long. They only had a small window of freedom to get his friends and get the fuck back to the palace.

When the lake and Letty's cottage came into view through the trees, Saffron had to resist the urge to sprint out into the wide clearing in an instant. He pulled Asche off the road, paused to listen for any voices that might be trailing them, before gazing down at the hematite ring on his finger. Wiggling them in curiosity, he let out a small breath before crouching down on the balls of his feet, gazing down at a patch of flattened grass as his mind turned over what to do.

Drawing an ogham circle, he added the feda marks for *expand, light, ripple, living, mine,* while clearly imagining what he wished to manifest. Smiling to himself, he watched as a glowing ring of red light lazily pulsated from the ring, extending outward until no longer visible. Crimson ripples bounced back from behind him where the light collided with Asche and Taran's feet, though Asche said nothing. Proof they couldn't see the action—though Taran watched it expand with silent focus. There wasn't any time for Saffron to unpack his feelings around that, either.

The ripple expanded outward, far enough into the clearing that Saffron lost sight of it. Another circle bounced back, like rain pattering the surface of a pond, but Saffron squinted though the overcast light to see it came from a deer grazing on the far edge of the lake. He waited impatiently for a few more to amble back to where he crouched, knowing if there were only two or three there was a good chance they belonged to his friends—but his agitation grew when none echoed back at all. Frowning, he cast the spell one more time—but once again, there were only responses from Asche, Taran, and the grazing deer.

"Where are they?" He asked under his breath, rising back to his feet. He crossed into the clearing, knowing for certain there at least wasn't anyone uninvited milling about to spot him. Asche hurried on Saffron's heels, making a noise like they wanted to ask something, but the question never came. Perhaps Saffron walked too fast. Perhaps they could feel the sudden anxiety emanating from him with every quickened step.

He moved swiftly, through the wild grass toward the lake, then the little cottage where Letty should have been inside reading, or baking, or practicing her herb magic. Nimue should have been trundling around on the edge of the water, or splashing in it and calling out something rude to Saffron on approach. Hollow should have been there cleaning up the yard or chopping wood for the fireplace or practicing with his sword. Where were they?

Reaching the porch and stepping up to the door, Saffron knocked, trying to keep his growing nerves at bay. No one came to answer; there wasn't even a sound on the other side to indicate anyone was home and simply missed by his ripple spell. Perhaps they'd spent the night in the ruins with the rest of the human coven? Well—Saffron wanted to at least leave a note for Letty to find when she returned. He moved his finger to the knob to draw another circle around the lock—but the latch slipped when he accidentally bumped it, as if wriggled loose from his knocking. Saffron hesitated, before pushing the door open with a squeak of the hinges.

Just like the first time he'd visited, signs of Letty's existence were everywhere. In the herbs and flowery bundles hanging from wire between every rafter; in the dangling, polished lake stones in front of the windows, carved with runes visible when Saffron trailed his fingers between them; in bundles of braided water plants soaking in a wooden basin, likely used to give Nimue legs when needed; and on top of it all, books. So, so, so many books, even more than when he first sat at the table and drank tea with them, many with water-warped pages and mud-smeared covers as if Letty had shared them with Nimue on the edge of the lake.

One of the books was facedown in the middle of the floor, pages bent beneath its own weight. Saffron finally stepped inside, picking it up to return it to its place, before realizing he wasn't sure exactly where it'd fallen from. He left it on the nearby table—then noticed a pot of cold food hanging in the fireplace, untouched. Loose herbs scattered over the table alongside it, as if Letty had been interrupted while cooking. That in itself wasn't particularly strange, either—perhaps someone needed her at the ruins without warning? Perhaps something had happened? She could also be forgetful, maybe she just forgot there was stew cooking in the fireplace...?

He could make justifications all he wanted—until he realized, perhaps he only did so because otherwise, his heart would be pounding. Something was wrong. Something definitely wasn't right.

"Saffron?" Asche asked from the doorway, and Saffron realized his ears were ringing.

"Something's wrong," he whispered out loud, surveying the

room again. Searching for something more specific to prove it. "I think... something's wrong."

He turned back to where Asche stood, just as a sudden wave of red raced over the ground, crashing against his feet and surprising him. He thought the lake had suddenly turned to blood and flooded the house—until he realized it was his ripple-spell, still in effect. There was a group of people headed straight for them.

He almost felt relief. Only the smallest taste of it sparked in his chest—but he stopped himself. He stood in the doorway, staring at the porch outside. Straining his ears. Something was wrong. Something was wrong—

Those voices did not belong to his friends.

"Icarus, be gone!" he declared, and Taran vanished in an instant. Saffron then lunged for Asche, yanking them off the porch, shoving them into the narrow crawl space beneath the cottage's floorboards. Fiachra refused to let go of Saffron's shirt when he attempted to toss her into the sky, next, making him swear and scoop her into his arm, pinning her to his chest as he crawled under with the daurae. Asche's nose wrinkled in annoyance, pulling faces every time cobwebs tangled in their hair or they squashed a hand into a puddle of mud or their horns scraped against the bottom of the floor above them. Saffron clamped one hand over the daurae's mouth, the other still clutching Fiachra, holding his breath as the ripples intensified. All the way until boots stomped along the wooden porch.

"...because the solstice is only a couple weeks away," someone argued. Saffron and Asche glanced at one another. "We still don't know what the fuck Ryder wants. Why won't he just tell us?"

"We just have to trust him. Like we always have." Saffron recognized that voice. It was Breton. He sounded tense as he said it, like they were words he'd repeated often, but wasn't sure he believed himself.

"You really believe that rowan witch is gonna help?" Someone else asked in a frustrated mumble. "Ry keeps talking like they're madly in love with him and will do anything he says, but... from the way he's been acting lately... I dunno, Breton, I just worry that—"

"No more chatting, come on," Breton finally snapped. "Get this place cleaned up. Just like last time."

"Are they really with Chandry?" Someone asked. Saffron's heart thudded against his ribcage.

"What did I just say? Get a move on."

Saffron stared straight ahead. He didn't blink, he didn't breathe, until the scattered footsteps overhead finished what they were doing and finally left again. Voices disappeared into the distance as they went, but those words still echoed in Saffron's mind. It wasn't until Fiachra moved in Saffron's arms and Asche asked if he was alright—that Saffron returned to his body at all. Saffron stared at them for a long time, before turning to crawl out from under the porch without answering. Fiachra wriggled from his grasp, circling before returning to his shoulder. Saffron stared in the direction the voices had gone, words echoing endlessly in his head. Endlessly, endlessly.

He wished Breton had answered that question.

"I..." he trailed off. Mouth dry. He turned his tongue over, before finally glancing back to Asche. "I can't... go back to Avren with you yet."

"What!" Asche cried, grabbing Saffron's sleeve. "You can't stay here, either! Cylvan is worried sick, too, you should have seen him—!"

"I can't go back yet!" Saffron said, voice cracking in worry. Asche closed their mouth, but the uncertainty was all over their own face. Saffron swallowed back the emotion in his voice, shaking his head. "I think Ryder may have taken them, Asche. My friends. I have to know where they are before I go anywhere. I'm not going to leave them."

"But—"

Saffron reached into his pocket, digging out the amethyst pendant. He squeezed it tightly, though his chin quivered in overwhelm when it flared with heat in reply. Again and again and again, as if Cylvan was begging him to come home. Saffron blinked back the rush of heartbroken tears that flooded the backs of his eyes, shaking his head and stuffing it back into his pocket.

"I'll stay for three days. Maximum," he said. "Tell Cylvan. Tell Cylvan he can come get me after three days, and I won't argue with him."

"Three days is a long time!"

"Two days, then."

"Saffron!"

"If something happens before the end of two days," Saffron said, reaching up to scratch beneath Fiachra's beak. "I'll send Fiachra back with my amethyst. She'll take it to Cylvan, just like she did last time. That will tell him to come and get me even sooner."

Asche wanted to argue. Their mouth dangled open with the weight of everything they wished to say—but they knew there was no arguing with him. They knew there would be no changing his mind. And Saffron could see it on their face, too—they were worried about where the others may have gone.

"A—alright," Asche finally whispered. "Alright, Saffron, I'll... I'll tell him."

"Make sure he doesn't come until two days. Or until Fiachra takes him the pendant."

"I'll try. I don't know if he'll listen—"

"Cylvan trusts me," Saffron said, giving Asche a reassuring smile. "I know he does. He'll listen. I promise he will."

Asche closed their mouth. They pressed their lips together, nodding stiffly. Like they didn't believe it—or, perhaps, because they couldn't believe they were about to turn and leave Saffron behind. But Saffron just kept smiling. He pulled Asche into a hug, then nudged them away. Back toward the trees. He wished them luck, then a safe trip back. He told them to be careful on their way out. He told them he would see them again soon.

When they were finally gone, he made the walk back to his cottage.

He went inside and sat on the bed. He waited.

Taran's voice in the back of his mind warned him before a knock ever came. Saffron thanked him—it was the reason he was ready with a practiced, perfect beantighe smile the moment Ryder opened the door and stepped inside.

33

THE TEA

Saffron's finger traced the rim of the teacup, far too elegant to be from the ruins, themselves. Perhaps stolen, just like the new, clean clothes he wore. Just like the decadently carved silver sword on Ryder's belt.

The cathedral study was bright in the sun, light shining through the colorful panes of glass and casting art on the rug covering the stone floor. Saffron's eyes skimmed over the spines of books crowding the shelves in every direction, though his thoughts raced by too fast to read any of the titles. Between the shelves, he gazed at the hung paintings, some of clearly generic landscapes, another of a knight on a knee at the feet of a princess, the third bearing a striking resemblance to the place Saffron kept dreaming about. That quiet, snowy place where he'd walked alongside the beast who would be his familiar, never knowing it.

His finger circled the rim around, and around, and around, thoughts popping in and out of his mind like flowers emerging through winter permafrost, daring him to say something, to incite something, to accuse Ryder Kyteler of doing something to his friends, to explain how he'd found Saffron at that failed burial the night before. How he knew exactly when and where to be to rescue Saffron yet again. All while Ryder cooed over him like he was a fawn found in the icy woods.

"You hurt people, Saffron," he said with warmth and caring in his voice, as Saffron feigned uncertainty at his memories the night before. A part of him telling the truth, a part of him curious to hear what Ryder would say. "I wish there was an easier way to tell you, but your magic let loose on a half-dozen witchhunters in the woods outside of Avren. I warned you that this might happen. I only wish you'd listened to me."

"I think they kidnapped me from Cylvan's gala," Saffron stoked the fire, mumbling like he was deep in thought. Just wanting to hear what Ryder would say to him. "How did you know where to find me...?"

"I had a feeling they suspected you. Your prince did a poor job of keeping you hidden. Once one of my people told me they were headed for the palace, I tried to step in. I tried to get you out, first, for your own safety. Do you remember when a beantighe approached you to ask for help? Saying there were high fey moon-hunting humans in the woods... imagine my surprise when they came back and told me you'd brushed them off. I almost stormed into the ballroom right then, subtlety be damned."

Saffron's finger continued circling the rim of the cup as Ryder chuckled like what he said was funny. Charming, chivalrous. Saffron barely reacted, just continued watching as steam from the honey-lavender brew ghosted over the sides of the ceramic before being whisked away by his touch. Again and again. Fighting the urge to lunge and throw the boiling liquid in Ryder's face, demanding he shut the fuck up and tell Saffron where his friends were.

"I have to ask... did you tell him?"

Ryder waited for Saffron to react. That time, Saffron did, raising his eyebrows as the question caught him off guard.

"Tell who what?" He asked. Ryder watched him, before approaching to sit on the arm of the chair across from where Saffron sat.

"Your prince... did you tell him about your magic? About how dangerous it's growing?"

Saffron couldn't resist the tiny twitch of his jaw, fighting to keep his composure. He knew from the beginning this would be part of the act, that he would have to play damsel-in-distress before he could weave his words to get Ryder talking. He mentally apologized to Cylvan for speaking ill of him, those lies, even if it was for a reason.

"Yes," Saffron said. His voice cracked perfectly. "The day before the gala... I told him everything. I thought I could trust him, I wanted to prove you wrong... but... he acted so strangely toward me afterward..."

"I was afraid of that," Ryder breathed. He put out a hand, placing it on Saffron's knee before lifting it again to nudge the bottom of the teacup for Saffron to drink. Saffron did. He wondered if it had a spoonful of alcohol in it with the way every swallow made the room wobble slightly. "I worried... even your royal knight in shining armor would have a breaking point. I really did try to warn you, Saffron—but I'm so sorry."

"What are you trying to say?" Saffron asked, a flicker of sincerity slipping through. He already knew, but he wanted Ryder to say it. He wanted to see if Ryder was so far up his own ass—he would say the absolutely outrageous thing Saffron thought he was implying.

"I worry your prince may have been the one to call the witch-hunters to take you away. Once he realized the danger you posed to him, his reputation, the courtiers..."

Saffron bit down hard enough on his tongue he tasted blood. He would have fully snapped otherwise. He would have thrown the hot drink into Ryder's face then smashed the ceramic into his nose.

"Oh..." he managed to grind out all the same, before sipping at the tea to give himself a moment to temper his anger back down again. "I can't believe it..."

Ryder's hand returned to Saffron's leg, that time placed a little higher on his thigh. Saffron stared at it, feeling the muscle in his cheek twitch as he finished the drink in his cup. Trying to keep himself composed. He was a good beantighe; no amount of time masquerading as a high fey would wear those parts of him down. And Ryder, despite being so all-knowing and smart and always in control, seemed to be believing it, at least.

"Thank you for coming for me," Saffron went on, offering Ryder a pathetic smile. "Even though I left after our argument last time..."

"I'll always come for you, no matter where you are," Ryder promised. He squeezed Saffron's thigh. Saffron bit back the urge to smack his hand away. "And, selfishly—I'm glad I did. Now I don't have to worry about you being mistreated where I can't step in to help you. You can stay here, Saffron, with me. With our growing coven of arid witches. We can finally do this together, like I once told you. Until the solstice, when we can finally show the high fey we're something to be reckoned with."

"You have something planned for the solstice?" Saffron asked with real curiosity for the first time, watching as Ryder returned to the tea-cart to pour him another steaming cup. His doe-eyed look was an added bonus for the man who, apparently, melted as soon as someone gave him a naïve little gaze. Big strong man with all the answers Saffron needed, and Saffron was finally begging for it.

"Not now," Ryder said, driving Saffron's irritation a little higher. "We'll talk about it as the date comes. We're still a few weeks out, after all. Don't worry about anything until then—just focus on yourself. On trying to feel better. We have plenty of time, since... well, since..."

Saffron watched him. He didn't say anything. Ryder's smile was innocent. Awkward.

Fake.

"Since I guess you'll be staying here with me in the meantime after all, won't you? Considering, well... what your prince has done. Since he broke your trust like that. It isn't safe for you to leave right now."

"Oh... right," Saffron said. Ryder looked relieved—but only because he couldn't hear the snarling, the teeth gnashing in the back of Saffron's mind as more pieces all clicked together. Teeth that didn't even belong to Taran. "For how long? Until the solstice?"

"I mean for longer than the solstice," he said gently, with a nod. Saffron smiled awkwardly in response, playing dumb, because he truly didn't know how else to react except to burst out laughing at how fucking tightly-wound his nerves were growing. "Every time you came to see us, before now... I saw it on your face, Saffron. Relief. Peace. Like you knew this is where you really belong. With these people. With me." Ryder's smile softened. "And every time you came, I hoped it would be the time you decided to stay. To stay for good, I mean. Until we've overcome every obstacle ahead of us, for the sake of the people we're protecting. For our growing coven. I never wanted to pressure you, or even ask outright, since I knew you were in a precarious situation with your Night Prince—but I still hoped it. And now that you're finally here, safe, with me, I'm realizing more and more how badly we can use someone like you. I've said it before—but you and I could do amazing things together. Not only for ourselves, but for the people down below us right now. And those beyond that. Better things than you would ever be able to do trying to make changes from the inside out. And I think you know that as well as I do."

Saffron didn't know what to say. Even if he was genuinely only a naïve, timid, frightened little fawn, he wasn't sure he would know what to say. All of that was so inviting, hopeful, inspirational—but at the same time, empty. A whole monologue of empty platitudes, empty words. Promises without details. Flowers without roots.

"Yeah," he said with a pretty smile, even sighing pleasantly before sipping his tea again. "I'm so glad to finally understand where I truly belong. Here, next to you. With these people. Where I can best help them. Ah, speaking of these people... when do you think I can go see my friends?" Saffron wasn't going to wait any longer. His nerves weren't helped as he swore he even heard Taran laughing at him in the back of his mind, like he was as disgusted with the innocent act as Saffron was having to do it.

"Soon," Ryder answered after some consideration. Saffron knew by then how to tell when he was forming the perfect velvet lie behind his eyes. Watching as it came together before slipping like honey from his mouth. "But perhaps not right away. Just like Letty had to stay put in her cottage for a week or so in order to avoid the risk of anyone spotting her who shouldn't—I think you should do the same. Especially since I can't imagine your prince is just going to let you go without searching, first. But since I like you so much—I'll let you spend your days in my study here, with me, when I'm doing some reading. We could explore the ruins together too, if you like. Maybe practice your archery some more, since there's a chance you may still perform at the Midsummer opening ceremony... hmm, we'll talk about it later."

"Ha..." Saffron attempted, but it fell flat. He drank more tea. "Alright... that means you'll finally let me browse the books you have here, then? I'll get started—"

"The more I think about it, the more practicing your archery sounds like a good idea," Ryder smiled, patting Saffron on the leg before getting back to his feet. Saffron hated how, even with the promise of rejecting his prince in favor of Ryder—the man still seemed to find any excuse to put off any actual research. Actual work toward finding the witch's mark he'd promised Saffron from the very beginning. "I'm sure you could use the fresh air, anyway. There's a private breezeway in the neighboring building where we can go and don't have to worry about the rain."

Damnit—Saffron wasn't ready to leave the cathedral, yet. Not when there were groups of people in the nave down below, groups of people that may actually contain his friends if he was given any chance to look. He just needed one chance. Just a moment, at least, without Ryder there breathing down his neck and asking questions.

"Is there anything for me to eat, first?" he asked, fluttering his eyelashes. "I—I haven't had a proper meal since the gala last night, where I just snacked on the buffet table..."

"Danu's mounds. No wonder Cylvan fell for your tricks so easily. How do you get your voice to sound like that? Don't you hate yourself?"

Shut up, Saffron thought back to the bitter dog living in his head. He focused on the way Ryder chuckled, clearly taken by Saffron's innocent act even if Taran teased him for it.

"No problem. I'll go get something from the kitchen downstairs. Hang tight, alright? Keep drinking your tea. When the rain comes it's only gonna get colder in here."

Saffron raised the tea to him with a smile. Ryder nodded back, then turned to leave through a side door. Saffron watched him go. The moment the door closed, Saffron was on his feet, moving so fast the tea spilled over the rim of the cup and splattered his hand. He barely felt it. He knew he didn't have a lot of time.

He went straight for the door Breton once brought him through, knowing it led down to the nave—cursing under his breath when it was locked. He tried the door Ryder took, instead, holding his breath when he found it also locked. His heart thumped in his ears. He rushed to the clerestory bannister, last, overlooking the nave below. Knowing he was too high up to see faces up close—but he didn't have to be up close. He would recognize his friends even from afar. He definitely, definitely would—and Saffron's stomach only sank more the longer he looked, the longer that passed without spotting them at all.

Where else could they be? Somewhere else in the ruins? He chose to search the nave first on the grounds of giving Ryder one final benefit of the doubt, thinking perhaps they were milling about in the cathedral where he could keep a closer eye on them— and maybe they still were. They could have been in one of the adjoining rooms. They could be in some fucking dungeons down below, for all he knew. They could be somewhere else in the ruins, entirely. Saffron's fury only grew higher the more he considered exactly all the places Ryder could have stashed them, especially if he wished to do to Saffron what Sunbeam said he'd once done to her. With Chandry.

Saffron petrified when he recalled exactly what Sunbeam said Ryder had done with Chandry. His hands tightened over the railing, fighting to keep his breath steady. *Ryder put Chandry in the human world. He trapped her over there.*

"Focus, beantighe."

Saffron squeezed his eyes closed. Fine—he would just have to wait for Ryder to get back to ask. To continue playing innocent. To learn what he wanted to know by fluttering his eyelashes and pouting his lips. Until then, he was going to use the remainder of his time alone to scour that man's library for anything useful at all. He wouldn't get another chance, what with Cylvan on the other side of the trees likely chomping at the bit to steal Saffron back the moment two days ran out.

Fiachra, perched high on one of the bookshelves, sensed the beginning of his search, flapping to the floor and scuttling around in search of whatever she thought might help him. So helpful. She was so helpful.

He moved quickly, skimming the spines of the books on Ryder's shelves, barely reading them except in search of very specific words. *Witch's marks. Acacia Kyteler. Veil magic, veil knocks. Arid magic. Arid anything. Witchcraft. Witchhunters.* Anything, anything, as rain came to patter the glass of the lancet windows. As the light in the room gave way to dull, overcast darkness, making it harder than ever to see in the low light. Forcing him to slow down and search with a little more intention, squinting and touching every book as he passed it—but that was a curse in itself. Because as he was forced to look a little more closely, Saffron quickly came to realize—Ryder's collection was not as broad as Saffron had been led to believe.

"What?" he snapped. He shook his head, moving to search

another shelf, instead. Disbelief tangled in the back of his mind as even Taran seemed surprised at exactly how little there was to find. Those books, nearly every one of them—were no different from the ones Saffron could find in the general sections of Mairwen's library.

"You have to be shitting me," he hissed, growing more and more frustrated. He grabbed one that looked familiar, snapping it back shut and slamming it back in place the moment he read the title. It was the same one he used in his Ancient Alvish and Arithmetic class. "This son of a bitch... all he does is lie!"

Fiachra crooned from the oak desk by the windows, summoning Saffron's attention. She hopped onto it with clumsy talons on the polished wood, opening her wings wide and flapping them slightly to really get his attention. He hurried over, asking what it was, curiosity sparking when she flapped her wings again and pecked the top drawer. Knowing there was nothing else in the room to help him, Saffron humored the bird, attempting to pull the drawer open and finding it as locked as the doors to leave. Huffing, growing more embittered than ever, he nudged Fiachra out of the way and pressed his hematite-ring finger to the wood, drawing a circle around the lock—

"Saffron? Wake up. How are you feeling?"

Saffron swam through heavy thoughts, crashing against the inside of his head like angry waves on the lake. His mind spun, around and around until he thought he might be sick. Lurching forward, he pressed his hand to his mouth, shivering as Ryder said something before pulling the blanket tighter over Saffron's shoulders.

Saffron sat in the study armchair, soaking wet from the rain. His teeth chattered in his mouth, breathing hard and heavy like he'd been running. The palms of his hands were scraped, stinging as he pulled the blanket closer around his body. His knuckles were split. His jaw hurt, stiff as he tried to open his mouth to ask what was going on—

"Here, Saffron, let me make you some tea," Ryder said, touching Saffron's face all over, wiping rain and wet hair from his eyes. "Shhh, it's alright. Just hang tight."

Saffron's tongue turned over in his mouth, finding a bitter, semisweet layer of film coating the back of his teeth. A bitter, floral earthiness he knew. He knew, he knew, before the wolf's voice ever rang in his head at all.

"Don't drink the tea again."

Again? Saffron lifted heavy, bleary eyes to where Ryder crouched down in front of the fireplace. The man's hands shook as he removed a matchbox from the stone shelf alongside the hearth, plucking one out and striking it. In the added light of the flame, Saffron saw three others scattered on the floor. The wood in the hearth caught in an instant, as if still warm. In the light of the fire, as Ryder glanced back over his shoulder to meet Saffron's eyes and smile, Saffron saw the pink swelling of a split bottom lip.

Saffron's heart pounded in his ears. He didn't hear what Ryder said—but he heard Taran's voice clear as day. Like wind chimes in a storm.

"Don't say anything. Don't let him know he missed anything."

What happened? Saffron's head ached, thoughts scattered like fingers had raked through him to leave trenches behind. Like gathering mud from the bank of Quartz Creek. Only one thing remained loud, undeniable above the disorientation—

He knew the taste of weaverthistle. It took him back to Danann House, when Eias tried to give it to him the morning after he and Cylvan saw the wolf on the road outside the ruins. He was reminded of all those times he and his friends in Beantighe Village had brewed and swallowed that same taste whenever something particularly terrible happened that they would rather forget. The taste every member of Beantighe Village, every student of Morrígan Academy, had swallowed back the morning Saffron and his friends left the Spring Court for Avren.

What happened? He demanded more firmly.

"Check your pocket. Be careful not to let Ryder see."

Saffron sank heavily into the cushions of the chair while Ryder's back was still to him, busy hanging a kettle of water in the open flames. In his pocket, Saffron felt something he couldn't remember putting there.

"You found it in the drawer of the desk."

Where's Fiachra? Saffron asked immediately, hand carefully removing the parchment as his eyes skimmed every corner of the room, before forcing himself to focus. One thing at a time. One thing at a—

Saffron stared at the page unfolded on his lap. Baba Yaga's words stretched across the parchment, her handwriting as familiar as Cylvan's was. His eyes skimmed the words as fast as the shock would let him.

Saffron—I am sorry to hear you are still unwell...

I think Fiachra is a lovely name... human witches have always familiarized with such pets... familiarizing with Fiachra may help to ease your burden...

... If you are unable to familiarize... seek your witch's mark. Also sometimes called a rowan mark, an arid mark, or a veil mark... generally given by the veil when first making the oath...

If you can find a way to force your mark... even without a bridge partner... I wonder if it will help to ease the pain your body is in...

Please write me again soon... to reassure this old woman of your wellness...

—Your henmother.

Ryder's voice rang in Saffron's ears, standing on the edge of the ruins for the first time. Stealing words from Baba Yaga's hand and passing them as his own. From that letter she sent back with Fiachra—who Saffron assumed had lost it. Fiachra, who stole a Morrígan access ring before returning back to Avren. Where she must have been captured by Ryder—all over again.

His stomach turned. He sought out his friend in the room again, thinking only of how terrified she must have been. How close he'd come to losing her. How she could have very well ended up nailed to the palace gates, just like all the others. When he still didn't see her, his heart skipped in horror—before he realized, he'd put his amethyst pendant in the same pocket where the letter was stowed. If it was gone, and Fiachra was nowhere to be found, then maybe—

Ryder stood from the fireplace. Leaving the kettle to boil. Saffron shoved the letter back into his pocket, just as the man returned with a weary smile, placing his hands on Saffron's thighs and running them up and down as if trying to warm him.

"Do you want a change of clothes?" He asked. "I can find something dry for you to wear."

"Alright," Saffron croaked. He spoke a little too quickly, saying anything to get Ryder's hands off of him. To get Ryder away from him. Ryder nodded. He went to a chest against the wall, flipping it open to dig around through garments inside.

"You need to get away from here."

Something tells me I already tried once.

"Then you've realized it, too."

Saffron's mind went silent. Not in so many words. He knew —but to put that understanding into words terrified him. Taran offered to do it for him. Taking all of the fear Saffron knew would come—and burning it with flames of pure rage.

"He's plucked your memory threads. He may have done it more times before now, even."

Last night, Saffron interjected. He pressed a hand to his chest with how it jolted. He was almost sick at the vague recollection of a finger touching his forehead the night before, when Ryder appeared at Saffron's failed burial.

"This time he was sloppy," Taran added. *"He didn't think to*

check your pockets, to see what made you kick down the door and run in the first place. Careful, now."

Ryder returned with dry clothes thrown over his shoulders and a cup of tea. Clearly knowing better than to leave the weaver-thistle bulb in the cup, but it didn't matter. Saffron knew from the smell of it. Despite his ability to keep the shock and disbelief from his expression, his hands shook as he accepted the drink. His smile twitched as he gave it. His fingers trembled as he hooked one through the loop of the teacup. It rattled against the saucer as Saffron couldn't find an anchor of composure to cling to.

As the reality of his situation fully sank in, hooking under his skin, through his bones, he didn't know which realization was worse.

That his mind had been rifled through, memories taken at Ryder's whim whenever there was something he didn't wish for Saffron to know—

Or—how the only way Ryder could do any of that—was if his blood was equal parts opulent as it was arid.

34

THE BEAST

Tea spilled over the rim of the cup. Saffron couldn't stop shaking.

He took a sip. Just a tiny one, knowing it wouldn't be enough to have any effect on his memories. Hoping it would be enough to blur his emotions in that moment. An attempt to calm himself. As the world came crashing down.

A half-fey man posing as human. Teaching taboo magic to the rescued Spring Witches of Alfidel. Promising them freedom and peace and happy lives. A chance to live in the sun.

"He comes from Fjornar," Taran said right as Saffron remembered that, too. Their dance on Beltane that told him so. *"The King's Keep."*

How do you... but then Saffron recalled his most recent dream. Where the wolf told him outright: *This is where I became what I am. This is where they trained the oracles who turned my bones to silver.*

"It's where Eias trained as well," Taran grumbled. *"I should have recognized it sooner."*

Of course Ryder was from Fjornar where they trained oracles —of course he was. And yet Saffron had trusted him implicitly, simply by the curve of his ears. They must have been glamoured. Ryder must have glamoured them to be round no differently than how Saffron glamoured his into points.

He suddenly recalled how they'd been pointed on Beltane. Saffron's stomach turned over on itself.

"What happened?" Ryder asked, catching Saffron off guard. Saffron, despite everything, could still rely on his beantighe instincts. By some grace of god. A smile appeared on his lips.

"I think that's my question," he said. Meaning far more than his innocent tone put on.

"I don't know why you left, but... you got lost in the ruins. Maybe you went looking for me. I'm sorry it took so long for me to come back," he said with a weary smile, like he thought Saffron was quite the handful. Saffron gulped back vomit when Ryder's hand brushed down his cheek. "It's easy to get turned around out there when you're not familiar with it. Especially at night. *Especially* with the rain. I went out looking for you, heard you scurrying around, caught you right as you slipped off a wall. Bonked your head. Which explains why you don't remember much, I guess."

He took Saffron's hands, turning them to show off the scrapes on his palms. Saffron could only smile at him, fighting to keep the expression as blank and empty as possible. In reality—it never ceased to frighten him exactly how easily Ryder lied. How easy those words came to him with only a moment of consideration.

"I'm glad you were there to catch me," Saffron said. His blank smile remained. He forced himself to relax, to focus. He reminded himself of his missing amethyst. His missing owl. What he'd told Asche earlier that morning. Knowing it was only a matter of time before a certain Night Prince came for him. He just had to keep Ryder talking until then, to keep him distracted. Perhaps to even finally learn what all of it was for.

"I guess you've always been there to catch me, though," Saffron went on, sitting up in the chair and putting a hand on

Ryder's chest. He smiled demurely, innocently. Ryder's blue eyes flickered over every inch of Saffron's face, like he was finally getting exactly what he'd wanted since the beginning. "I'm sorry it took me so long to... understand, I guess. To listen. I was just so... I just wanted to believe Cylvan actually... But you were there for me all this time. Right in front of me."

Ryder placed his hand on Saffron's chest in return. Saffron had to resist jerking away.

"I knew the moment I heard about this," Ryder whispered. "He says he was compelled to shoot you? That he didn't do it on purpose... but remember what he first meant to do to you, Saffron. How he meant to use you, then throw you away once you gave him what he wanted. I just don't believe someone so cruel could have such a change of heart. And the timing of it... to try and kill you an instant after you saved him from Taran... don't you understand?"

Saffron grit his teeth. He grit back against everything he wished to say, until his teeth creaked beneath the pressure. *How do you know any of that? How do you know what Cylvan first intended to do with me, you cocksucking—*

"Saffron," Taran suddenly said. *"I think I know this man from somewhere. Somewhere other than Fjornar. I don't know exactly, but I think... oh, godsdamnit..."*

What? Saffron snapped back, eyes going wide as he stared at Ryder. Silent with his mouth, though his lips parted slightly. But Taran didn't answer again. Saffron even sensed him pull away, to tuck himself into the furthest corner of Saffron's mind, as if to recompose himself. Saffron's pulse raced as he waited, but knew he couldn't just sit there in silence while Ryder waited for a response. He had to focus. He had to stay grounded. There wasn't much time.

"Since we'll be together every day, now—you'll be able to help me find my witch's mark, won't you?"

"Oh, yes," Ryder chuckled. "And more. We'll do so much

more. These people will finally have their symbol of hope—their rowan spirit. The one I promised would come and drape the moon in crimson, to send the message of their grief... *Iron reaps its bloody night; rowan tears the moon shall weep...*"

Saffron's smile tightened.

"That's from..."

"The adage on the red cards, yes," Ryder grinned, sitting back on the balls of his feet. "Our call for anyone who wishes to come and see. To bask in the crimson moon the night of the solstice. And it'll happen, thanks to you. All thanks to you, Saffron, my rowan spirit—"

"Wait," Saffron interjected. He sat forward, on the edge of the chair. "You have something planned...? For the solstice? Do you mean—like when I asked you to speak to the kings? As part of our deal?"

Ryder's smile turned mischievous. Saffron's heart sank.

"I never intended on meeting with the kings," he laughed. "Sorry. I would have agreed to anything you said, though—that's how sure I was that you would eventually see through your prince's guise."

"Then what?" Saffron insisted. He buried fingernails into the arms of the chair. Trying to keep himself anchored in his body.

"We'll have plenty of time to talk about it later, Saffron. We have all the time in the world now. Let's just focus on getting you warmed up. Come on, you really should change your clothes."

"No, Ryder—" Saffron threw his hands out, grabbing Ryder by the front of his shirt. Pulling him back. Back down to his knees. The desperation in his voice was suddenly very real, squeezing him from the inside. "Please—tell me what you're planning. It has something to do with—with me, doesn't it? Since you promised me my witch's mark by the solstice, too. Right?" Saffron's mouth was dry. He licked his lips, but it didn't help. "If you'd just tell me what I should be focusing on, or what I should be preparing for... the last thing I want is to be there and not know what I'm doing... what if I accidentally hurt people?"

A mix of lies and truth. An act rooted in genuine restlessness. He wouldn't be on Ryder's hip on the solstice. He'd already learned how to control the wolf in his arm, even though Ryder didn't know that, yet. But with every other lie Ryder kept from him, mixing them with scattered truths, promises and reassurances, all while wasting Saffron's time every time they met, just like Saffron said the last time they were together...

"You're just going to have to trust me, Saffron." Ryder's smile was so calm. Collected. There wasn't an ounce of worry anywhere on his face, even though the solstice was only a few weeks away. If he really believed Saffron was going to help him do something on that day, during the Midsummer Games—why wasn't he more worried? He should have been panicking. He should have been scrambling to find out how to get Saffron's witch's mark like he promised. Wasn't he worried Saffron might let the beast loose and tear apart every single person within reach...?

Oh.

"You..." he trailed off. Ryder raised his eyebrows in question. He waited for Saffron to continue. But for Saffron—there was only snarling. Gnashing teeth. He saw only red filling his vision as it dawned on him—exactly why Ryder fought so hard to get Saffron to come to him in the ruins, but even once Saffron did—he was in no rush to offer any help. He was never in any rush to practice magic together. To let Saffron into his study. To teach Saffron anything new. Even though he believed, as much as Saffron did, that Saffron's magic would only get more intense. More out of control. Wilder. Even though he believed, as much as Saffron did—that the vicious beast that manifested from his arm—would only be more bloodthirsty than ever on the solstice.

Ryder wanted Saffron to be wild, untamed. Ryder wanted Saffron's unbridled rowan magic to harm people. To kill people. To rain destruction across the games. He knew how desperate Saffron was for help—and he knew how Saffron would never agree to something like that, even if he earned

Saffron's trust. Even if Saffron came to hate Cylvan, he would never choose to kill innocent people on purpose. Just to send a message.

Ryder was betting on Saffron not knowing how to control it. Ryder was betting on Saffron's magic being untamed enough to wreak havoc. To spill blood; to hurt and maim anyone and everyone he could within reach.

Perhaps there was a reason he decided to rescind his promised romantic summer to Saffron, after all. The moment he saw what Saffron's magic did to that human outside of Ériu's shrine—he must have realized exactly how he could use it to his advantage.

And had Saffron never had the courage to face the beast in his arm, to reason with it, to come to trust it, to be vulnerable enough to come to an understanding with it—Saffron may very well have let it happen. No—he would have been forced to let it happen. Exactly as Ryder designed it.

And less as Ryder imagined it, but still by his own design— while Taran was not the wild incarnation of Saffron's magic, something else was. Something else that might grow stronger as time ticked by, all the same. Perhaps it was how Saffron was seeing halos again, perhaps it was the way he could grip iron magic in living things and tear them apart. Whether it was to tame the wolf or something else—Saffron still needed a witch's mark. And Ryder had tricked him into thinking such a thing was within reach.

"You... were supposed to help me get my witch's mark..." the words left him, flat and cold. That statement was raw, it scraped up the back of his throat, riddled with thorns.

"What do you mean?" Ryder said with a laugh. Saffron buried his nails deeper into the arms of the chair. He may have kept himself in place—had Ryder not put out his hands to caress Saffron's face so gently.

Saffron's hand snapped out. It grabbed Ryder's in a vice grip, staring at him—before pressing it backward. Bending Ryder's fingers like he'd once bent Lady Callan's, except that time he wouldn't stop until he felt them snap. Ryder flinched, then frowned, leaning forward on his knees in confusion.

"Stop lying to me," Saffron ground out through his teeth. "All you ever do—is fucking lie, you piece of shit."

Ryder's friendly expression vanished in an instant.

"How could you say that?" he asked, voice low. "After everything I've done for you?"

"You—!" The word tore from Saffron's chest. He slammed his hands into Ryder's body, knocking him backward. "You—! You were going to let me slaughter people, weren't you! Innocent people! You were going to put that nightmare on me! You were going to trick me into—!" His throat closed up, emotion swelling higher and higher until he tasted blood. "You did everything you could to get me here, and then—! And now—! You'll do anything to keep me here! I fucking know it! Sunbeam told me so! She—!"

He overflowed with rage and magic and all the wild potential Ryder wanted so badly. Until Saffron could see the aridity in the air, he could see the undulating pink glow of Ryder's half-arid, half-opulent blood. Until he could feel Ryder's heartbeat under his own skin, beneath his fingers, like something tangible. Like he could close his fists and crush it in an instant. Until he couldn't stop the words from bursting out: "What the fuck have you done with my friends, you bastard!"

His hands slammed into Ryder's chest a second time—and it sent him crashing backward into the bookshelves. Ryder collided with them with enough force to knock books loose, clattering to the ground as Ryder buckled forward, then slowly straightened up again. He clutched his chest, and upon meeting Saffron's eyes again—blood dripped from the corner of his mouth. Saffron remembered that witchhunter on top of him outside the beantighe ruins. How Saffron saw them, their magic—how he grasped at their insides, their blood, ripping into it like the rowan vines that nearly suffocated Fiachra at Ériu's feet. Standing there, staring at Ryder, breathing heavily—Saffron felt it all over again. He felt the invisible tangibility of warm, flowing life, bloody iron

—and how easy it would be to rake his fingers through it. He could kill him. Saffron could kill Ryder right there. To shred him into pieces, just like rowan vines. To nail to the cathedral doors like a barn owl slaughtered to prove his own strength. It would be so easy—

The memory of killing that witchhunter with his hands, with his magic, flooded Saffron's mind. As if to remind him how he did it the first time, how easy it was, how easy and quick and painless for him—but then the scene suddenly unraveled in a thousand directions, the entirety of that nightmare crashing into him like a wave against the cliffs of the shore. Those witchhunters at the palace dorms. Uninvited, unexpected. How they interrupted the gala in front of everyone—when they could have just taken Letty and left. If they'd never made a scene in front of everyone, Saffron never would have known at all.

Those beantighes in the wall. Behind the wainscoting Saffron used to escape.

You're one of us, aren't you?

How did they know? He was always so careful. Letty would have never said anything. Hollow, Nimue would have never said a thing at all.

We've only heard rumors. That's all...

Saffron had turned to leave. To get away from those in the ballroom, without another thought—

There were others gathered at the beantighe dorms, to be taken to the ruins tonight. You don't think...? Could someone have told them...?

Could someone have told them? Could someone have told them?

"*Ground yourself, Saffron!*" Taran snarled, sensing how Saffron spiraled. How the memories crashed over him, swallowing him, claiming every inch of him. Forcing him to pay attention as every piece came together. Saffron stumbled backward, nearly tripping over his own feet as the floor wavered beneath him. He tried to do that, he tried to find his body, to settle back into it— but another realization came. Crushing him.

Could someone have told them?

Ryder was there that night. He knew where to find Saffron, where to take him. At just the right time.

Could someone have told them?

Ryder appeared the night before when witchhunters tried to bury him. Had Saffron not fought back, they would have. Ryder would have come with just enough time to dig Saffron back out again. Right when Saffron would have given up hope.

Could someone have told them?

Ryder knew the witchhunters would be at the palace during Cylvan's last gala. He sent the beantighe in under the guise of luring Saffron out. He admitted it. He admitted it like something chivalrous.

Imagine my surprise when they came back and told me you'd brushed them off...

What if Ryder never meant to lure Saffron away from the witchhunters waiting in the darkness—but straight to them? In order to rescue him, to bring him back to the ruins? To trap Saffron there one final time, after hours earlier, Saffron screamed he would never, ever come to see Ryder ever again?

"Did you... use witchhunters to almost arrest Letty?" Saffron asked, holding his head. Searching for Ryder through blurry eyes —spotting him standing with hunched shoulders, as if on the verge of lunging. Eyes bulging slightly. Saffron tasted more blood. "Did you bring her here so I would finally come...? Because I wasn't agreeing fast enough...?"

Ryder said nothing at first. Saffron couldn't breathe. He was no longer in his body at all.

"Saffron—" Ryder attempted. He stepped forward—then lunged, throwing out his hands, trying to grab Saffron where he stood. Saffron screamed when the man's hand lashed out, extending for his forehead. Saffron shoved Ryder back again, back into the shelf, knocking more books to the floor.

"I know you've been taking my memories!" he shrieked. "You think I don't know what weaverthistle tea tastes like, cocksucker!

But you won't get anymore—you won't take anything else from me!"

"Saffron!"

"I know only oracles can weave memory threads, too!" Saffron continued, voice rising higher and higher as his rage grew with it. "And oracles are all half-fey, you piece of shit—!"

He grunted as Ryder lunged once more, throwing an arm around Saffron's back, opposite hand smashing against his mouth to silence him. Saffron attempted to shove him off again, tangling their feet together and crashing to the floor. He slammed an elbow against the side of Ryder's face, twisting to push himself upright again, but Ryder grabbed him by the hair and wrenched him back—then slammed him face down against the floor.

"Be still!"

Saffron petrified. Every muscle locked, paralyzed. Ryder waited only a moment longer, before sitting back, still straddling Saffron's waist and crushing his hips into the stone floor. He let out a long exhale, raking fingers back through his hair before pinching the bridge of his nose.

"Godsdamnit... goddamnit," he groaned. "Not like this, I didn't want it to be like this, Saffron. God*damnit*, I didn't want it to be like this. God—I've never met anyone as fucking stubborn as you. Whatever I've had to do is because you refuse to listen. Even now, you refuse to fucking listen, Christ!"

Do something, Saffron begged, searching for Taran in his mind. Taran answered, though his voice was far away.

"I rely on your own ability. If you're debilitated, so am I."

Useless, he growled. *Absolutely fucking useless!*

"Speak for yourself, beantighe."

Fingers suddenly trailed along the bottom of Saffron's shirt, before sliding it upward and making Saffron gasp. He strained against the enchantment, clenching his teeth together until they nearly turned to dust.

"All you care about is your prince," Ryder repeated under his breath, hand traveling up Saffron's spine, pushing the fabric with it. "But does he touch you gently like this? Does he even caress you lovingly, the way you're meant to be? Would he even notice if a witch's mark appeared on your skin? Does he know how much you've been suffering? Would he ever know if something changed...?"

Saffron focused on the tips of his fingers. Straining to feel them, to move them. Fingers were always the first things to loosen. The moment they twitched, he could force his way through the rest.

"Does he know about these?" Ryder continued, drawing over every letter of the scars on Saffron's back. "They have been... so cruel to you, Saffron. I'm only asking you to let me show you kindness, for once."

Sensation returned, and Saffron threw his arm back, breaking free of Ryder's grasp, slamming backward. Knocking Ryder away, he rolled onto his back, bending his leg to crush the man's ribs with his heel—but Ryder was faster, lunging and pressing his body into the bottom of Saffron's foot. It pinned Saffron's knee into his chest, making him gasp and claw at Ryder's shoulders as his sternum bent beneath the weight and screamed with pain.

He tasted the bitter, earthy flavor of weaverthistle tea on his lips and tongue before he could reel his head back, the rim of the cup smashed against his mouth before invading fingers shoved inside to force him to swallow. He choked, tea and spit and over-whelmed blood dripping from his nose as his body fought to breathe. He clawed at Ryder's face, his hair, his shirt as the man stretched back his arm and grabbed the teapot, forcing Saffron's mouth open and pouring the hot liquid down his throat. Saffron spluttered, choking and coughing, shoving his hands out to try and knock it away—only for the porcelain to slam against his head, shattering and making his world spin.

He groaned as Ryder finally sat back again, breathing heavily. Even as he stepped off of Saffron's stomach, Saffron struggled to reconnect to the rest of his body, eyes rolling back and vision blur-ring as his head throbbed and the hot tea drenching his hair and shirt turned cold. Ryder's hand returned, though that time his touch was gentler. He scooped his arm under Saffron's back, sitting him up and pressing something into his teeth. Saffron was too disoriented to fight back that time, clutching at Ryder's shirt, weakly trying to push him away. He didn't have to see to know what split between his teeth—he knew the moment he tasted it. A ripe strawberry; one with the tinge of wild fairy magic.

"I'll make this up to you," Ryder breathed, pressing his face into the side of Saffron's hair. "I swear I'll make this up to you, my rowan spirit. I'll explain everything once I have you somewhere safe. I'll take you to your friends. I promise no harm has come to them. You'll understand everything, Saffron, even why I have to do all of this for us—"

A deafening bang crashed through the cathedral. Screams erupted from the humans below—only to be swallowed by the deafening snarl of wind tearing through the stone building, over-turning furniture and shattering glass.

"*Where is he!*" the voice tore over stone and debris, booming and echoing off the high ceilings with all the ferocity of an old god seeking retribution. Saffron's king of the forest had finally come to collect.

Ryder was in the process of yanking a thick blanket from the nearest couch when the sound of feathers and a screech got Saffron's attention. On the ledge overlooking the nave below, a white-faced golden owl landed on the railing. Saffron smiled at her, mouthing the words '*good bird*' as Ryder's arms slid under his back and legs—but a moment before he was lifted from the floor, a second creature sewn of nighttime darkness appeared over the railing. Ryder managed barely a sound in warning—before a gale of wind tore from the shadow, crashing into him, slamming him into the high vaulted ceiling—then whisking away. Ryder crashed back to the floor in an unconscious heap.

Cold hands found Saffron half a moment later. So different from the ones that had torn at him, dragged him, pulled and yanked so roughly only moments prior. Saffron much preferred the ice that time, knowing they were wet from the rain. Making him shiver. Still—he managed to crack a smile. Even as everything spun, as every inch of him ached, as his thoughts danced and couldn't seem to click together—he knew, the moment he turned into Cylvan's body and breathed him in, he was safe. That was the safest place he could ever be, right there in his raven prince's arms.

35

THE WOLF

"*Wait.*"

"Wait," Saffron mumbled, mimicking Taran's voice in his head. He cracked his eyes open as they rushed through the ruins in the dark, with only the crashing of rain against crumbling stones and rooftops, the splashing of Cylvan's boots in the mud, and—the patter of giant paws running alongside them. Saffron nearly asked when Taran had manifested, but the question caught on his tongue when he realized the creature keeping pace wasn't the wolf whose magic he commanded. Despite being the same in size, the beast was the color of orange leaves, coppery and fiery with a sharper snout and upright ears. Its long, thick tail confirmed what Saffron's woozy mind first thought—it wasn't a wolf at all. Cylvan was joined by a massive fox.

"Wait," he groaned out one more time. Images flashed in his mind, put there by Taran. Images from their shared dreams, the stone buildings, emphasized by how Saffron was certain there were more protective charms in those ruins than any of them could count. There was no way they'd be able to escape without notice—and he knew Ryder was going to do anything, everything he had to, to not lose Saffron like he'd already lost Sunbeam.

Cylvan, however, didn't listen. He pushed wet hair from Saffron's eyes, kissing his forehead, promising everything was going to be alright, they would be away from that place soon and back somewhere warm and safe where Saffron could rest—but then the fox clamped teeth on Cylvan's sleeve, yanking him back right before he turned the corner around a building. Saffron strained to look through the darkness, stomach turning at the sight of lanterns clutched by a group of wet humans, clearly searching. Looking for Saffron, probably told by Ryder he'd been stolen away by the Night Prince of Alfidel—and if they indeed found him in Cylvan's arms, it wasn't going to end well.

Another mental image blurred into view in his mind, and Saffron rolled his heavy head backward, then to the side, finally spotting what Taran was trying to direct him toward. He muttered Cylvan's name, tugging on the front of his shirt, before wearily pointing toward it. Cylvan bit his lip, before cursing under his breath and pulling Saffron closer, racing through the darkness where he indicated.

AFTER BARRICADING THE DOOR WITH WHATEVER OLD furniture they could find, the giant fox paced back and forth at the head of the room. Back and forth, back and forth, while Cylvan settled Saffron on a dusty pew, stripping off his own damp cloak to try to cover Saffron with it. Fiachra preened from where she perched on the back of the wooden bench, occasionally clicking in threat whenever she thought Cylvan rubbed Saffron's arms a little too much. Cylvan said nothing at first, even bearing the brunt of the owl's sharp beak so long as he could keep his hands focused on warming Saffron's chills.

"Who is that?" Saffron finally asked. His voice was hoarse, but he was glad to be able to string sentences together, again. The chilly rain must have helped to clear his head of the fruits. He was glad Ryder hadn't had a chance to force any more into his mouth.

Cylvan glanced over his shoulder to the orange beast, before turning back with a sarcastic smile.

"What, you don't recognize him? Think hard about it, púca. Try not to hurt his feelings. Come on, think of the feast in the woods."

Saffron frowned. His heart pattered uncomfortably when his instinct was to wonder if whoever the beast was was something Ryder had taken from his memories, not sure how he would reveal that fun detail to Cylvan without inciting another windy tirade. There was no way it was Sionnach—despite their name meaning *fox* in Gaeilge. Oh, had he ever told them that? He wondered how they would respond...

But then he churned over Cylvan's last comment about the *feast in the woods*, knowing he only ever used that tone when referring to some myth Saffron should have known—and he jumped when it finally struck him.

"Bricriu's feast! C-Copper!" he exclaimed. At the sound, the animal turned with ears back in what Saffron thought might be embarrassment, snorting and turning its nose up before trotting over. He sniffed Saffron up and down in greeting, before licking his face, then head-butting Cylvan and knocking him off the pew. Saffron laughed more, throwing his arms out and embracing his friend's giant, soft, fuzzy head, petting his snout and pinching the velvety skin of his ears, complimenting him, telling him how pretty and good and handsome he was. Behind them, Cylvan grumbled to himself while getting back to his feet and brushing himself off, like he was jealous of the shift in attention.

"Is this your Sídhe magic, Copper?" Saffron asked affectionately, scratching his ears. "Why didn't you tell me? Why didn't anyone ever tell me? We could have had so much more fun in the woods, aww..."

"Don't worry, he didn't tell me either," Cylvan grumbled, flipping out his hair and reclaiming his seat. "Until his animal nose could be useful in finding you. It's so ironic, isn't it, considering the way he bullies poor Sionnach for their legs and tail and ears... how ironic and cruel of him, don't you think?"

"You're one to talk, dragon-prince," Saffron cooed, before nuzzling Copper's head one more time.

When Copper finally returned to the head of the room to continue his on-guard pacing, Cylvan reclaimed his spot on the pew, rubbing Saffron's arms up and down again to warm them, as if he didn't know what else to do. How else to help. Saffron finally put his hands on Cylvan's, just to hold them. Only then did he realize how badly he trembled, even his breath shaking with every exhale. The adrenaline of it all, to finally understand the full extent of how he'd been misled. The shame and guilt anchored to it. How he was so embarrassed to have been tricked. How it took Taran mac Delbaith, of all people, to snap him out of it. To guide him through the realization.

To bring him back from a spiral that devoured his conscious thoughts like fire eating parchment, when he'd been a moment from flaying Ryder into pieces. He closed his eyes, then closed his hands into fists where they rested on Cylvan's palms. He could still feel the thickness in the air. That clutchable, tangible intangibility. Like a thinning of the veil at the tips of his fingers. As if he'd knocked into the space between his touch and Ryder's body, allowing him to grasp it.

He let out a long, heavy breath. It was true that Taran, the wolf, was not a manifestation of his rowan magic at all. Perhaps it was that rush of fury, rage, bloodlust that all-consumed him in moments of emotions high enough to boil his blood, instead. The wolf living in the scars on his arm had been a balm the entire time, after all. Like Baba Yaga had tried to tell him in her letter. How ironic, that the wolf haunting his nightmares was actually proof of a familiar's ability to keep his magic tempered. And that what he'd been going through—was *tempered* at all. It was the best possible outcome. Oh, god. God help him. Ériu, Danu, Lugh, anyone else who listened—fucking help him.

"I'm sorry," he finally whispered, the first to speak between himself and the raven seated across from him. "I just keep causing you trouble, no matter how hard I try to be good. And now I've caused my friends trouble, too, because I was so foolish..."

Cylvan made a sound of incredulity. Like he truly couldn't believe a single word out of Saffron's mouth. Saffron averted his eyes; he didn't know where to start. He didn't know if he wanted to talk about it at all. Not right away, at least. He needed to process it. He needed time to grieve. He needed a chance to just— accept what had been his reality all along. And the humiliation it took to finally get there.

He suddenly felt exhausted. His body bent beneath the weight of it, sighing and pressing his forehead into Cylvan's open hands on his knees. Cylvan didn't say anything at first, just lifted a hand to gently comb fingers through Saffron's hair.

"I hurt people," Saffron whispered. He didn't know where it came from. Instincts. An attempt to release even an ounce of the pressure building inside of him, locked behind his own silence. "The wolf... in my arm... it's not my magic. It's a familiar. It protected me when witchhunters took me from your gala. It... killed all of them. And I just let it..."

Cylvan's hand in Saffron's hair paused for only a second.

"Good," he whispered. Saffron lifted his head with a frown, and Cylvan pursed his lips. "Not that people died—but that you had something to protect you. Gods, that's all I've ever prayed for, that there would be something, anything, to keep you safe when I can't..."

Saffron grimaced. "And who will be there when I inevitably hurt you, too?"

"Hurt me," Cylvan said in an instant. Like an invitation. Saffron had been mostly facetious, and Cylvan's sincerity surprised him. He took Saffron's face, lifting it to meet one another's eyes again. "I've told you before, I'm not afraid of you. I'm not afraid of anything you can do. And if it means you'll stay where I can keep you safe—hurt me as much as you need. I will never hold it against you."

"No, Cylvan—"

"I mean it. I mean it," Cylvan repeated, pulling Saffron close, holding him with a sense of desperation. It left Saffron breathless, heart pounding as he closed his eyes and wrapped his arms back around him.

"I'll stay with you," he promised. "I won't hurt you. I'll never hurt you, Cylvan. I want to become the person who protects you, too. I'm going to be the one who keeps you safe one day, too." In a quiet voice, one only for the raven prince in front of him, he whispered: *"I love you. I love you."*

"It appears Cylvan finally has the naïve, frivolous romance he's always wanted," Taran grumbled. Saffron pulled away from Cylvan's embrace, gazing at him for a moment, before swallowing against the tightness in his throat.

"Oh..." he breathed, thoughts racing. He rubbed his thumb up and down the bumpy scar on his arm before pressing his lips together. "I... I have to show you something. I think you'll be shocked, but— you need to know. You deserve to know the truth about... him."

"*'Him'?* Who, Saffron?" Cylvan asked, immediately concerned, cupping Saffron's cheek. Saffron's heart continued pounding like crazy, sitting up and carefully wiggling free from where Cylvan had him caged against the pew. He met Copper's eyes, next, and smiled awkwardly at him, too.

"You're about to be a lot more confused, I think, Copper," he said. "I'll explain everything later, alright? Until then, just... no one panic. You're going to want to."

"Saffron, what's going on?" Cylvan asked, rising slowly to his feet. Saffron avoided his eyes, just wanting to get it over with. He gazed down at the scars on his wrists, rubbing his palm up and down the length of it.

Can you obey me now? He asked the voice in his head.

"I suppose we'll find out."

"Asshole," he grumbled. He rubbed the scars one more time, before taking a deep breath. *"Icarus, come."*

Saffron didn't realize how accustomed he'd grown to the smell of death and rot and wet fur. That time, his heart no longer raced at the sight of him materializing. He'd grown so familiar with that beast in his arm, both due to the number of times he'd accidentally summoned it, but also by the way it had lived inside of him. How the opulence he stole and named had intermingled with his own magic, until he felt no distinction between where his ended and Taran's began. To the point of sharing dreams, of walking alongside one another, as if the veil was attempting to ease their animosity slowly before they came to the realization of what was actually happening.

That was the first time he'd ever seen the exact moment and place where the wolf manifested on command—and it proved that it still was not Taran mac Delbaith physically appearing at his feet. Though he was still birthed in the darkness, it was from nothing. His physical form only condensed into one of striking teeth and weighty paws when Saffron commanded it, whether he did so consciously in the moment or not.

The thought made him straighten up. He squared his shoulders, emboldened by the proof right in front of him. That wolf was his. That nightmarish beast belonged to him, and only he could control it. The wolf that once stalked the Agate Wood outside of Morrígan—was Saffron's familiar, who lived only to serve him.

Cylvan stepped from the pews, drawing the sword from his belt and walking backward to where Saffron stood at the mouth of the aisle. Staring at the beast that stood almost as tall as he did.

The wolf let out a long, hot breath, eyes on Saffron before traveling to the prince.

"Hello, Cylvan."

"T—" Cylvan choked. Saffron reached out to take his hand in reassurance, but Cylvan had gone pale as a ghost. "Taran?"

His voice cracked. Not in fear, or apprehension—there was

something broken about it. Saffron nodded. He watched Cylvan's jaw clench, then his tongue rolled in his mouth, trying to find the right words.

"Why are you here like this?" he asked. Taran made a sound like a miserable laugh.

"Your little beantighe-witch trapped me in this form. What do you think? This is the first time you've seen me up close like this, isn't it? Not drenched in blood, at least."

Cylvan's jaw clenched. He glanced down at Saffron, just for a moment, before back to Taran. He never lowered his sword. "Where have you been?"

"That's a complicated question, since I'm not sure I'm really here now."

"What is that supposed to mean?"

"It's—not really him," Saffron spoke. Cylvan looked down at him again. His expression flickered into a little more of a frenzy. "Well, I mean, it is, but it isn't. I think it has something to do with how I cursed him on Ostara—but I think I accidentally... somehow... linked our magic together. My magic summons him when I'm in danger, and for a long time, did so without my permission. But I'm beginning to understand, I think. When I cursed him—I accidentally set down the inevitability that, when I finally needed him, he would manifest as my familiar. A protector, and carrier of the extra weight of my magic. Which means he's not a manifestation of my rowan magic at all—but, maybe, the only reason I haven't done anything worse all this time." He didn't want to think about that.

"There was a time where I didn't understand, either," Taran grumbled. "I acted on instinct without realizing who I was or where I was. I think we've come to an understanding together."

"Those dreams we shared," Saffron said. "They didn't start until after the first time I summoned you. At the statue of Ériu. That was the first time my magic made you manifest, since I never felt in danger before that."

Taran nodded.

"If—if you're not really here, then where are you?" Cylvan went on.

"It's not safe for me to tell you," Taran said. "Ryder has already tampered with your beantighe's memories, I don't want to risk anyone finding out where I'm hiding. I'm not in any position to defend myself—and I am not eager to return to court any time soon."

"Your—your memories?" Cylvan's voice ignited with rage, snapping to look at Saffron again. Saffron grimaced.

"Taran thinks so," he said, averting his eyes to the floor. "I think he might be right. I didn't realize until just before you came."

"But I thought he was..."

"He's half-fey," Taran finished what Cylvan couldn't bring himself to say. As if doing so would prove himself as much a fool as the rest of them for not realizing, either. "He wouldn't be able to threadweave, otherwise."

"Yes, Taran, thank you. I realize that," Cylvan growled.

"It took your little beantighe-pet long enough to figure out anything on his own," Taran replied in the same annoyed tone. "He's lucky I was there to hold his hand through it. He might have given that man everything, otherwise. What a fine king he'll make one day."

"Watch your tongue," Cylvan hissed, lifting the sword again in threat. "You will not speak of him like that in front of me."

"Oooh, what chivalry," Taran muttered. "You couldn't ever defend me like that, Cylvan? Maybe we would have gotten along better from the start if you'd shown even an ounce of respect for me, too."

"It's because you demanded it that I would never give it," Cylvan snarled. "Perhaps that's the difference."

"Your pet will destroy you."

"You've already done that well enough."

Taran's snout wrinkled. He bowed his head in irritation, snarling flatly.

"I did nothing except fight to protect you, Cylvan, don't be so fucking naïve—"

"You ruined me!" Cylvan shouted, making Saffron flinch. "You killed my friend and framed me for it. You killed those beantighes at Morrígan and were going to blame me for those, too. You took my already festering reputation and rotted it from the inside, all for the sake of *saving me?* To tame me? You were supposed to be my friend, Taran, but you ruined me in ways I will never recover from."

"I kept you alive!" Taran snarled. "Had I not done what I did, they would have killed you years ago and I would have married Asche, instead. It's only because I insisted you would choose me that you were ever left alive long enough to fall in love with a human rat—!"

Wind sliced the space between them, and Taran yelped before stumbling backward.

"You will not speak of him that way again," Cylvan threatened once more through clenched teeth. He threw up another hand, and a second blast of wind tore through what remained of the ancient building. At the far end of the church, the wooden door crumbled, revealing a frozen courtyard on the other side. Saffron's mouth dangled open in surprise when he swore he smelled winter chill. "I do not care if you're only an illusion in front of me now, Taran mac Delbaith—I will find where you're really hiding and I will shred you into pieces if you dare disrespect him one more time."

A growl emanated from the back of Taran's throat, head bowed and ears flat back on his head, again. Saffron finally broke free of Cylvan's grasp before he could send another shockwave blasting through the building, putting himself between the prince and the wolf with his hands up.

"Don't defend him, Saffron," Cylvan growled. "Let me finally take out all my anger for what he's done to me. I promise I will be much more agreeable for the rest of our long lives, afterward."

"It's no use," Saffron insisted in frustration. "You said so yourself—"

"Even better. He can clearly feel it just as well every time I hit him. Let me enjoy it."

"As expected for you to lose your mind in a rage, Cylvan," Taran snarled. "You say I ruined your reputation, but it wouldn't have been so fucking easy if you hadn't already struck the match. You've always needed someone to keep you under control."

"Stop it!" Saffron shouted. "Both of you!"

Cylvan ground his teeth together, but slowly lowered the tip of the sword.

"Ah, the Night Prince fucks a beantighe and can suddenly be compelled to his knees," Taran growled bitterly. "If I'd known that earlier—"

"Icarus, sit down!"

Taran's mouth snapped shut. He slowly lowered his stomach to the ground, paws placed nicely in front of him. Cylvan barked a laugh.

"Look who's bending their knees now, you fucking mutt—!"

"Cylvan...!" Saffron threatened. Cylvan narrowed his eyes, but slowly closed his mouth. Saffron's eyes flickered to the floor, then back to him. Cylvan silently pleaded, but inevitably gave in and knelt to the floor with a sigh, too.

Saffron let out a long breath, putting his hands down. He ran fingers back through his hair, trying to make sense of the throbbing in his head. The tidal wave of information crammed into his skull all at once, given no time to process. No time to think. Ériu above, grant him a moment of fucking peace.

"I am not allies with him," Saffron told Cylvan matter-of-factly, thrusting a finger at the wolf on the floor. "I hate him more than words can describe, so don't, for one second, think I've forgiven him. But I am going to use him. I took ownership of him, so I'm going to use him. He's a dangerous weapon, if anything. And once I'm done... I'll be the one to find where he's really hiding, and I'll shred him into pieces with my own hands before you ever can. Do you understand?"

Cylvan sighed, rolling his eyes, clearly wishing to answer something sarcastic, to argue—but instead answered a mumbled, *"Yes."* Taran snorted a little laugh, and Cylvan narrowed his eyes at the dog once more in annoyance.

"All we can do now is..." Saffron trailed off.

He... didn't know. He didn't know what to do next at all, not when Ryder had scrambled his mind, making it impossible to know what was real and what wasn't; what he was missing, and if it was important. Not to mention Sunbeam, Ryder's intentions for the Midsummer Games, even his and Cylvan's earlier plans to find Eias Lam in search of Saffron's witch's mark... god above. He groaned, pressing hands to his face to try and compose himself again.

The only thing to pull him out of it was the whistling of wind through the broken door at the end of the building. The bitter-cold breeze that broke through it, carrying what Saffron realized in surprise—was snow. Flurries of snow, as if the rain clouds overhead had burst with a sudden chill. Taran noticed him looking, and glanced back that way, too, before letting out a sharp huff through his nose.

"I didn't tell you to come here for nothing," he grumbled. "There's a veneer on half the buildings in these ruins, but only descendants of Aryadne or Clymeus can pass through it, or lead others through. It opens up to—"

"The King's Keep," Saffron finished for him. Taran tucked his ears back, nodding. That place they'd dreamed of together. Where Taran had his bones replaced, where Eias studied oralcry; where even Ryder had come from. "The one in the Winter Court. In Fjornar."

"Ryder will not be able to follow us through it," Taran went on. "If we enter it here, we can pass through the other side into the woods outside of Avren. It will bypass their search and their charms entirely, without them ever seeing us leave."

"Can someone please explain what the fuck is going on?" Copper's shrill voice echoed off the stone ceiling. Taran rolled his eyes and returned to his feet, turning toward the far door as Saffron whirled around to find his friend suddenly standing naked and wide-eyed at the front of the church. Having changed back to normal just so he could speak. Saffron didn't know what he could say to possibly explain, grabbing Cylvan's cloak still draped over the pew and hurrying to cover Copper up against the cold.

36

THE VENEER

Following on the heels of the great wolf in front of them, Saffron watched as flurries of snow collected in the beast's black fur. Wondering how a creature could be there, but not. Intangible but tangible. He squeezed Cylvan's hand.

Taran led Cylvan, Copper, and Saffron through thick snow that had clearly sat undisturbed for decades in the King's Keep. It was practically a mirror image of the Finnian Ruins—the Queen's Keep—on the other side, though the stone and metal buildings there were far less crumbling. More cared for, kept pristine, almost every structure still standing like it was new. That place that was familiar despite being brand new to Saffron—that place he saw so many times in his dreams, but never entered until that moment on his two feet. Even Fiachra seemed unsettled by the atmosphere, keeping close to Saffron's head while perched on his shoulder, before soon flapping down to be held in his arms beneath the warmth of Saffron's tunic.

He couldn't wrap his head around what a *veneer* was, no matter how many times Cylvan tried to explain it—"*... like a glamour on a place, a thin layer of a torn veil that stretches through it to somewhere new; stable but rare as most were broken at the end* *of Proserpina's reign, but any that had special circumstances could have easily gone unnoticed. Just like this one, if Taran is right when he says only descendants of Proserpina or Clymeus can see and pass through it..."*

Saffron wanted to ask if that was really the place where Taran grew up, where they cursed him with the wolf king's silver bones, but every time his mouth opened, the echoing silence of the Winter Court stifled it back again. Not only around them, but in the back of Saffron's mind. Empty, while Taran existed in his form in person. Saffron hoped Taran wouldn't exist in his subconscious for the rest of his life.

God—he would have to send another letter to Baba Yaga. To ask for more advice. That time, for suggestions on controlling and subduing a wild familiar who came to life already hating Saffron's guts. And vice versa. Oh, god. Ériu help him.

They passed through the abandoned snowy Keep, then through a piece of the surrounding fence that had rusted away, crossing through the snowy woods on the other side until the chill slowly gave way to summer warmth. Then humid air, then rain, until the snow vanished beneath their feet and was replaced by thick mud. Until Saffron could smell the distant bakeries of Avren, hear her nighttime harp music in the distance, taste the sweetness of her seaside air. A seamless transition he didn't feel at all. Once they were on the other side, he turned back to seek out the snow again, but there was only the rest of the woods for as far as he could see. Every day he was reminded how little he understood of the veil—and how powerful even the oldest spells could be.

Taran vanished back into the shadows without another word, without even a goodbye, and Saffron felt the weight of him return to his mind the moment he did. It made him itch, scratching at the markings on his arm until Cylvan touched the side of his waist, pulling him close. He tucked the amethyst pendant into his hand with a small smile, and Saffron sighed, pulling it back on over his head. Next to him, Copper, who was still naked beneath

Cylvan's cloak, made a small sound like he'd been kicked in the chest. Saffron smiled weakly back at him, reaching out to take his hand as Cylvan kept an arm around his waist. They continued through the thick woods toward the lights of the city.

At the edge of Avren, Copper's eyes lingered endlessly on how Cylvan and Saffron held hands, even while pulling on a pair of clothes from the crook of a tree where they'd hidden them before seeking Saffron out. He kept gazing at Saffron with his mouth hanging open slightly, always on the verge of asking something. Even when Cylvan and Saffron finally let go of one another in the main city streets, Copper's eyes lingered. Saffron pretended not to notice. Not until later.

As they arrived back on campus, and then to their dorm, where Cylvan whispered that he would meet Saffron at his bedroom window, Copper still didn't get his chance to ask questions as Sionnach burst from their room the moment he and Saffron arrived in the hallway. They crashed into Saffron with clinging arms, nearly knocking him into the wall and exclaiming how worried they'd been, how happy they were that he was back. Saffron choked on a laugh, hugging them back and apologizing quietly. Copper frowned in growing frustration. Everything he wanted to ask clearly bulged at the base of his throat.

It was only when they finally made it into their dorm, with Saffron wishing Copper goodnight in order to head straight for his room, that Copper finally grabbed his hand and stopped him. Still, he struggled to find the words he wanted to say, before closing his mouth and swallowing back something he decided to keep to himself.

"Are you alright?" he finally asked. "I mean—you know you can always ask me if you need help, right? I can—I can do lots of things, too, just like Cylvan, so just... just rely on me, too, alright? And—and don't worry about your secret. Um—any of them, like how... how you're wrapped up with those humans. Or, erm, how... apparently you *are* human... and control Lord Taran... damn, I really thought he just ran away... anyway, I think there were a lot. Of secrets, I mean. But either way—I'm not going to tell anyone anything. You can trust me, Saff. I promise."

Saffron sighed with a gentle smile, pulling Copper down to kiss him on the cheek.

"Thank you for helping Cylvan find me," he said. "And you know, you shared a secret with me, too. About your fox-form. So I'll keep yours if you keep mine, alright?"

"Oh... yeah. Um, actually, wanna see more of it? That even Cylvan doesn't know. To try and keep the balance between your secrets and mine."

Saffron laughed, about to tell him he didn't have to worry about it—but then Copper pulled away one of his earrings, and his pointed ears vanished entirely. Replaced by two fiery red fox ears on his head. A fluffy tail even appeared behind him, swishing back and forth in anxiety. He let Saffron look for exactly one minute before returning the earring and clearing his throat. "That's it."

"Oh my god—I can't even touch them?" Saffron complained, leaping forward to try and grab the tail, only to find it missing entirely. Damn. It must have been a physical glamour. Like Cylvan once told him. Saffron pouted his lips, before pulling Copper into a hug.

"Your secret's safe with me, Copp. But I actually do want to wander around in the woods on your back one day."

Copper laughed, rubbing the back of his neck like he flushed in embarrassment. "Yeah, sure..."

Wishing Saffron goodnight, Saffron wished him the same before hurrying to his room. He hoped his raven would already be waiting for him on the other side.

Barely closing the door behind him, Saffron was swept up into a pair of strong arms in an instant. He clung tightly to Cylvan in return, before being thrown on the bed in a turn of the prince's feet. Before he could utter a sound, a demanding mouth crashed against his, stealing his words, his breath, every thought between them. Saffron tangled fingers in Cylvan's hair, pulling him closer, kissing him as if it were possible to express every apology and wish for understanding through the breathy movement of their mouths against one another.

"I was so worried about you," Cylvan spoke first, hands cupping under Saffron's jaw, pressing a thumb against the center of his lips. "Never, ever leave me like that, ever again. Kidnapped or not. As your king, I forbid it."

"I'm sorry," Saffron said for the hundredth time, at least.

"Tell me what happened to you, Saffron. Please. Everything."

Saffron kissed Cylvan a moment longer, before sitting up beneath him. He kept their mouths connected for as long as he needed, before finally pulling away with a defeated sigh through his nose. Cylvan's eyes searched every inch of his face, a mix of relief to have him back and burning questions he was resisting to ask. Just like everyone else. Saffron owed all of them so much.

Crossing his legs, Saffron's anxiety rose slightly as the clock ticked loudly from the common room. Telling him exactly how long it took him to gather his thoughts in that silence. As Fiachra tidied up her nest in the broken clock on his mantle and settled into it after too long away. God—there was so much to say.

He started with Ryder's first promise made in the infirmary—and told Cylvan everything. Not realizing how much there really was, but at least finding comfort in how hardly any of it had been kept from Cylvan on purpose. There were no secrets, only unshared details. Only specifics kept close to his chest.

The agreement he and Ryder first made, including Saffron asking Ryder to speak to the kings on the solstice as equals.

How his friends were missing when he and Asche went to visit them. How Saffron still didn't know exactly where they were —but he had a sinking feeling, since he spoke with Sunbeam. Knowing where Ryder had taken Chandry in comparison.

Ryder's library being nothing but a façade. Baba Yaga's letter in the desk.

How Saffron knew Ryder had influence over the witchhunters, but didn't know to what extent. Or, better yet—*how*.

The way Ryder always intended to draw out Saffron's getting his witch's mark in order to make his magic as wild and dangerous as possible, to be unleashed on the bystanders at the Midsummer Games.

Saffron rubbed his thumb in circles over the back of Cylvan's hand. Feeling every vein, tendon, bone. Memorizing them. Debating whether or not he should tell Cylvan about what else was happening to him, despite Taran's numbing influence. His magic-sight. His manipulation of the intangible. How he'd killed one witchhunter outside the palace, how he'd almost killed Ryder. Had Taran not stopped him, he would have. He would have killed Ryder right then.

A part of him regretted not—but he swallowed that guilt. Ryder was dishonest, a fraud, a façade, nothing more than a mask of what a leader of human rebellion should be—and a leader all the same. Ryder might have ill intentions, but he also had all of those humans under his wing. Whether or not he genuinely wished to help or protect them didn't matter. If Saffron had killed him in the cathedral, it would have left all of them abandoned all over again. And while they might have been able to re-organize, Saffron couldn't deny having a leader with influence over witch-hunters and their activities was, objectively, not a bad thing. Maybe. He could only pray.

God, his head hurt. He pressed his palms into his eyes, groaning before collapsing back onto the bed.

"Asshole," Saffron whispered. It was childish, but he didn't know how else to keep his anger down. Little did he know, anger would soon give way to misery, and tears would drip from his eyes as he spoke. "I can't believe I fell for it so easily. That asshole, that absolute prick... how could I have been so stupid, I'll never forgive myself for being so stupid again... All because he was human... I thought he was human... and he used it against me. It's not fair, it's so cruel..."

"I'll let you have Taran," Cylvan interjected. "If you let me shred Ryder Kyteler apart."

Saffron laughed weakly. "I don't know if I want to agree to that, either. What if I want them both all for myself?"

"That's not fair," Cylvan pouted. "I want to bloody my hands a little, too. What kind of loving husband would I be if I couldn't exact revenge for you at least once?"

"I suppose that's fair. Hm... I guess I might enjoy watching you tear him apart on my behalf."

Saffron pulled Cylvan down onto the bed, turning him on his back and draping himself over his chest. Cylvan's hand found his hair, combing fingers through it. It eased Saffron's nerves in an instant. His body turned heavy, sinking into the pillows, the blankets, across Cylvan's body. Listening to his prince's strong, healthy heartbeat thumping in a steady rhythm.

"What kind of magic are you using on me?" Saffron asked softly. Cylvan's fingers slowed in his hair.

"What do you mean?"

Saffron closed his eyes. "I... should be more upset. I should be more worried. I should be...panicking, pulling my hair out in anxiety. But instead... I feel... like I could just go to sleep."

He lifted his head, resting his chin in the center of Cylvan's chest. Immediately, he knew why. He knew why he felt none of the panic and concern he should. He knew it the moment Cylvan smiled at him, so handsome and perfect and comforting.

Cylvan, against everything else in the world, made Saffron feel safe.

Maybe no one else would ever believe it—but Saffron knew. He knew, he knew, he knew.

Night Prince or not, Cylvan was inherently good. And there was nowhere else Saffron would ever sleep so soundly, even in times of such worry and uncertainty, except held in his arms.

37

THE WAIT

Saffron knew Ryder wouldn't leave him alone for long. Ryder, who had lost two of his golden sheep, who wouldn't get a chance to find and groom a third for whatever he had planned on the solstice.

Eventually, Ryder would come for him again. Either posing as a friend, or perhaps with a threat, but either way with nothing but lies to tell. Saffron knew it would happen, eventually. He only hoped for a few days of peace to recover from the drugs in his system, a chance to really process through what he'd seen, heard, learned, done. As badly as he wished to find his friends, he knew they would be safer if he didn't prod the beast. Until Ryder decided to use them as leverage. Being patient would kill him, but —he didn't want to act recklessly, either. He didn't want to give Ryder the thrill of hurting Saffron by hurting his friends.

Instead, he wrote down everything Ryder had ever said that might be a clue as to what he had planned to do had Saffron obeyed, and what he might resort to since Saffron left him. He tried to piece together any memories he had taken, following Taran's instructions offered in the back of his mind. Saffron didn't have to ask how Taran knew so much about manipulated memories, fully aware of the fey lord's own dabbling in memory weaving with Eias—but there was something about the way he spoke that told Saffron there may have been more to it than simply those moments. Saffron wasn't sure he wanted to know.

Until Ryder came looking for him again, Saffron would attend classes without leaving campus; he would spend his free nights in his dorm or at Luvon's townhouse; he wouldn't go back to the Finnian Ruins. He might not even return to the palace, not with knowing Ryder had some level of influence on the witch-hunters of Avren. Not when that man had a record of bypassing guards and barrier charms with ease. He who could slip in and out of the veil with a magic ring or circles carved into doors.

Saffron didn't even want Cylvan going. He managed to convince the prince to skip his next gala in favor of wandering the woods together, all the while as Saffron clung to his hand and wouldn't let go of it. The hand of the person who helped him feel calmest, safest, most at peace, even when things were falling apart and all he wanted to do was scream and tear himself to ribbons with worry.

He still wasn't sure exactly where his friends were, though a part of him knew. His only comfort was thinking Ryder wouldn't hurt Hollow, Letty, Nimue so long as Saffron was still within reach. He wouldn't do anything to break whatever trust he thought he could regain.

Saffron would busy himself with preparations for the Midsummer Games and his role in them. He would perform as he was asked to do, knowing he wasn't as dangerous as Ryder tried to make him feel like he was. Ryder would learn, eventually, that Saffron's magic was never meant to go as wild as he'd hoped. Not with a familiar to calm it, at least.

Until then, Saffron, for the first time, didn't mind wandering the woods in a group. Sionnach, Copper, and Cylvan joined him in hunting pixies for Saffron to draw and for Sionnach to study, all while Cylvan and Copper made a big deal about who could lift the bigger rock and throw it the farthest. Arguing about who could move faster—Cylvan on his wind or Copper in his fox form

—though Copper refused to try it out because he didn't want Sionnach to see. Every time there was a sound out of sight, Saffron would jump and turn, which wasn't like him—and every time, Cylvan's eyes turned to meet his, too. To nod in reassurance that everything was fine. Saffron hated it—not to be cared for, but the fact that Ryder could even take the vulnerable comfort of the woods from him.

He reclaimed some of that comfort by practicing archery in the embrace of the trees. Copper and Cylvan constantly argued over who could teach him best, who had the better form, whose arrow had hit closest to the center of the target—but in the end, it was Sionnach who actually did the most good in teaching Saffron anything. Their father was a satyr, and satyr were known for how they hunted with speed and precision in the thickest forests of the Fall Court, after all.

He wrote another attempt at a letter to Baba Yaga, that time focusing on things that wouldn't make her worry, telling her he'd found the first missing letter she sent and thanking her for her words of advice. He described his time at Cylvan's galas, then some things about his new friends, then talked briefly about his work with Ryder—as well as how Ryder ended up betraying him, though didn't include too much detail so she wouldn't worry. He asked if she knew anything about magic being more balanced on the equinox and unbalanced on the solstice. He asked if she knew anything about veil magic, specifically veil knocks. He thanked her again for her previous words of advice, then thanked her for being someone he could trust implicitly, then apologized for being so needy. In many ways—she was all he had left. And the realization made him break down into tears, sobbing into the grass even as Sionnach hurried over to kneel next to him and ask if everything was alright.

Taran didn't bother him in the meantime, either, except for the occasional shared dream where they wandered the King's Keep in the Winter Court. Saffron didn't mind. He didn't have any reason to speak to Taran mac Delbaith, either. If anything, the relief from worrying about accidentally summoning a blood-thirsty beast in the middle of his classes was the greatest gift he could be given at all.

More than once he sought solace in Asche's dorm room on Mairwen's Prep School campus, where he could read in silence alongside the daurae, or find distraction in their passionate chatter. He asked about the charms they used in the Finnian Ruins. He asked if there were charms that did things to the veil. He collapsed with a groan when Asche told him all about how, technically, wild fairy fruits were a natural charm formed by the veil like any other.

When he ran out of other ways to distract himself from the worry, the stress, Saffron had Asche buy all the supplies he needed to attempt painting a courting locket. He did so with legs crossed on Asche's bed, growing more and more agitated as he couldn't decide whether it should be his human face or his glamoured high fey face to give to Cylvan. Asche finally got through to him when they assured him courting lockets weren't anything actually formal, they held no real weight, it was more of a lighthearted matchmaking game than anything else—then they talked Saffron into finding something else. To give Cylvan something else that no one else would. Saffron was not, after all, like anyone else who attended the prince's galas and gave him painted portraits to show their interest.

Asche, meanwhile, never asked about Ryder. They never mentioned the ruins at all. Saffron debated endlessly whether he should tell them that Sunbeam was not only safe, but accounted for—before reminding himself he'd promised to keep it a secret. He wouldn't tell anyone, especially not while he didn't know where Ryder was. Especially since she'd apparently, by some grace of god above, managed to skirt Ryder's detection while he scraped through Saffron's memories. Saffron didn't like to think about that, either—more than once it ended in nausea rolling so intensely in his stomach he had to stop where he was and bend over his knees until the dizziness subsided.

He spent time hiding in Mairwen's library. A few times, he even convinced Sionnach to let him back into the restricted section, in exchange revealing to them that Prince Cylvan himself was banned from it since, according to him, he'd been unfairly caught stealing books and never returning them. Sionnach smiled the whole time Saffron told them, like they loved having that dirt on him. From those prohibited books, Saffron finally learned what *hell* was. He learned about human demons and devils and some of their religions. He finally understood what everyone meant when they spoke from the perspective of the human world —that only he knew nothing about. It reminded him of a conversation he'd had with Cylvan a long time ago while walking to the henge in the Kyteler Ruins, where he told Saffron about his brief journeys into the human world. How the humans who spotted him thought he was a 'demon' by the horns on his head. Saffron asked if Cylvan could find a way back into the human world again, like he used to—but Cylvan told him the veil tears he once used to sneak back and forth had long since been closed. Something told Saffron Luvon would say the same thing if he ever asked.

Eventually, Saffron had to accept—he could only do what he could only do. Even though it was like being skinned alive, slowly, every day as the solstice crept ever closer.

The night before the games, Saffron was surprised when Balor suddenly returned with a letter from Baba Yaga, the bird looking grouchier than ever as it delivered the message in the library before flapping off again. Saffron tore it open in an instant, skimming the words as fast as he could, just wanting to make sure there wasn't any serious reason why Baba took so long to reply. When he saw the explanation, he laughed for the first time in what felt like days.

I apologize for the late reply, little spice. I do hope you haven't worried too much. This bird simply refuses to leave when I try to shoo it away. It seems to prefer scuttling

*around in the village. Are you sure Prince Cylvan is taking
proper care of him?*

Saffron thought he might go mad over it. How simple of an explanation, after the horrible things that happened to Fiachra in comparison.

Reading the rest of the letter, Saffron sank into the comforting sight of his henmother's handwriting, reading the paragraphs about every mundane chore and task and thing she did every day that were like relaxing music to his ears. He nearly disappeared into them entirely, daydreaming about Beantighe Village and all its simple comforts, until one last thought at the bottom of the page caught his attention, written with slightly more urgency than the rest. Like it was something she remembered just seconds before rolling up the paper to attach to Balor's leg.

*I know nothing specific of veil magic, only a rhyme I learned
while attending school. I don't know if it will be of any help:*

Split knocks are memories, one knock's to give;
 Two knocks for passage, three knock's a bridge;
 Four knocks set a trap, five knocks make a vow,

"'Six knock's a devils' snare, you'll fall beneath the bough,'" Saffron read aloud under his breath. Asche asked if he'd said something, but Saffron shook his head. 'Six knocks aloud, they scatter like mice'—Saffron thought back to the adage on the red cards, how they specifically mentioned the solstice, and how it must have been some sort of clue to what Ryder was planning— but even with the rhyme Baba Yaga shared, there was no more illumination on what anything might mean.

Saffron's anxiety, his apprehension only grew as the hours passed, until he accidentally snapped at the daurae twice. Then almost cried while apologizing, twice. Only when Asche finally pressed their book shut and declared they wished to spend the night at the palace did Saffron finally relax a little bit, instantly calmed at the thought of sleeping in bed next to Cylvan. Cylvan, who had been away from campus more than he'd been on it in the days leading up to the solstice. Preparing. Preparing for something no one knew how to prepare for.

Passing through the palace gates, over the long windy bridge, into the main courtyard, Saffron only felt safe again once the doors closed loud and echoing behind him. Asche took him to where they thought Cylvan might be, in one of the many meeting rooms where the prince indeed sat at a long table with a dozen other people Saffron didn't know. Who all looked very official, important, powerful. From the few words Saffron overheard, they were discussing the dead barn owls nailed to the gatehouse doors, the human terrorists behind it, how they were still trying to find where they were hiding. Saffron didn't want to hear it, feeling weak, vulnerable, like he worried that information would leak aloud through holes Ryder had left in his mind while digging out threads. He at least found reassurance in how the continued discussions of human hideouts meant Cylvan never revealed the location of the human coven in the ruins, either. Knowing of the innocent people who gathered there.

Asche knocked on the door. They motioned a hand to Cylvan, who looked at them, then to where Saffron hovered a few feet behind them. He said nothing to the others in the room, rising to his feet in an instant and hurrying to the door, as if he could sense it. As if he could sense the swirling emotions in Saffron's body without having to see him up close. Cylvan went straight for Saffron and wrapped him in an embrace, asking if everything was alright.

"What are they talking about?" Saffron asked after a weak smile. Cylvan glanced back over his shoulder, before reaching out to close the door the rest of the way, then place a hand to Saffron's back to lead him away. Saffron wished Asche a good night before they went too far, before taking Cylvan's hand and allowing himself to be pulled into the side of the prince's body.

"You know about the barn owls," Cylvan muttered. "There have been three more killed and nailed to the palace gates this week alone..."

He trailed off as Fiachra opened her eyes from where she dozed off on Saffron's shoulder, narrowing her gaze at him in warning. Cylvan attempted a slow pet of her head with the back of his finger, and when she allowed it, he cleared his throat and straightened back up again.

"They—*we* are simply discussing the extent of the danger to the kings, especially during the games tomorrow, and the precautions to take."

"Are they going to—"

"They will not do anything to cause any scenes," Cylvan promised before Saffron could fully unravel. "The royal guard, especially, are very good at suppressing threats without drawing any attention."

Saffron cracked a weak, uncertain smile. Still, despite the reassurances, he couldn't shake the nausea in his gut. He thought of all those people living in the cathedral—all those people who simply wanted a better life. Who thought they would be given one by Ryder Kyteler. Saffron hoped Ryder had changed his mind about the solstice. He hoped the people in the ruins wouldn't suffer at the hands of that man's rage for having lost both himself and Sunbeam. He hoped Ryder would think clearly and know, even with veil magic, even with whatever *falling beneath the bough* meant, he wouldn't stand a chance against an entire armed guard.

Saffron squeezed Cylvan's hand tighter. He blinked back a flicker of tears, swallowing the lump in his throat.

"I'm sorry for interrupting the meeting," he whispered. "I just wanted to be with you, tonight."

"I will always come when you call," Cylvan answered in an instant, pulling their interwoven hands to his mouth, kissing Saffron's knuckles. "Always."

38

THE GAMES

He didn't expect to sleep; he also didn't expect Cylvan to stay awake with him for as long as he did. But his prince was clearly worried, it was all over his face, though he never said anything out loud. He knew Saffron wouldn't like that, he knew Saffron would get embarrassed and brush it all off as nothing. Cylvan knew Saffron just needed a safe place to exist with all of his emotions, and he provided it. God—Prince Cylvan was all Saffron would ever need. For the rest of his life.

They laid in bed as Cylvan read from *The Odyssey*. He showed off all of his favorite pieces of clothing and jewelry as Saffron raided his closet and asked a thousand questions about every single thing. They drank wine from his secret stash, then grabbed a pair of bows and quivers and went down to the palace gardens to drunkenly shoot at clusters of wisteria at two in the morning. It was reckless, it was childish—but it made Saffron laugh. And every time he got a little quieter because the worried thoughts crept back in, Cylvan would interject with something else and draw him back to the surface. It ended with them kissing, then fondling, then softly fucking in the dimly-lit gardens as the rest of the palace slept soundly in their beds. One moment without the world to reach them. A taste of peace where he could find it, like taking a bite from a ripe, sweet fruit.

But eventually, morning came. The sun rose, and Saffron couldn't avoid it any longer. He would be expected at the opening ceremony within another few hours. At least he wouldn't be alone. There would be guards. There would be oracles. Cylvan would be there, too. And, while still the most unsettling, surreal reassurance ever—Taran would be at Saffron's command. Without worry about hurting anyone else in the process. If Ryder appeared to make a threat, Saffron could simply summon his familiar to tear him apart.

If, for whatever reason, even that failed—then Ryder might even finally learn the true extent of Saffron's wild magic.

Despite the festival meadow sitting right along the edge of tall seaside cliffs, despite the rows upon rows of tents stretched over the grass and flowers a mile from the nearest Avren street, it was still too busy to hear the sea. Over the chatter of patrons, festival-goers, fans of the sporting events who cheered with every bang of practice swords and bodies overturned while preparing for actual judged rounds. Even an hour before the opening ceremony, tents wound through the countryside clearing like multicolored scales on a monstrous sea snake, goods ranging from clothing, to jewelry, to betting counters, to every kind of food Saffron could possibly think of. If he could imagine it, he could smell it. He could find it. He *would* find it, once the opening ceremony was over. Once he knew it was safe. He would drink himself silly like on Beltane, but that time dance hand-in-hand only with the people he knew.

In his private preparation tent, the words on the red card wouldn't leave him alone. He repeated them again and again, sometimes whispered under his breath, sometimes echoing in his skull as he stared at the closed flaps of the tent and anticipated someone walking in. He still didn't know exactly what else Ryder could have planned, but was sure the red card gave clues. Enough to act as a warning. Damnit.

Saffron had cycled through every word, line, rhyme, idea a thousand times, enough that he wasn't sure there was anything else to think about at all. The world revolved around those words, around what might happen in the next hour. Two hours. Maybe three. He didn't know. God, not knowing was the worst part. Not knowing when. Not knowing how. Not knowing *if*.

All while he stewed and mentally tied himself into knot after knot, Sionnach helped him dress, eyes low as they focused on every detail and clasped the buttons down Saffron's back. Saffron's hands unconsciously combed through Fiachra's breast feathers where she perched on his hand and purred.

"Sionnach," he said quietly, the first voice out loud that wasn't his friend's mumblings of concentration or his own frenzied whispers. He thought of the adage on the red card, again. "Tonight's not a blood moon, is it?"

"Definitely not," they answered right away. "That only happens every century or so. Alfidel always has a day of mourning when it comes, too. We definitely wouldn't be here celebrating. And you definitely wouldn't be looking so pretty in your little outfit—so come on, let me finish getting you ready."

Outside the tent, music swelled. Voices grew as more guests gathered around the ceremony space. Saffron returned to petting Fiachra's soft feathers so Sionnach could continue what they were doing. Closing his eyes, he held his breath, attempting to purge the tension from his body. Reminding himself he wasn't alone. Cylvan was there. Cylvan knew what was happening. There were guards—even more than previous years, he was reassured. Saffron wouldn't miss anything, either. Fiachra would react. Taran had his own way of sensing danger. Saffron had to relax. Saffron needed to *breathe.*

Someone jangled the little bell hanging on the outside of the tent, but Saffron's voice caught before he could invite them in. Sionnach took over and did it for him without blinking an eye.

Without even looking up from their work. God—Saffron was so stressed.

At first, Saffron didn't recognize the person who bowed their head through the opening in the canvas and stepped inside—but only because he'd never seen Cylvan dressed in all white before. He gasped the moment his heart restarted from awe, leaping off the perch and summoning a huff of annoyance from his friend in the process. But Saffron couldn't resist.

"Cyl—your highness!" he exclaimed with a bright smile, meeting Cylvan at the mouth of the tent. Cylvan wore a fitted doublet in cream linen, embroidered with golden thread designed into shining suns and sparkling stars, tailored specifically for him as he took on the role of the Oak King in the opening ceremony. The Oak King—Cylvan—who would battle the Holly King—Copper—for dominance over the coming seasons, as told in myth, where the Holly King would reign victorious and allow for the harvest months to come. Cylvan and Copper only learned who the other person was a few days prior, resulting in nonstop taunting and mockery as Cylvan threatened to rewrite the myth in the Oak King's favor to watch everyone laugh at Copper from the audience. Copper responded by tackling Cylvan to the ground and shoving his own hair into his mouth.

Appreciating the myriad of details on Cylvan's doublet, Saffron trailed tips of his fingers down the designs on Cylvan's chest, losing himself in their intricacy. Finally, Cylvan chuckled, taking Saffron's hands and whispering for him to remember where he was. Saffron blushed, pulling away in an instant. He took a slight step back.

"You—you just look so handsome, Prince Cylvan," he said weakly. "Such a light color suits you, Oak King."

"I could say the same about you," Cylvan laughed, pinching one of the layered pieces of fabric at Saffron's hip, where the belt of his quiver would settle. "We make quite the pair, don't you think?"

Saffron kept smiling. Cylvan smiled back at him, biting his lip as if he couldn't resist reveling in that tiny shared moment between them, either. Saffron wondered what Sionnach must think, watching them in silence, until Cylvan cleared his throat, straightening up and glancing over Saffron's shoulder.

"I was actually wondering, have you seen Daurae Asche? They're supposed to sit with the kings at the head of the field for the opening ceremony, but they appear to have run off again."

Saffron's smile slipped slightly, like heavy moss sloughing from a rock. His stomach sank, but he forced himself to stay calm. To not let the anxiety eat at him when there wasn't any reason to worry, yet. Cylvan didn't appear worried at all. He and Saffron both knew how much the daurae hated parties with all their noise and crowds and people wanting their attention—it was likely nothing. Just nothing. Saffron let out a long breath, exhaling as much stress as he could with it.

"I haven't seen them, no, but I'm not surprised to hear they've run off. Probably hiding behind some rock somewhere, or looking at glass beads at one of the vendor stands."

"Oh—that's actually a great idea. You're probably right. Why didn't I think of that?" Cylvan muttered, furrowing his brows and glancing over his shoulder. "I'll go sniff around that way, then. If any guards poke their heads in, they're just looking for the daurae, too, so don't worry."

"There must not be anything else going on for guards to have time to play hide-and-seek?" Saffron asked. His voice dripped with unspoken worry—which was easily quelled as Cylvan's smile remained easy. Handsome. Reassuring.

"Oh, yes," he nodded. "No trouble at all so far. Not even a belligerent drunk to escort out. Perhaps Danu will bless us with a peaceful day."

"You've cursed us with those words," Sionnach joked. Saffron turned to them, going pale and catching Sionnach off guard. They smiled awkwardly, shaking their head. "I mean, probably not really, though. I was only teasing. What could possibly go awry at an event like this, anyway? The stands break under fey ass?"

"You hear that, Lord Saffron?" Cylvan said. "The goat teases me now. We've become great friends."

Saffron pushed Cylvan toward the exit, making him laugh. They exchanged whispers of *'I'll see you soon,'* before Cylvan excused himself. Saffron caught the briefest glimpse of the crowd on the other side, cheering and singing and laughing. Enjoying themselves. Without a hint of danger at all. It helped him breathe a little better—but the tightness refused to leave him entirely. Not until Asche had their ass in the chair alongside the kings.

"Sionnach, do you think you could get me something to drink? Um, for my nerves," Saffron asked. Sionnach nodded, happy to stretch their legs and see what other stalls were selling for snacks. Saffron thanked them, watched them go, then paused for exactly three seconds before turning, hurrying to the center of the tent, pacing back and forth a few steps, before closing his eyes. He summoned the image of Taran, the wolf, into his mind, knowing that was one way to lure him to the forefront of their shared thoughts. Once he sensed the beast's arrival, he let out another held breath.

"Icarus," he whispered. *"Come."*

His forearm burned enough that he flinched, but Saffron kept his eyes closed. He kept his focus, all the way until he felt the hot breath of a beast trickle over his face. When he finally looked up, he met Taran's crimson-red eyes gazing back at him.

"Asche is missing," he said, hurrying to snatch up the quiver of arrows and cinch it around his waist. Growing restless despite Cylvan's reassurances. "Can you find them? Without being seen?"

Taran's ears twitched, taking in the sound of the Midsummer activities all around them on the other side of the tent. His nostrils flared and tightened as he fought through the cacophony of smells drowning him in an instant. Finding a place to ground himself amongst all the excited chaos on the other side of the world.

"What happened?" he asked, voice low and unexpectedly sincere. "Where should I look?"

"I don't know if anything has, erm, *happened,* yet. They might just be hiding somewhere, or maybe don't know what time it is. Can you track them somehow?" Saffron insisted, placing a hand on Taran's nose. "Like the good dog you are."

"Funny," Taran growled, but perked his ears and lifted his head all the same. "I'll try."

"Well... even if you can't find Asche... maybe circle the meadow to see if anything strange is going on at all. Just in case." Saffron added, voice going soft. The stress, the worry nibbled at him again.

"Let me save you the effort, your highness."

Saffron whirled, barely catching sight of Ryder stepping through the opening of the tent. He moved faster than even Taran could anticipate, lunging and slamming Saffron on his back against the ground.

Before the wolf could attack, Ryder threw a hand out, burying a fist full of yew leaves into Saffron's mouth. Fire erupted on his tongue, down his throat, and Taran flinched in tandem, before vanishing with a snarl cut short. Fiachra screeched and bolted from her perch, smashing into Ryder, tearing claws through his hair and raking talons down the skin of his cheek—until Ryder cursed at her, throwing out his arm and battering her into the ground.

Saffron thrashed beneath Ryder's weight, managing to free one of his hands enough to spit and scrape the yew from inside his mouth, pink-tinged spit staining the front of his white outfit as he did. Ryder didn't give him a chance to try anything else, grabbing Saffron's wrists and shoving them to the ground of his head. Saffron cursed and spit at him, stopping only when he saw the pink shimmer in the man's eyes digging into him. Bright pink, like a vivid sunset, glowing around the rim of his irises. Drunk on fairy fruits, enough to kill a normal man. But Ryder wasn't a normal man—Saffron knew that much by then.

"I see you've gained control of your beast," he growled, squeezing Saffron's wrists until the bones scraped against one another. "But it's no matter to me. I thought I'd come and wish you luck in the ceremony this morning. Turns out I don't think I'll need you this time—but I still have to ask." Leaning forward, Ryder hovered within an inch of Saffron's ear. "Did you consider —for even a second—what would happen if you made me angry enough to tear everything you love into pieces?"

Saffron opened his mouth to scream, but Ryder's hand clamped over it, first. Trapping his voice, his breath, the remaining yew leaves that scorched his tongue and dribbled lines of fiery spit down the back of his throat.

"Before it comes, I need you to know—that what happens next is a consequence of your choice to leave me. Your choice to abandon me and what we could have had together. I am not afraid to force a hand that will not fit into mine—nor am I hesitant to break the legs of someone who refuses to kneel, no matter if they're royalty or peasant."

"I won't let you hurt him—!" Saffron snarled, breaking free of Ryder's grasp for only a moment before the hand returned, grabbing Saffron by the face and crushing his cheeks into his teeth.

"It would be too easy to take him from you, now—that pain would be sharp, but quick. No, no—I'm going to be worse than that. I can do worse than that. I'm going to make you watch as these high fey tear him apart, piece by piece, *slowly*. But—listen to me, Saffron, and don't forget this—my coven will stay with me, through life or death, especially after what happens today. These fey will reckon with the cost of their comfortable lives after today. They will finally understand—their reign is coming to a swift, abrupt end, and there's nowhere to run. And your prince—they will never forgive him. They'll never trust him again after what you've forced me to do. I'm going to strip Cylvan dé Tuatha dé Danann of any pitiful slivers of grace he had left—and you'll spend the rest of your long, charmed life knowing it was all your fault."

"Get off me, damnit—!"

"One last thing I need you to know." Ryder's hot breath cascaded over Saffron's ear, before lips gently kissed the curve of it hidden beneath the glamoured point. "I will wait for you. I will always welcome you back. I will never hold any resentment toward you. You don't know any better right now—but one day, you will. Mark my words, you will. And when that day comes, when you realize I am your only ally in this life—I will take you back with open arms. And we will continue right where we left off. Remember that. Remember me when, soon enough, you finally feel what cruelty your beloved prince is capable of."

"Get—off of me," Saffron snarled one last time, finally shoving his elbow into Ryder's stomach to knock him back. Clambering to his feet, he leapt for the bow on the side table, nocking an arrow against the string and reeling back—

"Be still."

Saffron turned to stone. Every inch, hardly able to inhale into his lungs. Ryder took one of Saffron's limp hands, pulling it to his mouth and kissing the back before returning it gently to Saffron's side.

"I'll see you again in a moment, rowan spirit."

Saffron was forced to watch him go. Without another word, without a scream or a snarl for Ryder Kyteler to turn back around and face him. All the while—he suddenly understood, in the deepest reaches of his soul, exactly the terror Cylvan must have felt the first time Saffron ran away with his true name on his tongue.

39

THE SOWING

Sionnach returned right as the enchantment broke, yelping and throwing their arms out to catch Saffron before he collapsed to the ground from nearly suffocating. Saffron clutched his chest, heart slamming against his ribs until he was sure it would reopen that old wound. Sionnach held him upright, frantically asking what happened—but Saffron pushed from their arms. Grabbing his bow once more, quiver still attached to his belt, he stopped only to scoop Fiachra from the ground and pull her into his chest.

Outside, the promenade was crowded with people in every direction. Walking into him, snapping at him to get out of the way, stepping on his feet and tangling up in his bow. Saffron's nerves grew. They festered, higher and higher without Taran his familiar, there to tamp them back down again. Blood dripped from his nose, a drop of red splattering into Fiachra's snowy white breast feathers where she laid unmoving in his arm.

"Hey!" he attempted to shout at a group of passing guards, but they hurried by without noticing. Saffron tried to get the attention of another, but they just smiled at him, saying they would be right back, they were still looking for the daurae—and Saffron swore at them as they left. Festival goers passing by threw him strange looks, giving him a wide berth where they could, but Saffron still felt every single one of them. Their eyes, their breaths, their—fucking—*opulence*. Damnit, without Taran to numb the undercurrent of rowan magic in his blood, Saffron felt himself treading water. On the verge of drowning beneath it, that glowing white opulence that made his head throb, flickering into beaming halos behind heads that passed. Squeezing his eyes closed, he had to turn away, to avert his eyes—gaze landing on the bird in his arm, instead. Fiachra, who Saffron was sure had only been stunned—wasn't moving at all.

"H-hey..." he started. His heart skipped. He nudged her slightly with his arm. "Fiachra... Fiachra, hey!"

Saffron stumbled out of the way of the moving crowd, scooping his bird under the head, petting his thumb down her beak, attempting to summon her back. But she wasn't reacting—she wasn't responding. Saffron's blood ran cold, staring at her, mouth hanging open in disbelief.

No, no, no, no—Saffron wasn't going to allow that to happen. He wasn't going to allow Ryder Kyteler to take anything else from him. He had to—he had to do something—

Pulling her protectively into his body, he shuddered, clenching his jaw and squeezing his eyes closed. There had to be something. There had to be something, anything he could do—he was a rowan witch, goddamnit, there had to be *something!*

He placed his hand on her. He stared at her as his fingers flexed. More blood swelled up the back of his throat, dripping from his nose, his mouth. She, who was neither arid nor opulent —she who wasn't wild fey or anything else—but Saffron had once watched as his hands dragged the opulence from the body of a witchhunter; as he'd flooded them with arid magic until they burst at the seams and collapsed, dead, on top of him. He had dominion over magic, he could see the glow of magic on every opulent and arid-touched thing in every direction. If he could flood a person's body with aridity to kill them—perhaps he could do the same to save something, too. To infuse it with aridity no differently than wild charms or wild fey were infused with opulence, giving them long life and longevity.

He summoned that same flood of energy as what he felt before killing that hunter outside the beantighe dorms. He channeled it from his chest where it swirled hot and boiling, down his arm, to his hand where he wore the hematite ring. He flooded his touch with every ounce of magic he had, until blood dripped from both nostrils and slithered over his lips, his chin. Until he saw the faint glow of arid magic escape the tips of his fingers, pulsating between the bird's feathers, disappearing into her body.

She suddenly thrashed with life, screeching and flaring out her wings, her talons, writhing and tearing within Saffron's arms. Saffron threw his body around her, holding her close, bracing against the sharp edges of her beak and claws. Holding her until the convulsions stopped, and she was nothing but a gasping, heaving mass of feathers in his arms. Pulling away, he didn't know whether to be relieved or unsettled by the glow of red newly surrounding her—he just released a sharp breath, pulling her in close again and kissing the top of her head.

Over the crowd came the sound of rising music, summoning his attention. Opening his eyes, he stared down the length of the thoroughfare, knowing it was a summons for him. For Cylvan, for Copper, who would battle as the Oak and Holly Kings to mark the start of the games. Saffron closed his eyes one more time, grounding himself. Digging his heels into the earth as he held the trembling, arid bird protectively into his chest.

He wouldn't allow Ryder Kyteler to take another single thing from him.

Reclaiming his silver bow with one hand, Saffron kept Fiachra pulled into his chest with the other. He pushed back into the crowd, not bothering to wipe the blood from his face. His nose, his mouth. He wanted Ryder to see. He wanted Ryder to feel even an ounce of vulnerability the moment they finally faced one another again.

· · ·

APPROACHING THE EDGE OF THE FIELD, SAFFRON HEARD none of the excited cheering, the swelling music; he smelled none of the incense or burning candles or ocean of flowery bouquets; he saw none of the crowd of thousands of people in the wooden stands surrounding the grassy expanse, felt none of their eyes as they watched him approach and released calls of excitement. Too far to see the blood spilling down the bottom half of his face. Too far away to see the barn owl that twitched in his arm, black eyes finally opening again before twisting and righting herself. Taking her place on Saffron's shoulder. As if nothing had happened at all. But he felt her—he felt the softness of her feathers against his cheek. He felt the warmth of her new, inherent aridity filling him to the brim with his own.

"Rowan tears the moon shall weep," he whispered. Like a promise, as he pulled a silver arrow from his quiver and nocked it into the string. He moved his feet, finding the perfect placement of them. Grounding his heels back into the earth like Ryder once taught him.

Cylvan and Copper emerged from the side of the field, dressed in garb of the mythical kings to commit their battle for ownership over the rest of summer. Had Saffron not been so distracted, so focused on searching the edge of the field for someone else, he might have been able to appreciate the impressive ways Cylvan moved, the grace of how he and Copper found their places in the center of the field and bowed to one another like steps in a dance. How Cylvan lifted his blade with clear practice, how handsome he looked settling into starting position, even with his face behind a mask.

Copper, on the other hand, looked like his outfit had been improperly tailored, half a size too large, cuffed at the pants like originally sewn for someone with longer legs. Saffron assumed it was a prank at Cylvan's hands—and wished he could find amusement in it. But there was nothing except ice and fire in Saffron's blood. He held the bow at the ready, arrow tucked into the string, prepared to fire at an instant. Clenching every muscle in his body so tightly, his head throbbed. He wished Taran would ease back into his mind. He wished that stupid dog could be useful and search while Saffron couldn't—while another part of him quietly hoped he was alright at all.

Something drew his attention, out of the corner of his eye— and the world turned beneath him as, on the edge of the field, a cluster of veiled shadows suddenly loomed, silver chains and bottles dangling from their waists. He almost reeled back to fire at them, but locked his body in place. *Not yet. Don't move, yet. Don't get distracted.* He had to keep his eyes on Cylvan. He couldn't look away from Cylvan for even a moment. He didn't even dare to blink as Cylvan's blade clashed against Copper's in the sunlight.

When the crowd spotted the witchhunters, next, their cheering shifted in tone. It scattered into gasps and frenzied chatter, reduced from a deafening roar to a dull thunder. The shift was substantial enough that Cylvan paused his attack, pushing up his mask and turning to look. His eyes skimmed over the witchhunters, then sought Saffron in an instant, meeting eyes and offering him a tiny nod to acknowledge the unwelcome guests. A reassurance that Saffron need not panic despite them, like he was confident they wouldn't cause a scene without guards stepping in first. Before Saffron could nod back, the Oak King at Cylvan's back lifted his own mask and threw it to the grass.

A choked scream escaped Saffron as Ryder's hands moved, taking Cylvan by the horn with one and lifting the blade to his throat with the other.

Saffron pulled and released the arrow before realizing he'd moved at all. Ryder jerked out of the way, barely skimmed by the flash of silver whisking past him. The wild grin splitting his face summoned bile up the back of Saffron's throat, quickly replaced with blood as the white and red halos shimmered back into his eyes. All around him, nearly blinding him.

The world around him went quiet. Cylvan's eyes found his, though otherwise he remained still. As if he'd been taught, long ago, exactly how to act if ever held at the mercy of a blade. Saffron's heart quaked. The glow in his eyes flickered, then intensified. Cylvan's opulent white outline was so bright, almost blinding, and tinged with flickers of gold that must have been his Sídhe power. It overtook Ryder's pink aura behind him. Saffron's hands twitched, realizing he wasn't sure he'd be able to grip Ryder's lungs in his chest and squeeze them into paste even if he wanted to. He didn't know if he might accidentally hurt Cylvan, instead, not knowing who he raked his hands through before it was too late.

Perhaps Ryder knew that. Perhaps he really did know more than he led Saffron to believe. All he did was smile at Saffron like the look on his face was worth the growing cacophony of the crowd around them. The commands for guards to engage. So many guards against one man. How could he possibly keep smiling like that?

Saffron knew exactly what Ryder mouthed alongside Cylvan's ear, reading his lips. Perhaps knowing, already, without having to hear it. Despite the clamoring of feet and voices ringing in every direction, Saffron knew exactly the two words Ryder had offered him.

"Choose wisely."

His heart drummed faster. His fingers unfurled then clenched again, tingling with want to tear, but he resisted. He avoided the spiraling pool that would suck him in if he dared gaze into it, just like in Ryder's study. He couldn't. He couldn't get it wrong. He couldn't hurt Cylvan.

Where the hell was Taran?

"Lord Saffron," Saoirse raced up behind him, but Saffron raised a hand to her as Ryder's eyes flashed to the guard, before adjusting his grip on the sword. Cylvan flinched when Ryder's grasp on his horn tugged down, straining his neck backward. Presenting the gentle arch of his throat where the blade nearly kissed.

"Take everyone away," Saffron told Saoirse under his breath.

He never took his eyes from Cylvan for an instant. "The kings, your guards, Sionnach. Fiachra, go find Copper. It isn't safe—"

"I will not—" Saoirse attempted as Fiachra took off from Saffron's shoulder—but Saffron turned to the fey guard, nostrils flared and erupting with a flash of rage. She stumbled backward, perhaps in surprise, perhaps something else as she lifted a hand to her chest. As if Saffron had slammed his heels into her sternum.

"Do not say no to me," he growled, rough as he forced the words past the yew-inflicted burns. "I say this as your harmonious prince—take the kings and my friends away from here. *Now!*"

Saoirse stared at him. She wanted to say something. She was on the verge of protesting further, perhaps even laughing in his face—but saw how much blood spilled from him. His nose, his mouth. She saw how heavily he breathed, how sweat beaded on his forehead. Fighting everything inside his body for control. On the verge of splitting apart—and taking the earth with him. Finally, she nodded once, took a step back, then turned. Saffron returned his attention to Cylvan and Ryder just as Saoirse called out for the rest of the guards to find the kings and take them away.

Choose wisely. Saffron opened his mouth to ask what Ryder meant by those words—but his answer came before he needed to. It came on the sound of hissing and cursing, with snarled demands on the edge of fire erupting from hands. Daurae Asche, dragged out from behind the wood stands by one more black-veiled witchhunter.

Choose wisely. Choose wisely—

Choose Prince Cylvan, or choose Daurae Asche.

"Help the daurae!" someone suddenly shrieked from the stands, making Saffron jump. His head snapped to search; one spectator slammed backward as his magic struck them like a bludgeon, taking down a few others around them. As if struck by a crashing wave. He nearly wondered how they managed to hear what even he couldn't from Ryder's mouth—before realizing, they didn't have to. They could see the options in front of him.

They didn't have to know Saffron was being told to choose—they were ordering him to do it, either way. Before long, a cacophony of crying voices erupted to join them.

"Protect the daurae!"

"Leave Prince Cylvan!"

"Save Daurae Asche!"

"If Prince Cylvan will ever do a good thing for Alfidel—let it be this!"

Saffron turned slowly back to Ryder, who clucked his tongue in pity. He stroked a piece of Cylvan's hair between two fingers, then pressed it to his nose, all the while keeping Saffron's eyes. Saffron couldn't look away, even with how badly he wished to gaze at Cylvan. But he couldn't bring himself to meet the prince's eyes in comparison—he wasn't sure he could stomach the certain look on his face as the people of Alfidel pleaded for his death in favor of saving their golden daurae, instead. Their child of the sun.

"Don't do this," Saffron whispered, instead. He spoke with clarity on his lips so Ryder would know exactly what he said. Ryder's smile grew more insistent, confirming he understood every word, even as Saffron continued. "I promised you once before—you don't have to do it like this. You will have an audience with the kings before the sun sets. I swear it."

"But this is already the most intimate of audiences I've ever had with anyone," Ryder said with a grin. Saffron heard the words that time, only then realizing exactly how silent the crowd had gone while waiting for Saffron's answer. All watching him in breathless silence, waiting for Saffron to make his choice. "I suppose I should thank you either way. I never would have gotten this close without you, Lord Saffron."

"Ryder, please!" Saffron's voice cracked. He lowered the bow slightly, though never shifted the head of the arrow from its place at the ready. "Please, just—not like this. You've already taken everything else from me. That's enough for me to listen. Please—this is too much. They're just—they're just a child."

"Is that your choice, then?" Ryder said. "You choose Daurae Asche, the innocent child—"

"Wait!" Saffron cried. An uproar tore through the crowd, but Saffron ignored them. He saw only Ryder. He focused only on Ryder, who just kept smiling, fed by the chaos around them.

"Come on, then. I don't have all day. Choose your Night Prince. Choose your Night Court. Or choose the sun. Choose a Day for everyone to live in. It shouldn't be this difficult."

Saffron couldn't keep holding his breath. He released a cracked exhale that shook his entire body.

He finally met Cylvan's eyes, who stared at him. Pale, motionless, terrified—but not for himself. Not for the blade pressed to his throat. The hand at his side was stiff, extended slightly in the direction of his sibling held by the witchhunter only a few yards away. As if both reaching for them—and begging Saffron to make the right choice. Silently pleading for what even he thought to be *the right choice*. The same as all those witnessing it. *Save them. Save Asche. Please, save my sibling. Save the daurae. Not me. Not me.*

Saffron's pulse slammed in his ears. It warped the edges of his vision where not already strained by glowing halos in every direction. He didn't know—he wasn't sure—he was trapped. He didn't know what to do. God, what was he supposed to do?

Saffron's eyes turned to the daurae in uncertainty, who glowed as bright white as anyone else—but then he saw the witchhunter that held them. His drumming heart came to a halt.

The witchhunter, who should have been highlighted in pink like all the others—was draped in crimson, as intense as rowan berries in summer.

Saffron's ears rang. The witchhunter saw him looking—and nodded. Just slightly, just once.

Saffron's heart thumped back to life. He turned, raising the bow. He drew the taut string back with a practiced hand, aiming it at Ryder. Knowing the consequences of choosing the Night over the sun—and facing the approaching darkness without hesitation.

"I've made my choice."

"Saffron, *no!*" The plea tore from Cylvan's mouth, the desperation in it rough as it shredded his vocal chords. "Not me, Saffron, not me, please, gods—!"

Ryder shoved Cylvan away. The prince stumbled to his hands and knees, turning again in an instant to throw a swell of wind at the witchhunter pinning Asche where they stood—

Knock, knock.

Asche vanished into a shimmering pink light.

The crowd went silent. Cylvan was silent. Paralyzed on his knees, arms outstretched to where Asche stood moments before. The prince trembled over every inch, shoulders rising and falling faster and faster with growing panic, hands curling into fists. An attempt to summon his sibling back from the other side. When Asche didn't return, a horrible sound spilled from Cylvan's mouth, before he sank to the grass, clawing at it. He screamed, and the crowd joined him. Shrieking curses, spewing hatred and vitriol and threats as Cylvan wept.

Saffron called out his name, taking a step forward, but Ryder's voice lifted over the crowd one more time.

"Once silver sows their longest day, iron reaps its bloody night," he recited, slowly at first. Saffron stiffened, turning back to him. "As yew trees pin our suns in sleep, rowan tears the moon shall weep..."

"Ryder—" Saffron attempted, but the words caught with sharp edges the moment Ryder lifted his hands, and Saffron saw the rings he wore. Pixie rings, just like the one he showed when they first met. Just before disappearing into the floor of the infirmary.

Six of them. Each one on its own finger.

Saffron's eyes snapped back to Cylvan, who remained motionless on his knees. Staring blankly at the place where Asche had vanished. Saffron threw his bow to the ground and raced to meet his prince. Grass stained his skirt as he dropped in front of Cylvan, grabbing his shoulders, attempting to pull his attention back as Ryder continued behind them.

"Not once, nor twice, nor thrice..."

"Cylvan, please—! Get up, please, *get up!*"

"Six knocks aloud, *they scatter like mice.*"

Saffron threw himself over Cylvan, pulling him close and bracing for whatever came—just as more deafening bangs echoed into the sky from every direction around them. Six knocks, reverberating through the earth like canons.

Knock, knock, knock, knock, knock, knock—

The ground shifted, warping and twisting and bursting into bright colors and shrieking sounds. It sucked the air from the field, and Saffron could only once again grab and heave Cylvan backward in a desperate attempt to pull him free of the circle's reach. A circle that glowed beneath the grass, as if placed there the day before. Donning six knock-knots, each one wider than Saffron was tall. No feda markings to indicate direction or intention, no marks of where to end up—and Saffron realized what was coming just as Cylvan erupted back to life, sweeping Saffron into his arms and leaping into the sky. Away from the man and the undulating earth. Away from the glowing light of the veil renting open, earth turning over itself like how humans described the gaping mouth of hell.

Within moments, it collapsed back in on itself—swallowing everything and everyone within the boundary.

Thousands of people, stolen through the veil in an instant.

Saffron barely had a chance to catch his breath when Cylvan suddenly gasped, gravity shifting beneath them until there was nothing but plummeting back to the ravaged earth.

Saffron slammed into the dirt hard enough to disconnect from reality, spinning in darkness before finally emerging again at the sound of Sionnach's screaming voice. He swam through the blurry darkness, fighting to rekindle his vision and thoughts, finally turning onto his side to wheeze and cough up remaining blood as his crushed lungs struggled to inflate again. Sionnach was there; Copper was there; Avren guards and even the kings were there, though they raced past Saffron to where Cylvan laid motionless a few yards away. Hair scattered in a dark halo around him, spilling over his closed eyes and pale lips when turned onto his back. One of his horns dangled from a single obsidian fiber, before breaking away from the movement and thudding to the grass. Saffron clawed at the ground, screaming, attempting to drag himself closer, only for his strength to vanish as King Tross uttered:

"That tear in the veil was too large—he must have been made ashen."

40

THE CIRCLE

Saffron sat in one of the five capitol palace libraries, facing the fire burning brightly in the hearth that stood taller than he did. On his lap, nestled in a piece of cloth, he stroked his thumb endlessly over the bumps of his raven's wind-carved horn, heavy and black like stone.

Saffron wanted to be relieved Cylvan hadn't been hurt worse —but that felt too selfish. He should have been grateful that Cylvan hadn't been taken with the rest of them—but that was too selfish. Selfish. *Selfish.*

Had Saffron not commanded everyone else away in time, they, too, might have been taken. Into the mouth of the churning earth, or the air, or the sky, or whatever the veil technically was. He already knew there wouldn't be any bodies in the soil once it was turned over in search. Those people hadn't been buried. They'd been taken. And the rest of the people he cared about were nearly taken right with them. He and Cylvan would have been taken right with them. They would have all vanished into thin air, like water into steam beneath a hot sun.

If he allowed himself to think about it too hard, he sank too deeply. If he sank too deeply, he wouldn't be able to speak again. He already found himself touching his throat every few minutes when a lump formed a little too large to swallow. If he couldn't speak, he wouldn't be able to react when someone finally came to get him. He wouldn't be able to act normally. With the confidence of a future prince.

A part of him wasn't sure he wished for anyone to come and find him at all.

Hollow. Letty. Nimue. Daurae Asche. Sunbeam, in her own way. All of them, claimed by Ryder, taken through the veil. Somewhere Saffron couldn't reach them. Somewhere Saffron couldn't find them. Even if he had the courage to knock through the veil in that very moment—he wouldn't even know where to start. He had no way of knowing where to find them. There was simply— nothing he could do at all.

The only minuscule reassurance came in what Sunbeam once told him. The same reassurance he offered to himself every time he thought about Hollow and Letty on the other side of the veil before the games ever came and went.

Time passed differently between the human and the fey world.

While it had been exactly six hours since the moment Ryder stole Asche and those people in the crowd, wherever they ended up—it had only been two hours on the other side. Give or take. Hollow and Letty had only been there for a few days, at least, if it really had been a few weeks for Saffron.

Saffron hated not knowing exactly when they went. He hated himself for not checking in on them sooner. God—he hated himself for a lot of things.

Closing his eyes, he hung his head forward. He bit back a wave of emotion for the hundredth time, clutching Cylvan's broken horn in his hands. That piece of heavy but lightweight obsidian bone. That piece of glasslike, bonelike, solid piece of his prince, a reminder that Saffron could have lost even more. He could have lost even more on top of what he already had, both in front of his eyes and without even knowing it. If he only hadn't been so—

"Thank you."

Saffron jumped. He stared into the fire, turned over his shoulder, searched around the doorway trying to find who'd said it, before realizing the words hadn't come through his ears at all. They were nothing more than a distant whisper, like spirits moaning on the wind. *Thank you,* Taran had said. Saffron didn't know the fey lord even knew those words. He almost asked *'for what?'*—but instead, squeezed Cylvan's broken horn a little tighter.

It could have been so much worse.

KING TROSS CAME TO GATHER HIM NOT MUCH LATER. Saffron wrapped Cylvan's horn in its cloth and tucked it into the back of his waistband like he used to do with his sketchbook, following the king out of the library and down the hallway outside. Down, down, down, through long winding corridors that once swelled with dancing, laughing, drunken courtiers dressed for a gala. That night, they were empty. There wasn't a single breath of even the most hidden of beantighes in the walls. The entire palace had been locked down the instant Cylvan was carried inside, no one allowed to enter or leave. Not until they determined exactly how long Avren's ashen state would last—including Cylvan's. Including King Ailir's, and King Tross's, Sionnach's, Copper's—everyone. Not until they knew where to find the daurae. Perhaps not even until they found Ryder Kyteler.

There were still so many hallways, grand atriums, staircases, corridors Saffron had never walked through in the few times he'd been there, so he walked as close as he could behind the king without tripping him. Tross smiled kindly whenever Saffron accidentally met his eyes. Otherwise, they walked in silence, nodding only when passing at-the-ready guards and advisors and other palace officials who hurried by and exchanged hushed messages between one another.

"A raven has been sent to summon Gentle Naoill come right away."

"Are the oracles prepared to leave, yet?"

"Families are still being notified—there are simply too many to make quick work of it..."

They never slowed their pace, except when passing Saffron directly. Easing down just enough to give him a look, to examine him up and down, and Saffron knew why. Ryder implied that night would be the end of what remained of Cylvan's reputation, but he didn't warn how it would affect Saffron's, too. He didn't have to—Saffron knew the moment Ryder first posed the question. *Choose wisely.* Saffron knew his own reputation, the one he'd agonized over for so long, fighting to cultivate himself into a fey lord of politeness and perfection, despite all of his mistakes and flaws. All of that work. All of Cylvan's work. Luvon's. Catrín's. Baba Yaga's. Adelard's. Even King Tross, who ensured Saffron dressed impeccably for every event.

The people of Avren, and eventually all of Alfidel, would soon only know him as the one to sacrifice Daurae Asche in favor of a Night Court. Had Saffron been told that the day before, he would have scoffed. Laughed. Invited it. But beneath the mantle of incoming darkness—he couldn't understand how Cylvan still walked upright with how heavy it draped over his back.

They arrived before two grand doors bookended by sentries, who gave the king one look before one stepped forward to open the door. Tross swept inside with Saffron on his heels, and Saffron paused in surprise at all the faces seated at the long table filling the room. Sionnach, Copper, even Maeve flanked King Ailir at the head of the table, as well as three figures wearing forest green and silver, sheer veils pulled back to reveal their faces, ears semi-pointed and capped with decorative silver on the ends.

Everyone but King Ailir stood as Saffron and King Tross entered. They bowed in respect. Sionnach, to Saffron's surprise, was the first one to break out of the formality, hurrying from their seat to throw their arms around Saffron with a small sound of relief. Saffron hugged them back, tightly, whispering how glad he was they were alright. They repeated the sentiment, and Saffron swore he felt a few warm drops of tears on his shoulder. But when he pulled back, Sionnach had already wiped them away, stepping aside as Tross motioned for Saffron to follow him to the head of the table where King Ailir and the oracles sat. Cylvan was nowhere to be found.

The oracle with the most decorated veil stood as Saffron approached, smiling and extending her pale hands, sparkling with rings on every finger. It reminded Saffron of Morrígan beantighes. Her hands were turned palm up, like Saffron used to do when scooping water out of the creek to wash his face, and he watched as Tross placed his hands in hers, palms down, as if the tips of his fingers were the offered water. She briefly bowed, pressing her forehead to his knuckles before lifting her head again and smiling.

"Pleased to find you well, all things considered, your highness," she offered to Tross, before smiling at Saffron. "And it's a pleasure to see you again, Prince Saffron."

Saffron recognized her in an instant—she'd been there the morning he left Beantighe Village for Avren, to administer weaverthistle to all of his old friends. All he could do was nod, offering an uncertain glance to the king, before back to the lady. "I'm glad to see you as well. I apologize for not introducing myself properly last time. Erm—how should I... call you?"

The briefest awkward silence rang out in the room like the tick of a clock, but the lady continued smiling as warmly as ever.

"We offer our names to Lugh in exchange for the power to give true ones, your highness," she said. Behind Saffron, Tross added:

"You may call her *high seer*," he said, understanding what Saffron meant. "Behind her, those are diviners. Highly trained oracles who cater to the Tuatha dé Danann, specifically."

The high lady seer kept smiling. "I was honored to give true names to all of King Ailir's children, you know, including Prince Cylvan. Should you be pleased with my work in the future, I will be honored to do the same for your own one day, as well."

"O-oh," Saffron nodded, flushing in embarrassment.

King Ailir motioned for Tross and Saffron to take a seat as the head oracle's two associates rose to their feet to offer their chairs. Saffron's instinct was to politely refuse, but Tross was already leading him toward one of them, turning it out so Saffron could sit. He did, not wanting to cause any more trouble.

"I was just informing the kings we may already have a trace on where the daurae has been taken through the veil. Oracles are preparing to pass through in search," the high lady seer said, and relief washed through Saffron like cold water.

"And what of the crowd of people taken second?" Tross asked. The high lady seer's smile faded slightly, and she shifted where she sat.

"Unfortunately... that human used a very old veil spell that we are currently incapable of tracking or recreating. It requires a certain type of magic-user to perform and understand it. But I've asked some of my brightest diviners to begin work in the National Library's archives first thing in the morning to seek whatever training they need in order to counter it. Should we come up empty, I may ask that we send ravens to neighboring kingdoms and ask for their assistance."

Saffron's heart beat hard and slow. He knew exactly what kind of magic the seer spoke of, of course, and it was difficult to keep his mouth shut. But if it meant he might be able to help all those people who were lost, then perhaps speaking up would be better? The moment his lips parted, though, the scars on his forearm throbbed, and his mouth clamped shut again. Like Taran was warning him to keep quiet.

"Thank you, seer. We will rely on you and the work of your diviners in the meantime," Ailir broke the silence.

Saffron didn't hear whatever words were exchanged, next,

barely noticing even when the oracles excused themselves as Tross offered to see them out. He rubbed his thumb up and down his arm, waiting to hear Taran's voice in his head. To say something, anything, since he clearly wished to be noticed. But the beast never showed itself, his voice never materialized, and the burning sensation faded back into Saffron's skin. He forced himself to swallow the confusion and return to the conversation, finding King Ailir had risen to his feet. His golden hair was slightly askew, nose and chin red from being rubbed in apprehension for hours and hours.

"As you may have all realized by now," the king began, that time addressing the others in the room. Copper, Sionnach, Maeve, who all straightened up to attention. "Lord Saffron, here, is Prince Cylvan's intended fiancé. He has been for some time. I will not go into the details, as they are not mine to share, but he is your future Harmonious King of Alfidel."

Ailir's golden eyes traveled to meet Saffron's, and Saffron meant to smile, but it wouldn't come. He'd never been on the full receiving end of King Ailir's gaze like that—and something about it was startling. Partially because of its intensity—partially because he could so vividly see Asche in their father's features. He thought of what Ryder once told him about how even King Ailir, embodiment of a Day Court, had nearly lost the throne entirely by the nature of his birth—and Saffron wondered how much it must hurt the king to watch the same happen to Cylvan. To be forced to walk a narrow line between protecting him and having to let him endure it. A king who, on the surface, appeared so powerful and loved by all—but who secretly walked the thinnest line that could be drawn.

"Saffron is also a human. A very powerful human, who can perform equally powerful feats of arid magic. The royal family knows this and has already accepted it. We have already embraced him as a member of our family and our court. I expect the rest of you shall do the same."

Saffron squeezed his hands together, not expecting such kind words. He bit down on his bottom lip to fight for his composure. He couldn't bring himself to look at his friends, otherwise, only hoping he didn't look too pitiful.

"As you may assume, it was never our intention for Saffron's identity to be revealed so early in my son's courtship. He was meant to attend school at Mairwen as a high fey, to receive a proper education, in order to best prepare him for kinghood in the future."

Saffron finally lifted his eyes to Sionnach, first, who sat pale and staring unblinking at the king. As if they thought Ailir's next words would be a call for their execution now that they were made aware of such a big secret. Copper, across from them, looked equally colorless, but stoic. Maeve looked intrigued—and did so with her eyes directly on Saffron the entire time. He thought she might freeze him to his core, having to turn away again quickly.

"In any other circumstance, I would have asked the high lady seer to strip your memory threads here in this room," Ailir continued, tapping a finger to the table. That time, the blood drained from Saffron's face. "But considering what we've just witnessed, and the clear threat to my family, Saffron included—I have a secondary proposal for you, if you wish to keep your memories intact. Hear me: from this day forward, you will act as guardians for both Saffron and Prince Cylvan, in cases where royal guards would be inappropriate. On Mairwen's campus, in the city, any place they may travel where a full escort would draw too much attention. You will protect the crown prince and his fiancé—as well as his fiancé's status and true identity—with your lives. Otherwise," he trailed off, reserving a moment to meet his victims' eyes one at a time, emphasizing his point. "I will have your memories stripped bare, and your families will be banished from Alfidel for the next three centuries."

A chill fell, but it wasn't from Maeve. The silence was equally deafening, vibrating Saffron all the way to his bones, pricking him with a needle of fear. It buzzed and tingled under his skin until he itched all over, leaping to his feet and making everyone jump.

"Um!" he exclaimed with a sharp breath, before putting his hands up in apology. "I'm sorry—erm, I mean—I don't mean to interrupt, your majesty, it's only that..."

Saffron struggled to find the right words, to maintain that composure he'd clung to with a weaker grasp than ever before. He turned to his friends, reading the mix of emotions on each of their faces. Fear, anticipation, apprehension. He couldn't stand it. He couldn't stand the thought of them being threatened on his behalf, not unlike—

Not unlike Ryder had done with Hollow, Letty, Nimue.

Swallowing back his nervousness, Saffron cleared his throat and straightened up.

"I didn't mean for anyone to come to any harm today," he said. His voice shook, but he spoke clearly. Just like he'd practiced so much with Catrín during his weeks in the Winter Court. "I don't mean trouble for any of you, and I never did. Yes—I'm human. And yes, I can perform arid magic; and, yes, I've made plenty of mistakes in how I've tried to keep it all under control while also trying to navigate pretending to be a high fey, but..."

He swallowed against the thorns tangling in his throat, attempting to shield him from revealing every secret he'd clawed at keeping for months. He rubbed at his neck in habit, before clearing it.

"I want to be completely honest with all of you," he went on, voice softer in anxiety. "I want you to understand everything that's going on. It doesn't feel fair otherwise—and I want you to be able to make your own decision when it comes to... if you agree to... to be my guardians, going forward. I want you to know my true intentions, and that I mean no one any harm."

No one protested, so Saffron closed his eyes. He wished Cylvan was there. He wished Cylvan was there smiling at him in encouragement, squeezing his hand. His fingers twitched in response.

"As recent as Imbolc this year, I was only a beantighe at Morrígan Academy in the Spring Court..."

How he and Cylvan met. Their conflict with Taran mac Delbaith. How Saffron turned to arid magic to first try and help Berry, and then to eventually help Cylvan. He left out the Morrígan's Kyteler Ruins and the beannighe, he didn't mention Sunbeam, he barely hinted at his oath with the veil, but those details didn't matter—only what he wished for all of them to understand.

Saffron wanted to be a king for humans. He wanted to be a king for the high fey, too, but not the ones who already lived luxuriously in Avren's highest courts. Not for any of them who already attended galas and tried to court the prince, all while gossiping about a Night Court behind his back; those confident that, even in a Night Court, they would not be touched. They would be protected by the embrace of power and affluence. No— Saffron wanted to be a king for low fey, wild fey, half-fey, fey who had never worn jewels or attended prestigious schools. He wanted to be a king for beantighes and foundlings and changeling children everywhere—even those that had already been passed back through the veil, who didn't know how to be humans. Like Luvon had once intended to do with him.

"Prince Cylvan asked me to be his king because I understand what it's like to live as the lowest of creatures in this world—and I agreed. But also—because I love him. I love him more than anything, even if it seems outrageous from the outside. I've seen parts of him that are kind and gentle; parts of him that have suffered beneath the same expectations and cruel systems as I have. I know it will not be easy to follow me ahead of this, especially after what just happened with Ryder Kyteler and his connection to humans and human magic. It's terribly complicated, and even dangerous, but... before anyone decides if they want to help me, as King Ailir has asked, I wanted to make sure you all knew exactly what you were agreeing to. I would also like to gently ask his majesty..."

He glanced to Ailir, who had watched him speak that entire time with shiny, curious eyes.

"That he rescinds his threat to strip their memory threads and banish their families, whether they agree or not. I know how it feels to have memories rifled through, and even stripped—and, with all due respect, I would rather not be involved in agreements that leverage such threats. Let them choose on their own accord. If they refuse and leave the palace straight to the nearest gossip parlor, telling them everything I've told them here—then so be it. We'll deal with it. But I will not lie about who I am or where I came from to people expected to put their lives at risk to protect me. That is not the kind of court I want to build for myself, or for Prince Cylvan."

Saffron's words lingered in the wide room for a few moments, before Sionnach noisily leapt from their chair. Face flushed, standing stiffly, they put a hand to their chest.

"I'll do it!" they exclaimed. "I'll do it, Saffron! I'll watch over you. I'll help you, whatever you need from me. Whatever I can do. Since we first met, I knew you were different—but someone I felt like I could trust right away. I don't care that you're human. Honestly—I knew from the very beginning you weren't all you said. I never could have imagined it would be *this*, something so— so—amazing, but—but I don't care. I'll do it."

Saffron smiled at them in relief, before turning to Maeve, who sat back in her chair with arms folded. Her smile was different, edging on shit-eating.

"Hilarious. I never thought someone as prissy as Cylvan would have it in himself to fall in love with a *beantighe*," she muttered, before sitting forward. "I can't commit to endorsing you forever, Prince Saffron—but I don't see the harm in keeping an eye on you for now. Not because you and I are friends, but—I too know Cylvan has secret soft spots. I've seen them, too, and if he feels safe enough sharing them with you, then I'll trust his judgment. Though gods know it'll be fun to watch Cylvan flounder in being a good husband and all, too."

Saffron offered her an uncertain nod of thanks, before his attention drifted to Copper. Copper, who remained pale. Who stared back at Saffron with a face like he was in pain, like he wasn't sure of anything at all. Like the world had been pulled out from under him. Despite knowing already that Saffron was human, perhaps even connecting the dots that he and Cylvan were closer than Saffron's attendance at suitor galas implied. None of it should have been a shock to him, and yet...

Saffron nearly whispered Copper's name, but the fey lord suddenly rose to his feet, stammering a few times before shaking his head.

"I... I have to..." he attempted, before raking fingers through his hair and putting his hands up again. "I need some air, I need to think, just... hold on."

He turned suddenly, hurrying from the room. Through the great doors at the end, they slammed shut with a banging echo, leaving Saffron feeling like Copper had looked only moments before. Pale, pained, confused. The silence lingering was a return of needles pricking him all over, but then Maeve surprised him.

"I would never say a kind word about Copper dé Bricriu," she said. "Ah, but... give him some time. We'll see what he decides."

"Why would he...?" Saffron asked weakly, glancing to the doors again, hoping Copper would come right back in laughing like it had all been a joke. But he didn't. The silence remained. The needles scratched deeper.

"Copper's family situation is... complicated," Sionnach whispered with an awkward smile, and Saffron realized there was something everyone but him seemed to know. His self-consciousness intensified. Maybe Sionnach noticed, because they added: "Even I can see why this might all be difficult for him to accept, let alone agree to. Just... give him some time. We'll see if his little fox brain can untangle a way to move forward."

"You may need a new roommate, soon," Maeve added with a sigh. Said sarcastically at first, before her dorm prefect-instincts kicked in, gazing at the ceiling while calculating where Saffron could go, instead. Or perhaps where Copper might be moved. Saffron's heart only sank deeper. Of all the people he anticipated to have such a reaction, Copper was the last. It unraveled all the confidence he had remaining in his chest, and the heavy mantle of darkness draping over his back made his shoulders slump again.

41

THE REAPING

Once the palace fell as silent as the rest of the city, Saffron began his search for his missing raven. He exchanged a mouse from the messenger paddock for Fiachra's help, the owl finding it no problem to fly through the high-ceilinged corridors and around the wide-corners at every end. In his hand, he clutched a wooden hair pick he'd carved in the days leading up to the solstice on Asche's recommendation. *Don't bother with a courting locket; give Cylvan something only someone like you would...* Saffron had nearly forgotten about it, buried beneath an ocean of stress—which only stressed him out more, wondering what else he'd done or said or agreed to that he couldn't remember.

When Cylvan wasn't in his own bedroom, wasn't in the gardens, or the dining hall, the ballroom, any of the studies Saffron knew he liked best, he followed his gut to the final place he thought his raven might go. His heart squeezed and pounded and twisted in on itself the entire time he walked the corridor, not entirely sure he was even headed the right way. He had to ask one of the guards for directions, and even then lost his way twice. But when he found it, he knew from the moment he cracked the knob and glanced inside.

Asche's bedroom was not much different from the one they inhabited in Danann House, though obviously much, much larger, and much, much more cluttered. Floor to ceiling, shelves and bookcases and glass-door cabinets were piled high and loaded to the brim with crystals and knick-knacks and bottles of mysterious dirt and other liquids. Saffron knew every single object in that room, surely, had roots in wild charms, and because of that was careful not to accidentally bump into anything. The last thing he wanted when seeking out Cylvan to offer comfort was to be turned into a frog.

His raven prince blended in well with all of the trinkets, hidden away on the cushioned windowsill in the dimmest part of the room. He must not have heard Saffron enter, because he never moved, never said anything, only gazed out the open window across the flickering lights of Avren on the opposite side of the ravine. Saffron nearly spoke his name, but it lodged in the back of his throat as he fully observed the state of his prince.

The scuffs and bruises from the fall at the games remained on his cheek and forehead, though bandaged in the infirmary. Saffron knew why they hadn't been healed, yet—all of Avren was ashen from the veil Ryder tore open then closed again. Saffron had never seen his raven like that before—and it squeezed his lungs until he couldn't breathe. A hot protectiveness overwhelmed him. Making his blood boil.

Cylvan's makeup had also been wiped away, hair washed and combed and braided over one shoulder. He wore no jewelry. No hair clips. No rings or bracelets or even gold buttons on a fancy tunic. Only a thin poet's blouse, not even tucked into the waist of his pants. Cylvan dé Tuatha dé Danann, even draped in moss and mud, would never look anything other than perfectly handsome —but that night, beneath the bandages, Saffron saw the return of worrying chips in his demeanor. Hairline cracks evident, maybe only to him, just in the way his prince sat leaning against the corner of the thin window frame, as if he wouldn't care if he suddenly slipped and was swallowed into the sky. He wouldn't be able to catch himself if he did. He would fall and fall and fall with nothing to catch or cushion him at the bottom. He was no more or less opulent than Saffron in that moment—and perhaps that was why the cracks were so much more obvious. Perhaps that was why he looked pale, why his hair looked slightly duller than normal.

Still, Cylvan was perfect. To Saffron, he would always be perfect.

"Cylvan?" he asked. He clutched the hair pick behind his back. The way Cylvan didn't even jump, just turned to look at him slowly, before smiling just as softly, almost broke Saffron's heart.

"Púca," he said gently, adjusting how he sat. "I didn't realize how long I've—"

"No!" Saffron put his hands out, before straightening back up again. "No, don't get up. I'm just here to... make sure you're not alone. If you don't want to be."

Cylvan watched him with such curiosity. Like Saffron never said the things he most expected, like he still wasn't used to being caught off guard. Saffron didn't know what was so strange about his offer, worrying his hands over the pick behind his back before finally approaching.

Saffron lowered to his knees. Cylvan opened his mouth to protest, before closing it again as Saffron gently tucked the pick beneath where Cylvan's hands were folded on his lap. It was carved from a branch of cherry-wood he found in the forest outside of Mairwen; a crescent moon crowning two prongs decorated with scratchy stars and clouds. Cylvan stared down at it for a long time, brushing his thumb over the hand-carved shape.

"It's nothing, really," Saffron whispered, breaking the silence. "I know it's not carved very well—my expertise is more in charcoal and paper, as you know—and I know it won't match any of your outfits, and it'll probably break after a few uses, but... it was Asche's idea."

Cylvan's fingers went still. Saffron bit his lip. He reached into his pocket, removing the still-unfinished courting locket he hadn't brought himself to throw out, yet, just in case Cylvan laughed at the presentation of the pick. He cupped the ugly little portrait in his hands like a sick bird, then sighed again.

"I thought about painting you a courting locket," he explained, feeling a little pathetic. "But I just couldn't decide... exactly how I wanted to do it. If I painted myself as a human, well, you wouldn't be able to carry it around, would you? It would be something shameful, at least for a little while. But every time I tried to paint myself as a high fey, instead, I just... my thoughts would start racing. All I could think was how doing that would be like turning my back on who I really was, which was especially hard with everything going on. Maybe a part of me also worried you would start to prefer me like that, like when I was glamoured and beautiful, and I just... couldn't really stomach it. Ah..."

He smiled awkwardly, but didn't meet Cylvan's eyes. Closing one hand around the locket, he placed it on the floor and straightened up on his knees. He took Cylvan's braid, trailing the dark plait over his palms.

"Um, in Beantighe Village, we had a tradition of gifting hair picks to one another as a way of showing affection. Picks and clips and other little hair trinkets were the only accessory we could wear with our uniforms that wouldn't get us in trouble. So long as they were still covered by our veils and weren't too flashy. So when you'd give one to someone you loved, they could wear it for everyone to see. It sounds stupid, I know, but—but I was complaining to Daurae Asche about the portrait on the locket, and they asked why I was trying to gift you something like a high fey, when I should be gifting you something more meaningful to who I really am, so I... so I thought..."

Tears dripped against the back of Saffron's hand, slowing his words and summoning his eyes upward. Cylvan was staring at him, lips pressed together tightly, chin wrinkled and jaw clenched. The emotions spilled freely from his eyes, the rest of him trembling as if fighting to keep it all down. To push it all down, away, out of reach of where it all hurt him the most.

"It's alright," Saffron whispered, cupping his hands on either side of Cylvan's face. "You can cry, Cylvan. Please, cry if you need to. You don't have to pretend like you're fine. Not with me. Never with me."

Cylvan's expression twisted, going tight—then broke. A choked cry tumbled out of him, hunching forward and pressing his hands into his face as an agonized sound spluttered out of him. Saffron's heart shattered, and all he could do was pull Cylvan into his chest, holding him, pressing his face into his prince's dark hair as his own tears pricked the backs of his eyes.

Cylvan's weeping devolved into body-heaving sobs, which tumbled into cursing himself and everything he was, everything he'd ever be. He tore at his hair, his clothes, begging Asche to forgive him, begging Saffron to forgive him for being such a blight on his life—and as much as Saffron wished to grab his face and kiss him, to declare it wasn't true, it was never true—he let Cylvan cry. He wouldn't get in the way.

He pulled Cylvan off the edge of the windowsill and onto the floor, then down onto his lap, where Cylvan wept against Saffron's stomach with arms locked around his middle. Curled tightly within himself, weeping and screaming and begging until the things he spoke were no longer words. Saffron held him. Held him, held him, and would continue to do so for any amount of eternity Cylvan needed to grieve.

All the while, even with how tightly his body clenched on itself, how severely he ground his teeth, how he gripped Saffron with the ferocity of someone being dragged away for execution—Cylvan's hand around the hair pick never tightened. It clutched the prongs of wood with such care and gentleness, never snapping even the most delicate connections. He pulled it into his chest with both hands, as if it were something so much bigger than the size of a pen. He nested it within two cupped hands, sometimes going quiet except for shuddering breaths just to gaze at it and gently run his fingers over the details. Saffron only held him. Held him.

When the emotions finally released their tightest grip on Cylvan's body, when he finally relaxed enough to allow his head to recline fully into Saffron's lap, Saffron's hands finally found his hair. Petting it back, unweaving the tousled braid to re-plait it with gentle hands. He bit back his own emotions every time his knuckles brushed over the shattered rim of his prince's once-beautifully carved horn.

"I need you to know… that I didn't send Asche into danger without thinking," he finally said like a confession. He nearly explained everything he'd seen, the arid glow around who he knew had to be Sunbeam—

"I trust you." The words escaped Cylvan's grief-swollen lips like a confession of his own. Saffron leaned forward, tucking strands of hair from Cylvan's eyes. His face was wet and splotched red, hair barely untangled and wild from all the tearing and pulling of his own hands. "There was never a moment I didn't trust you knew what you were doing, Saffron—even though it terrified me. Even though I reacted without thinking—I knew you would never send Asche away without thought."

Cylvan might as well have pressed his hand into Saffron's chest, tangling his heart between sharp nails. He took his prince by the face again, pulling him into a gentle, tear-salted kiss.

"You chose me," Cylvan went on in a croak. "It would have been so easy to throw me away. Everyone would have praised and loved you for it, you would have been deified for saving Asche, for saving all of Alfidel. It would have been so much easier for you, for everyone—but you still chose me."

Saffron kissed him again. "I will always choose you. You're mine."

Cylvan released a trembling breath.

"Ryder is intent on proving you and I aren't meant for one another," Saffron went on, wiping fresh tears from Cylvan's cheeks. "And I am intent on proving him wrong, all while taking back everything he's taken from me. I've never been blessed with so much at once, in all my life—and I'm not going to allow someone like Ryder Kyteler to take it all from me. I promise, Cylvan, we'll have Asche back. I'll get Letty and Nimue and Hollow back. We'll find Eias Lam and threaten them into helping me with my witch's mark—or, if the next equinox comes first, I will bypass them entirely and open the veil myself and ask it to make you my bridge partner. My one and only companion, in life and magic and eternity. And then we'll be kings together, one day, no matter how long it takes or what terrible things come as we go. Day or Night. I will always choose you, Day or Night."

"I do not think there is much hope left for a Day Court," Cylvan breathed. Saffron smirked, gently pulling the crescent-moon pick from between Cylvan's fingers. Finishing the braid in his hair, Saffron tucked the prongs into the highest knot beneath Cylvan's ear.

"So be it," he whispered. "But I will remain by your side in the darkness."

Cylvan's mouth pressed flat again. His hand searched for Saffron's, and Saffron found it. Pressing their foreheads together, Saffron closed his eyes, squeezing Cylvan's hand firmly in his. He wouldn't let go; he wouldn't lose that person like he almost had so many times, already. No matter how little light there was to guide them.

If they were destined to walk in darkness—Saffron would learn how to bend light. If he couldn't bend light, then he would bend shadow. If he couldn't bend shadow—then Saffron would simply never let go of Cylvan's hand. He already knew, that was where he best belonged, anyway.

CYLVAN FELL INTO A GENTLE SLEEP ON SAFFRON'S LAP. Lips parted slightly, dark eyelashes flickering back and forth as he dreamed. Saffron only knew they were merciful visions by how he never moved or twitched at all. Saffron brushed fingers through his hair endlessly, endlessly. Wishing to help keep him there for as long as he needed to rest.

"There are few people I would trust enough to let Cylvan sleep in their arms."

Saffron closed his eyes.

I don't think I will ever understand the relationship you have with each other. Do you hate each other? Or do you care for each other? What a way to show affection.

Taran hovered in the front of Saffron's mind, and it made Saffron itch. As always. Clearly, the fey lord had something he wished to say, so Saffron eased the discomfort by summoning him to appear. Speaking in a whisper, hardly more than a breath of wind through the window. When Taran materialized in front of him, he offered a tiny nod of thanks, before lowering his head to gently press his nose to Cylvan's broken horn.

"I could never hate him," Taran said, voice as soft as Saffron's. Neither stirring Cylvan for even a moment. "Even if it may have appeared otherwise. I know I was cruel to him, but it was never because I hated him."

"Then why?"

Taran didn't answer at first. He gazed down at Cylvan for a long time, before slowly lowering himself to the floor. Even still, he never turned his crimson eyes away.

"I was afraid of what they would do to him, otherwise. I had to prove I had control of him."

"Who are they?"

Taran's ears flicked back, like just thinking about it made his hackles raise.

"My family. Of course. You saw my memories, it should come as no surprise."

Saffron bit his lip. He turned his eyes down to his sleeping prince as well, gently tucking a few dark pieces of hair from his forehead, then trailing a finger around the smoothed rim of his broken horn.

"Why did you ask Eias to pull your memories of killing

beantighes? The ones at Morrígan. My friends," he asked, next. His voice shook as he did, though he didn't know why. Even if Taran got angry, Saffron was no longer afraid of him. Perhaps he was simply scared to delve into those painful memories at all.

Taran took his time before responding, again. Saffron was in no hurry. He wouldn't offer a way for Taran to get out of it, either. He'd been given an opportunity to understand every terrible thing that had happened to him—most of those things at the very hands of the person he now had total dominion over. Saffron was going to understand every reasoning. Not in favor of forgiveness—but so that he might learn and recognize such warning signs in future high fey growing mad with power.

"I didn't need my family knowing I was struggling to keep Cylvan under control," the wolf finally answered. "I did not need them knowing I was resorting to killing beantighes and searching for wild fairy fruits to get something as simple as a proposal. A proposal should have been easy. If I couldn't accomplish that much, they would have no faith in me to rule afterward. To do their bidding as I ruled, afterward."

Saffron nodded, recalling that conversation he'd witnessed between Taran and his sister, Anysta, in his memory thread. Right before taking on Cylvan's appearance and killing Glass, who changed into Nimue after drowning in the ocean.

"You were expected to marry him... because then your family could have their ashen curse lifted, right?" he asked, also recalling the conversation he had with Asche right before diving into Taran's memory threads at all. Taran gave him a look of surprised curiosity, as if he never expected Saffron to have figured that out. As if Saffron could possibly catch him off guard with exactly how much he knew, despite having demonstrated time and time again that Taran wasn't as good at keeping secrets as he always thought. He didn't answer out loud, only nodded. Saffron's stomach turned over, knotting in on itself. He calmed his nerves again by stroking Cylvan's soft hair.

"If they're so desperate... why haven't I seen anyone from your family at any of the suitor galas I've been attending?" he asked quietly.

"I can assure you, they are not as isolated as you may think. They do not need to attend galas in-person to know exactly what goes on at them. I know my family is still desperate to reclaim their magic, though I no longer know what means they will take to get it. You sensed the warning I gave you in that meeting with the kings and the oracles, didn't you?"

Saffron nodded. He gazed down at the scars on his forearm, which had burned slightly when he was on the verge of revealing the little bit he knew about veil magic, if it would help Asche. In that moment, he understood.

"You think the royal oracles are influenced by your family?"

"I cannot know for sure. But I encourage you to proceed with every interaction going forward as if it's a possibility."

"Do you think..." Saffron trailed off. Feeling only a little bit foolish. "Is there any chance they're working with Ryder, too?"

"Doubtful. My family wants to *rule* on the throne, not overturn it."

Saffron sighed. He didn't know if that was a relief or not. If they'd been working together, it would have tightened Saffron's focus somewhat. If they were separate threats entirely—he would have to split his attention both ways.

"You once said... if it didn't work with Cylvan, they would have killed him. They would have had you court Asche, instead. Is that true?"

"Yes. I would rather not discuss it."

"I would. I want to know. I want to know everything that could be a danger to Cylvan, even if it's long in the past. It's my responsibility to take care of him now. Especially once he starts openly courting me, once we actually announce our engagement, which I imagine will happen sooner rather than later all things considered... not to mention with the daurae gone, they must be starting to panic."

"I imagine so. But I cannot tell you any more than I already have."

"Why not?"

Taran's snout wrinkled in annoyance. His ears flattened back again.

"Because Eias' fingers in my memories were the only ones I ever consented to; all the others were done to me against my will. For the same purpose Ryder Kyteler tore out yours. My family has been weaving my memory threads since I can remember, to keep me obedient. To keep me docile and submissive. There are few things I know to be absolutely true, and not false threads planted to change how I perceive the world."

Saffron stared at him. With that confession, he felt like he suddenly understood Taran mac Delbaith just a little bit better. His desperate, frenzied demand for control. His insistence on following the rules and giving them, to always know what was happening even if he wasn't there to witness it for himself. His slow unraveling as Cylvan grew less and less willing to obey; the pressure he must have felt from his family to act accordingly, the fear of losing Cylvan if he didn't, never quite knowing exactly what was real or what was fake. How much of his own perception of Cylvan wasn't even real? Were there even parts of their relationship, their friendship, that Taran's family had manufactured for the sole purpose of keeping Taran obedient?

"Why did Eias pull your memory of killing Glass?" Saffron went on. Taran clenched his teeth.

"My family would have taken it, otherwise. To hide the evidence. I wanted to keep it—not only to remind myself of the horrible thing I'd done, the lengths I was willing to go to protect him—but also so that, when I did one day rise into power alongside Cylvan, I might have at least one thing I could use to illuminate all of the horrible things they forced me to do."

Saffron didn't know what to say. He gazed down at Cylvan again, seeking comfort in the way he continued to sleep so peacefully. Saffron couldn't help but trail a finger over the curve of his eyebrow, through the soft ends of his lashes.

"Thank you for telling me," was all he could think to say. He wasn't about to offer forgiveness, he wasn't about to offer sympathy, not to the person who had still acted with such cruelty despite the harshness of his circumstances—but Saffron understood him. Just a little bit better.

More than that—he understood the depths of cruelty that high fey were willing to go to get what they wanted. The people they would manipulate and harm in the process. How even their own children were such easy prey.

"What will you do now?" Taran went on. Saffron's mind wandered toward an answer as his fingers drew a line up the point of Cylvan's ear.

"We're going to try and find Eias Lam," Saffron whispered. "Both to see if they can get us through the veil to find my friends, and to see if they can open a dialogue between me and the veil. So I can beseech it for my witch's mark. If we can't find them, or if Mabon comes sooner—then we will perform a veil oath ceremony, and I'll ask the veil to make Cylvan my bridge partner. Then we can open the veil together, to search the other side. All of this, of course, assuming the oracles don't get through and find them first, but..."

Saffron closed his eyes. Taran asked his next question before Saffron could answer it, himself.

"What of Ryder Kyteler?"

He exhaled a long breath. He shook his head.

"I don't know," he whispered. "I don't know *what of Ryder Kyteler* at all. I don't know where to start, especially if even the royal oracles can't get a trace on Asche or anyone else. What's someone like me supposed to..."

Saffron trailed off as something fluttered into the room through the window, dropping a piece of paper into his lap no bigger than a coil of cinnamon. He stared at the little blue fairy wren that perched on the arm of an electric desk lamp, hopping back and forth, peeping at him in announcement. In one moment, confirming what he'd hoped since witnessing that glow of arid magic around the witchhunter clinging to Asche.

Barely taking his eyes from the bird, he pinched the scroll, unfurling it over his leg and recognizing Sunbeam's handwriting in an instant. Cylvan jumped awake the moment Saffron burst out laughing, squeezing the paper in his hand, then throwing his arms around his prince as the laughter melted into sobs of joy.

Found them. London.

ACKNOWLEDGMENTS

My partner, prince, and peach, Mo, who continues to awe me every day with their talent and skill in creating some of the most stunning art I've ever seen. I appreciate your dedication to making this series so visually beautiful—and every day I wake up reminded how lucky I am to create worlds with you.

https://morlevart.com/work

Twitter: @morlevart

Instagram: @morlev_art

The Rowan Blood fandom and my Ko-fi subscribers, new and old, who continue to awe and inspire me with their interaction, creativity, and support. Everything I do, I do for you (even the sad, angsty stuff).

Anyone who has ever left a rating, review, or spread the Rowan Blood series through word of mouth—you are the beating heart and lifeblood of indie authors, specifically, who rely so much on your time and dedication. Thank you so much for contributing to my ability to do this, and continue doing this. I have so many more stories to share with you.

My friends and peers, near and far, who show support in a myriad of ways, whether it be through online interaction or one-on-one chatting. I am so lucky to be surrounded by so many gifted and hardworking people, I can't wait to share long careers side by side with one another!

ABOUT THE AUTHOR

Kellen Graves (they/them) is a queer indie writer and artist from the Pacific Northwest, where they live with their partner, two cats, and crystal collection. They also enjoy digital illustration, photography, collecting planners, and disappearing into the ocean.

You can find more info about this release and upcoming releases, see their art, and connect by following Kellen on social media or checking out their website.

ALSO BY KELLEN GRAVES

ROWAN BLOOD

PRINCE OF THE SORROWS (VOL. ONE)

LORD OF SILVER ASHES (VOL. TWO)

HERALD OF THE WITCH'S MARK (VOL. THREE)

THE FOX AND THE DRYAD

ROWAN BLOOD VOLUME FOUR WILL COME 2024

www.ingramcontent.com/pod-product-compliance
Lightning Source LLC
Chambersburg PA
CBHW031232310726
48971CB00004B/978